Over Brooklyn Hills

The Steep Climes Quartet:
Book Three

The Steep Climes Quartet, Book One: *Kill Well*
The Steep Climes Quartet, Book Two: *Dear Josephine*
The Steep Climes Quartet, Book Three: *Over Brooklyn Hills*
The Steep Climes Quartet, Book Four: *Farm to Me*

Over Brooklyn Hills
[The Steep Climes Quartet, Book Three]

Printed in the United States of America

ISBN 979-8-9885055-4-9
LCCN 2026910627

CMTI Publishing
21 Corashire Road
New Marlborough, MA 01230
www.cmtipublishing.com

What reviewers and readers are saying about *Kill Well* (The Steep Climes Quartet: Book One)

Murder is another dire effect of climate change in Guenette's labyrinthine thriller. This first installment of the author's Steep Climes series envisions a near future in which catastrophic heat, droughts, and floods are fraying society, hobbling the economy, and nurturing deadly conspiracies.... Even global-warming deniers will enjoy the resulting page-turner. Despite overdone soapboxing, vivid characters and hardboiled writing make this an entertaining suspenser.

—Kirkus Reviews

Set in a near future where the DSM 7 includes a diagnosis of "climate anxiety," **Kill Well,** *the first entry in The Steep Climes Quartet, Guenette's pointedly realistic thriller series, opens with a bang... A pointedly realistic thriller of murder, the fossil fuel industry, and climate activism.*

—BookLife Reviews

Introspective and solemn, **Kill Well** *by David Guenette is a story of murder and danger, written by an author with a beautiful grasp of the English language, and an obviously deep, powerful, and intense passion for the harsh and shocking realities of climate change. There is everything to be said about an author who can turn that much knowledge into a thriller that often catches the reader off guard with its stunning realism.*

—Independent Book Review

Kill Well *is a smart, taut thriller that grabs you on the first page and keeps you guessing all the way to the suspenseful conclusion. David Guenette knows a lot about hacking and corporate skullduggery, and he knows a lot about people too.*

—Tom Perrotta is author of *Election* and *Little Children*, both of which were made into critically acclaimed, Academy Award-nominated films, and for *Little Children* he received an Academy Award nomination for Best Adapted Screenplay. His novels *The Leftovers* and *Mrs. Fletcher* have been adapted into TV series on HBO. His most recent novel is *Tracy Flick Can't Win*.

David Guenette manages to show that the climate crisis is already affecting our energy and food bills and intensifying the drama of local politics. **Kill Well** *is a fun ride but uncomfortable, too, as we get another way to think about where we're heading all too quickly.*

—Karen Christensen, CEO and Publisher, Berkshire Publishing Company and author of *Eco Living, The Green Home*, and *Home Ecology* (book and Substack newsletter)

No drowned worlds or climate-ravaged zombies, but a solid story with compelling characters that leaves you thinking that you haven't been thinking nearly enough about climate change. I can't wait until the next book in this series hits.

—Larry D. Gussin, Gussin Climate Action Fund at The Sierra Club Foundation

Kill Well *is more than just a suspenseful murder thriller. It combines the reality of climate change and climate activism, the potential devious tactics that the fossil fuel industry has at its disposal, and how difficult it is to exist without surveillance tracking you.*

—Amazon Review

This is a terrific book and the first of its kind that I've read. It deftly combines a page-turning thriller with the dangers of climate change and the dark forces behind it, all the while giving us rich characters that you either care about greatly or strongly loathe.... One of the things I love is that there's plenty of climate change consequences, but experienced the way most of us experience these, which is in the background, lurking, and so easily put out of mind. This tension between real danger and our lack of recognition of it reflects the plot's progress that likewise moves unthinkingly through self-centered interactions, but all with the punch you want in an entertaining read.

—Amazon Review

The detective story is gripping and unfolds in the context of dark corporate forces working to maintain the corporate status quo. Guenette gets us inside the heads of his characters, even into the minds of evildoers. The balance between the ordinary Main Street concerns and the bigger picture takes surprising twists and turns.

—Amazon Review

It is amazing how David Guenette is able to blend emotions, anxieties of ordinary people who besides facing the challenges of everyday life, live at a time when drastic changes the environment will be very soon real and frightening. Yet, the language of the novel is so down to earth and friendly that makes the reading of this breathtakingly seductive.

—Amazon Review

What reviewers and readers are saying about *Dear Josephine* (The Steep Climes Quartet: Book Two)

The second installment of The Steep Climes Quartet turns up the heat on the Berkshire residents introduced in **Kill Well***. Their daily hustle to make ends meet forms the deceptively calm eye of a gathering storm involving oligarch-stalking assassins, Cat 5 hurricanes and oil-financed think tanks bamboozling voters and Congress with insidiously calibrated disinformation… Parallel plotlines serve up tasty examples of Bad Acting. Tech-savvy paranoids clash with high-stakes dark money operatives, bloodthirsty political activists, and the FBI, leaving a trail of burner phones and dead bodies in their wake. Fans of the suspense-thriller action that propelled Kill Well will find plenty of satisfaction here. Read that book before devouring this one.*

—Amazon Review

Loved this, the second book in a projected quartet! It gets into the nitty gritty of life in a climate changed near (very near) future—plenty of catastrophe but not in the apocalyptic manner of most books in this genre: it feels personal in the way it renders what ordinary life might come to feel like before too long. The plot is driven by an entertaining mashup of noir-ish procedural and psychological narrative. It gets inside the heads of a wide range of characters, including fossil fuel flaks, newspaper publishers, climate activists and researchers, and divorced suburban homeowners at loose ends, not to mention a killer with a meticulous plan to even the score with corporate oligarchs. The book's strength is in all these alternating perspectives. Very enjoyable!

—Amazon Review

Dear Josephine *pulls off a difficult feat--it describes the real life near term impact from environmental changes while delving into the ruthless steps bad actors will take either to preserve the status quo or to strike out for what they see as justice. The action scenes are compelling, convincingly detailed, wholly believable, and not like anything else I've come across. Other chapters focus on one particular family and their network. The interpersonal interactions and detail are really well realized.* **Kill Well***, the first book, shares these characteristics. A good read--someone should option these for a film!*

—Amazon Review

David Guenette does a great job of making personal the future reality we all face with our current climate trajectory. The struggles of people living day to day while navigating frequent climate related issues helps to illuminate what we all face in the very near future. The level and depth of knowledge and detail, not only around climate issues but also around day to day life, really helped to draw me in. A strong second book in this series, it was hard to put down

—Amazon Review

Dear Josephine*… is a masterclass in literary thriller writing—a chillingly plausible vision of a near-future climate crisis wrapped in a gripping,* *intelligent murder mystery. What makes this book extraordinary is not just the intricately woven plot – though that alone is reason enough to read it – but the profound depth and texture of the characters…The near-future world Guenette envisions is frighteningly believable. With extreme weather events, supply chain instability, AI-driven research, and simmering civil unrest, this is speculative fiction that reads like tomorrow's news. And yet, amidst this realism, the novel's pacing never lets up. The appearance of radical climate groups, the mystery of coordinated murders, and the shadowy forces resisting environmental reform all converge in a narrative that is urgent, nuanced, and utterly absorbing.* **Dear Josephine** *doesn't preach – it implicates.*

— Amazon Review

Dear Josephine *continues David Guenette's The Steep Climes Quartet with an absorbing mix of personal reflection and societal unease. Set in the very near future, the novel captures the feeling of living in a world where climate disruption is no longer an abstraction but a daily reality – felt in rising insurance premiums, food costs, political polarization, and personal doubt… The plot touches on big themes – corporate influence, AI-driven research, direct action movements – but it's the character-driven realism that gives the novel its emotional weight. Thoughtful, serious, and unsettling in the best way,* **Dear Josephine** *isn't just speculative fiction – it's a mirror held up to where we might be headed next.*

— Amazon Review

Contents

We are entering a period of consequences.

Al Gore

The Earth is a fine place and worth fighting for.

Ernest Hemingway, Author

Over Brooklyn Hills

The Steep Climes Quartet: Book Three

David Guenette

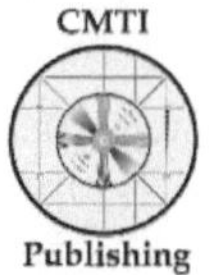

CMTI Publishing, New Marlborough, MA, USA

Chapter 1: Hide and Seek, Snap to It

Early April, 2035

Allen Randolph, who's never liked his name and who hasn't used it with others for the better part of a decade, does like other things. He likes getting deep into figuring out how to carry missions forward for No One is Safe, even if he worries about collateral damage, and when he speaks of *collateral damage*, he's talking about innocent people who sometimes get hurt. He's talking about people who aren't part of the malicious class of fossil fuel assholes, the criminal executives and financiers of the wide-ranging companies and corporations and banks that have no problem killing the world for whatever money they can grasp, in their crimes against humanity.

He especially likes building things. He'd probably be a furniture maker or some sort of inventor if the world wasn't so fucked up. He likes all the work he's done with drones, although that work has slowed. He'd been one of the architects of the drone campaigns before the anti-drone tech deployed and made that sort of attack infrequent. Before the advent of effective anti-drone measures, he'd been customizing off-the-shelf drones often. Still, the two pipeline breaks that have been in the news recently are, he's sure, his handiwork, and he's got three more drone requisitions on his schedule for the weeks ahead.

He likes the puzzles his skills put before him, figuring out builds like the one he's hunched over now, as weird as this one is. He's making a container for the explosive pack of soft form plastic explosive. The explosive is his own home-built version blend of PETN and RDX but using a plasticizer closer to what the British use in their PE-4, but even softer, more moldable.

He's been making bombs for years now, bombs for blowing up refineries, cars with executives within, and some pipelines.

The explosive he's just made needs to be very flexible but keep its integrity along the twelve-inch strip of it, which is why he's created a sleeve out of cloth cut from an old shirt fished from a clothing drop-off bin.

Thinking of the source of this cloth makes him laugh, an almost silent outward sniff through his nose. Getting the clothes that night a year ago had been one of his closest calls, the police car rounding the corner at the end of the shopping strip, coming from the backside of the long L-shaped group of one-story buildings off the downtown of a suburb of Peoria. He doesn't remember the name of the town. He was just passing through.

The cop hadn't seen him, or hadn't stopped, at any rate. More likely, when he'd later reconstructed his luck, he might have been seen in the solid sweep of the headlights over him, but there was a young woman, or girl, sitting right up against the cop, and the cop had just driven on.

Not that anything much would have happened if the cop had stopped. He was just some late-twenties guy rummaging through discarded clothes, after all, and he'd been neat about it, no piles strewn. But cops can be assholes. He'd learned that the hard way when he was still in high school, back when ICE agents were getting violent when confronted by protesters, back before the LA and Minneapolis killings that had helped the new Congress push back against the round-up programs.

He'd been at one such protest, having driven with other like-minded classmates. The local cops had gotten crazy, as if trying to outdo ICE and the cosplayers attracted to squad actions like flies to shit.

His first experience getting arrested. He'd been surprised by the viciousness of the police, but that was the last time he found himself surprised. He'd gotten more involved with climate actions and was arrested two more times, but he was considered a minor, still not eighteen, and his records should be out of bounds. Still, if he were to get picked up, detained for whatever reason, he's not one to bet on those records being off-limits. That kind of data never really disappears. But he might not get flagged, or if he does, with the last arrest being almost ten years earlier, it might be a non-flag flag of sorts. That's his best guess, but he knows there's still danger in that.

That's why he feels lucky that the cop had probably been out back of the stores, probably getting a blow job from some town girl, some girl who's probably younger than he was when he first felt the pain of the zip ties.

He's not in Peoria, that's for sure, and he's no longer going to climate protests but running dark. These days his NOS contacts are all unknown but proved true by codenames and numbers and postcards and letters and online classified listings that guide the meetups. There's always a chain of code that points to the next message source, and the book-based transposition cipher they all use is simple, effective, and completely apart from the digital world. Clear message intercepts are far too likely, and now that AI has been loosed upon the world, even encrypted messages in phone texts might as well spell everything out in plain English.

The assignment he's working on now was described using a series of plain language codes, a custom jewelry order job. The real content and details are pulled from alphanumeric cyphers. The current transposition cipher is using *The Agony and the Ecstasy*, but it has to be a particular edition, one specific one among the many.

This assignment is a challenging project, for the cartels, and must be a torture or interrogation or kidnapping device.

He focuses on the puzzle, not the real-world intent.

He checks his cloth sleeve work. The darts and stitches across the sleeve are needed to keep the thin joints of the plastic explosive from tearing. That's the point.

The trickiest part is getting the explosive's precursors sent, which means coordinating the deliveries and drop-offs. The equipment he needs for the cook up, that's all available in any well-stocked high school chemistry lab, which is where he's gotten his essentials. One full score from his old high school. That was the first time he'd been back in his old hometown for seven years. First and only time. The risk had been moderate. He'd taken forensic precautions. There was no way any connection would be made, even if they'd gone through the school break-in with a fine-tooth comb, which they wouldn't do—just some juvenile delinquent stealing shit from a school.

He lays the thin, explosive-filled sleeve down on the table and sits back. He pushes the head of the light with the ten-times magnifying glass, the arm swinging away smoothly from its clamped base anchor. He'd found this lamp in a used store years ago and it's been put to good use, but having this sort of thing and his other tools and bits and wires and electronics in his old pickup truck camper could be a problem for him. He's got the story prepped if needed, though, along with samples of his craft work that he makes to sell at various flea markets and shows. The stock is a mix of things he uses and a bunch for items he's never made, like the intricate bead bracelets he picked up in bulk to build up the inventory.

Much of his own work is in the form of oddly ornate tiny clocks that look the part. He's even got a product sheet, but that needs updating soon. He updates his print maps with pen marks and highlighter with the next trade show destinations, and he'll update the calendar on his phone, too. *Just on my way to sell more of this stuff I make, Officer.*

He makes sure to have gone to such previous events because it's easy to have your travels recorded in some database or another, with toll responders and video cameras and cell phone location records just a click away.

He's never yet had to test his stratagem, but he's confident. Trays of bracelet beads look much like the tiny glass isolators he runs wires through, and the wires themselves are obvious for his craft products, as are timers, clocks, batteries. Of course, what might happen if there's a thorough search, when less easily explained precursor material is overturned or his cache of cash discovered, that's a different story, but the solution there is to not provoke a real search.

He's in another month-to-month furnished apartment rental in… where? Buda. Yeah, Buda, Texas, south of Austin, off Interstate 35. It's a crappy garage apartment joined to a small house on Pinafore Street, the sort of neighborhood he favors, that's down at the heel economically. Cash rent payment is a plus. Another essential is driveway or yard space for his pickup camper.

He's been here for less than two weeks and will be gone in a month, maybe more. Losing security deposits and last month's rent is just part of the cost of doing business. And people are grateful, likely as not. A little bonus for the landlord.

He's scheduled to meet up with his cartel contact in Encinal on June 22 in a town well south of San Antonio, at the junction with Texas 44, a middling town in the middle of agricultural lands, where his Mexican contact is as invisible as his own beat-up truck camper.

And Bob's your uncle. He's always been amused by these old sayings, an inheritance from his father, long dead now, from leukemia. Solvents his dad had worked with a likely cause, but he hadn't understood that, not exactly, not as a newly minted high school junior.

He likes the old expressions, and he likes that it helps him think of his father, although he's never been interested enough to look up actual meanings and origins. *Over, done, and gone. If it had been a snake, it would have bit you.* And then other phrases start cascading: *bee's knees, diddly-squat, hill of beans,* until he stops himself, getting back on track, considering the next steps.

His next step is to finish what he calls the *snap dragon,* the inspiration from his childhood, some party favor he's got no idea what it's called, a stiff plastic length that when hitting a wrist, circles tightly, snapping closed. Then it comes to him, *slap bracelet.*

He'd thought about calling what he's designing *armadillo* because instead of one piece of stiff plastic he uses convex beaten copper segments with space for the explosive sleeve underneath, and it can look a bit like a copper armadillo when it circles up. The segments are connected together by weak springs scavenged from retractable pens. The springs are anchored at the front and back edges of each segment, and he's used his tiny Dremel tool to place holes for the anchor points in the copper shells. When snapped against a wrist or arm—or a neck—the segments, if weighted just right, close around, and a magnetic latch secures it closed. He's made sure it's long enough to encircle a neck. That's part of the design spec.

Part of the magnetic latch is the detonator, armed when the magnetic latch closes. The detonator is controlled remotely. He's using a simple signal broadcaster with its own small button battery and a push button, with a reliable range likely no more than forty feet.

He's not sure if the additional weight of the sleeved PE-4 he's carefully placing into the underside of the shallow curved shells could throw the balance off, but he thinks there shouldn't be a problem. He's tested the device with an inert substitute that's close to the same weight and flexibility. The detonator latch's weight can be adjusted, if need be, to compensate for any differential.

He picks up the snake of copper shells and flicks them closed, admiring the look. It looks like an oversized bracelet or just-right necklace, the copper polished and textured with the tiny hammer strikes that shape the metal. Any absurdity in the scale can be argued as being for aesthetic effect.

He re-extends the device and it holds straight by the springs, but it seems on the verge of collapsing back into the round form. But if he doesn't move it about too abruptly and keeps his movements smooth, the segments stay in a straight line. He raises the copper snake gently, holds out his other arm, and brings it down on his wrist. The device snaps around perfectly, even though it goes around almost twice.

"Fucking A." But wait—when he puts in the detonator battery, will that throw off the weight enough to make the operation clumsier? Nah, won't happen.

He's due in Encinal soon, a town equidistant from Laredo and Piedras Negras, one extending down the interstate and the other a good connection away from Texas 83, then connecting with Texas 277 in Carrizo Springs, then the straight shot to Piedras Negras. He doesn't know which of these will be the crossing point into Mexico. Or it could be Hidalgo, or Raymundo de la Rosa. Columbia or Dolores are other solid crossing points back into Mexico, too. But Encinal it is for the rendezvous, unless he gets a coded text or call on the active burner. Smart rendezvous locations and procedures.

His Mexican contact, known to him simply as Biff, will have cash and the two long rifles and the scopes and boxes of ammunition once they cross back into Mexico. They'll get the device ready to go, plus he has the schematics to hand over. The plans look like a jewelry design under quick glance. The detonator is drawn as a small clock face. Tiny check marks at various parts of the build sheet correspond to a text file on a microSD that looks like a to-do list, which it actually is in a way, noting, in order of check marks, the specifications for the various parts and assembly processes, certain obvious names and descriptors left missing.

It had been tempting to draw the design and the specifications in a way that would make it hard for them to reproduce the device on their own. That could be useful leverage and might pry loose more funding, but he's playing it straight with these guys. He doesn't know why they want such a complicated and elegant device, but with the cartels, the reasons can have as much to do with the theatrics of terror; that's his guess.

He's supposed to meet up with another NOS field man, and that guy will have the briefing info, including the reason why he's coming into Mexico and why the long guns and the other stuff Biff has told him he's been assembling for him. *Biff*—odd choice of name. These guys are smart, great to work with, but they're dangerous. *If it had been a snake…*

"Hasta la vista, baby." Another one of those weird sayings his father used, maybe from some old movie?

This assignment's a bit disappointing, though. He misses the early days, back when he was the main drone architect, building and evolving fossil fuel refinery attack mechanisms, but the companies quickly countered every new twist he could come up with. By the time the large sweep net drone defenses had become widely deployed across oil industry facilities, NOS had shut down his efforts. He's been solo for a while now, following the encrypted directions of the *wheres* and *whats* of his life. He's glad that he's been back to the new drone work, but he still misses the ad hoc workshops he put together years before. He misses working with one or two others, designing and fabricating the various drones. The work he's back doing recently is simple FPV attack drones. He'll go by the post office in a day or two for the package he's expecting, a letter with transposed letter code and the new book he'll use to decode the new coded message and future messages. Hopefully, the new book will be a fun read, but that's happened only once in the last seven years, although he's liked skipping around the current book. He likes reading about Michelangelo, but the text is stuffy and on the ponderous side.

Fortunately, the letters themselves can crack him up. These are chatty, always from a different fictitious friend, the rush of words and phone numbers and page references surreptitiously pointing out key passages but obscured in long bodies of sentences. It's all hide and seek, and about as close to a fun hobby as he has these days.

Burn after reading. This is definitely from a movie his father used to talk about, but he hasn't seen it, ever.

Chapter 2: Happy Trails

Early April, 2035

Davin Caine is seeing his first backpacker of the season traipsing down Main Street, although he's been hearing from others about their own sightings for a couple of weeks now, often excitedly reported as if these hikers were red-winged blackbirds or one or another of the migrating birds in the early waves heading northward, as if the scraggly and too often musty-smelling would-be backwoods men and women are the new herald of spring.

He sits alone at a tiny café table on the sidewalk on Main Street, where he's trying to read his Google news feed on his phone, the minuscule tabletop wobbling as he replaces the cup in the saucer after another sip of coffee. He's been trying to read up on the Boston Sea Wall Project, partly funded by the National Sea Wall Act of 2030, which was passed after Miami and the Gold Coast were devastated by Hurricane Josephine, and if he scrolls through long enough there will be some article or another about that ongoing disaster. Late fall of 2034 saw a series of what amounted to battles between squatter reclaimers in parts of the city's abandoned waterfront buildings and adjacent areas where legitimate reclamation and rebuilding was going on, complaints on one side turning to armed confrontations. Something about sewer and water connections, or lack thereof, if he remembers right. There were a dozen dead and injured, and that was before police action finally brought an end to the violence and the casualties from that action. For now. What is popularly called the *Interstitial Interstate* or just *Interstate,* which provides a buffer zone of sorts between illegal domicile and legitimate, will continue to have problems. The demarcation line roughly runs along a portion of Interstate 95, finally reopened after three years.

People of limited means get angry when you try to take away the little they have, but basically, it's a problem of too many people with too few places for them to go, and the funding remains stupidly one-sided. The Florida government is no less racist, and if anything, those living in poverty are more villainized post-Josephine. If anything, the still half-destroyed major American city has become normalized, just another daily fact of life, and he's really no different in this way of thinking, too often the tragedy out of sight and therefore out of mind. Except when there are running gun battles, but there you go.

He gets back to reading an article about Boston's big project, one that won't be completed for years, a major infrastructure project that costs tens of billions of dollars, and that's just for the foundational engineering work and the half-built water redirect pumps and siphon-way pipelines. There are plans for some sea wall sections to contain housing, although the Massachusetts legislature is balking at likely cost overruns. The project as a whole has taken on the popular name *The Big Vig* largely because of interest costs for the growing overruns. The article is reporting on a new investigation of inside plays with the bond agency.

Same old, same old. He had lived in Cambridge during the Big Dig, and while he'd appreciated getting to Logan Airport in fifteen minutes instead of the typical hour plus, pre-Big Dig, the cost overruns were famous in the day, with Bostonians torn between disgust and pride in the amount of money that had been extracted from the Federal budget. He quietly laughs. He's still caught up in that mix of feelings, even after all these years.

His chair's cast iron seat is even smaller than the white-painted iron tabletop, and overall, the diminutive size of this café set and the four others in a scattered line alongside the curb makes him think of dollhouse furniture. It seems improbable that anyone would consciously choose to sit there, but he's lucky to have found an open seat, with the set's other chair holding his side bag with his laptop.

It's early in April, and the day is sunny and still on the cool side, although the forecast reports that tomorrow will bring the first early season hot spell. A backpacker advances up the sidewalk. It must be miserable to start from the northern terminus so early in the season. The guy *looks* miserable enough, even though the sun is shining and the temperature is a very nice fifty-six degrees, and not yet ten o'clock in the morning.

But then again, Davin will always assume the connection between hiking the Appalachian Trail and misery, based on his own, now-ancient, experience. Still, he's always liked that name for the Appalachian Trail, a simple but accurate enough description as he himself learned: *The Green Tunnel*. Not green yet, though.

As for the actual name, The Appalachian Trail, the only thing he would change would be to misspell the second part of the name as *Trial*. The summer before heading off to college, he had hiked the very northern start of the trail from Katahdin, along a stretch he belatedly learned was named, colloquially, the Hundred Mile Wilderness. The experience pretty much cured him of any further backpacking urges, despite all his preparatory research and anticipation, but then he's always been inquisitive, even, as it turned out, when he was young enough and foolish enough to lace up a Sears and Roebuck pair of hiking boots and set off to hike the Appalachian Trail. Sears and Roebuck, the Amazon.com of his youth.

The hills and mountains of the Berkshires, where he lives now, are part of the Northeast Appalachians, as he discovered back then. Most people don't know this, but rather think of the various geologic structures along the length of the trail as distinct elements, separate from the others. All these decades on from the time he found himself struggling up and down mud-encased tree roots and wilting in swelteringly humid and oppressive greenery, he still vividly remembers the geologic revelations back in his pre-hike planning, which was that all the multitude of mountains and ranges were part of the Appalachian Range, starting with the Mahoosucs, those mountains at the northern start of the trail, midway up the large state of Maine. These geological structures grow north of New Hampshire's White Mountains, which themselves are a close range over from Vermont's Green Mountains. The very same Green Mountains are themselves an extension of the Berkshire Mountains that range from southern Vermont through Massachusetts and into northwest Connecticut, and all of these are part of the larger geological structure known as the Appalachian Mountains, all the way down to the southern start of the trail in Georgia.

When he was reading up on all this, back in his youth, his biggest surprise had been that the Appalachians were once part of the geologic structure of the Scottish Highlands and, if that wasn't interesting enough, the Appalachians had once been geologically joined with the Atlas Mountains of North Africa that span Morocco through Algeria and Tunisia, all once connected, eons back, when most land was part of the Earth's giant landmass called Pangaea.

When did this supercontinent exist? Any numbers above seven figures mostly become static in his mind, but it has to be at least hundreds of millions of years ago.

He could look it up, the number of millennia and the name of the era now lost in his memory—he hates to lose track of any and all facts and figures he thinks may have once been in his possession, but he doesn't bother. In his seventy-first year he's slowly accepting such gaps and now more often than not doesn't bother querying Google. Is he even remembering the right name of the supercontinent? How is *Pangaea* even spelled?

The lone backpacker has now stopped and is saying something to the first table in the line fronting Beannie's, the latest coffee house iteration to inhabit the storefront that has seen near-countless versions of a coffee establishment over the course of his nearly two decades living in Great Barrington.

Seeing this hiker–patrons interaction, his thinking shifts to active defense. As best he can tell from the backpacker's posture and the corresponding physical reaction of the two young people sitting at the table, there may be some panhandling he'll want to cut short if the disheveled and trail-weary young man decides to request some tithe from each and every table.

The young couple at the first table hand the hiker something, and with a nod the hiker moves to the next table, and now Davin can hear him clearly enough to know that a donation request is being made of the single occupant of that table, and when that man turns enough toward the standing hiker, Davin realizes that he knows him. The man is one of his Housatonic neighbors, a couple of houses up from his, and hardly more than a waving sort of acquaintance, with the occasional *How are you?* if they've gotten their mail from the post office at the same time, although that may be as much Davin's failure as his. The man—Donny?—has always struck Davin as a bit of a jerk, and all the more so after the guy's uncalled-for complaint to him about Davin's poor trash barrel-securing technique after a bear spread the contents of ripped trash bags across the road. His dislike of the man had been compounded when, some years back, this same neighbor tried to NIMBY against the carrying capacity upgrades of the power lines that run a quarter mile or more from their respective backyards. That wasn't fun.

He'd won, but this may well be the biggest reason for them being little more than waving neighbors. He's still considered a newcomer by most of those who grew up here, although he moved from Cambridge to Housatonic sixteen, seventeen years ago.

Donny says something sharp and the young man steps back with a nod, and then both the backpacker and Donny look toward him. Both, almost synchronized, nod at him.

He nods back at Donny, with what he hopes is a friendly enough smile, but is this going to be seen as encouragement by the backpacker? He's stepping toward him. Sure enough, there's that wave of sweat and body musk that advances as the backpacker approaches, and there's the request for any extra change, and don't you know, he's telling him he's on his way to resupply, and Davin stops him with a raised hand.

"You started out from Katahdin?"

The young man seems delighted by the question, perhaps thinking it bodes well for his immediate future's finances.

"Yeah, sure, started end of February, went through that cold stretch," he's saying, apparently glad of an attentive audience. "Had to hunker down in a motel for four days."

"Tell you what, tell me the name of the mountain range Katahdin's part of, I'll contribute to your travel fund."

The young man no longer looks expectant; instead he's rummaging inside his Gor-Tex jacket and pulls out an obvious pair of smart glasses.

Davin says, "I'll call that a cheat," but the young man has donned them and is saying into the air "Mount Katahdin is in what mountain range?" and his gaze is that inward one that Davin still finds weird as the fellow reads off the information from his heads-up display.

"Mahoosucs," the young guy says, looking back at Davin.

He's shaking his head, but he's amused by the kid's fast thinking. "You know that before you started hiking? Before just now?"

The backpacker, who he sees now must be in his early

twenties, grins. "No."

Davin reaches into his jacket and pulls out his wallet, selecting a five-dollar bill, handing it over. "For your honesty."

The youngster grins more, nods, and steps to the next table, leaving his trail of odor, and then on to the next, and then is gone.

Donny is up from his table and steps closer to tell Davin that he shouldn't give handouts, and Davin can't even manage a *How are ya?* before Donny steps away.

His coffee has grown too cold and he abandons it. Down the street there's a big timber truck, its gurgling diesel engine unpleasantly announcing its approach. With more EVs on the road nowadays, outdoor dining can be more pleasant, but Route 7, which is also Main Street in town, still has plenty of noisy vehicles.

He pulls out his phone and sees that his meeting with Alicia Soares is getting close. She owns the digital newspaper he still sometimes works for, but then again, the office is just two doors down, so he still has a couple of minutes to kill.

He wonders at the glasses the backpacker carries. The prices for these AR rigs have fallen, although these remain twice or more the cost of a good phone, and you still need the right phone, most times, to use the glasses. And then he laughs; almost all of the Appalachian Trail has good signal coverage these days. He's heard that drone delivery on the AT is common and has been for some time now. He lives in a well-connected age. Certainly Great Barrington, with open 6G Wi-Fi all around, is a good example. These days are so different from his own experience and preparation for his ten-day hike decades earlier.

He laughs again, imagining backpackers wearing AR glasses while hiking, and as absurd as the image is, it must happen, at least on occasion. If he were there, he'd avoid using glasses, although this isn't an issue, really, since he doesn't own a pair, happy enough with his laptop and his phone.

He pulls his phone out again. He needs to get going, but as he picks up his bag and starts toward the office, he's still thinking about his long-ago time on the trail. Those boots of his had been a poor choice. Even though he'd followed the best advice about breaking them in, even to the point of repeatedly applying mink oil, the boots remained stiff and easily water soaked. The biggest problem with the boots, though, was how the eyelets for the laces had been made: a loop of metal with edges that tended to saw through the laces with alarming regularity. He still often tells the story most any time any mention of backpacking comes up, recounting in agonizing detail his frequent stops to repair his laces, and how that had felt a mortal threat, the mosquitoes so thick on those northern late summer days on the trail that he feared, whenever he had necessarily stopped to effect the lace repairs, he might prove sufficiently drained of blood to continue.

In his mind's eye, he can still see—even feel—the cloud of voracious mosquitoes and the ghost of panicked annoyance he'd increasingly experienced. He can also admit, and sometimes will still do, although mostly as a self-deprecating joke, that he'd found himself half-wishing that he'd break a leg or succumb to some other sort of injury that would require him to be helicoptered out, rescued from the ordeal of backpacking. Those first four days were anguish, the pack heavy enough for him to be always on the lookout for imbalance, and the trail up there well-churned and well-soaked dirt and a seemingly endless series of steep climbs with only muddy roots for handholds. The subsequent four days were actually something of a pleasure though, his nineteen-year-old body quickly adjusting to the physical demands even while the way grew more level and the pack lighter.

The Green Tunnel has stuck with him as the right description, given that vistas were surprisingly hard to come by. Two years ago, however, wildfires solved that problem for a stretch of the trail within White Mountains National Forest, ripping through the eastern slopes of Mount Jefferson in the Presidential Range and claiming some part of Franconia Notch State Park before traversing eastward as far as Maine's Lakes and Mountains region, stopped only by Kezar Lake and some luck in Lovell, something he remembers because an old friend's vacation house there was spared.

Southward, on Main Street, the parade of cars and trucks seems infinite.

That summer had been a rare dry spell for northern New England, but "rare" weather has become more common, of course. People are adjusting to these changes, and these days only dangerous weather gets any real notice.

In the southern part of Berkshire County, they'd escaped the drought conditions, and that summer had been a great one for his garden, fenced and hardened against the critters that otherwise had easy access from the woods that surround the back of his property, where he'd leveled off a good parcel of land. For some reason, his house in Housatonic, the odd village that is part of Great Barrington, Massachusetts, had been built on a slope. The valley constricted in this part of the river run, and that made for good waterpower. In the mid-nineteenth century, the big textile mill complex buildings had been built, and that offered prosperity to the region for many decades. Days long gone, and now the vehicles heading north are thinning, but the southbound lane is unrelenting.

Both to the south and to the north the valley widens out again. The Appalachian Trail runs through Great Barrington, crossing Route 7 and heading north, coming up from Sheffield across the Housatonic flood plains that run for miles in the broad section of the Housatonic Valley before it rapidly narrows between the geological structure of Monument Mountain and its companion run of other small mountains and hills on the eastern side of the valley. On the western side of this constricted run, there are gentler hills that rise toward Alford and build into the Taconic Range, and this range straddles the border of Massachusetts and New York. Further to the west is the much larger and longer Hudson River Valley, with the Catskills well beyond.

After crossing Route 7, south of the town of Great Barrington, the trail picks its meandering way across the flood plain and starts climbing again, a steep rise up the west face of June Mountain, and then dips down before going up the southwest ridge of East Mountain to follow the ridge around south of Butternut Basin, where the Butternut Ski Resort runs slope down northward. Past that, there's a stretch of the trail that lowers easily into the small Konkapot Valley, until, crossing Route 23 at the border of Great Barrington and Monterey, the trail begins another steep ascent, this time toward Livermore Peak and then up Baldy Mountain in East Lee. Then the trail heads up toward Becket, crossing at the Appalachian Trail footbridge over the Mass Pike. A short hike crosses Route 20, with hundreds of miles yet to go until the trail's terminus on the top of Mount Katahdin, in Maine.

Neither the trail's Route 7 crossing on the south side of Great Barrington nor the Route 23 crossing to the east of the town is all that far from the town's Main Street, and backpackers have long been a common sight, lone or in twos or threes, carrying their gear down the sidewalks on Main Street, or toward one of the two big supermarkets, one about three miles north of town center on Route 7, toward the village of Housatonic, and one south on Route 7, halfway toward Sheffield. Another popular destination is the Berkshire Co-op, just off Main Street in the new location on Bridge Street, that much closer to the center of Great Barrington, a purpose-built mixed-use development completed some dozens of years back. There's an ice cream shop on Railroad Street that's popular, too, with the backpackers, and restaurants, a laundromat, and the Barrington Outfitters store are common stop-offs for the hikers. All of these destinations could be tempting for through-hikers mostly otherwise suffering through The Long Green Tunnel.

Over the last couple of years there have been more of these backpackers around Great Barrington, more of them and earlier in the season, often well before July and August when through-hikers would traditionally make their way up from Georgia's trail start. It's not even May, and nights can still be quite cold and the weather generally messy, although, this spring it has been unusually warm. Or, perhaps, not that unusual anymore.

He decides to stop being lazy and walks down to the crosswalk, pushing the button that brings the metal chorus of *Wait, wait, wait.*

The ever-earlier influx of hikers is a solid topic in the two coffee houses downtown, and among acquaintances bumping into each other on the street or standing in line at the post office, especially when any number of the subjects of the conversation are standing nearby, all too often with the funk of trail life a far too noticeable miasma as they wait to collect their *poste restante*.

With a tone, the metallic voice changes to *Walk, walk, walk*, and he's stepping on to the crosswalk but jumps back, a rider and his electric bike whizzing by, seemingly unaware of any right of way.

Chapter 3: I Love New York

May 6, 2035

Victor Alturo is turning his small studio apartment upside down looking for his wallet, a far too common search. He keeps meaning to follow the habit of putting his wallet in the same place on the tiny entry tabletop as soon as he gets through his apartment door, but he hasn't gotten around to creating this habit in the first place.

"Come on, buddy boy," Alexo calls from the hall through the still open door, electing not to go in because the place is cramped and messy, presumably.

There it is, his stupid wallet, the cloth cover looking more like a sock than anything else. He must have kicked it partly under the armchair on the way to get the door, annoyed with Alexo and his habit of pounding on it, when anyone with half a brain can figure out that with such a small living space, even a gentle whisper through the old wooden door would suffice to announce one's presence.

The apartment on Clinton is tiny, can't be more than two hundred square feet, not counting the tiny galley kitchen and the bathroom. The management company claimed the space was bigger, but then he's long ago concluded that he's best doubting anything and everything those assholes say, like about the rent increase that's supposed to wait until his fourth year. Somehow, the rent has been boosted each and every year, something to do with costs rising, apparently, but he's never bothered to read the lease agreement that closely.

He'll not hold his breath for air conditioning, despite the management company's claim that it's coming. That claim has grown cold, as far as he's concerned, the latest excuse something about waiting on a grant of some sort of funding coming from the Feds. He'd put in a window unit, except that's not allowed, with the likely prospect of any electrical circuit being unable to carry the load and tripping a breaker, requiring a call to the management company and what always seems a minimum two-day wait. He works out of his apartment much of the time and the VR rig needs power and he needs the rig working. There's no winning.

Alexo is calling out again, and Victor plucks his straw fedora off the floor and steps through the door, turning to lock it, the damn key always finicky.

"Bro-bro," Alexo says in greeting, and they walk down the hall, heading to the four flights of stairs to get to the front entrance. The air is stale, heavy, and the heat's building already.

Victor grunts.

"Temp's going up today," Alexo tells him.

Victor really would like his friend to just shut up, just for a minute. He grunts in answer.

"Says the next four days, anyway, likely thunderstorms at some point, when it breaks," Alexo says.

"Coffee, then jibber-jabber, okay?"

This is the sort of thing his pal hates to hear—that he talks too much—but then Alexo doesn't have to work night hours at the pub, and Alexo isn't the one woken by some asshole of a pal pounding on his apartment door. Victor's work as a subcontractor designing and assembling digital objects to furnish VR environments somehow doesn't manage to pay as much as it should. He's just a contract provider, hence the second job.

They trot-drop down the stairs and through the modest front inner door that is old dark wood panels with its gummy shellac finish that probably hasn't been redone since the building was built a century or more before, and whose cloudy surface seems sticky enough to capture the bright light of the outside world. When they exit through the big glass exterior door, the metal shine of the seventies-era refit entryway is an unsettling contrast, and once through the metal and glass door, both come to a stop, blinking against the bright light outside.

"Jesus!" Victor takes a tentative step down but stops again. He's surprised by the temperature that heats him, the sun feeling like a searchlight trying to burn its way through him. He squints up, and the sun, this being a bit past noon, is not yet past the other buildings on the opposite side of the street.

"Like I said, bro-ba-de-bro," Alexo tells him as they head up on the sidewalk for some bodega coffee, "maybe four days of this shit."

Victor grunts.

"It's not even June," Alexo says. "Still, just a taste of the months ahead, my guess."

Tomorrow is May 7. Last summer Victor had barely made it through, especially the three-week heatwave in August when he had to get to the cooling center after his power was canceled because he was in arrears. He couldn't work without electricity for his online connection, and he couldn't work anyway, not with the temperature and humidity so high. His electric fan, even when set directly on him, was insufficient. That had been an unpleasant morning, walking over to LIU Athletic Center, and he almost fainted halfway as he was shortcutting through Fort Greene Park. He now viscerally understands wet-bulb temperature.

Tomorrow he's got a hard deadline for a big contract. Fuck. He grunts again, squinting. He wishes he'd found his sunglasses before heading out, and then he wishes for his sunglasses even more because now, halfway to the corner of DeKalb, a homeless woman catches his eye and nods at him. She's sitting on the second step up of a brownstone that's clearly undergoing a gut rehab, the demo tube hanging down almost to the first floor, but it's Sunday and there's no crew activity.

She's holding up a sign made of cardboard. The sign is held on a slant that makes reading difficult, but then he makes it out:

Geisha for hire

is scrawled at the top edge of the cardboard and underneath:

Shower and shade
I clean up good

He tries to look away, but that's never been a strong suit of his, as much as he keeps trying to learn this essential skill of city living, then momentum works to carry him past eye contact, with Alexo saying something.

Alexo, head down, is getting agitated at something he's looking at on his phone, and Victor is getting agitated, but only because he finds it very annoying when people walk and look at their phones. The least they could do is get a pair of AR glasses and read their screens in heads-up mode while looking out for other pedestrians. Or trucks, e-bikes, cabbies. Cabbies can still be found in the outer boroughs, although Manhattan has gone car-free. Mostly. Plenty of the rich are happy to pay the fees to get their vehicles on the streets.

Alexo is no longer beside him; instead, his friend is standing stock-still, peering at his phone screen, others on the sidewalk moving around and past him.

Alexo looks up, a frown building. Victor steps back toward him.

"Don't you work with a woman, Elise Groöstrum?" Alexo asks.

"You talking about Big E?" He doesn't know her that

well, just through the meetups with other subs. She lives somewhere around his neighborhood, not that he's ever run into her on the street. There's been a couple of parties over the years. "Up near the Navy Yard."

"Doesn't say. Says she was a resident of Brooklyn, lived on Hall Street, so yeah, the Yard."

"Was?" is the only thing Victor can think to ask. Whatever Alexo is seeing has to be Big E.

"Yeah. Shit, yeah, she pulled a Buckel yesterday. Shit."

Alexo is now looking up, showing him the screen, but the sun is glaring full on and he can see nothing. He feels others walking around him. He's standing dead still, so close to his friend that Alexo is radiating additional heat his way. The sun is hitting him full force now that he's still, but he's not seeing anything, really, as he processes the news. Buckel? A flush washes over him. The name of the guy who set himself on fire protesting fossil fuels a decade ago, maybe even earlier, up in Prospect Park, the name now lent to those climate-concerned maniacs who join the growing ranks of suicides to ease environment and carbon burdens.

"Yeah," Victor finally answers. "I know her."

Fuck. He now knows three people who have suicided as protest, although he can't help but suspect that all of the three must have been fucked up in some way, even though he knows you aren't supposed to be judgmental that way, not with what they're calling these days *sincere suicide*.

"Fuck." He gestures to the opposite sidewalk. "Let's cross, I need the shade."

Chapter 4: What Fletch Finds

Middle of May, 2035

Marion Fletcher-Gray, or Fletch, as she prefers, still often feels new in the job of town manager of Great Barrington, even though she just marked her first decade working in this post. She doesn't know why she can still feel this impostor syndrome after so long on the job, or what prompts her insecurities to override her good sense, and a good sense of confidence is what she, at fifty-two years old, should be feeling.

It's not the job, though, making her feel bad today.

It's closing in on the middle of May, the big town meeting last week went well, and all of the town warrants she wanted to get passed did, in fact, get voted in. Her exhaustion has finally receded and she's looking forward to the next couple of weeks. She's been looking forward to coasting a bit, no final budgets to wrestle for the vote, no last-minute crises. Except for her own personal crisis. In her house!

Her husband Robbie has been fucking around, but in some way, this anger is less about Robbie's infidelity and more at Robbie's stupidity, his thinking that in a small town like this he could be seeing—*fucking*—two women and somehow keep this quiet. Two, as far as she knows.

She counts slowly to ten.

She glances around her office at the plentiful pictures taken with state reps and senators and two different governors, and her various awards and citations.

She looks at herself in the mirror over the credenza off to the side. She's in decent shape for a woman her age.

And why wouldn't she feel great? Except now maybe she's arguing with herself because she most definitely doesn't feel great, but she knows why she's feeling unsure and critical and bad about herself. It's not her usual raft of self-doubt, or her general worry about how she's doing. Knowing why she's feeling awful just makes her angrier.

She's had consistently good job reviews and she's at the start of her third five-year contract. Administrating a town like Great Barrington can often feel like a thankless job, a Sisyphean task, like bailing out a boat with a sieve, even if she knows she's doing a good job. She's gotten a lot of things done. She's made a mark on the town.

The bond program she marshaled through for the adaptation plan that includes fixes on culverts and bridges, that's a victory worth crowing about, and even the flood mitigation bill for which she found herself taking on an advocacy role statewide. Three years into the job she read an article in the local interactive about the history of dams in the upper Housatonic, some thousand of them, if she remembers this right. That article came out of a study or some local history book and out of that, these years later, has come a new flood management program based on the siting of a series of control catchments in locations where dams had run sawmills and other small operations going back to the early history of the county. Even today significant dams still exist that once powered textiles and papermaking into the twentieth century.

The build-out of catchments and flood control dams should keep deluges from causing widespread damage along much of the Housatonic River. The dam and headgates of the old Monument Mills in Housatonic is one such dam getting restored, and the Risingdale dam basin has gotten dredged and now boasts in-line flow hydroelectric generators, that project paid for in large part by GE's PCB settlement money, when finished.

For a town manager, she has become somewhat popular. Nothing like being in the right place at the right time.

Nothing is feeling right at the moment, though.

Maybe, in some way, her husband's betrayal is her fault? She's always too busy with the town's business, but she's always made time for him. She keeps to her rule that they have sex at least once a week, although the rule has been more lately the exception, but that's Town Meeting, with all its pressing prep. And what if she's picked up some sexually transmitted disease from Robbie? Berkshire County has been ranking near the top in per capita cases of venereal disease statewide for several years, and she personally pushed for a town panel discussion on the very matter last year. And now Robbie's been messing around God knows where. In God knows who.

She knows one, actually, for sure. She knows the name and address, marital history, number of children, and employment of one of the two women, and unlike the rumored second woman, Fletch has no doubt about this one. Walking into one's house and seeing Robbie on the living room rug with the woman riding him tends to erase any such doubt completely.

Of course, she just turned around and left, but not before her cry of surprise had registered her presence to Robbie and the woman. She has no clear recollection of exiting the house, nor does she have any real sense of driving away, although, of course, her ending up back in her office in town hall was strong evidence that she did both. Even now she's not sure if it was surprise, or shock, or whatever exactly her reaction might have been, but it's definitely anger now.

The woman's name is Marjorie Klandorf and she's a friend of Fletch's from yoga class. Yesterday, Fletch went home because she'd forgotten her yoga mat. She missed that class and however many others to come.

Marge missed that class, too. Fletch almost laughs at this thought, but laughter and panic and confusion don't mix well. She'd love to see the absurdity of the situation, but her anger is dominant, even if in one way she feels more disgusted by having thought a woman who liked to be called Marge could ever be a friend. She must have known *Marge* is the name of a betraying friend, a husband stealer; she should have known. The woman isn't attractive, her body soft and saggy around sharp hips and skinny legs, without any bum to speak of, but now Fletch is sliding back into an odd anthropological state, her sight of the two of them yesterday, there on the living room rug, a field observation.

Yesterday seems unreal.

She learned about the purported second woman that same day, her assistant Kara coming in at the sounds of Fletch's angry mutterings and tears, and she wasn't able to stop herself from telling the younger woman that she'd just walked in on her husband with another woman. The assistant, looking appropriately shocked, said something about her distress and disappointment that the woman had actually gone through with seeing Robbie, which confused Fletch, although not nearly as much as Kara mentioning a different name, an unknown name.

Fletch takes a long breath, then exhales slowly. She picks up the police department's proposed budget for 2036 that's been on her desk for several days already, and she opens the folder and tries to work.

She puts the folder back down.

She knows the publisher of the local, although *Berkshire Interactive* has grown to encompass far more than just South County. She counts Alicia Soares among her friends.

She's supposed to be talking with Alicia about another big issue these days, and that's the cost of housing. She's supposed to be at a housing forum within the hour, up at the South County Community Center. She pulls a pad toward her, searching for a moment before finding a pen.

Of course, she knows the problems. Too many Airbnbs and second homes, and all despite all the efforts and plans to build more housing. Massachusetts remains caught up in a statewide housing crisis. Great Barrington has made less progress on housing than many other towns and cities. A good plan for a large quantity of affordable housing is on the books but can't move forward until the site gets sign-off from the bonding agency that the location is protected from flooding. That's the reason why she fought so hard for the flood mitigation bill.

She sighs. She swallows her anger and starts in on her notes, getting ready for the meeting.

Chapter 5: I'll Take a Medium Meditation, Please

May 24, 2035

Davin sits in his outdoor spot, his meditation spot, at least when the weather permits and when he remembers that this practice does him good.

But he's not meditating. He's thinking about Gwen, his ex-wife, and her height, and how she was chronically after him to straighten up, liking him better at his full height.

He closes his eyes again. He stretches his back, sitting straighter. He opens his eyes, moving his head one side to the other, then up and down. His neck feels tight.

He's been talking about Gwen and the marriage and the divorce to his new therapist. He and the therapist, Jochim Green, meet through video calls, and he isn't really all that new anymore—he's been using him long enough for the sessions to be only once a month now, mainly check-ins, and it isn't that Jochim hasn't been brought up to speed on such major events in his patient's life. But Davin's lately been thinking of Gwen more. This might be because of the latest long stretch of bad dating, or maybe simply just because when one was married for the better part of three decades, the ex-spouse will still haunt you now and again, even after fourteen years pass. Not quite fourteen years yet, since it's still spring, but summer officially starts in less than a month.

Perhaps he's thinking of Gwen because he's been trying to get back to some sort of meditation practice that he learned from her originally. He's outside, sitting on a large pillow he uses for this purpose, kept in his studio, and there's an old throw rug underneath for keeping off damp and dirt. He's under the big shag bark hickory that grows at the crest of a small slope of earth that rises from the near driveway edge. This is the start of the swale system that keeps hard rains from flooding downhill to his studio and from overwashing the terrace and second floor living room beyond.

He glances up at the flat solar panels on the studio's flat bumped-up roof.

Now he looks up to the east-facing slant of the three-story house's roof, but it looks like a two-story height, the house built into a slope and the back length of the first floor below grade on this side. The panels up on the roof are new, too, part of a purchase in 2033 through a low-interest loan from the Massachusetts's Climate Bank. He would have gone solar sooner, considering that the Climate Bank has been online since 2031, but the southern edge of his driveway that makes up a property line had tall trees blocking too much sunlight for the panels to make sense.

That particular neighbor had been resistant to any suggestions about taking these trees down for years. But ash borers had been busy, and that was fortunate for him because in 2032, after he'd forwarded his neighbor a letter from his home insurance company, noting the dead or dying trees, his neighbor, fearing a potential suit should a tree fall onto Davin's property, allowed him to pay for their removal. That wasn't cheap.

There are other trees along his property line, mainly black cherry, that are well on their way to problematic height, but he'll worry about that in a few years' time. He'd just as soon wait as long as possible, not just because the neighbor is onery, but because he likes the look of these trees.

He eyes the four-foot-high studio bump-up wall and sees the three battery units there, mounted, along with control boxes or whatever exactly those covered plastic boxes are. When his distributed energy service provider needs to come by for some servicing or sensor upgrading, they have all the access they need. The provider he's contracted with is Earth Solution, a franchised VPP management service that shows up to maintain his solar panels and batteries on an as-needed basis, flagged through real-time data collection that is part of the service.

He again looks at the flat panels on the framed-out half of his studio's roof and sees that they're getting dusty again. Earth Solution's service techs tend to be grumbly about this—their having to come by more frequently because there's no appreciable slant and the dust and dirt and snow can be a problem. This year the service is talking about installing an auto sweep.

He lets out a long breath, but it isn't meditation breathing but worry about how much the auto sweep might set him back. He closes his eyes and takes some slow breaths, but an image of Gwen, from the last time he's seen her, pops up again. The haunting has mostly faded away after the first six or seven years, but he has flare-ups on occasion.

The last time he saw Gwen was when their daughter Skip and her husband Marco finally came stateside, last August, to celebrate Penelope's fifth birthday. They all met up at the Housatonic House on the Hill. That's what he calls his home, and it's the house Jimmy lived in after the move out here from Cambridge, during those four years at Monument Mountain high school before heading off to college. Housatonic House on the Hill, the house he and Gwen had bought, that had taken far too much time and money to fix up, and then his studio build had finally happened.

That couldn't have helped make Gwen feel more secure, although she never mentioned financial anxiety was a problem. Or maybe he'd projected this onto her. He'd certainly been anxious about money, in part because he hoped to distance himself from his professional work to have more time making art.

Gwen had dropped them off and there'd been little beyond a hello, or maybe it was just a nod, but that made sense considering that he only had eyes for Penelope. That day was wonderful, but full of odd feelings, too. He was overjoyed to see Skip and Marco and his young granddaughter. That day, his granddaughter showed some confusion about who exactly this stranger was and seemed a bit perplexed, he assumed as to why this old guy was crying, but soon he and Penelope were hand in hand as he walked with her, showing her the yard, the garden, the house.

He sits on the cushion, and the sun is on his face, but he's being revisited by the odd mix of longing and loneliness he can feel when he thinks of his kids and his granddaughter. That first day last August was his first time holding Penelope since she was still an infant. He'd managed to brave the flight and swallow the costs of jetting to Barcelona, which is where his daughter, Skip, and her Spanish husband and their first and only child, Penelope, still live.

It had been great seeing Jimmy and Cyn, too, that August day. They live in Boston but had driven Skip and Marco and Penelope out to Gwen's Lenox house before coming over to see him. He sees them less than he'd like, but it was great to see them with their niece in the flesh, too, although their own video calls with the niece and two trips to Europe served to make them known to her.

He'd put Jimmy and Cyn up in what had once been Jimmy's bedroom, on the third floor, the house sharers down to two at the time, just Marsha and Charlie, the awkward and odd Jerome having moved out the previous month. He'd put Skip and her family in the first floor Airbnb apartment for two nights, having blocked out the time exactly for this purpose. On the third day of the visit, they'd all set out back to Boston for one of Skip's interviews, and then she and Marco and Penelope were off to Seattle for a series of interviews with an ocean conservation research facility. They then flew back to Boston for a follow-up interview, staying at Jimmy and Cyn's Comm Ave. apartment, and then the next day it was back to Barcelona.

He'd come east that last morning, driving his Blazer EV, navigating Boston's Back Bay with care and trepidation, but the congestion pricing made the traffic far gentler than what he'd long grown to expect. He'd come to drive them to Logan, aching to see them even just for the few extra moments, and by the time he said goodbye to Penelope he was calling her Pee-Wee, which she concluded suited her just fine, and they both cried a bit when he dropped them off at the airport. Since then, he too video calls with Pee-Wee most every week, getting up early on Saturday mornings to catch her back from her kids' gymnastics, sometimes pretending to have lunch together if he calls a bit early. She looks like his daughter, who looks like her mother, and there's not much trace of his side of the family, but he's always enjoyed the look of Gwen, so he has no complaints.

He opens his eyes again, annoyed at the run of his thoughts. His eyes rest again on the solar equipment, and he's proud that he owns the panels, batteries, and electronic hardware outright and pleased that this allows him to choose to use his own solar generation when electricity prices are at their highest. His electricity bills are much lower since he's spent the money, but payback is still some years away and the loan payments mean he spends close to the same each month as he ever did. The tax credits for the installation have been only marginally helpful because he also has a backlog of business loss from his art that already reduces income tax owed, but he's allowed to defer taking solar tax credit through next year. One can always hope.

Meditate, asshole. He laughs. It's a beautiful day.

For meditating, Gwen had used the space above their bedroom on the third floor, what both she and he called her loft, but these days he's in the small bedroom on the second floor, the bedroom with an exterior door and small deck, at the opposite end from his office. This second floor bedroom, accessible from the inside through the long library that separates the bedroom and his office, is above the main Airbnb apartment bedroom, and sometimes he hears more than he likes when there are guests, and his having a woman over has proved a bad idea when there are guests, the sounds of sex as easily going downward as they do upward.

He's been taking a break from dating of late, frustrated by the results from the dating service, but then again, his most recent dating was a woman he met in real life, a fellow citizen of Great Barrington, and someone about whom he quickly developed hope. Now, though, his takeaway from the sudden implosion of that new relationship is embarrassment and the anxiety that he could run into her anywhere, at any time. Who knows what went wrong—the woman must be mentally or emotionally unstable, and that's not him projecting.

Probably.

He sighs and rolls his shoulders, trying to settle down. He pivots on the pillow to face away from the house, but this means he's stealing a look across the backyard. The garden's plantings are getting bigger each day, the green of coming summer suddenly everywhere, the trees at the back of the property full and lush already. The weather has been on the spectacular side, with only one hot spell, and that dissipated quickly, and the rains have been gentle.

They've avoided the series of heat waves that have been getting locked into the Mid-Atlantic states. These heatwaves have been tough, at least if the news he keeps up on is accurate. The latest heat wave has its northern edge a bit north of New York City and the Palisades, the demarcation line stretching west to Erie and beyond, capturing all of Pennsylvania in its embrace and down into North Carolina.

Nice day here, though. He's trying to settle into something like a relaxed head space, closing his eyes once again and trying to slow his breathing, but he can't get thoughts of his family to quiet.

He opens his eyes, but closes them again quickly, intent on meditating, but he's now thinking that over the long years of the marriage he gradually lost touch or minimized contact with his various siblings, and his parents each died young, younger certainly than his own years now, although he's loath to count those years exactly. This topic of his growing estrangement from his birth family worries like a tongue probing a chipped tooth, unavoidable without great effort. Post-divorce, albeit slowly, he's come to understand that his growing too distant from his own siblings and parents may have been an error, one compounded by Gwen's difficulty dealing with the argumentative ways his siblings related to the world, and he's long realized his parents had made her uncomfortable. Not that any family is without issues.

He pushes the pillow to the edge of the rug and lies down, his hands coming to rest on his chest. He gazes upward. The tree's branches are letting sky and light peek through, the movement like a dance of static.

All four parents gone now, her mother the first to die and her father the last, and both of his parents dead within one year of each other. Gwen and he had found it remarkable that the estates of each family contributed about the same amount of money to the next generation, which, split among the numbers of siblings of hers and his, was no great fortune, but certainly a much-needed blessing. Some of this money helped reduce the debt load that they had gotten themselves into, overspending on the Housatonic house renovations and his new-built studio, but the overwhelming share went to their kids' education. Without this money, they would have been hard-pressed to help the kids in any significant way, and as it was, Jimmy, the last to graduate, came away with college loans.

They had both thought they knew that there was a lot to like about having a so-called empty nest—even maybe anticipating it, him teasing that they could now have sex in all the rooms of the house—but the transition away from Gwen's fundamental identity of mother was difficult in some basic way, not surprising, perhaps, but difficult nonetheless. What surprised them both about this transition was how the marriage and their relationship were affected. The difficulty they faced in re-inventing themselves for each other was like dusting off old outfits and finding the fit tight and uncomfortable. The isolation of COVID provided another strain on the marriage, and his on-again, off-again struggles with depression yet another strain.

"Fuck it." He groans as he staggers to standing, his knees still tight from his earlier attempt at a semi-cross-legged position. He'll go into his office and get a jump on the new additions to the system architecture his recent hire, James Seconds, has put together for his review. They're trying to determine whether the platform *Berkshire Interactive* runs on can be extended to incorporate micropayments for content consumption.

The New York Times has finally come around to that revenue model and so they're wondering how this could work for *Berkshire Interactive*, a thought that makes him laugh, finding himself accidentally thinking, even if just for a moment, these two efforts comparable. On the other hand, *The New York Times*, while still considered an important media presence, has been steadily fading in relevance.

"The old gray mare, she ain't what she used to be," he half sings, more tunelessly than not, as he walks down toward the living room's French doors, rolled rug and pillow under his arms. But what is?

Chapter 6: High Crimes and Misunderstandings

End of first week of June, 2035

The weather is warm for the first week of June, not that there are never outlier hot days that feel like July, but such record weather rarely lasts for more than a day or two or three up in the Berkshires, and Marion Fletcher-Gray, the Fletch of Great Barrington Town Manager fame, has been at her desk trying to write up a proposal for the Selectboard to consider sabbaticals, since she is past her ten-year mark on the job.

She's also well past the time she usually heads home. It's nearly summer solstice, just a couple weeks from the longest day of the year, and the windows outside her office are growing dim. These days, she finds herself staying longer in the office, getting to her empty house later and later.

She hasn't had a sabbatical, not in the last ten years, just a modest vacation package, but doing this job too long without some sort of renewal takes its toll. Ten years of her reign. She loves being sardonic, but it's more habit than choice for her these days. She needs to keep this tendency of hers in check, because sardonic comments don't work well in a public capacity, especially when you're trying to get something you want.

And boy, does she need some time away. She's feeling like she'll explode at any minute, the whole thing with Robbie, who she's asked—demanded, actually—to leave their home, is really doing a number on her. She could end up going off on someone, someone who matters, something that will hurt her professionally and make it that much more difficult to do her job.

The chief of police is one such example. Yorkie Sullivan, Chief of the Great Barrington Police Department, has of late been a particular pain in the ass. There's a battle brewing over the size of the department, with his latest draft budget proposing an increase in the size of the force, adding two more officers. She's long thought that the police department for her modest town is already overstaffed, and last year she commissioned a comp report. The analysis of similarly sized, similarly situated municipalities has provided her with useful arguments, and, perhaps unwisely, she's made the report public. The clear conclusion of the report is that Great Barrington already has a higher number of police officers than the norm. The report will be useful, perhaps, in swaying some constituents, not that she'll prevail, especially considering the old boy network that lives on in what amounts to something of a jobs program for locals. The Department of Public Works, the fire department, and the Great Barrington Police Department traditionally provide enough support to enough Selectboard members to serve as a bulwark against change, but this has been shifting, although she doesn't know how fast. The demographics and economics of tight housing and ever-higher-creeping property taxes play better with the professionals who have become a significant percentage of the town's population. The previous Selectboard election may have finally shifted the balance of the board away from old townie power.

She's also been getting pestered for release of overtime for this department, Yorkie playing up reports of more young people around town, some possible increase in shoplifting and public sleeping. There's been one incident of assault—a mugging, basically—a young man aggressively asking an out-of-town guest for money, and the perpetrator, according to Yorkie, right in her office just two days back.

The young man looked like a homeless—*unhoused*—person. Both labels make the case that people without a place to live are a big problem.

On the other hand, the young person is claiming he's a tourist and that he lives in New York City, and Yorkie has a Bronx address for him on record that squares up. The young man is claiming that he'd only been panhandling and that the other guy just freaked out, that he wasn't screaming at that man but was just trying to calm him down.

Small town police bullshit. She was inclined to say that Yorkie was just posturing, but over the last week she's been hearing from other people about similar encounters, although one frantic citizen, a neighbor, had detained her over the fence talking about *great herds of the unwashed*. She hadn't laughed, but then she wasn't likely to at that moment, sitting out back with a glass of wine, thinking of exactly how she should handle all of Robbie's clothes and things, all that he'd left without, having taken only a small suitcase a few days before. Burn, rip, destroy, throw out, or give away in a big tag sale were the current options.

There had been an edge of panic in her neighbor's remarks. The neighbor is new, and as good an example of the type of people buying into Great Barrington as one could hope to find: ex-urbanites, awash in the fear of crime or in search of a child-raising paradise or more affordable living. The well-off newcomers, these upper middle-class people, like strong services and seem compelled to push for stronger schools, public works on climate mitigation and resilience, and affordable housing, at least as long as the efforts to build multi-family units don't happen in their neighborhoods. The well-off also complain about high taxes, but more out of habit than existential challenge.

If she's going to push back against the expansion in police hires, she knows that she'll have to tread carefully. Fortunately, this new budget is due next May, when it needs to be ready for the vote of the town meeting, so she's got time.

Her phone rings; it's Chief Sullivan on the line. Speak of the devil.

"Yup," she says.

Sullivan's phlegmy rumble is the first thing she hears, but this is so much part of the man that she barely notices it anymore. Gone are those days where *consumptive* comes to mind when listening to the chief speak.

"A head's up," he says, voice momentarily clear. "There's been a report of a gunshot or gunshots up in Housatonic, likely around or in the park and playground."

The recently renovated park. "What do we know?" she asks him, but he tells her there's nothing more yet; his officers are canvassing the neighborhood and the construction crew finishing up the rebuild of the Housatonic Elementary School, whose old playground had become the village park too many years back for her to guess. The closed school had been underused or vacant for decades before her own tenure started, and a number of proposals and projects have started and stopped across the years, but four years ago the town finally found the right developer, which, in the case of this building, is a developer who actually carries through from the planning into construction. A mixed-use building was the proposal; offices and apartments, and the old school, reborn, will open by the fall, at least if the work remains on schedule.

The town has basically given the building to the developer, with plenty of tax breaks, and the only real concession is that two of the twelve apartments are to be rented below market rates. The ten-year property tax abatement looks to keep the taxes unpaid for another six years, but this has been one of her big triumphs, even with the giveaways.

She tells the chief to keep her informed and cuts the connection. She rests her forehead on the desk, eyes closed tight, then pushes back in her office chair and stands. A shooting!

Chapter 7: All Aboard the Wahwah Express

First week of June, 2035

The online newspaper seems to be going as well as expected, but Alicia tries not to acknowledge positive news too directly, long having surreptitiously practiced the superstition of denying good news in order to ward off the evil eye. She's sometimes more conscious of this practice than at other times, and when so aware, she chides herself and resolves that this superstition is an insignificant cultural fragment that means nothing, really, about how she actually reacts to the world.

Alicia is startled out of her thoughts, seeing a woman who also waits for the train, who Alicia flashes on is her mother, but now that Alicia has a better look, she sees that this woman looks almost nothing like her mother, really, just a trick of the mind—has to be anyway; her mother's dead. There are similarities, though. The way that woman is dressed, a kind of corporate casual, and her hair is similar, too.

She calms herself, and that's easy to do with such a beautiful day, standing in the shade of the station's wide overhang, listening to the twittering of the birds.

Alicia's a practical gal, lets reason lead, all things to be figured out, capable of being figured out, and very much preferred to be figured out. At least that's what she believes. She's innately proud in proving absurd the adage that women are emotional, while men are rational. Alicia's among the proud ranks of the long and struggling line of feminists that included her mother, God rest her soul, although every time she thinks about her mother she feels a bit down. She doesn't usually think of her mother by choice, or only rarely so, not that she keeps track of such things, but this is one of those rare flares of feeling down. And angry. This isn't her. She pushes the insistent apparition away.

She's standing near the railroad tracks waiting for the 11:10 train to arrive at the Great Barrington Train Station and Annex, which brings to the fore a memory of the Annex opening being her first ribbon-cutting coverage after her being enthroned at *The Berkshire Record*. Her fall from that editorship had been a blow, but she's long since resurrected her career with *Berkshire Interactive*.

She's looking down the track, looking around, enjoying the warmth of the day, listening to the birds among the nearby trees, and eavesdropping, too, another mostly unconscious habit, all in a not entirely successful effort to not notice the converging thoughts of mother and track, but this fails. Here come those feelings again, the guilt, and the anger about her mother's suicide, when she was twelve years old. She thinks of her mother's death as suicide, although her death was ruled accidental. The few potential witnesses on the late-night platform hadn't noticed anything. No one saw exactly what happened, a slip or stumble maybe, and no one ever seems to have questioned the circumstances or raised the question of intent.

And the alcohol blood level was high. She only learned this bit of information years later, going through her father's things after his own passing, in his early seventies, but by lung cancer, not hit by a train. Her mother had died just before turning forty. She was an elegant but distant mother, her beauty a thing of mystery observed from the vantage of remoteness. Mind the gap.

Jesus. Why is this mood dogging her? She's here to meet an old college friend whom she hasn't seen since. She thinks about her old therapist, and about how much he'd love the

Berkshires. Well, he certainly wouldn't be the only one.

The chamber of commerce is forecasting a record year for visitors, which should mean more of these visitors will be signing up to *Berkshire Interactive,* which she can confidently claim offers the best, most complete local news, the most usefully interactive services, and most comprehensive events calendar in the area, although, compared to the anemic alternatives to *BI,* the claim may actually be less significant than it sounds at first blush.

Of course, what is most significant is what the advertisers think, and that's been looking good. Already, two of the alternative publications in print have shuttered their operations or will be shuttering them. The demise of one of these publications was reported to her by some of her advertisers. The information about the other publication's closing down has come from its own publisher-editor, who recently met with Alicia to declare defeat and to ask to join her winning efforts.

Of course, she immediately—and graciously, she hopes—accepted said surrender, and named the now ex-publisher-editor as *Berkshire Interactive*'s new galleries editor—on a freelance basis, of course—and has been courting the several advertisers that publication had managed to hold on to exclusively, albeit possibly because of the absurdly low rates that, she suspects, have helped contribute to the publication's capitulation. The first galleries editor had lasted for several years, but had been petering out slowly and painfully, until Alicia had suggested retirement. Several remaining online competitors to *BI* are competitors in name only, too weak to challenge her.

The Berkshires has long had the reputation of having a depressed economy, and long before the rest of the country joined with the county in that regard. Steadily rising prices and costs have dug into employment while keeping wages down, and COVID, more than a dozen years before, largely shut down the tourist economy for a while, and a number of businesses never made it back to successful active status. The housing market crisis is another contributor, despite the post-pandemic boost temporarily enjoyed when so many New Yorkers sought to leave the city. This time the crisis is in availability, with prices still too high. Homelessness has been a big problem in many local places, as is hunger, largely because of food price pressures.

Fortunately, Massachusetts is still doing fairly well compared to a lot of other states, but the Commonwealth's resources aren't unlimited, especially when Congress remains budget gridlocked in the ongoing fight about defense spending, and federal aid remains locked for most programs. There are simply too many Defense Department-related jobs spread across too many districts, and the last congressional election showed that incumbent candidates had every reason to be cautious about calling for those cuts.

Her thoughts drift into current politics.

I like Ike.

The old slogan has taken on new currency among progressives, even to the point of a tentative resurrection of Nixon as patron saint of environmentalism, the EPA still recovering from Trump. Otherwise, the fight for renewable energy has gone well, post-Trump, but that delay, according to her columnist, Jeannie Louise, who writes about climate, has allowed fossil fuels to entrench new gas-fired power plants and that, according to her, has suppressed many solar and wind projects.

She gets a kick out of having Jeannie Louise on board, or at least as on board as Davin gets her to be, since there's really little financial reward they can provide compared to the big publishing outlets that hire Jeannie Louise for her detailed analysis of climate change policy issues. She lets Jeannie Louise do what she wants, and there's been some great results, including her new column about weather and climate change causality.

Attribution, that's the term.

Jeannie Louise has a knack for making subjects into

popular reading that should otherwise cause eyes to glaze over. She also creates content that *Berkshire Interactive* can syndicate, and while the fees gained through such content are modest, they all add up.

South of the Berkshires, she's been seeing in the news, a heatwave is building and the forecasts say it could remain a stable condition for a while. New York City will be in the thick of it.

There are other opportunities for Alicia in neighboring areas like North County and Northwest Connecticut, while the greater Hudson area—which easily could include Albany—would be tougher competition. She's also mentally bracing herself for more buy-out offers, but there's no way that's going to happen, not while she's having so much fun, even if most of the income is going right back out, still building the business.

The rail service coming back had been big news, although much of the drama behind the restoration of train services—the fights between Massachusetts and Connecticut and the budget battles within the legislature—preceded her arrival in the Berkshires. She did, of course, familiarize herself with the rather torturous development of the effort. There'd been the usual starts and stops, and a couple that could hardly have been expected, but the passenger service finally stuttered back into existence, as fuel costs made the argument for the service obvious.

Perhaps she could get someone to write up an updated cost comparison for using the train, or maybe she can do this herself and save the writer's fee. Of course, the steady rise in EVs adds further complication, but something regular about the train service would be nice. This is something else that could become an ongoing index feature, along with the costs such as fuel prices, tolls, parking fees, and all the other factors that will have to be considered.

Nice. Another index. People love indexes.

Another index might be a running guesstimate on the population in South County as the season grows, especially if the numbers continue to swell far beyond normal expectations and far earlier than in previous years. So far, this is rumor more than established fact.

Maybe Davin can show her—yes, again—how to generate a response template that will encourage the motels, inns, B&Bs—and Airbnbs, of course—to self-report, although the chamber may have enough of these data points already. She should be able to get the Airbnb information—basically, availabilities and numbers of guests over the defined locations—although, Airbnb allows only registered users to view offerings. How long will it take Airbnb to shut down this kind of robotic data collection? Maybe this will be too big a pain.

The blast of the train's approach whistle makes her jump. Like the other dozen or so people waiting, she turns to look southward down the track and, of course, sees nothing, the train probably still a couple of minutes out, the sound of its approach growing slowly, except for those repeating whistle blasts.

She's here to greet an old college friend, Max—although she's stumped to recall her friend's actual first name, having always called her Max for so long. If Max's email and follow-up call to her is any indication, Max continues to be her preference.

Max, Max, Max.

Probably Maxine—yeah, she's pretty sure she has the name right.

She and Max were in the same dorm for their first two years at school, and then roommates off campus junior year. Junior year was the year Max told her that she thought she liked other women, when they were both drinking—What the fuck were they drinking?—some mango-tequila-lime concoction Max had named a *Signorita*.

The drink isn't the main recollection from that evening as much as is the vivid memory of Max cajoling her, coaxing, pleading for Alicia to show Max her breasts—*Just that, promise?*—and she had been flush with the request and

Max's desire for her that was driving it. It felt good, but that was the liquor talking. It had felt quite good to take off her blouse—a dark red thing with those puffy short sleeves—Oh God, she used to dress like that—and stand before Max, drinking in Max's drinking in of her, and pleased, joyful, simply in feeling admired, desired.

That feeling continued until Max reached out to touch, and she stepped back and reminded her that she'd made it clear this was a *look don't touch,* and it was only the next morning that Alicia wondered if she'd been a bit mean to Max, but it was Max, after all, who had asked, and she was very clear from the start that this would go no further and that she was not a lesbian, although, obviously, she was less inhibited with drink.

She's not a lesbian.

Not that there's anything wrong with that.

She's been in a relationship with Deidre, and she still thinks of Deidre, a lovely young woman, someone who had been living at Davin's house back then, and Alicia still doesn't entirely understand what happened, but she knows that they loved each other. But Deidre moved out, just months after moving in with her at her Sheffield home, and Alicia knows that this had something to do with how busy she'd been with *Berkshire Interactive.*

When she allows herself to think about Deidre, Alicia misses her. She doesn't let herself think about Deidre very often. She sighs.

The train's moving slowly, rounding the last corner.

She and Max had continued to be close friends, or so she'd thought, although senior year saw different living arrangements and they got in touch only infrequently post-college. They still liked each other, although she also always had in mind that Max, despite her frequent assurances that year, long ago, wanted more, and Alicia felt a certain nervousness with Max after that.

The train is entering the station, having *Mother-May-I'*d down the track without her noticing. She's waiting for this good friend that she hasn't seen in quite some time, waiting to catch a glimpse of her stepping from one of the cars, and it's a beautiful day, and Alicia's feeling good. She's excited about giving herself a bit of time off. She's been nose-to-the-grindstone, after all, but now she's out and about, footloose and fancy-free, a moment in the sun.

And then she's scanning from one car to another to another, watching the passengers spill out, or cautiously step, or struggle with bags, backpacks, and suitcases of all sizes.

The disembarking passengers are mixed, many, no doubt, tourists, and then there's one of the commuters she knows, and they acknowledge each other with a wave. Then there's a gang of leather-vested, tattooed black guys, and Alicia's alarmed for a moment, just like that, followed by a spear of guilt.

Following after this group of guys is an elderly black woman—Gang Mother!—but the woman is struggling with a roll-on that seems to be almost her size, so she steps forward to lend her a hand getting the suitcase down to the platform, and right behind the old woman is Max, looking great, and grinning, and they're on the platform, screaming little high screams into each other's ear, hugging and swaying, and Alicia's glad that Max is here, the night long ago once again put in its place, and Max is asking her if she's going to show her around *Rockwell Region*. There's a young woman with sparkling black hair walking toward them, and the leap of excitement ebbs when she realizes that this is not Deidre. But Max—*Max!*—is here.

Beyond her, more and more people are getting off the train, mostly young men, some with luggage or like backpackers, but more are jumbled, sleeping bags under arms and wearing street shoes, and all those short-brimmed straw fedoras, and the number is striking.

Brooklyn hipsters go a-hiking!

Chapter 8: Sweeng Batta Batta

First week of June, 2035

Freelance journalist Derek Waalewi most often thinks of himself as an anachronism, something out of a Graham Greene novel, or part of that spike in online journalism, the old Substacks and podcasts that blossomed in the mid-2020s, only to again become a rare breed halfway through the first Democratic administration following Trump.

Trump the Muttonhead. That blot, that embarrassment, that enemy of America, and that gift to a whole generation of journalists and opinion writers who escaped from the dying legacy media only to be threatened with being drowned by the baby bath water of online hyper-consolidation. But where there's a will, there's a way, his papa always told him, and the last year or so has seen another re-emergence with the anti-trust cases triumphing, and with the widespread adoption of micro-payment systems, and the tentative re-awakening of American journalism is up and drinking strong coffee.

He's done well financially with his reporting on the excursion into Mexico by American soldiers reacting to an attack on one of the many forward operating post border camps manned by personnel of the 2nd Brigade, 4th Infantry Division. They, like other divisions and brigades and the 1st Combat Engineer Battalion, 1st Marine Division, occupied both fixed and changing forward operation installations under the Joint Task Force-Southern Border, within the proscribed areas of operations, FOPs, and FOBs, and base camps. He smiles at the military gobbledygook. His ability to translate the parade of acronyms and stilted phrasing and definitions has been part of his success in what's evolved into a short series of articles. One thing he helped make clear was the scope of the US Joint Task Force–Southern Border's area of operations across the two thousand-mile US–Mexico border, from San Diego, California, to McAllen, Texas. It was really that first article of his that had gotten him back in the freelancer game, the one reporting on the growing number of armed conflicts that have been occurring, at least sometimes, with one or another cartel butting up against the military presence.

The recent three-month lull is hardly likely to remain status quo as long as the border's migrant problem grows. Smuggling of all sorts goes on across the border and it represents huge opportunities for the cartels. He's hoping that he can learn more about the size of these smuggling operations and gain a clearer sense of the economic scope. It's why he's here, but when he looks around, where he stands in the hot sun looks like nowhere.

He'd been in the right place at the right time to cover the initial incident or, more accurately, the initial reaction to the attack, when he managed to tag along when a self-assembled QRF responded to the soldiers' call for assistance. The first group of soldiers, eighteen men in a light platoon, pursued what was assumed to be a small, armed group sniping with small arms and mortar fire at the temporary camp, and these soldiers were engaging in what became a mobile firefight, and using their two joint light tactical vehicles, or JLTVs, they found themselves advancing across the border. These sorts of border intrusions had happened before but had been minor, sparking only pro forma complaints by the Mexican government.

Production of JLTVs had been ordered closed during the Trump administration but plenty made it into the field. They became one of the workhorses of US Joint Task Force–

Southern Border and were capable in cross-country maneuvering, and the soldiers simply gave chase.

The big difference was that those soldiers soon found themselves facing an ambush by greater forces, and the base camp's QRF set out to RTB these soldiers in force, two gunships and a Stryker group in lead deployment. Shortly after, the 4th Combat Aviation Brigade dispatched two AH-64D Apache gunships to catch up and assist in covering the growing reaction forces.

QRF, Quick Reaction Force; RTB, Return to Base; CAB, Combat Aviation Brigade, he mentally recites, shaking his head, then thinks of how hard he's had to work to keep all of the names and jargon straight. The way the military speaks, it's like some sort of neurolinguistic virus.

Before long, a whole company deployed from 2nd Brigade, 4th Infantry Division using a bevy of CH-47F Chinook for cargo and troop transport. Another three helicopters, aging UH-60M Black Hawks, were flying in Mexican airspace too, mainly for evacuation of the wounded and the several casualties who were KIA.

He'd been there. He wrote a long set piece about it, his accidental embed, although it hadn't been a happy accident for the staff sergeant who allowed him to hop on the JLTV, back in the heat of the moment. No one had had any idea of what was ahead. It was just a scoot and shoot.

Six dead, ten wounded, number of enemy combatant casualties officially undetermined, but the US soldiers had met a significant force, which the Apaches chewed up hard, but word from US command yanked the American forces back, and the tug wasn't gentle.

Nor was the diplomatic shitstorm that followed.

His next two articles followed the repercussions, and his coverage of the Mexican government's complaints and UN accusations sold well enough, but by then the competition was all over the story of the aftermath. His third piece tried to present the conflict from the Mexican side, and it had become clear through both US Military intelligence and the Mexican government that the other side was the cartels, with the best guesses about whether the initial attack had been an attempt to either clear a smuggling route or distract from one, but speculation had remained just that.

Not battle but armed interaction. The US government has been frowning on the use of *battle* to describe the incident.

He had found it thin going, his efforts to dredge up information about the cartels and what the motivation might have been and who, or rather, which cartel or cartels were involved. Rumors were flying about cartel-to-cartel cooperation.

His third piece had done much worse than his second piece and here he is, in Sinaloa cartel land, just up from two months in Oaxaca working on his Spanish.

And the señoritas.

But as a journalist, he's bound by ethics to tell the truth, and except for one four-day stretch, he hadn't exactly been a winner in the *señoritas* department.

"Yeah," he says quietly, looking around at the dusty countryside, up near Hermosillo, waiting for a contact. As mediocre as the sex may have been, the thoughts of those four nights are helping him ignore the hint of distress in his bowels as he waits.

The work to acquire a cartel-adjacent contact willing to talk off the record hasn't been easy.

Cartel-adjacent is scary enough for him.

The success he had, especially with the first article about the battle, raised his profile to the point where his contract editor was willing to invest time in his new efforts. His contract editor had worked hard.

The contact has been verified, and the meet point should be safe, but should he have verified the verifier, a sort-of colleague who knows the same editors? He laughs at this thought—that he's been set up out of some play for competitive advantage.

And this nameless contact might not even show up, so

he might as well enjoy the view, but the dust and scrub and brown hills in the distance aren't all that inspiring. The landscape is dusted with green in patches made muddy through the dun-colored haze that thickens with the distance. It's pretty fucking hot, too.

"*Hace mucho calor hoy*," he says out loud.

He can't believe he forgot to bring a fucking hat.

There's been plenty of talk of new rounds of violence, cartel on cartel, and reports of heads missing from corpses and bodies strung up from bridges, but he's heard something more interesting. The cartels, or some of them anyway, are trucing or even working together, the threats from the US border enforcement and the military patrols resulting in a few armed engagements with the *yanqui*, although nothing on the scale of the incident he covered. That could be bringing them together, Sinaloa and another cartel, although he's heard three different cartels named as the other one.

He's been seeing the term *yankii* used in speech and graffiti and figured it was a variant spelling or typo that's gotten caught up in some algorithm's embrace, but the usage seemed, yes, disparaging, but in a different way than Yankee can get used. One slow Oaxacan evening, prepping for this assignment, he did some reading up and found that *yankii* was an actual thing, a sort of Japanese movement that originated from working and suburban youth, a movement that much of Japanese society still associates, despite its decades-old history, with juvenile delinquency. Not one of his priority questions, but if the opportunity presents itself, he'll ask if this is how the cartels look at the armed forces arranged along the border.

Juvenile delinquents.

He sees the dust from a vehicle and, squinting, he makes out a truck, and as he awaits its approach, he hopes it's the contact, someone he will know by the hat and boots, the hat a gimme cap for the Oakland Raiders, the boots, red leather, silver trimmed. A red carnation, so to speak. He's trying to take his mind off his rising stomach and the ghost of a sense he will need to take a shit, and he compulsively, yet again, runs down the list of what he's eaten, what he's drunk, assuring himself he's been good, following the guidelines of bottled water only.

If only he'd brought out the half-empty water bottle, but he's left it in the rental, and that's too far behind him to retrieve it now that the likely contact is coming toward him. His walking away would look weird and might spook the meeting.

Just this morning, he emailed the assignment editor he's contracted with the meet plans spelled out in as much detail as he could, the rendezvous location, the time, but that detail now looks thin as he stands, the truck slowing, then stopping.

Derek wipes his palms on his jeans, left outside thigh, right outside thigh, twice, and when he looks at his right hand, ready to shake hands, there's a dampened smear of desert dust there.

"Hola," he says, with a wave as the man steps down from the truck, and he smiles, the Raiders cap and the red leather boots right there, but behind the man, two others jump out of the bed, the three converging on him, a baseball bat swinging in the hand of one of the other two men.

The other man behind Raiders Cap is saying "Sweeng batta batta, sweeng batta batta," but Derek's eyes are on the man with the bat, and his body figures out what's going on first, his bowels letting loose, and Derek's last emotion as a conscious, living man, with no sense of embarrassment, is surprised wonder.

Chapter 9: Outward Bound

Second week of June, 2035

Walk in the heat, or stay in the heat, is what Victor is telling himself, wanting to get the walking over. He notices he's scanning for storefronts or coffee shops or bars where he could duck in for some AC. But ducking into a place is not the same as getting to where he's heading, which is Grand Central Terminal, to take Metro-North to Danbury in Connecticut, to transfer to the Housatonic line for service to Great Barrington, Massachusetts.

He started on the B Line, getting off at Broadway–Lafayette Street, where he planned to grab the 6 Train up to Grand Central. But of course, he hadn't checked that the line was in service, a stupid enough move in any case, but especially since the heat is causing all sorts of problems across the whole transit system. So now he's hoofing it from Lafayette, and he's made it through Union Square and on to Park Avenue South. Best he figures it, he has another twenty blocks or so, and he's feeling it. He's already stopped once, but at this rate he'll need two more rest stops, and he's already gone through his water bottle.

There's little in the way of tuk-tuks in this stretch and even then, he's reluctant to spend that money. One quick glance at the Uber app trashes that idea, the priority fees about as high as he's ever seen, so that means self-driving cabs and Ubers are right out. As is the still-new Checkers service, which sometimes strikes him as something right out of *The Fifth Element*, that old movie that his buddy Danny had pushed on him repeatedly, although now he wonders if he's thinking about a different sci-fi movie, one where old-style Checker Cabs had a goofy-looking mannequin in the driver's seat.

He hadn't even known about the original Checker Cabs, not really, but these new versions have caught on in NYC, with similarly formed bright yellow bodies put on an EV chassis, and this is something that has become a pervasive fad, with pseudo-1950s Bel Airs and Mercury Montereys and Dodge Royals and several others periodically spotted on the streets. He's been told that these fifties-era car models work well, with their large sheet metal bodies, now reproduced through digital scans and 3D printed forms of resin and fiber, but with the safety features hidden under the big envelopes. The best looking one is a recreated Figoni et Falaschi Delahaye 135MS Narval, originally made in 1946, low and long, sweeping lines across a bright red body, but he's only seen pictures of it online, and it might well be a one-of-a-kind custom job or AI.

The Checker Cabs look like the original models, but the interior is larger and certainly more comfortable, and the cost of a ride is prohibitive for someone economically marginal. But the heat is tough and he flags one down. He notices the engaged light too late to stop his arm before the car slides past, its four passengers peering at him from within their air-conditioned comfort. The way they're gazing through the glass, maybe they're tourists, perhaps dazzled at this New York denizen in the wild.

He manages to flip them off, but the Checkers cab has already passed and the effort of it all exhausts him. He doesn't have the money to spare, anyway. Smarter people than him are riding in comfort. But his rent is so high and the temperature, too, and he's having trouble mustering up much in the way of resentment.

He could have bought a parasol five blocks past, but earlier he'd felt too silly. He'll stop again to rest in nine blocks, but even a swing through Madison Square Park, as tempting as the tree canopy is, is too out of the way on a day like this.

He dated a girl who lives in the Murray Street House apartments, and that's a fourteen-block push, but he's not thinking right, considering that he had dated her early on in his move to Brooklyn. Doing the math, that was almost six years ago, which means he'd dated her during that time when he was salaried, back when he was working for that app engineering company, Divisys, his first and last great job, before the layoffs.

That early relationship hadn't really gone well anyway, and he might have ghosted her. No, wait—she ghosted him after that layoff. He's glad for the shade the tall buildings provide.

Fuck.

It all seems like a lifetime ago.

Fuck, it's hot. He laughs at thinking about stopping in at his old girlfriend's apartment for a bit of cool air—the chance she's still there is next to none, and she's probably not even in the city now. She'd probably been thinking about kids, the house in the suburbs, who knows?

She's likely done him a favor.

He shifts the backpack, some garish orange thing, maybe older than him, a dirt-stained nylon piece of crap with a light aluminum frame that's slightly bent in the left vertical bracing. He just bought the backpack a week before, in the thrift shop in Queens, back when the heat wave was still growing, and he realizes with surprise this trek now is his biggest recent outdoor experience, this death march to Grand Central. He doesn't count the short runs to the bodegas or to the pub as real time outdoors, just quick walks to nearby destinations, not like today's out-and-out ordeal. The shoulder pads are thin with a lifeless compression and his shoulders are complaining, but he's only got twenty blocks to go.

His friend Nick is up in Sheffield, which is supposed to

be near Great Barrington. His friend's staying with his folks up in their summer house, and Nick has reached out and invited him up. Nick's parents are off on some trip soon, not that he's got all those details down, exactly. It sounds like there may be a couple of others taking up this invitation, and an ADU is part of the property, but any place out of the city sounds paradisiacal, no matter the details. Nick's text mentioned that the Berkshires are running ten to fifteen degrees cooler, and that's the official average, not the extra heat island effect his corner of Brooklyn is trying to survive, running another few degrees hotter.

The Bronx, overall, is worse.

He steps into a Duane Reade but is disappointed that the AC is not working great. He strides over to the cooler cases and buys three bottles of water that are cold. Back on the sidewalk, he drinks one down, and so quickly that the cold is cramping his sinuses, but the relief is worth it. He sticks a second bottle into a side pocket of the creaky backpack, the frayed elastic closure making him nervous about the hold, and then opens his other bottle. He leans over and pours the water in fits and starts over his head and neck and wrists, then wets his straw fedora and puts it back on his now relatively cool crown.

"Yo, yo, coolie-cool," a passerby says, and Victor nods, and there are others on the sidewalk, crowding the shady side with him or walking past.

He hitches the beat-up backpack higher up onto his shoulders, feeling every ounce of his various changes of clothes, his VR rig, a ziplock bag of sundries, a tarp and bedroll, some netting, some trail mix. Nick had suggested these last items, not sure if there might be some renters for a day or two or three after his folks leave, but there's the backyard and plenty of woods and hiking trails and even the Appalachian Trail, just for the interim, if so.

"Fuck," says Victor, but it's not in any mean way, and no one passing reacts or even notices, except one older man, responding with a nod.

There are another eleven blocks to go.

Chapter 10: Code Bomb Deluxe

Second week of June, 2035

Jimmy is restless, tired, and he'd rather be working from his apartment, but these days that doesn't happen anymore, not with how busy NoNolo is, has been, with all the climate court cases piling up, seething and ready for action. These days the long hurry up and wait of the legal system seems like a logjam breaking.

The last four weeks have been a dizzying flurry of work for him, systems admin for NoNolo, *clearinghouse to the gods*. The lengthy buildup of important responsibilities his company has claimed, handling the legal documents and documentation for a hundred climate cases in the courts, even more. Too many of the climate court cases are being prosecuted by armies of tiny Davids who are up against still-mighty Goliaths. Although the past two years have been tougher for Big Oil, they haven't been so tough that the various defendant corporations can't still easily outspend the plaintiffs.

NoNolo is one answer to that disparity, where the complex and time-consuming management of case documents and their timely dissemination can be expanded across the many cases that share the documentation. Of course, there are other ways to fight Goliath, and one such way is to be a Goliath too, like the huge class-action suits brought against fossil fuel companies by a collection of state attorneys general. Another change in the balance is the sources of funding that are large enough to cause worry even for the biggest multinationals, but big donors and NGOs and environmental and electrotech member groups must pick and choose their battles.

He's mostly stopped noticing the case count board that's pinned up in the small reception room, but this morning he'd taken a look and noticed that the number was up to 157 as he passed through, with a quick nod to Mary Ann, the receptionist, office manager, and all-around Girl Friday. Mary Ann reigns all-powerful in institutional importance, second only to McAdam's executive administrator, one Dolorie Sanchez, who guards the inner sanctum known as McAdam's office, and Jimmy knows that in all fairness, each of these women knows her stuff and keeps everything running smoothly.

On the other hand, it's his responsibility to keep the network humming and running smoothly and the structured documents database healthy. Somewhat to his chagrin, his responsibilities also seem to include helping people with their email accounts and passwords and the occasional hands-on reboot, even though that isn't strictly his job. Except it is if either Mary Ann or Dolorie deem it so, since he wants to keep things copesetic and otherwise happy, because he does like each of these two odd women, and besides, it keeps his job from getting too tense, since for him, power battles are *contraindicated,* as his father tends to say.

He should text Daddo—it's been a while. They've seen him east only twice since being back for Skip's triumphant return. He should telephone his father, but that's a habit that has always eluded him, and writing an actual email is something he mostly only does at work. Mostly he sends notes and messages via Slick, the Slack work environment that's eaten the older collaborative work system. Good riddance to Slack, with its clumsy and constrained interfaces and kludgy apps. About the best contribution Slack has made in the last half-decade is to amuse many when that silly court case about trademarks blew up in its face.

His office is the warmest space in the building, with the NoNolo servers in the next room, and he keeps the adjoining door open, usually, so that the air-conditioned cool in his cramped office helps the servers keep cool. To get to the servers, a person needs to pass through his office, a space neither impressive in size nor orderliness. Two shelves are packed with system documentation and tech manuals and looseleaf updates he keeps meaning to place into the right three-ring binder, and there are boxes big and small scattered about, some empty, some unopened, any one of which might contain fiber modems, network bridges, or several old keyboards. One box holds a still-working—barely working—monitor that he's already replaced with an upgrade. His eyes pass over the box holding the black oblong shape, half hidden, the top poking out behind a bankers box full of old test runs long overdue for filing or dumping. He's been meaning to pay closer attention to troubleshooting the problem with this otherwise-nice monitor. An irregular and infrequent unrequested shutting off means he should check out the power supply and whether it can be replaced, but this hasn't yet made it to his to-do list.

One of the things he's got on his to-do list is reconfiguring one of the three email servers the office uses, but his fight to consolidate the three platforms to one email platform keeps running into McAdam's bizarre loyalty to a wheezing Outlook software, McAdam a well-known victim to the dread of learning curve, even if he should move, by all sensible arguments, to the new and far better email platform Jimmy's been pushing. The other outlier is a more serious challenge, in that many of their clients use a legacy document management system long entrenched in the legal profession. This system has an email service built in, and the resistance to changing the DMS is strong. Ferocious, even. Last October, he'd gained the blessing of McAdam to propose to the clients a change in DMS, but the effort felt doomed. He'd undertaken the push, nonetheless, but this went about as well as he expected and he's still getting shit from some of the clients about his request, with a handful getting lawyerly about it in their reactions. He's concluded that one of the better options is to see if he can find or write an API for the in-house file and document server and thus let the clients keep using their old front ends ad infinitum. This despite his chronic arguing that the older DMS poses potential security vulnerabilities, but he's found the whole effort too much like herding cats. In fact, he's only come to know this expression after a colleague used it in his summary of Jimmy's far-too-long set of complaints during one meeting months ago. Meow.

Cyn is supposed to be heading back to their apartment, and the last time they texted, she thought she'd get there on the early side. Of course, the early side for her is, at best, the close of business for most others, but he knows a gift when he sees it. He's hoping that she'll want to go out for dinner or at least for a drink or two, especially since he's proposing a new cocktail bar that he wants to check out in case Daddo visits.

He'll put off putting out the fires Mary Ann or Dolorie keep lighting, but not for too long. He's something of a pet of theirs, and it's funny, because they keep thinking he's a young one, and they're both protective that way, despite the fact that he's been at NoNolo for six years. Of course, he is a young one, relatively speaking, given that most other employees are either older lawyers or much older lawyers, at least if one ignores the interns that march through at a steady rate. NoNolo offers progressive climate bona fides for all of the law school students passing through, and, if he says so himself, NoNolo is pretty fucking great.

But now he needs to get back to the job at hand, and that is reviewing and analyzing the new network security software he's installed. It's a new version of an AI software designed to scan and analyze all digital traffic, and there are now a bunch of these to choose from. But what's gotten him to move forward with the installation and testing of this product is that there's an additional level of protection for databases and content going to the backup server. The AI creates a virtual backup for deeper iterative scanning and analysis.

The relevant forums, Reddits, and other tech security sites have been forecasting double-trojan codes that are viruses encased in such a way as to avoid tripping common scans, but once in the backup servers, the trojan activates and takes over functions. The worry is that these new trojans are an escalation, since ransomware has been declining for years, with better cybersecurity. Ransomware attacks haven't disappeared though, of course, since there are plenty of networks that still fall short in effective cyber security implementation. Still, for any organization whose data and enterprise processes are valuable, ransomware attacks are no longer a problem, if you do the work.

A ransomware attack that had been reported on just last week had brought down a major investment company, but these days the news focus is more on who's getting sacked for such avoidable breaches. Still, cyber security is always playing a game of catch-up, with new workarounds and tech for intrusions regularly popping into existence.

He starts reading the latest report produced by the new AI software that covers yesterday's document handling. One of the things he appreciates about this new package is that the hold terms are infinitely adjustable, so setting a one-year hold can be specified, not that this makes sense for any enterprise with active backup requirements. He's selected a twenty-five-hour hold for the testing, and so far today, he's only gotten one query about a new document not being available because of the evaluation he's running, but he's taken care of that complaint by claiming system maintenance. Well, it is, isn't it?

He changes some program parameters and delimitators in the hold pool, where initially scanned content that is declared clear gets queued into the virtual backup server and re-analyzed within the backup server environment. He's mostly interested in the algorithmic tree that takes the second and more analytical look, at least as claimed by the software vendor, the AI running probability iterations and assigning weights after each iterative scan until it develops target focus or passes the data as clean. He only half understands how the AI runs its processes, but he understands the company's claims and he can adequately test them.

He sits back, hands behind his head, and with his six-foot-seven-inch frame, the spread elbow to elbow matches the width of the line of three monitors in front of him. It's a cool desk setup.

But then the monitors change. The one on the left throws up an alert, even as the middle screen seems to be continuing running processes.

He brings his arms down and leans in close. The AI has identified a probable threat in an innocuous-looking document sent in from a legitimate source, but there's a flag for extra code, and when he looks closely, he sees that there may indeed be something interweaved through the otherwise-expected metadata.

"That's weird."

He pulls up the analytical engine. What could this be? And is it a threat or just the AI being nervous, twitchy? That's a prevalent complaint about AI applied to network security. The left and middle monitors are back to running processes, but he doesn't bother to read the streaming code—not that he could. He's interested in the report of action on his right screen. He quickly glances back at the scrolling code vanishing upward on the two leftward screens. His level of code experience isn't great. He can muddle through, but the AI is fast. A million times faster, though he's got no real basis for speed comparison.

His phone rings. It's Cyn.

"Hey," he says, "You on target for 6:00 p.m. ETA?"

"Well," she says in the voice he loves so well he'd be

happy to listen to even if she were just reading a shopping list. "Well, I think so, but I'm waiting for a call from Kansas," meaning the other main office, the one that focuses on reducing methane generation from livestock.

She's been in a fight to refocus on cultured meats, and she doesn't really believe there's a big win working traditional livestock, but there's politics involved, and he knows this makes her cautious.

"He doesn't want to do this by text," she adds, but that's nothing unusual for Cyn's colleague, who has this particular peccadillo of mostly using phone or video, a fanatic in his belief in the benefits of synchronous communication. "I'll set up a time, schedule it, and then head out."

"Okey dokey."

After he ends the call, he finds himself hoping his reply sounded friendly. They've been having conversation about her Middlebury apartment and whether she should push to bring the Vermont office to Boston, but this never goes far. He's been making a good effort to keep a certain tone of petulance he can sometimes on his part contribute to such conversations, but he'd rather refrain from triggering an argument.

The main point he argues is that she's the Executive Director of MMEAT, which stands for Meat, Methane Emissions, and Agricultural Technology, and she could use that to force action. She doesn't want to disrupt her employees, and she likes to be off on her own at times. He tries not to take it personally.

The program in front of him beeps for his attention. What he's looking at, even though the code assembly isn't yet finished, is something that looks like a timing sequence. He scans the flooding results as the program continues. An activation sequence, for sure.

And the mess of code following could be any set of instructions and distinct programs, but the AI is having a slow time solving the puzzle. He's halfway out of his chair, but before he can pace, before he even fully stands, the code reassembly completes. He resettles himself and looks over the code analysis.

A code bomb.

A full body sweat rises and he pushes back his office chair in a flush of panic, but then calms himself. The danger is contained in the virtual backup hold server, all air-gapped to the actual servers and real back up servers. He can let the hidden code run and safely see the action. That should prove interesting. He steels himself to select the run option, and then does just that, and sits back, just waiting.

His phone rings again, and it's the IT from one of the client law firms, and Jimmy can hardly make out the name for all the panic in the man's voice as he's breathlessly telling Jimmy how all their documentation is gone. The voice keeps rising until Jimmy finally breaks through to let him know the clearinghouse is sound, but then he tells his fellow IT that he'll call back in a minute, because he's noticed the Slick notification pop-up screen, and when he clicks through to it, there are already eleven messages from different law firms, all reporting that all their documents have vanished, are gone, lost, and he quickly composes a message that NoNolo is extant, and that he'll follow up ASAP with more information.

His phone rings again. It's Cyn.

"I'm sorry," are her first words, and then she's explaining that she needs to stay late, has to have this video call with Kansas, new problems are blowing up, and she's sorry, again, and Jimmy's sure she means it and thinks he'll be disappointed.

"No problem, something's come up here, too, so just let me know when you hit the road." He ends the call, switching screens to get to his real backup server's scheduler and cancels today's automatic backup, with a good eleven minutes to spare.

He takes a long breath, and then pulls his chair up, pulling the keyboard close, and begins typing up an email to all clients about the danger. He's hoping that the

Mountain and Pacific Standard Time clients can kill their back up process until further notice.

Chapter 11: Pakistan and India Heat Up, Cheers

Second week of June, 2035

Jeannie Louise knows that monsoon season for the Indian subcontinent is June through September. She also knows that the season is late, that a heat dome still covers most of Pakistan and the western third of India, and that people are dying.

It's strange to be seeing this here, a drink in front of her. She's at her current favorite bar, having walked down to Railroad Street as she sometimes does if the day has grown late and she's been cooped up all day working. And if the weather's nice.

The weather here *is* nice. Today is a warm, normal day for the second week of June. She's gotten to the bar right at opening, the proverbial five o'clock somewhere. She likes to get to such places early and enjoy the quiet before business starts filling the place. She likes this because she usually gets to talk to the bartender, who, at this bar, is also the owner—unless he's behind on his shift setup, in which case she'll let him get on with his work. Even then he and she might sneak in a little talk about cocktails or bourbon, but she's not gabbing today, not beyond her ordering a Left Hand. There it sits in a pretty Nick & Nora glass, the drink a variant of a Boulevardier, with Campari and a favorite Italian sweet vermouth, but up, and more bourbon-forward, with the addition of this bar's house-made chocolate bitters, and a pretty brandied cherry stick.

She's ignoring her drink, eyes fixed on her tablet.

She sits up straighter, reacting to the story reporting on the subcontinent's heatwave, now close to a month in duration, with only intermittent drops in temperature. These slightly lower temperatures would themselves have been high enough to be newsworthy on their own not all that long ago, but this article is focused on the political tensions between India and Pakistan. The conflict seems silly considering the heat wave disaster that is happening, but then, any finger-pointing when both fingers can press the nuclear button demands attention. The heatwave death tolls are inching toward six figures, with the worst of the dying mostly in Pakistan, but there are also fatalities in some affected parts of India that share national borders, and especially in lower Kashmir. Tensions within Pakistan are significant, but far more dangerous is the growing hostile rhetoric between the two countries. Estimates are that as much as half of the casualty count is being attributed to military, paramilitary, and individual violence, all directly connected to the hundreds of thousands of people on the move. According to one NGO, the number of displaced people is well past the million mark and parts of the borders are collapsing.

The article reports that a further escalation of violence is expected. She skims more claims of Pakistanis killing Indians in some areas and Indians killing Pakistanis in other areas. It seems clear in the coverage she's skipping through that most casualties are due to rampant internal paramilitary activities, although one report specifies that the exact scope of such activities is hard to verify. Something that needs no further verification is the recent withdrawal of UN efforts to mobilize relief, where personnel on the ground in the worst-affected provinces of Bahawalpur and Rahim Yar Khan in the Punjab region have been recalled due to the hostilities.

The UN, *The Guardian* reports, has called on the two

countries to constrain the substantial military forces coming into play, but a rise in border crossings by Indian residents to the west of Tanot, in Rajasthan, has been spiking, further envenoming the rhetoric and setting up more violence.

There is another article referenced, via the algorithms in play following her interests. This linked article is about the Mid-Atlantic heatwaves that include all the boroughs of New York City and some way up into the Hudson Valley, in what is a near-identical weather system reappearing after a three-year absence. Even the algorithms think every news story really has to be about America, but any use of nuclear weapons affects everyone, doesn't it?

The US heatwave article focuses on the new climate model that has forecast this extreme weather event, although, extreme is a relative state when comparing what's happened on a big chunk of the subcontinent. One big difference is that much of the US grid has remained stable and there are copious resources for coping, unlike what's available in the subcontinent.

She clicks back and scrolls through her synopsis tool for her Google News "See all articles and perspectives" feature, but she doesn't see anything she hasn't already read. News about Pakistan and India is something she and many, many others have been following the last few weeks.

Nothing like nuclear weapons to sharpen interest. She puts down her tablet.

"Something wrong with the drink?" the bartender asks her with a slight frown.

She picks up the glass, nods cheers to him, and takes a sip. "No, no," she tells him. "All's good."

She's a bit worried how he'll feel when her next order is a glass of bourbon, straight.

Chapter 12: Disappearing Daikons

Second week of June, 2035

Davin's just sent in his annual contribution to Climate Consensus, the group he supports by sending in 10 percent of his previous year's art income, as figured in Schedule C of his federal tax return, and that's 10 percent on his net income. It's a modest amount but, hey, every little bit helps.

He's up in the garden out back, the tall black plastic deer fencing looking looser and wavier over the years. It's just barely into mid-June and the garden is already well underway, the early crops, like radishes, already producing. At least they're supposed to be.

The garden went in early, as usual these days, although the old saw of New England gardening suggests waiting until Memorial Day, just in case there's a late freeze. His might be the last generation to think this way, though. Even as far back as 2019, when he first put in the large vegetable garden out in the back part of the property, the planting started before Memorial Day, but the start date has crept earlier and earlier, until May Day is the common starting point for first seeds in the ground, or as he's been doing more often, hardening the seedlings from the greenhouse he put in four years ago.

He's recently turned seventy years of age. He's been thinking a lot about this, knowing that this is just another number, but some years seem more potent in meaning and it looks like he's going to keep having trouble shaking this one off. He remembers clearly enough that he wasn't all that happy about turning sixty-four that particular February barely three months ahead of Hurricane Josephine that wiped out Miami Beach on Florida's Gold Coast.

The name is a misnomer these days, that's for sure. The city has never been properly rebuilt and recovery has been, at best, an ad hoc affair. Most estimates of the current population are somewhere around two million, many residents *off-book*. That's the term in use these days.

Those who remain are mostly poor people, although some are now in homes that were once quite fine, but fixing them up after the sea had moved through all those structures, those places aren't nice these days, not that there hasn't been an occasional magazine feature article about people still living in area homes restored to glory. There have been many more articles, news stories, and even online trackers of the repeating storm damages in that area since the 2029 devastation. There's something of a cottage industry surveilling the people living in the wreck, and these days such stories—including a goddamn reality show—carry what strikes him as the tone of prurient fascination. These days it's mostly poverty-stricken people and illegal aliens living in towers and apartments and tract homes that still stand, even as some of the surrounding areas that had flooded and been torn apart by the terrible storm now almost seem normal after six years of cleanup and rebuilding. In the last several years, the relationship between the people in those areas left largely abandoned and those living in the rebuilt areas has been growing more tense, with something akin to border skirmishes or street wars breaking out periodically. There was one of these flare-ups in the news yesterday, one of the bigger outbreaks of violence, and as of this morning, there are sixteen dead.

One recurring element of these conflicts is sanitary infrastructure, with large parts of the city and its environs without working sewer systems. Fresh water too is often improvised or needs to be trucked in.

Another thing not to think about. He sighs. Feces and less-identifiable garbage floating down the Intracoastal is not the right picture for *Florida Living*.

He looks around the garden, appreciating the fresh wood chips put down last week on the pathways. The compost bin in the back south corner looks like Marsha may have worked at turning it again, because he sure hasn't done it. Marsha is the longest house sharer now in residence here in the Housatonic House on the Hill. She has one of the third-floor bedrooms and has been living in the house for, what, seven years? Yeah, that's right. He was sixty-three when she signed her first lease. She's always been one who is hard to read, although after all this time, the two of them have settled into a comfortable acquaintance, but he doesn't see that much of her unless she's in the kitchen putting up food or out here in the garden, helping to grow it.

Seventy. He shakes his head. Where does the time go? He arches his back, a tic of sorts, for the last few years, of his halfhearted efforts trying to straighten out, but all his time spent working on the platform of *Berkshire Interactive* and its several sister publications, and the editing and writing for Alicia's company have left him with a stoop. Of course, there were the decades before that, of content management consulting work, something else that doesn't make him happy about his posture.

The focus of his current unhappiness, however, is the series of holes in the dirt where the radishes are planted. *Were* planted.

The garden these days is well hardened against pests, although mice and voles and shrews and moles—or whatever tiny creatures that like compost bins a lot, and actual vegetables even more—those creatures can be a problem. But they don't carry off whole radishes.

Something seems to be picking at the early sweet peas, too, even though these plants are barely beyond full bloom. There are some young pea pods that have gone missing.

He'll have to talk to Marsha about rigging some netting,

in case the tiny pea pods are being taken by birds. He'll need her help putting up the sunscreens soon, too, although he's ordered new sets of SunSails because, while the brand does a good job, three or four years seems to be all he can get out of them before too much ripping or fraying makes them useless for protecting the crops from the high summer's hot sun and the downpours that can push many growing crops back into the mud. All it takes is one of those hailstorms to kill a growing season's effort.

He steps over to the lettuce bed. Some of the small plants have had parts torn off, although this might just be Marsha starting in early on a spring salad. But the way some of the modest lettuce plants have been torn out by the root makes him consider this isn't her handiwork.

He hasn't bothered using the cameras and security lights he rigged years back, back when trying to determine which animals were devastating his corn crop, but with the additional hardening of the garden, he hasn't needed to bother. His latest hardening effort, two years back, included placing hardware cloth along the bottom of the deer fence, dropping the metal screen down into a ten-inch-deep trench he'd paid a high school kid to dig. He has intentional amnesia over the kid's name and the cost. Spending money still often feels like some terrible misstep.

He stopped growing corn, anyway. He's still annoyed about that lost battle, but the math is pretty convincing. Corn, when his crop would be harvested, is local and cheap, so he leaves corn to the big farmers. He's learned to concentrate on greens and vegetables and root vegetables that he's gotten better at cold storing in a purpose-built part of the basement. He has potatoes and carrots and turnips that keep almost through the end of winter, and he still had three butternut squash left in April, although that's because he's not a fan of that particular winter squash, so he tends to have at least a few rot out. He must clean the root cellar. He's learned the hard way that rotten root vegetables can really stink up the place, and rotted potatoes are the worst offenders, smell-wise. He's also learned that the area needs a good cleaning, with disinfectants, between seasons if there's to be any chance of the stored vegetables lasting.

He's curious about the missing radishes, and he goes back to that part of the garden for a closer look. There are still a lot of radish plants, and some will be ready to pick in two or three days, but the ones he was hoping to get this morning are MIA. Maybe Marsha has picked them, but then she's been at her mother's nursing home for the last two nights, her mother doing poorly, so that theory fails.

Perhaps he should reinstitute his rodent hunts, using a break barrel .22 air rifle that dispatches his main nemesis effectively, as long as he's willing to put in the time to shoot the damn chipmunks that still manage to get through the fence, but the hardware cloth addition still should be at least halfway effective, fingers crossed. He'll put the lights and cameras back to active status, although he'll want to check positions, since the garden screens, when put up, may interrupt good line of sight. The smaller rodents tend not to trip the motion sensors, because if he sets the sensitivity that high any and all breath of wind and swaying crops will keep up a night-long light show that comes close to a strobe-like effect, an outcome worse than a bit of garden loss. They're not the top priority, anyway.

According to the weather forecasts, the end of the next week could see the start of a weeklong hot spell if the front that has socked in the Mid-Atlantic coast as far as New York City shifts further northward. He can only hope that the SunSails arrive early enough, although a June or even an early July hot spell is likely to be okay if they adjust watering schedules right.

He heads to the greenhouse, an eight-foot by ten-foot cheap polycarbonate structure from Harbor Freight, which he's strengthened with pressure-treated wood. The greenhouse has its entrance up against the six-foot-high deer fencing of the garden wall, where the narrower garden gate toward the back provides access. He'd gotten the greenhouse up in Pittsfield, bought at their liquidation sales months before the whole company went belly up, a victim of another trade war with China. He's got seedlings to check on, but he hopes to be quick about it, since he's got time this morning to spend in the studio.

The deadline's looming for what should be a good gallery show, prime time for the high season and all those visiting tourists with money to spend, but this hopeful note is swamped by doubt that he's likely to sell any piece of art. People find his assemblage sculptures interesting, and he's gotten some good press lately, but few would-be buyers seem to know what exactly they should do with his art. Is his work really that weird?

While his joining Climate Consensus has apparently upped his status with both Jeannie Louise and Cynthia, he's worried about how little he might contribute to the group this next filing, and whether this will make Cynthia—*Cyn*—roll her eyes. Not that she needs to know. He could use other money to make his annual contribution less embarrassing if the art sales fall. Cynthia's more or less made him uneasy over the years. He's well aware of her judgments about his climate change *bona fides,* but that's finally been shifting.

Climate Consensus has been around for some years, going back to the 2028 election, but back then it had just been getting going. The 2032 elections had Climate Consensus spinning off a 527 in the form of Climate Consensus Action, although the two entities work hand-in-glove, with the 501(c)(3) doing the work of climate action education that includes ranking the climate action standings of candidates, drilling all the way down to local elections in many cases. The related PAC had been surprisingly effective in campaign funding in the 2032 elections and even more so in the following midterms. These days, he thinks of his donations to both organizations as tithing, where he regularly sends in a fixed percentage of income from art sales, split between the two sibling outfits.

Maybe the sales will be solid with the two shows. Be's

been really great helping out with preparations for these shows, although that may be because he's incorporated some of her architectural slabs into his recent pieces, including as tops to some of his free-standing, furniture-like pieces.

But wait! It's also a lamp! Now how much would you pay?

He shakes his head. This is a long-running joke he's come up with, since many of his pieces are self-illuminated, with lighting as part of the overall piece.

Now how much would you pay?! It's a reference to some ancient Ron Popeil cable television ads. This sort of spiel on his part isn't really all that funny. More a nervous twitch.

Inside the greenhouse a few of the empty flats have been moved around, and the bench, with its spread of hand tools, is off, and one of his garden trowels is gone, but he doesn't think much of it. He often forgets to put tools away, instead abandoning them in the last spot he's put them down.

He walks back through the garden and out, carefully closing the big front garden gate to make sure that the additional hardware cloth covers the slim gap between fence posts and the gate's frame. This gate faces the back of the house, which shows the second and third floors, since the house is built into a sloping grade, his studio, closer to him, is mostly below grade, except for the south façade facing the driveway and the four-foot high framed bump-up that raises the ceiling height to fourteen feet for half of the floor area, and lets a lot of light into the studio from the many windows running on the east and west sides of the bump-up. It's a dozen steps toward the big gravel parking area, and then he's dropping down the steepening driveway to get to the studio's entrance, his thoughts already shifting to his hopes and fears for the selling show.

Everything ten dollar!

He sure as hell hopes the declaration is just a self-deprecating joke.

Chapter 13: Blood Trail, Mud Trial

June 22, 2035

Fletch is in her car heading to Housatonic, but she can see that Great Barrington is far more crowded for even this late in the shoulder season, with the high season normally starting in July. Tanglewood opening up in Lenox, with its Fourth of July program, is as much the normal starting gun as any other, but the whole South County seems already hopping. She assumes that restaurants like it, motels and the inns and B&Bs like it, and the usual rise in summertime employment is playing catch-up, for once, and that's something that should delight the many people who've been struggling for work.

On the other hand, it's the third Friday before July's start, so there's nothing surprising about the number of visitors.

Except, after her talk with Sullivan this morning, the mix of visitors seems different. She's probably not the best at judging this, even after a decade in office, because she's always busy and doesn't get out that much. Sure, she goes to events and parades and meetings on this or that subject, at the Southern Berkshires Community Center or the VFW or Senior Center or the Housy Dome in Housatonic, and she walks through the halls of the various schools and survives the May town meeting and the many board hearings, as need be. But otherwise, she has her group of friends and some of her neighbors she relaxes with, though she and

Robbie have always been something like homebodies. When she's done with work, she wants downtime. She guesses she's the homebody, thinking about Robbie, but she shuts this thought down. She needs to keep her head on straight, and she knows that the betrayal—the shock!—of Robbie's secret life is still all too new and all too maddening.

She hasn't heard much gossip around town about Robbie moving out, but then again, she's not interested in advertising the implosion of her marriage. The chatter around town hall is all about the early flurry of activity in town, and while the news lends a certain giddiness to the air, there is also already talk about the housing crunch. With word getting around about some people taking in boarders in their spare rooms, and rents jumping, something feels new. She's hearing complaints from more locals getting forced out as more housing shifts to summer rentals. This is something that happens pretty much every tourist season, but more calls have been coming into the town planner's office or to her office, with the main inquiries lately about zoning restrictions and covenants around housing use and the legal rights of tenants at will.

Fletch has just come from a meeting with her town planner in a perhaps vain effort to get ahead of this, whatever exactly this is, before it blows up. This will almost certainly be on the agenda at next Monday's regular meeting, but that's ten days away because of the holiday weekend. Selectboard meetings are held on Mondays, and July Fourth is next Tuesday, so they're skipping over into the Monday after. This will give her more time to spend calling around the various departments and the town counsel to get a handle on what the town can and can't do, and she's already pretty sure it will prove to be a matter of mostly what they can't do. She asks Kara to call around the neighboring towns to see if their experiences are similar.

The biggest item for today, however, and the reason why she's heading to Housatonic, is the new development around the reports of gunfire in Housatonic a week back.

Sullivan reported to her that his officers spent the next day in the neighborhood canvassing, but there's no concrete evidence pointing to a shooter or shooters. Numerous witnesses reported the time consistently, however, although the odd theory or two of some of those interviewed was ignored.

Ear witnesses, Sullivan called them, and she suspects that had been some effort toward a joke on his part, and so far, that's proved the most unsettling aspect to the whole thing. Until the phone call she's just gotten from him, telling her they've found a blood trail, at any rate.

One witness claimed that the shots came from the old mill buildings, although the person, one of the window installers working on the old school renovation, refused to pinpoint which building because he simply couldn't tell. That witness did go on, according to Sullivan's report to her a week ago, to talk about how he'd jumped at the sound of the shot or shots, a perhaps pertinent point considering he'd been suspended in a cherry picker bucket, but it was late enough that it was unlikely he'd been wrestling a new window into place high up on the top floor of the building, and the reports mentioned beer cans and "alcohol smell."

The mills lie across the park. There's Park Street first, and then the rail tracks that are elevated at that point, on earthen and stone retaining structures as the tracks come down from the rail bridge overpass where Park Street takes a sharp left turn under it before heading over the bridge. After the bridge, Park Street turns right another ninety degrees to head south toward Route 7 and Great Barrington. The mill buildings—eight or nine altogether—are tucked in beyond the tracks and the river, with some on the opposite bank of the river. The whole complex, severely underused and mostly empty, runs northward, where the two largest mill buildings are.

She knows the area. Davin Caine lives up near Park Street, on that street where a car would go if not turning right to follow Route 183. "Keep going straight up and my street will turn into my driveway, and there's parking at the top," he told her in his email inviting her to the first of several cocktail parties she's been to since. She remembers the phrasing because that first time Robbie had followed these directions, they were shocked at finding how steep and long the driveway was, and the two of them had laughed when they'd parked, maybe with a touch of hysteria. There were jokes about rollercoasters and black diamond ski slopes, and the feeling was a bit surreal from the ordeal.

She can't figure that her Robbie then can be the same Robbie she walked in on two weeks back, and there's another woman, too.

She's heading over to Housatonic now, the chief already on site, for a fuller story on this new development. One big question she has is Why did it take a week for this discovery? *More* than a week—nine days in fact.

All she knows at present is that blood has been found on the scene, except it's taken this long to find it, and that's not a confidence booster. When this gets out, this is bound to add more concerns about public safety, especially given the news of a recent mugging in the Co-op parking lot, and an assault—what was probably a failed mugging, the responding officer had written in his report. The assault had happened a few blocks south, the target a pedestrian walking past The Great Barrington Bagel Company, and less than an hour later that same evening.

When she'd called the chief first thing yesterday for details, he told her that he'd quickly dispatched a second car to the location of the reported assault, but somehow pursuit of the *perp or perps*—Sullivan had used that term—*wasn't possible*. She managed to keep herself from mentioning that The Great Barrington Bagel Company is not very far south of the Great Barrington Police Station. Apparently, the suspect or suspects took off through the woods and floodplain scrub, toward the river, into the late evening darkness.

Sullivan had taken the opportunity on this morning's call to also fill her in on other police activity, including what he described as a "big bump in disorderlies," whatever exactly that really means, and tell her that his guys had only taken names and issued warnings. He then told her of other such reports, now totaling seven in all, and from all across downtown, the fairgrounds, and up near the closed Simon's Rock college campus that may or may not be getting developed into village plan housing. Hearing about Simon's Rock caused a bit of panic, and she's been scrambling through her to-do list to see if she somehow might have missed filing an appropriation request for a feasibility study, but, luckily, she still has time.

By the time her attention returned to the chief's phone conversation, she was hearing that out of these seven incidents, only one involved a local kid, and the others were from all over, but mostly the city or, in one instance, Danbury. She asked Sullivan to get somebody at the station to assemble a summary each morning to send on to her, and while there was some hesitation, he finally grunted out an "Okay."

She and Sullivan have been on good terms, mostly, so Fletch chalks up his reflex hesitation to tradition. Police is police, town manager is town manager.

His guys, he also told her, have all been seeing more young men they don't recognize, and some young women, too, and often with backpacks, but two different officers both mentioned that they didn't think the ones they saw were like the hikers who come down from the Appalachian Trail, which transects the town on its way south into Sheffield, meaning hikers often use the Great Barrington walkout for supply stops and laundry.

Sullivan seemed to be thinking out loud when he mentioned that he'd have his guys do some stop and chats to try to get a better sense of who these guys are, where they're from, and why they're here, and Fletch was surprised that this wasn't already in place, but she held her tongue. A lot of what's going on is new to them all if, really, there's anything much different happening, and maybe it's just a weird week.

As she turns right over the bridge, the police car light bars are flashing behind the Hive on the other side of the bridge, opposite the mills. The Hive is the newest name of the bar that's been here for decades, but in recent years attempts to make a go of it have proved short-lived. She pulls into the building's driveway and stops her car when she sees Sullivan leaning against one patrol car, talking to one of his cops.

She's out of her car, closing in, when he begins talking to her. Sullivan grumbles out a throat-clearing coughing fit that carries phlegmy overtones and is about Fletch's least-favorite thing about talking to Sullivan, but she patiently waits it out.

He tells her that they've gotten a call about what the person thought was blood, and he points toward a dumpster on the edge of the gravel parking area, away from the back of the building.

"Actually, the owner, or manager, called. His dishwasher was taking trash out and saw it, came to show him. He called us. I had Giardi go back to the site," Sullivan says, referring to his senior sergeant. "He found more traces of blood. We've found more blood trail, looks like a body sliding down, pulled down through there"—he points toward brush near the riverbank—"and it looks from the stones, rocks, like a body could have been pushed into the water. It's looking like a body dragged to the river, maybe from behind the mills." He mentions that he's getting the river searched.

Fletch looks at the activity around the dumpster, yellow tape already sagging, fluttering in a breeze that's picking up.

"I'll let you know," he then says, with another throat grumble cough, and only after she's back in the car and underway does she realize that she only nodded her response.

And then a squad car, and then another, screams past, lights and sirens blazing. Fletch asks her hands-free to call Chief.

Chapter 14: Alicia Über Alles

June 22, 2035

Life goes on. Business grows or dies.

Alicia shakes herself free from the threatening cliché parade; she'll be late in getting into her office, the second downtown space *Berkshire Interactive* has occupied, and she likes that the building she rents space in, taking up the whole suite of offices on the top floor, is on Main Street.

What she doesn't like is the parking situation. It's one of the chronic and common complaints she and all downtown visitors have. She has only two spots in the back reserved for *BI* and she often has to chase off interlopers. Calling the towing services is a great way to lose a subscriber.

Sometimes, like this morning, she likes to ruminate in the comfort of her home office, and at the moment she's again wondering if continuing growth is actually essential for *BI*, at least other than the ongoing work of expanding ad sales and building up direct marketing mechanisms.

She's caught up with the newest expansion planning, even while some part of her is still anxious about having brought in an investor, six years back, to fund the transition from *South County Interactive* to *Berkshire Interactive*. On the other hand, the expanded coverage area has done her proud, even if this has meant hiring an ad sales manager. Not that this woman manages Alicia's own ongoing sales efforts, but a title is less expense than a salary sometimes.

That investor was the result of her finally deciding to abide by the long-worn advice to use other people's money instead of her own. Now it may be time to find someone else's money again. Or two someones or three—she's been approached by several potential investors with the funds to expand the operation into competing territories. She still doubts the wisdom of seeking investors, even though the choice has proved out so far, with the expansion of the platform and coverage area yielding more revenue. The return on the initial investors' capital has been positive, and all the milestones have been met and then some.

Now, again, her doubts clash with her ambitions. A big play. That had been almost six years earlier, although the details and ownership breakdown had taken some further months to finalize. Still, it's a confusing step, adding another outside investor or two. There's value in what she's doing and it's great that the first investor, one Derek Babayan, a second generation Armenian American, Ivy League schooled, with a strutting MBA, has remained an easy mix with his 19 percent ownership, but he's been growing vocal lately about the opportunity for expansion, and he's been gently pushing Alicia to meet with a former classmate from his MBA days, talking up the potential for expansion. *A new model for publishing* has become his catchphrase of late.

It's a great line, even though it has many echoes of near-countless failed efforts. But, yes, the time is finally right, and the combination of self-erecting, self-defining platforms tied to local businesses and services is working, and working well. Her efforts are not unique, and a rebirth of hyperlocal online newspapers is taking place in many locations and across different-sized markets, but the Berkshires represents a particular sweet spot for success, small enough for comprehensive coverage, and she's got in early enough.

Can she do this again? Another time? They've built a compelling tool to match readers—locals and visitors alike—with desirable editorial and commercial content, and they've been successful enough to keep potential competitors at bay while proving out the efficacy to the advertisers, following Davin's motto: *Reach, Act, Track.*

She's even built up editorial remuneration for the growing list of contributors and contractors who are often more like reviewers or fact-checkers of the directories, and not reporters, not really, since a lot of the content is populated by the businesses and services and organizations and event producers themselves. Many of the editorial-side contributors act first and foremost as checks on accuracy and as help for relevant posters, and in only some cases as content providers themselves, mainly with reviews and overviews and the occasional in-depth piece. Davin's become something of a news reporter, and he's helped shape a couple of others, too, although he's steadfastly refused to involve himself in local sports coverage. Local sports coverage means school sports coverage, and even he admits that this is too rich a topic to ignore, not that she would have listened to him if he held an opposing opinion. She's hired an old sports reporter—old in experience, but also in age, evoking her chronic worry about long-term staffing and the problems of aging out. Davin is seventy years of age, at least, she's pretty sure, and the sports guy, Renalto, is close enough to Davin's age.

Another investor could help fund new hires, not that this would be the primary driver for new investment. Much of the editorial side remains inexpensive. Much of the content that drives visits and, more importantly, interactions, is less expensive than many might think. Less well paying than many might hope, is the other way to look at it.

Still, the galleries editor, Kathy Brogle, who'd been one of her former competitors in the Berkshires publications space, now manages to make some halfway decent money with several galleries that pay for additional content assistance, and she's also succeeded in carving out fees for show reviews, gallery mentions, and art scene overviews. Kathy has recently added follow-on gallery show promotions to home decorator services, and the sales of art items to those decorators' clients brings in other fees. Modest income, however you look at it, but every bit helps in supplementing the woman's part-time job as a special education art therapist.

Berkshire shuffle, a term Alicia has become quite familiar with, is the term denoting the collection of jobs and self-employed businesses and whatever else it takes for so many residents to make ends meet. Like Deidre, with whom she had a relationship for a few years, and who has recently emailed her about a business opportunity, asking for a meeting. She still feels affection for Deidre, but now more burnished by memory and put into perspective by her decision to keep her life simple, not that she'd known that when Deidre had moved out, but she's quickly realized how her work, her little media empire, will always be her primary focus. There's still an empty space in her life, and her occasional efforts to date in the last few years have not solved that, but then the drive is weak.

She knows that the younger woman made the right decision. She hasn't heard from her for some time and has even stopped thinking about her, mostly, and stopped asking Davin about her, but maybe that's because Deidre moved into her own apartment two or three years back, and Davin's contact with Deidre seems minimal these days, too.

She's surprised by Deidre's email, but glad enough to get it. She's less glad to hear that Deidre is still working at Farm Table, now full time, or as full time as a restaurant can offer, given the variable seasons, and shocked to learn that her former girlfriend's other job, managing that strange downtown store up on Railroad Street, is gone, that it's finally closed. She still doesn't understand how such a store would or could ever open, never mind last the two-dozen years of its existence selling tarot and crystals and other alternative *heebie-jeebies* this and that. Crystals—Jesus.

She was surprised by this news, and even more surprised when she looked the store up and saw that it'd been gone for the better part of a year, and she's chagrined to learn this only now, and from the back issues of her very own newspaper at that.

Hyperlocal content platform. Well, they never took out ads. After Deidre had ended their relationship, it was likely she'd stopped trying to pitch the store to advertise.

But now Deidre is pitching her own business, if Alicia's reading the email right, and looking for an investor, or maybe just a loan, or maybe she's contacted her mainly to ask for advice, hoping to secure a lease in another Railroad Street storefront in order to start a thrift store.

Piles Compiled: Curated Great Style is the name Deidre's going with, at least at this early stage. One piece of advice she might give Deidre is to rethink the business name. There's more descriptive copy that holds more promise, with terms like *sustainable fashion, recycled rad, dressing smart,* and more, and it does seem like the basic concept—at least in the public message—is still a work in progress. She does like the tagline Deidre is using in her signature: *Save Clothes, Save the Planet.*

She heads down to the kitchen, tucking the printouts from one of the new would-be investors under her arm. She'll get back to Deidre, but right now she's wrestling with her own investor puzzle. She's trying to decide on the investor's offer in front of her. It's certainly intriguing.

Intrigue, treachery, and hidden agenda are the most worrying things. Is she being blinded by the scope and ambition of the offer? On her own, she bootstrapped the creation of *South County Interactive* and brought in her one investor to expand into *Berkshire Interactive,* and even now she has plans to extend her advertiser base into the Northwest Corner in Connecticut and over the New York line. She already has some participating businesses there. And these areas are considered part of the Berkshires, but she keeps going around and around about what to do.

One challenge is determining where *Berkshires-the-Concept* ends and where the Hudson region begins, which itself is indistinct from the Capital Region, otherwise known as the Albany market, at least in terms of present media coverage, since Hudson is in Columbia County, which has a total population of only around seventy thousand people.

She pulls the kitchen table chair out and plops down on it, slapping the plan outline onto the surface, where one edge catches on a drop of jam she's missed after cleaning up from her early morning toast, and she wipes it off with her napkin, a reddish smear the result.

Well, primary residents, anyway. The second-home owners are another part of the population she'll pursue. *Hudson Interactive* would be similar to *Berkshire Interactive,* although the geographical area is potentially significantly larger and the business base more modest, which is an unattractive condition for expansion, and Columbia County also falls into the sphere of influence of the Albany region, which already has a series of online publication efforts, although only one is thriving. Kinda, anyway.

She's not afraid of competition, but that means more money is needed to get up and running in any effective manner, battling for readership. No—*participants.* Davin would be disappointed to hear her use the term *readership.*

"Interactive means participation," he's said, possibly a hundred times. She smiles.

The smile fades quickly; there are decisions ahead of her. If she's going to do Columbia County, she'll want Dutchess County too. Dutchess County, to the south and closer to the city, has well over a quarter million residents. If she's going to do Columbia County, she'll want Albany County and Rensselaer County too, figuring the former has over three hundred thousand in population and Rensselaer another hundred sixty-something thousand. And then Ulster County, just west of Dutchess County, is another potential addition.

This big play will require a hell of a lot of money. What kind of play should she make? A modest incremental expansion or go all out? There are a lot of moving parts to the question.

One item that Davin has recently discussed with her is that a big expansion means the number of seat licenses would have to grow for the platform they're using for *Berkshire Interactive*, and it looks like the money choice would be to buy a full site license, which is a quarter-million-dollar invoice. On the other hand, over time, not having the individual service subscription fees would pay off.

And then there's the expanding workforce. Can she get Davin to help figure out that cost? Can he be relied on? He keeps showing reservations about adding more work for himself, although, to date, that hasn't stopped him from taking many different assignments.

She gets up and grabs a pencil out of the utility drawer near her sink and sits back down at the table, pulling the printout toward her. She makes some notes.

Piss or get off the pot, Davin. But maybe this applies to herself as much, or more, than him.

Density, Definition, Destination, read her scribbled notes. Can she cherry-pick Hudson and Rhinebeck or is that thinking too literally—too geographically? The front-end work of a *Columbia Interactive* could negate the geographical distances, the lack of density, and why not then *Dutchess Interactive* and build up organically?

This stuff is driving her crazy. She wants to have Davin weigh in and hopes she won't have to beg him, but she's pretty sure he'll come through. He tends to respond to the sense of being needed, of being valued.

Nagging doubts about the would-be investors persist. Deidre, no doubt, would tell her to trust her gut, her instincts. Maybe she should have bought the right kind of crystal or gotten a tarot reading. But the blush of such cynical thoughts makes her feel bad, and she doesn't want to think about Deidre right now, certainly not in this unkind way, and she doesn't have time to deal with feelings anyway. She's too busy, there's too much on the line, and too many things to figure out.

A small part of her is calling bullshit and another part of her is feeling something a lot like dread, and on top of that, the lyrics from an old song keep poking through: 'Take the money and run.'

Chapter 15: Dewers on the Rocks

June 23, 2035

When Allen Randolph has to use a name, he makes one up and coming into Mexico he carries a decently fabricated Arizona driver's license and a solid facsimile of a tourist visa for Maker Dewers. The name, newly minted for the operation, cracks him up, but he'll never whiteboard it for anyone, and this name is disposable, of course.

John Story isn't a real name either, but he now has a passing acquaintance with the man with whom he's sharing this small apartment in Mexico City, in a rundown building, part of a long block, really, like a town house or row house, each segment with two addresses. They're on the top, the third floor of 98 to 100 Bucareli, with its nice blue tile façade that alternates with red stone façades, with nice white stone trim work.

If he gets stopped, he'll argue that he's just lost his passport and that he's on his way to the embassy or, if it's late, planning the visit for the next day. The visa check should be sound according to Biff, who told him when handing over the new identity that they have a contact within the Mexican immigration office at Calexico, and the application is an online process, so the contact at the border there can mark entry and supply the right stamps before passing it on.

His getting stopped is unlikely, especially now that he and the man going by John are in place. During the first briefing, the other man stupidly told him his real name is Jim, but at least he didn't blurt out a last name.

The guidelines on an operation like this with another person otherwise unknown are to keep one's real name to oneself. There are a lot of guidelines, and when, now years ago, he'd gone through what he still thinks of NOS boot camp, he'd studied hard. The sort of tradecraft on offer was exciting to him.

Running silent seems tattooed on his brain, even after all this time. He likes the sort of work he's doing, proud, he supposes, that he's making a direct difference in visiting justice upon those who are happy to burn the future for the sake of some profit today. He often takes the time to relive his operations, and only one or two haven't made national news, but that was what NOS wanted. He's fine with not getting credit on some behind-the-scenes operation toward what end he'll likely never know. He's competent at what he does, the four killings to date producing little evidence leading back to him or any actionable exposure for NOS.

Running silent.

Could that trainer, whose real name he still doesn't know, still be active? He'd seemed pretty old, those years back, and must have been some sort of former spook or a spook wannabe, anyway, but a good study either way.

Most of his actions become known to the authorities because NOS often likes to make the claims as part of the bigger campaign *To scare the fuckers witless,* and that's what he's doing. Some NOS action is specifically directed at hitting these monster corporations where it hurts: money.

His role in operations, the running silent, is a lonely life, although not always isolated. There's been those recruitment assignments he's taken on, although he has mixed feelings about it, not liking the pretense of it, but the closest he's had to real relationships sometimes comes through such assignments, like Sylvia, or *Sylvie,* as he'd come to call her. His heart had gotten involved then. If only she could have passed vetting, because sometimes these relationships become their own action teams and he misses Sylvie. He still thinks about her a lot, and it wasn't the sex—which was great—but the contact, the connection, that's the real price of running silent.

Probably this isolation is why John came on to him two nights ago. He has sympathy, really, but this operation is complicated enough already. Besides, he's just never bent that way.

At least the other man, even if surprisingly young, seemed well-informed on the details of the operation, and Maker appreciates getting more thorough background. He's been in place with John for four days and he's got plenty of time to speculate about such things, but John is only talking about the logistics, the *when* and *how* and *where* of it all. They're living dark, which means no lights during the off-hours, except for the middle rooms that they can black out with the taped sheets of six mil black plastic, and it's here they cook their rations on a tiny camp stove and where there's a table where they service the rifles and the rest of their equipment, here where they split a bottle of cheap tequila and John came on to him, but he's got no interest, although things had gotten tense enough during that clarification.

The younger man seemed embarrassed, and then angry as a way to cover up his embarrassment, at least that's what he assumes, not that he cares. Nor does he care if the guy jerks off loudly every night, loud when he releases, something of a payback in the way he does this, but that doesn't matter any, either.

Since they've been here, they've talked sometimes, although he's worried that John will come on to him again.

Some operations are out in the open, when he doesn't have to hide, or rather, can hide in plain sight. Some are big team efforts, and he's had a couple of brief relationships, but he has no roots, is always moving on to the next assignment. As much as he likes women, as much as he likes fucking, it's holding another person, the company, that can seem the higher price he pays. It might be best to put an end to such contemplation, just stopping such thoughts—they're just complications. This is a complicated operation. Even getting into place was its own operation, Biff putting together a work crew, pickup truck and van outfitted to look the part, the guys carrying in boxes and equipment and food, and all kinds of construction material, including the absurdly bright work light he and John use in the blackout section of the third floor, best pointed off an inside wall, as they discovered after some trial and error and a lot of squinting.

The crew had brought in the uniforms. The crew had wrestled the long extension ladder up to the roof, put the ropes there, in two big plastic tubs. And then the crew left, the parade of workers exiting in two bunches, two short, leaving them behind. Both he and John have gone up to the roof twice now, at night. Not that it's all that dark in the city's night, but with the dark clothes they were hard to notice even when they were anchoring the end of each rope.

They've been going over the maps and diagrams, studying the distances, the escape route, both the primary one and the secondary, in case they need to improvise. They've serviced the guns, preset the scopes, inventoried and re-inventoried the equipment. Placed the incendiary device for afterward.

But mostly they wait, and they've been in place long enough for any memory of the earlier activity to already have leaked out of people's minds, or at least more likely forgotten already, anyway, and that's just in case there's a neighborhood survey before tomorrow's action. Before the big show.

Security drones are the most likely problem, but with the right timing and the already-missing panes of glass in the front windows, and the uniforms for after, the plans are solid. Nothing he wouldn't expect from NOS. Someday he'd like to meet the planners, but whoever they are, he'll probably never know.

This place they're in, that's got to be all cartel. The site selection is perfect. 98 to 100 Bucareli is the back street for Secretaría de Gobernación, or SEGOB, as John calls it but drawing out the long *e*. They're in a section of three-story mixed-use buildings on the other side of the street that runs behind the government complex. Their block has Autotronic, an electric auto shop, a Chop Chop Bikes, and Jazar Refacciones, an auto parts store, all scattered along the street at first floor level. It's not clear if any of these businesses are active – most of the apartments in this stretch of buildings are vacant. There's a lot of graffiti across all the connected building fronts, and the building they're in has a blue tile façade. There are a number of such façades with white stonework trim that make up the rest of the block-long building, with alternating segments of red stone and white stonework. Razor wire is spread at the base of the second floor all along this block-long structure. Metal shop doors and grates mark the front entrances. There's a solid smattering of missing windowpanes among second- and third-floor windows and more missing in occasional balcony-window doors all along the block.

The dignitaries, if the intelligence is right, will come in through Casa Cobián, right across the street, and he doesn't know why the main entrance on Abraham González on the other side of the complex of buildings isn't used, but he can guess that the historic landmark and pretty pocket park across the street makes a better entrance, since this goes through gardens leading into the plaza-sized paved stone courtyard and into the SEGOB Ministry of the Interior.

There's supposed to be a reception, and they've observed comings and goings the last couple of days that have them thinking the reception is at least already partly set up in the large plaza courtyard. This must be for after the signing. If all goes to plan, there won't be a reception. The target opportunity is when they're getting out of the car and being greeted.

Their operation post is on the roof, blocked from view from the four-story Unidad de Apoyo al Sistema de Justicia building at the far corner of Bucareli and Calle Gral. Prim by the tall roof access shed atop 98 to 100 Bucareli and those others atop other segments of the long building. These make for nice blinds. Other nearby buildings are three stories or less, so not a discovery risk. Still, they have a second position on the third floor, if needed.

He wonders what the name for this type of building they're in is in Spanish, what the word might be for town house or row house. He can ask John, who is supposed to be a fluent Spanish speaker, although the claim has not been tested. It would be helpful if John spoke better Spanish than he does, which is *más o menos*.

Their escape route is to rappel down into the back alley, then head toward Emilio Dondé, but well before they hit the street, they are to enter the back entrance of a building on the other side of the alley that connects to the long delivery alley. That delivery alley, or driveway, that comes out at Calle Tres Guerras 13, about a half block down from Teatro Ciudadela.

He's studied the area on Google Maps, exploring the area all around in both grid view and street view, but he especially focused on the escape route. There's a big metal roll-up door at the end of the delivery alley that lets out onto thirty feet of concrete driveway, and he's seen that this slopes up toward the street. The escape route has been double-checked by others and according to Biff, the report is that the roll-up door is typically open in the daytime and the slope up to the street ends at a tall iron double-doored gate, latched but not locked. There's video camera surveillance in the short span of concrete, one camera facing the roll-up door and the other the gate.

The cartel's reasons for this operation are somewhat opaque, although the expediency of it for NOS is obvious: the give and take of favors and mutual benefits. The drug distribution support or whatever other evil deeds may be committed by NOS for the quid pro quo are indefensible, though. Four kids in his high school overdosed in his four years there. But no one is safe, right? Fentanyl, killings, human trafficking—no illusions here about the cartels—but little matters when the world is burning, and that's what he's doing, bringing the impending doom to the attention of the public and bringing justice down on those who otherwise work for the mass murder and ecocide that their products happily distribute across the globe.

"Hey, John."

John's lying down on a sleeping roll, face covered by a dark T-shirt against the glare of the work light that seems extra bright within the walls of black plastic sheets. The stage whisper is plenty loud enough to get his attention. John, who he thinks must be at least a couple of years younger than he is or younger yet, pulls the dark T-shirt from his eyes and rolls on his side to look at him.

"Let's walk through the steps again," he says to the blinking young man.

Chapter 16: Hot and Cold Case Open or Shut

June 24, 2035

As if keeping straight the multitude of climate cases in the courts isn't tough enough, Jeannie Louise has gotten caught up in the latest legal maneuverings and hijinks in the No One is Safe case, now in its sixth week, and that just piles on another element of confusion as she considers the court cases. *Climate change in the courts* is the preferred term for the many dozens of climate change-related legal suits being pressed, and typically against oil companies, but there are other ongoing fights, too. The number of such cases has to be well over a hundred, with many of these cases going back a decade, some, more.

Davin's son has contacted her in regard to these cases, but she hasn't yet mentioned this to Davin, her walking partner today. However, her question about whether he follows the various climate court cases has led him down a different path, talking about a case involving No One is Safe, that shadowy operation she loathes with a passion.

The United States of America v. Spark Earth R/Evolution Action Corp. case also involves climate change, but only in that this climate change advocacy nonprofit may or may not be a funding conduit for No One is Safe, a domestic terrorist group, so designated in 2030. That case has been controversial from the start, with speculation from the start about whether any sort of prosecution would go forward.

She and Davin are at the point of the River Walk where

Searles Castle, now northward, comes into view across long spans of lawns and now half-wild landscaping. This spot offers a great perspective of the structure itself and the scope of the grounds, the path they're on at the edge of the Housatonic and mostly behind trees that block sight lines except for this short break. The River Walk runs alongside the Housatonic and starts just a block or two from her apartment on Cottage Street, and once a week, more or less, Davin joins her to walk through to Olympia Fields, the modest Little League groupings of baseball fields, but if they're both feeling ambitious they'll sometimes walk farther, to the northern start of the Sheffield flood plains. But today it's agreed to be a short walk, although twice already this summer, higher ambition has mutually struck them and they've walked as far as Bistro Box to stop in for an early lunch.

The two of them rest in silence as they appreciate the large acreage of landscape running toward the stone structure, a French château-style house designed by Stanford White of McKim, Mead & White and built in the latter part of the nineteenth century. She'd read about it back when she was still new to Great Barrington and she'd gotten caught up in researching the building's origin story. There's some story about Stanford White—something about an affair, something about a woman on a swing, and a duel maybe? No, perhaps not. Weird how the mind wanders in certain circumstances.

Originally, this structure was called Kellogg Terrace, although she draws a complete blank on why, exactly, it was so named. The man who had commissioned the design and construction was Mark Hopkins, at the time treasurer and one of the founders of the Central Pacific Railroad. One of the Robber Barons seems a safe assumption, given the time period and the excessive size and style of the buildings and grounds. Hopkins died well before completion of the structure, and Mary Hopkins then married Edward Francis Searles, a man twenty-three years younger and who was in charge of designing the interior. *A man with designs.*

"Seven stories," she tells Davin. "That includes a 'dungeon' basement, I'm pretty sure."

He only grunts.

"I'm not sure how big the whole place is, but I remember that it has thirty-six fireplaces," she adds.

Davin tells her, "I was told that this was used as a private girls' school for quite a while, and when we moved to Housatonic, the place was the John Dewey Academy, which was some sort of place for troubled teens."

They turn away and continue down the River Walk, and all the floating random facts about the building they've been looking at in the distance dissipate as Jeannie goes back to thinking about Jimmy's email. He was asking about the utility of the AI Dark Money project she's been involved in, on and off, for half a decade, that project one of many connected to The Laundry, the ad hoc group of academics, policy wonks, analysts, and any and all other varieties of professionals focused on climate issues. They've had early success using a Rutgers University facility to run extensive AI-driven textual analyses of climate denial and anti-climate-action white papers, speeches, and magazine and podcast content, and the findings had been illuminating. Revealed were a group of nearly thirty contractors and staffers who were the actual authors of hundreds of speeches and articles, the work typically instigated through one or another of a dozen think tanks backed by fossil fuel interests.

That first report had created quite a stir, but the follow-up AI financial analysis efforts, some years in the making, have helped clarify direct funding sources for much of the dark money driving anti-climate activity, and this is what Jimmy is interested in. After explaining to her the cyberattacks on many of the law firms involved in a multitude of fossil fuel-related court cases, he's hoping to see if the funding tracing might be part of some investigation.

Who's funding the hacks, is how he put it, although he admitted the work backtracing to the source or sources of the attacks is ongoing.

She's been surprised by the number of cases now active in the courts or inching toward their day in court. She's largely been ignoring such cases, the hundred-plus, because such cases have been threatening for years, and always seemed to be on appeal or awaiting rulings on standings or running silent. In her recent search, following Jimmy's call, she found a bitbytes newsletter on the topic that explicated the many cases finally moving ahead.

But Davin's talking about NOS, the case she's bewildered by, the wide-ranging opinions and views regarding that court case now underway. She's clear enough on the central focus for the court, and it isn't even NOS on trial but a climate fundraising operation accused of secretly directing funds to NOS. The charges being brought against that organization have to be proved beyond a reasonable doubt, and as far as she's concerned, she's not in the courtroom or on the jury, and so any speculation about what the verdict might be is entirely not her concern.

"The prosecutors seem to be floundering," Davin tells her, as they walk down the River Walk.

She says nothing in response – Davin is quite capable of carrying each side of any conversation when he gets caught up in a story.

"I mean, they have all those other cases, other convictions, going back, what, five years, for the Eagle murders," he's saying, referring to one of the earliest NOS attacks.

"I was actually at NOS's debut, the parking garage explosions," he tells her, as if he hasn't mentioned this to her any number of times already. No one had been hurt, not seriously hurt, anyway, in that first public showing by NOS, but what he's referring to as the Eagle incident had killed a family and was connected to – part of – the bombing of the Sunoco Eagle Point facility. The Eagle incident resulted in fourteen people arrested, tried, and convicted, all but one of the felons under twenty-five years of age. All fourteen convicted in the several Eagle cases are still serving time. The hope at the time was that the group had been ended. She'd certainly had hoped so, but they had gotten better after that.

The forensic evidence that had been found on the drone used to drop the shaped charges on the refinery's oil tank farm had led investigators to one person, and the case quickly developed from this one point of contact. Others involved, in the town near Philadelphia where the gasoline tanker caused the house and its four inhabitants to burn, were quickly identified through various CCTV images, since it was known what time the tanker truck hit the house, and the tanker easy enough to trace. Those identified and arrested this way led to others' arrests. The various trials were followed widely, but NOS hadn't waited until the trials were complete to carry out further actions.

She can't remember the damn name of the town where the executive and his family had been burned to death, but she's not going to ask Davin. It's a warm day, perfect for the end of June. The sun is shining through the trees along the river, and she'd simply rather just enjoy the walk. It's a long-held ability of hers to tune Davin out when he gets into one of his rants.

"Makes me think of the Sinn Fein thing," he says.

Exactly—the current trial isn't arguing that Spark Earth R/Evolution Action is NOS, but a source of funding with shared aims. Spark claims to be a political organization dedicated to moving the electrotech revolution forward through peaceful political means, and that any connection between Spark and NOS is simply coincidence, not active support. Electrotech revolution. This is a term that showed up almost a decade ago, but it's mostly adopted by the more extreme renewable energy transition advocates, even today, even as the transition is now well underway. That's just one more reason for the virulent anger she's long held for NOS.

Progress away from fossil fuels is well underway and getting stronger by the day.

There's an assignment she's been working on, an analysis of the Grid Stability, Renewable Energy, and Intelligent Integration and Transmission Act. The act is typically referred to as "Great, Too," "GREAT Two," or "Greta," although this last nickname's a little odd, since there's no direct connection to the activist. "GREATII," is the official acronym, but she tends to use "The Great Second Act," paying homage to the reviving of IRA's electrification tax credits cut off at the knees by Trump's last administration. She's likely to go with the title for her article "GREAT Two has Trouble Running Full Tilt Out of the Gate Too," at least if she ever finishes the piece. She's putting the article out on her RE:CC bitbytes, where she can loosen the reins on her frustrations with slow rollouts of many of the programs specified and funded by the act, but because this isn't a paid assignment, she's as likely as not to put off finishing the piece, frustrated with her own slow rollout.

Such moments of frustration can get her thinking longingly about her old Ritalin habit. Never again.

"I remember, albeit hazily, the whole 1990s thing, with Sinn Fein going legit," Davin then adds, surprising her back into the conversation. "Although there are probably old-timers still who refuse to believe it."

She's following the current trial closely enough to know the prosecution is focusing on money raised by Spark, and she's not sure there's a great case, considering all the infamous digital traps and misdirects and third-party hand-off procedures NOS follows, stymieing the work of law enforcement to identify and arrest NOS terrorists since the initial arrests. Terrorists, well, there you go. Not activists.

"Similar, Spark and Sinn Fein, both terrorists," she says, "but it's the proof that's required, not historical analogy. The concept of dark money has been brought into the light, but the flat cell structure of NOS is a whole different problem," and that explains the central problem for the trial, as best she can figure. Whatever evidence chain for any secret funding that may go through Spark to NOS seems shaky and circumstantial, and that's with the Feds' own AI computational financial transaction platform these days, and one more sophisticated than The Laundry's best efforts.

The IRS has used their AI computational financial transaction platform quite successfully for tax evasion cases, going after the wealthy after the tax reforms of 2032, but there's no dark money direct reveal that's been presented at trial, at least so far. Probably any connections between the two organizations would be old-school analog, including handouts of cash. The best lever the prosecution has is the records of surprisingly high levels of cash donations to Spark, very much an outlier in today's credit and chip payment world.

Davin clearly understands the dark money mechanisms, or at least should, since this past winter, at one of his cocktail parties, she went deep into the projects she's involved in about dark money tracing, more or less having been interrogated by Cynthia, Davin's son's partner. She's even written a simplified guide to how dark money distribution by fossil fuel interests plays out, spinning out an article on the subject for *Wired*, and her writings on the subject elsewhere have been well received, now that the AI trace programs are humming. She's even been one of the people testifying before Congress—well, the Joint Committee on Election Finance Reform—about the program and the results.

The fight in Congress on election financing law remains a perennial non-topic, mostly, with the focus on Congress overturning Citizens United. Another perennial nonstarter, but she's had her moment in the spotlight, for whatever that may have been worth.

The current civil court case is really about restricting NOS, trying to squeeze its money supply and starve it out, but it's not looking good. No One is Safe has managed to keep hitting oil interests and there have been the murders of several high-profile oil company executives. NOS is getting funds from somewhere, obviously, especially with the scope of recent operations. Near the close of 2034, in what remains the most recent operation in the news, attempted murder was carried out in a spectacular but failed effort to flood a seminar room with natural gas at a regional meeting of the Society of Petroleum Engineers. The would-be mass execution had hung up on a fouled supply line, according to some news stories, or a problematic remote-controlled servo, as reported in others. Still, the staggering scope of the undertaking and the false front company created to participate as a vendor in the modest exposition event had required enormous effort to leave no actionable traces other than what looks like a bunch of patsies, as much victims as the intended targets.

She tells Davin that she's heading back, mentioning that she needs to get back to Jimmy, and this appears to surprise him.

He quickens his steps to catch up to her as she reverses course. "What are you talking about?"

"He wants to know about the Dark Money Project," is all she says, but it's obvious that Davin wants more.

"Has he talked to you about NoNolo's clients getting hacked?" she asks, and it's clear that he knows nothing of the sort. She spends the rest of the walk back filling him in.

Chapter 17: Hold that House

June 29, 2035

Deidre is still falling behind on her bills, especially as she scrambles to cover the new lease costs, and this despite her best efforts to get as many shifts at Farm Table as she can.

She can do without her landlord ambushing her anytime she's even a minute late with her rent. He's a somewhat creepy guy in his forties, who inherited the house on Hillside after his mother's death.

She's just stepped outside on her way to the new store space, and here he is again, with bad news—her rent's going up.

Deidre looks directly at him. "How much?"

It's sickening, the way he looks at her and her roommates, his eyes a little too slow moving across her body, and with that little smile he never hides whenever he's scanning them. Probably has child porn. No, too far—she's being cruel now.

He names a new rent rate that drops her mouth open, and she's blinking, trying to do the math. She'll have to pay more than double what she does now, and since her current rent isn't any particular bargain, any guilty feelings vanish.

"That a joke? That's a joke." He's never been a joker.

"I already got offers."

There may be some deal anyway, maybe to turn the apartment into short-term rental. Unlikely—this means there's work to be done fixing up the space, so he'll miss this season for sure. So maybe he's just going for higher rent.

Housing has long been at a premium in South County and rents are already high in Great Barrington, but the location of this apartment means that she hasn't needed to buy a car, and that's kept her costs down, helping with her savings. Her last car gave up the ghost four years ago and she's done okay without it, partly because she gives her roommate Janice some money to use her car sometimes when she has to drive somewhere.

Sharing the modest apartment with two roommates has helped with costs, too, and Janice is okay, but their other roommate, Cokie, she'll be glad enough to leave behind, right along with Cokie's impressive ability to leave everything to be done by her and Janice, including throwing Cokie's clothes and every other kind of thing of hers back into her bedroom. Janice, in particular, is annoyed by Cokie, but Janice's so-called bedroom, a curtained-off side of the big front room, is a likely contributing factor. Not that Deidre's own room is that big, and what space she has is filled with boxes of vintage clothes and dresses and coats and jackets on hangers, the various hooks carefully placed into every other stud across two walls. Now there's the worry about security deposits, and, oh God, the curtain channel they affixed to the ceiling to separate Janice's space from the rest of the living room, which could also, and most likely will, cause the loss of their security deposit.

Of course, another way to think of what she's facing is not really a rent hike but an eviction. The tenant protections from evictions have gotten stronger in Great Barrington, but there's nothing the town can do if the property owner raises rents, and the one condition where eviction protection doesn't apply is late rent payments. The doubling of her current rent is just a pretext for emptying the house, she now clearly understands.

Deidre lets out a long sigh. "When?"

"End of the month." From the way he's now not looking at her, it seems that he just might be feeling bad about this jerk move. Oh, but he must be talking the end of July.

"Uh, not this month, like, it's one day away from July," is what she says.

He nods, but a one-month, one-day notice isn't him being any less of a jerk, really.

"This is bullshit." She's not really addressing her landlord as much as the situation that has turned her normal, regular day into a huge shitstorm of a day. "Shit."

He's squaring his shoulders, a growing "fuck you" posture if she knows this guy. Absolutely this is a done deal.

On the other hand, she'll likely get the security deposit back, or the equivalent, anyway, and that was all her money, not the roommates. Maybe he won't give back the actual security deposit? But then again, he has to because eviction protection remains in place while a dispute is unresolved, and she sure won't be paying rent for any extra months it could take for eviction to move forward.

Of course, she'll have to find a new place. She sighs again, staring into space, and then her focus is back on him. She asks him if her roommates have been told.

"I figured you'd tell them," he says, stepping back up the front steps toward the first floor door from which he's ambushed her. He disappears inside.

"Great," she says, but he's already back inside, and she's already turning back down the front walk, lost in what this all means for what comes next. Her racing thoughts and feelings of distress are mental states she knows all too well from her childhood, when her mother, always scrambling for work, had moved them a half dozen times.

Getting caught up in an overdue rent eviction won't help with her leasing the store space. The lease is still not actually signed, both parties thinking of the current arrangement as prudent, a get-to-know-you opportunity. Of course, he's happy that she's repainting already, while waiting for her to show she's got sufficient funds, which means she's waiting to see if Alicia will come through.

Her mom has offered a loan, but she knows that her

mom really doesn't have the money to spare, and besides, she's already helping by letting her store more of her vintage stock in her mother's small apartment living room, clothes racks and garment bags and boxes full of strange home furnishings she's been collecting from her Goodwill raids and other thrift sources, tag sales, and flea markets for the last four years. She can't even realistically consider asking her mom to let her stay with her for a while, not with the tiny apartment her mom rents and not with so much of the limited space already crammed with stock.

She's heading to the restaurant, and not for a shift yet but because she's helping out with inventory. She cuts across to East Street, her usual route, on automatic.

At some point, when she's thinking more calmly, she might call Davin, her former landlord back when she was a house sharer in Housatonic, twice. She's been out of touch, but maybe there's a room opening up.

She'd moved out of Davin's house to live with Alicia for a year and then was back again in Housatonic for another year, a bit more, after she left Alicia. Third time's the charm?

She still feels a bit like screaming.

Chapter 18: Be, Be, Be

July 1, 2035

Davin has liked all of Be's ideas for changes in his studio, especially with her prioritizing his use. At first he'd been worried she would colonize too much of the space.

Busy as a bee is the thought that occurred to him, when he'd talked to her about the house share opening. She mentioned her job, of course, but talked about her artwork, too, and the shows she's had and her hopes. She mentioned setting up a new studio for herself, and her yoga classes and trips for gallery hopping, all of which came across as a whirlwind, a mix of chaos and control, and all a bit breathless.

He'd kept his own comments about his studio to a minimum, balancing his worry about promising too much and compromising his own work. He's only recently invited her to take some space in his studio, although running the 50-amp circuit for her kiln had felt a bit uncomfortably commitment-like.

He's worried now that she's colonizing him in some sort of way. He knows in what way. He's been obsessing about her. For instance, he's finally figured out that he's been checking more frequently to see if she's in the studio, and he happens to drop in to work in the studio when she is.

It's not like he doesn't work with Marsha on the garden, but that's long been the case and he's never felt any particular need to be in the garden at the same time, except, of course, when there's a two-man job, like putting up the Sun Shades. He doesn't think of Marsha in terms of gender. He knows, of course, that she's a woman, but that's about as far as it's ever gone. *Just the facts, ma'am.*

The garden help from Marsha has been a godsend. The nearly two thousand-square-foot fenced garden has been a bit of a worry for him, but over the years he's developed a good plan to reduce one of the most time-consuming aspects of a vegetable garden—weeding. The high mulch approach he's long adopted doesn't avoid weeding, but the thick mulch suppresses them and makes them easier to pull. Some years the mulch has been chopped up leaves from the fall cleanup, other years, like this one, wood chips, and he likely has enough for next year's garden, too, the result of two big trees on the north property line he'd needed taken down, and the size of the chip pile is still impressive. High mulch, no-till gardens are a good way to build up the organic content of the soil, an essential objective, given the clay-like quality of the dirt he first had to work with.

Now that Be's in the studio, instead of adding to her rent, she helps out there, but it's nothing like his garden arrangement with Marsha. With Be now in the studio, she seems changed. Maybe she's lost in her clay prep or concentrating on texture or glaze experiments. Maybe he feels different in the studio, too, at least in those moments when he gets in the zone, the rough sketches of a concept suddenly merging in form and function, knowing the right piece, object, whatever, is needed in the assemblage, and how to frame it.

He sniffs and glances up at the stack of shelves on the far wall his long shallow worktable below them, more a deep low shelf, really. There are cartons and boxes and a few sacks of the miscellany he has collected over the years, and he's always meaning to organize these bits of things better.

His eye comes to rest on a bankers box up on the middle shelf, the terrible scribble of his handwriting that says *Dolls heads*, and the one next to it, but he can't decipher the label there, the magic marker providing less contrast across the brown of that old cardboard box. *Keys, locks chains*, that's what it says, and his eyes move on to other labels. *Bird nests, act. figures, lenses, Balls, Rope string cord*, are other labels, some nearly illegible scrawls, some illegible. *Toys, games, Electronics*, this last box one of the bigger ones, containing all sorts of old motherboards and modems and probably even a sound card or two, an Ethernet adapter or two, and probably all sorts of bits from the parade of his own computers he's plundered over the years of leaping obsolescence. The shelves read like a Dada poem.

He hasn't looked into the *Electronics* box since he did a piece that used an old chip-fat modem card tucked up to form the ceiling of an old box that presented an antique framed print of an eighteenth- or nineteenth-century lady, set on an upholstered back that used some crazy paisley fabric if he's remembering it right. That piece sold at least five years back, and he's got digital images of it somewhere. The name eludes him, although, the word *lady* is part of it.

He stops his scan of the boxes and trays and bins on the many shelves, looking back down on the wide worktable behind him, where he does most of his assembly.

Little Lady End Table, that was it. He sometimes wonders about his artwork now out in the world, and he sometimes gets anxious about one piece or another, wondering, worrying if his joints and tenons remain tight, or if the finish holds up, or if this piece or another of the assemblage has stayed put, or if a light fixture fails.

It's great to be spending more time in the studio. And over the last three years he's been so productive. Productive enough to have Be, the third house sharer, trade help as his part-tine studio assistant for her use of part of that space.

Be, Be, Be. Even after the five months she's been onboard, will he ever get completely used to her? She's always coming up with ideas about the studio—crazy ideas—that he sometimes has to moderate, often at considerable resolve. This can feel exhausting enough, but he's fortunate to have her enthusiasm and ability to dig into a project. She's in her fifties, but she seems fundamentally young, maybe because she's never been married, never raised a child. But she's a tonic, for whatever reason. Maybe it's just having another artist around.

Somehow, now feels even older than his seventy years, maybe because he's working with a lot of younger people, a lot younger, at *Berkshire Interactive,* and this can feel like a mixed blessing sometimes. But his working with them, mentoring the new contributors, has an invigorating effect. These responsibilities, this mentoring role, could easily enough overwhelm him, especially if Alicia's thinking about adding new digital properties moves forward, like the latest thoughts about *Hudson Interactive* and *Upstate Interactive* and who knows how many more markets. He tries to keep himself from getting too closely involved with Alicia Soares's efforts to expand what even he has come to think of as her empire.

But he does go all the way back with Alicia, having done some work for her when she was starting *South County Interactive,* for the first iteration of which he'd helped define the platform capabilities and then taken point in setting up the chosen content management system. This work had constituted an odd turn for him, since he'd moved to the Berkshires many years back in an effort to get away from just such work, having done well enough in his profession to have advanced beyond his interest. *But who knew you can't make money with art?* It's an old joke that has for some time now lessened in its bitterness. He is actually making money with his art these days, a surprising fact, even if a modest amount.

Still, he couldn't keep the Housatonic property without house-sharing, and the work he still does for Berkshire Interactive LLC continues to make the difference between the cliché of starving artist and his doing well, at least relatively. His social security helps, too. Fat cat. He gives a small laugh, but the self-deprecating joke fades because, actually, he has an extra twenty pounds, at least, that he's put back on after nearly a year having kept it off. He's gotten used to his new old pounds. It's easy to get used to things.

The Airbnb apartment also contributes close to a third of the income he has each year. The apartment is booked pretty much solid from mid-spring through early November, and after years of two-day minimums, he's shifted mostly to week minimums during high season, and he has hardly any empty weeks.

There's a young family there now, their one child still a baby but close to toddlerhood, the language sounds of nonwords a development stage he has always liked, and he'll open the kitchen door to say hello if they're enjoying the porch, but really, he just loves to hear the babble. Even the middle-of-the-night crying over the last few days doesn't much bother him, except one night it was persistent, and the long run of sonic rumbles of the parents were discernibly anxious in tone and pitch, not that he could make out what was being said. That night, two nights back, he had grabbed his blanket off his bed and retreated to his office and his ever-tattered recliner, serviceable as a bed of sorts, pushed back.

He hopes that Be's available to help him turn the apartment, the window to do so a short four-hour one.

He keeps the apartment listing marked *unavailable* from the start of December through March, mainly to keep it accessible for visits by friends from back in Cambridge and from parts unknown, and for his two kids and their families.

Jimmy and Cyn are out here typically for the Christmas holidays alternate years, one year in Housatonic and the next with Gwen, in Lenox, putting them up. So far only once have the two of them ventured to Ohio to see Cyn's family for the holidays. Cyn and her twin brothers are close, and the boys, singular or plural, now in their late twenties, manage to visit them in Boston a couple of times a year.

Skip and Marco and Pee-wee don't make the holidays,

but if they move back to the States, that should change for the better unless she takes the offer in Seattle, but since there's no news on that front, he drops such worries. Stateside anywhere would be much better than across the pond.

Air travel has become very expensive, and by the time he had pushed himself into action to visit the newborn Penelope—he can't help but smile thinking about her—the first carbon load assessments were being put in place, and all airlines had passed on the additional fees. The carbon assessment is another example of something he's in favor of for the sake of climate change efforts, but he doesn't feel all that favorably disposed when he has to pay for it. He's had a lot of practice with this odd disconnect between policies he supports and a dragging reluctance to support them if it costs him money.

Air travel has grown less and less attractive by any standard. An image comes unbidden into his mind, the long metal tube of the fuselage of his last airplane trip, that tube that seemed to stretch on forever from his seat, well toward the back, and after the plane landed at Barcelona airport—El Prat—he had fiercely wrestled with his claustrophobia, the indeterminate wait for disembarkation both too long and unprepared for, his coping mechanisms barely holding through the flight's long duration.

Back then, too, his money situation was problematic and the expense of the travel was quite real. He'd gotten divorced from Gwen just after COVID—another coronavirus divorcé, a demographic cliché—and the change in economic status to a single-income household with a sizable mortgage was a challenge. A new mortgage enabled him to buy her share of the house, but keeping up with the payments, that was touch and go, as were all the other house-related expenses. Before the divorce they'd done the Airbnb rentals, and that income remains a big help to him, but he also quickly started sharing the big house with others to meet costs.

He smiles when he thinks of that time, with the inaugural class of house sharers, young Chaplin and easygoing Deidre, who, as it turned out, as easily moved out from the Housatonic house and into his boss's place, the affair slow-building and quite sweet. Until it hadn't been.

And then she was back for a while, but then off to her own apartment. Now she'd love another turn, according to the email he's just received. He'd love to help, but he doesn't see how. Marsha, Charlie, and Be make for a full house.

Be, Be, Be. He's got his artist statement to do for the upcoming show in Hudson, and he always dreads putting this sort of thing together, the fear of sounding pretentious perhaps offset only by his worry about embarrassing himself. He'll ask Be to weigh in next time she's working in the studio. Be, Be, Be.

Chapter 19: No No No

July 1, 2035

Jimmy's come to Housatonic, and he tells Jeannie Louise that Cyn is coming down for the long weekend too. Jeannie Louise knows this visit will please Davin, since he tends to talk about his kids sooner or later in every conversation she has with him. She also knows that Jimmy's intent on getting as much from her as possible about the potential for financial tracking concerning the recent big cyberattack on most of NoNolo's clients. If she's reading his mix of pride and modesty right, he's telling her his own company has survived entirely.

"I've long been fascinated by hacking and security," is what he's just told her, "and I was evaluating one of the new AI security add-ons, and it was that work that kept NoNolo safe, but the timing was fortuitous, to say the least."

She's met him at her favorite bar, and right at opening, her favorite time, not that she drops in more than once or twice a week, except there's no end of the week in sight, not with all she's got on her plate. And it always helps to have a good cocktail at hand when the topic of a meeting is an ask. She knows of Jimmy and that his wife—or partner?—is involved in climate work, a methane effort, or maybe agriculture, could be both. On the other hand, she's only met him once or twice before, at a cocktail party or two at Davin's house. When did professional adults become so young?

It's hard to maintain her attention to him as he continues to speak. He's fleshing out what he told her in his earlier email, about how a number of his company's clients have had their document caches unrecoverably erased, even with those firms using Iron Mountain or other off-site backup, a very interesting detail. Some of the West Coast firms have escaped the destruction, but even those firms are paralyzed by their scramble for security solutions to keep the attack from activating.

"We've found some other code bombs across our clients."

He's giving the impression that this is a big deal, but she doesn't feel the need to ask him what he's talking about, and it doesn't matter anyway because he starts talking about how the data loss of documents for the various court cases could cause significant problems. He mentions that delays from having to re-acquire evidentiary material could set back cases for months or years.

"If NoNolo had also succumbed to the attack," he adds, and then repeats, "months or years, best case." He tells her that two cases have been dropped since the hack across NoNolo's law firm clients, but every other suit continues, in part because his clearinghouse still safely retains all documentation.

She makes the mistake of asking him what sorts of documents are involved.

He runs through a long list of the types and categories of documents required for prosecuting court cases but makes it clear his list is far from exhaustive.

"There are expert witness and testimony target lists, subpoena submissions and intentions, collaboration strategies and tactics, and prior case law and notes and arguments for legal principles and precedents."

He's obviously trying to be specific, although the list of document types is hardly necessary, but it's oddly interesting. She's kept an eye on various climate court cases over the years, but never all that closely.

"There are complaints, summonses, and court orders, too," he adds, before telling her that that the main body of documents is more mundane. "There are a plethora of agreements and contracts ranging from intellectual property agreements and documents related to patents, trademarks, and copyrights, and there are employment agreements and the contracts on terms of employment," he continues. "It's really astonishing to me all the details and records lawyers collect, have to figure out are important, whatever, the whole discovery results."

He stops, before adding "I could never do that, couldn't be a lawyer."

It seems like a good moment for her to sip her drink.

"I mean, partnership agreements outlining specific terms and obligations, parsing this, and purchase agreements, service contracts. I could never do that sort of thing, I'm a coder, a system architect, I know how to buckle down and hunt from errant code string, but yikes, I'd pull my head off."

He takes a gulp from his orange seltzer, right from the can.

"It's mostly information mining, finding the gold across tons of documents," and then he burps, then makes a face.

"All these, the documents hacked, represent hundreds of hours of legal work," he's now telling her, but then he declares it's more like tens of thousands of hours. "If the hacks had gotten everything, then many documents would probably have to be resubmitted for discovery or recreated through reinterviewing, and even the notes behind documents are part of the document pool, although in some cases, some documents never get backed up, maybe residing on various laptops, depending on how organized or strict a firm's document management is."

"Yeah, okay, got it," she tells Jimmy.

"Right," she then says, mainly to say something. "Huge numbers of documents, all kinds, and I imagine many cases are likely using many of the same documents and evidentiary material."

He nods. "We have hard-copy backup, an outside service, but there tends to be a big lag."

She jiggles the ice in her highball glass.

"If these documents disappeared, we're talking millions and millions of dollars of lost value and who knows the consequences of delays." He pauses to take another gulp. "We've added a second backup server, this one from Iron Mountain, and that's costing us." Another sip. "Overall, we've dodged a bullet." But here she sees a grin being suppressed, some sort of *ta-da!* wanting to come out, but maybe she's just imagining that.

She now knows more than she ever thought she would about NoNolo, and that it's a document management service provided to the law firms involved in one or several of the hundred fifty-five suits and prosecutions aimed at the big oil companies, or sometimes at various government agencies, regulatory bodies, and the occasional state or local authority. She knows now that NoNolo has protected most documents, but there are some likely irretrievable losses if whatever new documentation to have been filed with NoNolo hadn't yet been uploaded to their server.

"Right now, we're doing everything we can to identify the source of the attack." He stops for a moment. "Well, when I say 'we,' I mean technical services, consulting talent working with CISA, and fortunately, the Feds are interested in the case."

"Well, sure. Wiping out backup servers is a huge security risk. Catastrophic."

He nods. "A web search on how to identify actors in cyberattacks kept returning hits on The Laundry, and I remembered that you're part of that group."

She takes another sip of her highball, the one today chosen more for refreshment and not too boozy. She uses a straw to take a pull from the tall glass of Americano. The Campari and sweet vermouth and club soda makes a low ABV choice, considering she's got to get back to work. Maybe one more, though.

"What I'm looking for is any linkage between the hacker group or groups and the sources of payment for their work," Jimmy says.

"Okay."

And now it's her turn, and she's trying to explain as concisely and clearly as she can what The Laundry has accomplished with its AI Dark Money project, how patterns in the dissemination of amounts of money can be teased from public documents, the annual filings of corporations and organizations, and how such patterns map to salary, payments, and fee structures for those identified with actions corresponding to the aims of dark money. She speaks at some length about how their original project of AI-driven textual analysis of climate denial content helped identify the actual authors, who were typically contractors writing for others and revealed, too, in the authorship of various legislative bills through lobbying groups. With a sense of pride, she mentions how her long-running tracking of climate denial and climate action delay think tanks and PACs and other such entities and matching up contractor payouts has helped estimate the quantity of Dark Money coming in, but then she confesses that there's so much more that's been done with the AI Dark Money project which she can't well explain. She knows about groups claiming nonprofit status, with their associated obligations of public reporting, but there are other central mechanisms and machinations of the project she can't describe in any useful detail.

"I've helped point the team toward likely targets, but I've got nothing to do with the codes and prompt sequences."

He nods.

She picks up her phone and thumbs through to her email and tells him she's sending an introduction to the person at the project who can best direct his queries. She's just put the phone back down, but a tone sounds, and she picks it up again, checks which topic notification the alert is from.

Notifications are stacking, the tone repeating. These are all from her NOS topic alert.

She scans the latest update on the court case. "Hmm. Another move for dismissal by the Spark defense team, the judge will pronounce on Monday."

Jimmy's draining his can, and then, done, takes the beverage napkin and dabs his lips, rather delicately.

"Good example of how tracing can be difficult," she says. "The NOS case, well, the Spark case about funding NOS, there can be a problem with connecting transactions."

"Don't mention NOS in front of Cyn. She hates those people, that group, like, with a passion."

"Yeah, me too," Jeannie Louise tells him.

"They're guilty all right." It's hard to draw any other conclusion. "There's no real direct evidence or the prosecution would have delivered it, it seems to me, at today's defense dismissal request."

The bar is starting to get noisy as more people come in.

"There's a lot of money being spent, has to be," she says. Until the latest attack—the latest successful one, anyway—the biggest property destruction had been Matterhorn Express Pipeline, back in 2032, when NOS had blown up many critical junctions and valve substations using drones. But last year's target, the Saguaro LNG export terminal nearing completion, has outdone all other claims. NOS had managed to hijack an inspection crew servicing the Saguaro Connector Pipeline just south of Chula Vista to deliver a low-level dirty bomb through an inspection hatch and on to an inspection sled, sending the explosive package toward the as-yet unopen facility.

"They placed the whole Saguaro facility out of action for what is likely to be decades," she tells him. "That was a huge operation, big money, and there's been remediation capping, mainly to keep the medical radiation brew from spreading into population centers, since there'd been some

Cobalt-57 and Cobalt-60 detected, with a half-life of some five years, at least for one of those radionuclide."

It was big news when it happened, and there are still frequent follow-ups.

Jimmy's just nodding.

"The cleanup necessary to finish the export facility may never happen. The only lead in that case was the arrest of a medical waste facility manager in California, and if he'd known names to give the investigators, he likely would have provided them, considering he faced the twenty-year maximum sentence and the maximum fine of two hundred fifty thousand dollars."

"He didn't have actionable information, right?" asks Jimmy.

She doesn't bother to answer. She's not unhappy about the Saguaro LNG export terminal being offline, as far as that goes, and likely permanently so. She has no doubt that the point of the terminal was to further build Asian markets for LNG, and more natural gas electrical generation is the last thing the climate needs. Still, the Saguaro LNG export terminal action had been roundly and rightly condemned. That kind of illegal action hurt climate progress efforts.

The Spark situation is infuriating, and it's hugely frustrating that the Feds are struggling to make their case, despite the money-tracing systems in place, systems far more powerful than the work she and her colleagues at The Laundry created in their dark money project.

"Dark money is not the same as secret money," she tells Jimmy, but she's also reminding herself.

She stands.

"I gotta get back to work," she tells him, approaching the bar to pay the tab. "You have the contact, tell him I sent you, maybe we can help."

Jimmy stands, his large frame looming in the growing crowd.

"Uh, thanks," he manages, but Jeannie Louise is already heading for the door, and the last thing she does is a clumsy wave in the direction of the bar.

Chapter 20: Animal, Mineral, or Vegetable

July 1, 2035

Davin's excited about having Jimmy visit and thrilled that Cyn, too, will be making her way down tonight. He doesn't know when Jimmy will be done with JL or if anything can even come from the meeting. It doesn't matter—he'll take any excuse or reason to have these two to himself for the evening. He doesn't know how long they're planning to stay. He doubts it will be more than just tonight, but he'll ask them and tell them to stay longer if they'd like. It may be that Jimmy's planning on getting together with his one Housatonic friend who still lives here, although he doesn't know if that guy, Gus, has been living here all this time. It could be that his friend is back living with his parents, but he'll ask after him anyway. If he remembers to, that is.

He's sitting at his desk, replaying video from the cameras he's reactivated out back to see what's periodically taking the early vegetables. Lettuce has been going missing and he's asked Marsha enough about that, earning him a glare the last such time. The last of the radishes are now gone entirely, although at this stage this early yield gets a bit woody with the heat, and he may or may not reseed for a second crop. The spinach production, which he's been so pleased to have finally made a success of, has reduced yield due to whole plants being uprooted, half his planting decimated. Even the few tiny early zucchini are going missing, and leaves are vanishing off his still-small kale and collards.

He set the cameras a few days back, but he's been busy and didn't review the recordings right away, and when he finally got around to it, he saw that he'd used the wrong setting and the motion trigger hadn't activated. And then, after a couple more days, this morning he's finally gotten a good night's recordings of the nocturnal scene.

This morning also brought news of Jimmy coming out to meet with JL, so his mood is bouncing all along the spectrum, a mix of anger at the confirmation of his suspicions about the garden and excitement about seeing Jimmy and Cyn tonight.

It's a full house here, up on the hill, which means Jimmy and Cyn won't be using the Airbnb apartment, but he's already inflated the rigid frame air bed he keeps deflated in a closet off the living room. He's already put up the air frame in his office. One thing he doesn't lack, given his Airbnb apartment, is sheets, pillows, and towels, so the bed is nicely made up, but room dimensions don't change. While his office is nicely sized for an office, the bed and all makes it a bit tight to get to his desk, the very desk where he's again watching the video from the garden's infrared video cameras.

There's a man and a woman, as best he can determine with the indistinct IR images, opening the back gate and through the greenhouse into the garden, rummaging through the rows, small handheld lights held low to the mulch, and they're picking at the garden. *His* garden! It's as infuriating watching this for the third or fourth time as it was upon initial review. He's been suspecting human, not animal, for some days now, the culling of the vegetables too precise, although the foragers clearly don't have gardening experience. If they had, they simply would have taken off the top leaves of spinach, not plucked root and all at, according to the cameras' time stamps, 1:23 a.m. this morning.

The first camera picked them up coming in at the

southeast corner of the property, walking through the meadow his neighbor there keeps. They might be coming from a housing development about a quarter mile south, through woods and this meadow, but that seems unlikely. There's a lot of talk about strange hordes of young people, and the consensus is they're mostly out of the city. When he's been downtown, he's certainly seen what people have been claiming, and even here in the village, there are more young adults hanging in the park now, and the one time he went up to Ramsdell Library, a surprisingly large number of the same sort of cohort were in the reading room and scattered about. Probably using Wi-Fi—there were several VR headsets and plenty of laptops and phones in use among the crowd. Electrical outlets seemed to be in high use, judging by the groupings around the outlets. Electric outlets would not have been a common commodity back when the library's construction was completed—1908, if he remembers right. Ramsdell is a lovely, small library, a two-story Beaux Arts-style building, gifted to the village by a former owner of the mills across the street.

It's been warm, although not unpleasantly so, but the day he went down to Ramsdell, that day was something of a scorcher, so maybe it was the library's AC that was most in demand, or restrooms, maybe, considering public Wi-Fi is ubiquitous across most of Great Barrington and Housatonic these days. He asked the desk person about the crowding, but she was a new hire, and young, and he only got a shrug in answer to his query.

He clicks on the video files again. The two figures move stealthily about, going grocery shopping.

The simplest solution is to lock the gates and send a message that way, but that doesn't feel like it would come close to being at all satisfying. On the other hand, he's in his seventies, and popping out of the dark to yell at vegetable thieves may not be the most sensible course of action.

But Jimmy will be here tonight. He's in his prime and is six foot, seven inches tall, and on the husky side at that.

Maybe he should ask Jimmy to keep vigil with him. Of course, this means staying up late, but then, Jimmy has always been a night owl, at least since his college days. Might not be now, though—Jimmy's been a responsible member of the working world for years now. He'll ask Jimmy what he'd like to do, and there's always the chain and padlock choice.

He could wait by himself, of course, and take some flash pictures with his phone, but without company, he's likely to fall asleep on watch. Mosquitoes are on the prowl at night and they've been vicious this summer. Bloodsuckers.

Chapter 21: Fletch's Walkabout

July 1, 2035

It's proving to be a tough week. Fletch locks up her office in town hall and heads for the street. As she steps out the front entrance, she stops for a moment to look around and sighs. It's Sunday, so the beginning of another tough week.

The number of visitors in town is swelling with the extra-long holiday weekend with July Fourth falling midweek. Tanglewood is planning a James Taylor tribute. The artist himself no longer performs, due to health problems or maybe just old age. How long must he have been doing July Fourth shows before having to quit?

This is also the first year the Silver-top is ready, a series of retractable reflective awnings that can span much of the lawn area, something planned for years to combat high temperature days. As far as she knows, the Silver-top remains all rolled up, the temperature forecast is just fine for the show and the fireworks.

She's been meaning to walk the streets more, and now here she is, still thinking of all the new problems she's facing. The town of Synecdoche is facing. She is the town.

She's always liked that there's a city in New York called Schenectady, and in fact she used to transpose one word for the other until she finally wrestled the confusion, which may be why she's thinking in this absurd way as she makes her way to the sidewalk and crosses Castle Street to land on the west side of Main Street, waiting for the pedestrian signal.

Main Street's looking busy this summer evening, and exceptionally so given the hour. She's long known that Great Barrington tends to roll up its sidewalks around 8:00 p.m., even during the summer. Restaurants, she's well aware, aren't thrilled that this is so, but in the last few years there have been two additional places where their bar action does run later. Open till 11:00, woo-hoo! She sits in on the Selectboard meetings, and there are chronic complaints about how early downtown shuts down and chronic complaints too about letting anything stay open too late. What was that comment she heard at one such meeting? One of the restaurant owners telling the board how he tries to explain away the early close of downtown to visitors, including, everyone no doubt assumed, New Yorkers, from the City That Never Sleeps.

The pedestrian signal sounds, and she crosses Main Street. It's as if everyone in town has cows to milk in the morning. This town has a lot of wiseasses, and she loves this, except, of course, when said wiseassery is aimed at her.

She turns northward. She'll make a loop, maybe as far as Farm Table, maybe stop in for a drink, although that activity is one rarely exercised, what with Robbie and her being more inclined to be homebodies.

Or so she thought, but now that Robbie's acting like some sort of swinger, and now that Robbie's out of the house and who knows where, she now has to amend such long-held views. She's the only homebody, apparently. She's the only one happy to be coming home after trying days and welcoming a glass of wine and an episode of one or another of their favorite series, or reading and then off to bed to be up early for another round of workaday wonder.

She looks up to the sky, the evening's dim just suggested, and she pulls out her phone. It's almost seven thirty. Another long day, and a Sunday at that.

She continues up the sidewalk, slipping back into another round of speculation on how long Robbie's been having affairs. He's always been home in the evenings, but what of his days when she's at work? His freelance writing jobs give him plenty of flexibility. He's never been one to talk about projects, or not frequently, at any rate.

Or she's been the one to talk, her endless debriefings from work. There's a moment of guilt in this thought and tears spring up momentarily, quickly replaced by anger. Maybe he's just been fucking around.

A passerby nods at her. She doesn't recognize the person. Does the person know she's the town manager, or is it just out of politeness? She's good-looking enough but, now that she's in her solid middle age years, hardly particularly noticeable, a growing genericness about her.

She almost bumps into someone but is saved by the older man calling out, "Steady on there, Fletch!" and she looks up just in time to see that she's almost trampled the town counsel, a lawyer by the name of McKenzie Grant, who's the go-to for Great Barrington when legal questions arise. Or when the town gets sued.

They chat for a minute, mostly pleasantries, him noting the evening's weather clear and warm, as perfect a summer day as can be, and she agrees, inwardly cursing her earlier inattentiveness.

"Yes, quite a nice evening." Has he heard about her marriage? She almost laughs—she could ask him for recommendations for a divorce lawyer.

"Taking the temperature of the town?"

And he's right, this unusual walk spurred by the trickle of grumbles and the growing reports from the police of unfamiliar crowds, of young people more shiftless, less known, out-of-towners of another sort than the Berkshires' usual. She nods.

"Watch out, next block up, past Salimi's. The alley, a bunch of kids hanging out, take a look."

She nods and turns back to her walk, but it takes just a minute and she's passing the Italian foodstuffs store, the front windows full of cans, bottles of oils and sauces, various stacks of tins and pasta packages, and an arrangement of odd artificial grapes cascading from a wide vase with fake grape leaf vines wrapped around. These grapes are looking dusty.

And then, at the wide alley that connects to Saturday Farmers' Market behind the block of Main Street buildings, a young man steps out and there are others behind him, some clearly with him, others farther down, in their own groups.

She can smell marijuana, but that's hardly rare in Great Barrington, with its five dispensaries, down from the high of eight such stores back when she was hired.

"Ma'am," he says, stepping in front of her, "any chance you could spare some money?"

He's not a kid, on closer look, but maybe mid-twenties, maybe older, and he's a good-looking young man, but his appearance is rumpled, and as the slight breeze shifts, his unkempt quality adds a pressing need for a shower. The three others close behind him, forming a short wall of interest in the encounter.

"Sorry, gents," Fletch says, and she's amused, in part, with the spectacle, but the young man steps closer and now it's clear to her that she's being accosted.

"Let's keep the sidewalks clear, shall we?" she says to the group, and the young man is saying something about spare change, and one of the three behind him is grumbling, a *What the fuck* emerging, oddly neutral in tone, and she reaches up to her earbud and taps her phone active.

"911," she says, and then at connection, "This is Marion Fletcher-Gray, requesting a patrol car at the Farmers' Market alley," and then a pause, and then, "Yes, I'll stay on the line," and she's looking back at the young man and behind him at each of his companions in turn, her lips pressed.

"What the fuck, lady," the young man behind her interlocutor mutters, and the man in front of her is shaking his head, and turns and tells the others to go, and the four men are walking through the alley, telling others that something's coming and, indeed, there's a rising siren.

She takes a deep breath and waits, squinting as the strobing light bar nears, waving the car down.

The passenger side window rolls down, the police vehicle taking up one of the two northward lanes, the police officer leaning toward her.

She leans down. "Shut the lights, for God's sake and off with the siren." She recognizes the officer but can't think of his name. She keeps from shaking her head at the absurdity of the lights and siren, both now blessedly off, but this guy must be a moron.

"You see any patrols down here,"—she now remembers his name—"Officer Macowski?"

"Uh, um, what do you mean?"

She shakes her head at that. "Never mind. I just got panhandled by a group of men. Why don't you drive around a bit and ask some questions of any such group?"

Sullivan is supposed to be having his officers doing just that, but she's seen little evidence of this in the daily reports she's getting. She'll have to talk to Sullivan about this.

"Uh, sure."

She waves him on, and he drives to the next corner, taking a right, lights going on again, but that makes sense, since he's driving down a one-way street the wrong way.

She lets out another long breath and settles back into walking. Farm Table and a drink is sounding better and better, and maybe even some dinner, her stomach reminding her that she's last eaten many hours ago. She's got four blocks to go and she's looking around more actively and noticing that there are more young people around and more groups, too, and there's nothing, as she looks closely, to suggest they're local kids.

At Farm Table, busy for a Sunday night, she finds a seat at the bar open and she orders a gin and tonic and takes a menu, but before she can order dinner, the owner, an ex-New Yorker and now gentleman farmer, comes by and tells the bartender that Mrs. Fletcher-Gray's dinner is on the house, and she protests. He waves this away, and tells her she should order the special tonight, lamb chops from some of his own livestock.

"And besides," he grins, "I want to talk to you about something, so you're working for your dinner."

The bartender puts down the drink, and the owner, Lester Comers, tells the bartender to put in an order for the chops.

"Medium rare good?" he asks Fletch before the bartender moves away, and she nods, and Lester nods. The bartender moves to the POS screen, and Lester's already talking, so she swivels the bar seat to better look at him and to spare her neck from having to crane.

"Lots of strangers in town these days," he says, looking at her.

She waits for him to go on.

"Been a big bump in dine-n-ditch," he tells her, and then explains what he means, which is that some patrons, "these strangers, these mostly young people," are walking out without paying. He tells her that he's had three people do this tonight, and the frequency is growing, as is the use of credit cards that turn out to be stolen or counterfeits, and then he abruptly excuses himself. She watches him go to a table with three young people and pull out the table check from his back pocket, standing and waiting for them to pay. When they produce the money, he calls over a server and hands this off to her.

The server looks familiar, but Fletch doesn't ask Lester when he comes back, and doesn't even have the opportunity to, since he starts right back up.

"Nice, business is busy, but not getting paid puts a damper, right?" he asks, except this isn't really a question. "Talking with others," he says, and Fletch realizes he means other restaurant owners, "this is happening to everybody. We've called the police station, maybe you could ask Sullivan what's what."

She smiles. "That's the quid pro quo?"

Lester laughs. "Yeah, sure, and having a VIP here." His expression shifts to a look of concern. "How are you doing, you okay? What's going on with, um, your husband, Robert? Bobbie?"

Oh, the dread and mortification. "Robbie," is all she says.

"Right," Lester says, deepening concern in his expression, and then there's awkward silence, but that's broken by a clatter of dishes tumbling, toward the back of the front dining area.

Lester rolls his eyes, then puts his hand on her arm, a gentle gesture. Low, he says, "You want, I'll not serve him, didn't know he was such an idiot…" He keeps his eyes on Fletch.

"Hmm." She pauses. "Well, even assholes have to eat, I guess."

He pats her arm. "Well, just so you know, Robbie's acting like a moron," and he's shaking his head. It looks like he's going to say more, but then there's another clatter and he rolls his eyes again, nods, and heads toward the ruckus.

Wow. She's entirely mortified, naked to the world. Her body flushes with a sweeping heat and she's got to go. She nods to the bartender, offers a thumbs-up and is walking out of Farm Table when her phone rings.

She taps the answer button on her ear set and it's Chief Sullivan with his throat-clearing rumble, no doubt pissed off because she's directed one of his officers, but what he's telling her is that they've found the body, that they have the state police on scene, and there's been an identification already. A thirty-one-year-old male, Jorge Correio, Pittsfield, known drug dealer, and that he'll report details when he has them, after the coroner's through.

She needs to get herself home. "Anything else?"

Sullivan tells her that Macowski was on his way for crime scene control, but his officer had mentioned there was some trouble with her, some trouble on the street.

"Downtown?"

"Yeah, nothing, really, just some guys panhandling, but aggressive."

He tells her that she did the right thing to call it in, and this is the second time tonight that she hears concern for her and it almost undoes her.

"Thanks," she says, making an effort that her voice doesn't crack, but then she's growing angry again—at what exactly she couldn't say. Shit. Did that come through when she asked him to come by her office tomorrow?

Everything feels out of control.

Chapter 22: Be is for Dumbstruck

July 2, 2035

Sitting at his desk up in his second-floor office, Davin has just finished up with his work emails, but before he heads to the studio, he wants to respond to one from an old house sharer. Deidre has messaged him to see if she might come by to talk about rejoining the house, and while he likes her, and liked having her as a house sharer both previous times, he can't see how he can help.

No room at the inn sounds a little callous, but it's true—there are no spare bedrooms, and the Airbnb is solidly booked apart from a few small spots still open, a day here and there between two-day minimums and longer stretches.

There are already three house sharers—Charlie, the perfect one, and Marsha and Be, who both trade some help around the property for lower rent in his house in Housatonic.

Davin sighs. Well, only Marsha really helps in the garden in any substantial way, in residence at the house for seven years, and she has always liked the garden work and seems to count on the rent reduction, too, now for the last six years. Middle-aged Marsha, creeping toward retirement age, has been a good house sharer, although he still has little significant sense of her, despite her length of residence, because she tends to keep her own counsel and isn't prone to seeking conversation. Still, there are worse traits in a house sharer than keeping mostly to himself or herself.

Between the two of them and their efforts in the garden there's good food on the table, and Marsha is the one taking the lead on the canning and prep for freezing. In good years he doesn't buy peas or green beans for months, and the tomatoes, cooked up and jarred as sauce, mean he eats more pasta than he should. The sauce can be acidic, but he loves making marinara and Bolognese and, on occasion, American chop suey.

Be helps with the Airbnb apartment and, now, in the studio, mostly in exchange for free studio space, not rent reduction. She's often at work on those days the Airbnb needs to be flipped. He's only adjusted her rent three times in five months.

He shuffles some printouts scattered about his desk, wondering why he's sitting in his second-floor office when he had planned to get some time in his studio. He knows why, though. He's not in his studio for the same reason why he's struggling not to give in to the temptation to cross the library room and retreat into his small bedroom, at the other end of the second floor and, quite possibly, pull the covers over his head. Be. The reason for his thoughts of his bed and pulling blankets over his head.

Be, whose real name is Beatrice, from the Venmo she used for her rent—is a fifty-four-year-old ceramic artist, but she works as a part-time arts therapy counselor at Austen Riggs Center up in Stockbridge, and she's been at the house for five months, following Jerome's departure from the house's third house share slot. Jerome had proved an odd house sharer, a bit like Turk before him, who managed to stay for several years following Deidre's second exit. Jerome had been odd and had grown odder yet, his tendency toward iconoclasm overmatched by his interest in engaging in arguments and sullen slights and criticisms, none of which seemed in evidence during the interview and screening period but became apparent within the first month of his residency, and clearer still after that. Turk, on the other hand, was just young, self-centered and lazy, and

Davin needs only to mention Turk's name and Marsha will as likely as not recapitulate her long list of complaints. She had found it easy, for all appearances, to ignore Turk's replacement, presumably due to Jerome's competent housecleaning. Or maybe more simply, Jerome's aim was better in the bathroom the three house sharers used on the third floor. Davin lost a few months' rent recovering from Jerome's departure, but he considered that money well spent.

And then came Be and the studio-share arrangement that has been going on for only the last couple of months. He's a fan, likes her ceramic work, mainly architectural slabs and arches, with bold textures stamped or carved into them.

When she became a house sharer, the single biggest item she brought to his Housatonic house was an electric kiln, and its top stood close enough up to his shoulder and it must be a yard wide or maybe more. The brand and the model escape him, although it's a brutish one-syllable name. Skutt, maybe?

She asked if she could park it in the studio that move-in day, and there it sat, covered with a blanket for the first months. There's been one kiln firing so far, and just recently. He's anticipating the worst come the next electricity bill.

But that's not his problem with Be. The real problem is that he finds her attractive. So damn attractive. The absurdity of it all, with *Amarcord* having just been revisited a month or so back. "I want a woman!" This line from the movie has become something of a tagline during his dating career, but it's been a couple of months since he last went on a date, and the last several years after he ended it with Gloria, the first of post-divorce girlfriends, have been a string of Match.com dates, often fun, or fun enough, and he's met some nice women. And that's the problem—nice, not interesting. The sex has been interesting, and mostly all's good on that front, but that interest wanes, sooner or later, if he doesn't find the woman herself all that interesting.

Unfortunately, he finds Be all too interesting, and the

last couple of weeks, as they've worked in the studio together at various times, his interest has been rising.

He knows that starting something with a house sharer carries all sorts of potential problems, including such complications as what to do should there be a need to end the house share, or if rent stops, or attraction turns into detestation, or any of the seemingly hundreds of ghostly possibilities of things going bad. This has been taking far too much of his attention of late.

At fifty-four, Be is looking just fine, tallish, maybe five foot seven, black curly hair that cascades onto her shoulders, and there's the start of some gray, although she mostly wears her hair clamped up by huge-toothed clips that strike him as nefarious, trap-like objects. He's been struck by her gorgeous face right from the start, but he's been dating and he knew then, as he knows even now, how ill-advised any advance might be, and he's never considered the possibility of her interest as much as she's something of a natural flirt, quick to smile and even quicker to grin, her face lighting up easily. She's not beautiful in any classic way, perhaps, but her face carries a mischievous air, and she's easy to look at, frank in her gaze, and she's got great curves.

All this he noticed in the interview, of course, but she was the best prospect, regardless of her appearance, and he was eager to see the back of Jerome, his late-twenties house sharer who never inspired much house-sharing confidence and who, finally, decided to move in with his girlfriend down in Sheffield, even while somehow never quite getting around to paying the last three months' rent. Good riddance. And Marsha was glad to see him go, although it never got to the point it did with Turk and the several shouting matches between the two of them about Turk's piss-poor aim and seeming inability to clean the house sharers' third-floor bathroom. Jerome was just odd and he's sure everyone else in the house felt this, so his departure was welcomed by all. Davin's the one short on the money, though.

The other house sharer is a perfect house sharer, an IT professional, either an independent contractor or working for an IT service agency. Charlie, somewhere in his late thirties, at a guess. Charlie is gone on business more than he's here, and even when he's in the Housatonic house, he mostly stays up in his third-floor bedroom, working remotely. Charlie has a few oddities, mainly in the form of his ramen-oriented diet, as if he was still an undergraduate, although lately he's taken to using the rice cooker Davin's bought, making a full batch, mixing in some odd-smelling frozen Korean food that Davin refrains from looking at too closely. Sometimes Charlie does his computer work in the living room, with music playing so softly that it sometimes has Davin, not easily discerning the music, worrying that he's going deaf, but there are worse traits in a house sharer than playing music low. And worse traits, too, than using his smart rig, seemingly conducting an orchestra from the big club chair near the fireplace, although he's probably coding with the VR interface.

Turk's old third-floor bedroom, which then became Jerome's, is now Be's, and she's been great on the rent and considerate, too, and Marsha seems happier, maybe, with another woman around.

And about two months ago, more or less, Davin's studio became Be's too, although she's as considerate about his studio space as she is within the household itself. She's even had useful ideas about some rearrangement of worktables that make so much sense he wonders why he hasn't ever thought of this himself.

She's been working on a larger-than-usual slab, or so she informed him yesterday, asking for his help to slide a cut plywood sheet under the base canvas cloth so that she could put it aside as it greened. She wanted help because the slab was wetter than she typically worked, and she loves the texture work and was afraid she'd distort it, either stretching or compressing or both, were she to attempt getting the board underneath the slab on her own.

He was happy to help and he, too, was taken with the texture on the earthenware clay slab as he came to the table, admiring the work as he listened to her instructions. The goal was simple enough, which was for him to slide the plywood underneath, inch by inch, as she gently raised the corners of the canvas square the slab was resting on.

Her table was up against the wall, and he had to work beside her. She smelled great, but he kept his focus on the task at hand.

Halfway through the delicate process to push the plywood steadily, he moved behind her, for a better position to reach around, one arm on one side, the other to her other. She turned her head and winked at him and then shifted her body back, lightly pressing her backside into his groin, issuing a quiet laugh as she got back to the business at hand. Did he actually say "Oh, jeez?" Maybe he only thought it, and his groan was silent, or maybe, just maybe, it was some sort of moan that he suppressed? He'll never know, since once the slab was safely put away she had to scramble to get to work on time. Her grin, though.

"Oh, Jeez."

Chapter 23: Hurry Up and Wait on Me

July 2, 2035

Deadlines, Victor finds himself thinking.

The mosquitoes don't help, and yesterday's rain seems to have put them in hyperdrive, although he's draped in netting, the top clipped on to a large branch above him where he also keeps his pack and bedroll and sundries.

If only he could get himself in gear. His billings will take a hit, otherwise. He's got less than a day now to finish up the latest project, a furnished war room for the client's *Kaiserlicher Kriegsraum,* one of the most popular VR multiplayer games currently. He's never played it, but he's got access to near-countless image files and the physics engine mechanics and he knows the basic play structure.

How's he ended up doing this? It's like being in a goddam ghillie suit, sitting under the evergreen that might be a hemlock, but maybe a spruce—in any case, he's not ever going to look up any plant identification, ever.

Somehow, here he is, in the woods, facing south across a small clearing on Monument Mountain, having trekked in using the power lines, and he's only had to text Nicky once, getting clarity about the trail sign marker, a bandanna tied to a branch. He's stupidly green, so that despite having the pin for where the ad hoc trail veers off from the powerlines, he's missed the flag and spent far too long searching, until he gives up and texts.

His getting lost adds insult to the injury of having to

text Nicky, because he's mightily pissed at him. The bed promised has been delayed indefinitely while Nicky figures out when there will be space. Certainly not until after the holiday is the best he's gotten from him.

So now he's free camping, reduced to using his tarp and sleeping bag and shitting in the woods, and shitting in the woods among a collection of others who share his plight, which is that there's nowhere affordable—just fucking available, even—to crash, and for God knows how long. Thank you, fucking Nicky!

Fortunately, the 6G Wi-Fi is good even out here, even if he's a twenty- or thirty-minute walk from the nearest supermarket, but Taft Farms is five minutes away and while expensive, the vegetables and other food there are good. Fortunately, some of the other people out here have things like pots and pans, so he's been able to reheat the soups from Taft, although he's been mainly eating bread and cheese, or some donuts, for breakfast, along with coffee and bottles of water.

The to-ing and fro-ing takes a lot of time. Fucking hunter-gatherer. He's rethinking the whole city exodus thing, although, when he looks at the weather, with the heat wave to the south still going, he figures he's probably right where he should be. But in the fucking rental, in a bed! Not out here sleeping rough.

It's actually been overcast, and he's grateful, because the temperature is hot enough, even with the clouds. But at least he's gotten back to work on the project, his rig using a power pack, his visor fully recharged from his venture into town this morning, a hot breakfast at a table with an electrical outlet nearby that one of his fellow campers told him about. He's working on a set of custom virtual reality home furnishings, including an elaborate armored weapons cabinet, and the skin he's gotten has given him more trouble than it should have, another piece of AI-generated shit of the sort he's had to work with more and more. He's come close to building his own skin from scratch, but the client thinks it's cooler to customize from a name-brand catalog rather than a no-name one-of-a-kind. And hoping to save money. The customers are always penny-pinching.

He laughs. Pennies are now legally ignorable as currency, the decision to drop the minting of pennies finally happened during Trump's second administration. He doesn't remember all that much from the time, although his folks were virulently anti-Trump, and as a teenager he'd even gone with them to the slew of demonstrations that occurred during those years.

Not that he could charge enough for an original skin, even if he could convince the client. He has so little agency as a contractor, for fuck's sake. There's never even an opportunity for direct contact, because every bit of conversation from the client and information about what the client wants goes through the service he contracts through. It isn't all that difficult to find direct contact information, but that makes for automatic dismissal if discovered. Fucking blackball, more like it. This is a matter of some energetic discussion on the forums.

The service keeps client identities close, but this is the second job he's had where this sort of shit skin armature produced by one common program or another has caused him problems. Fortunately, clients don't know all the prompts needed for their precious attempts at custom creativity to work, and the market for customization—*after-market work,* great phrase—is becoming ever more popular. He's inclined to underbill for the extra time he puts in, not that the service offers much in the way of fee-flex, but he figures he's being kept busy with his high ratings in part because of the extra effort he makes. Hopefully he'll get bumped into premium fee level, but this can be more a problem than a solution, is what people are saying, and he tries to avoid using the billing bump option whenever possible. A few times he's had to, though, dealing with clear and obvious client-sourced code errors. He remains cautious, though, the word is that flagging source errors can become difficult if the service doesn't accept the flag, even though it's the service that does a poor job screening source errors, but try telling them that. He's gone on the thread plenty of times to see if anyone else has raised the issue or come up with solutions that could be more elegant and effective than the bit hacks he's undertaken, but it seems safer to keep his head down.

He's not eager to post to any of the threads. There's been a flurry of texts and discussion threads on the Slick community he's part of for the VR fabrication jobs, but he mostly ignores them, letting himself look only at direct messages sent to him by friends, including his pal, a runt of a guy going by Tee, who's thrown some parties where Big E would sometimes show up.

According to the message that came after the news spread of Big E's self-immolation, his friend had had a relationship with her, and this makes Victor think about her, something he'd just as soon not do, even if he wasn't already almost guaranteed to blow his current assignment's deadline.

Big E had been just fine at meeting deadlines, not that she'd ever gloated, but the assignment board on the agency's Slick list has her consistently at the top of completions. She'd even taken time to post various hacks and tips for others in that forum where he lurks and learns but never posts. *Was* the top in completions. Huh. Setting yourself on fire is not a great competitive move.

He checks his comms center, looking to see if the client has approved the last batch of deliverables, but there's nothing from the service.

She hadn't been all that pretty, or he was never attracted that way, but then he's never been into excessive piercing. She certainly wasn't big, but rather slight and none too tall, and if he's ever heard how she got that nickname, he has no clue now.

What happened to all the piercings? When Big E got cremated? Although he doesn't know for a fact that she was, despite how she died... His grandmother, now dead a half dozen years, was the subject of a conversation at the time of her death about her titanium hip pieces and gold crowns, which his father insisted be recovered at the crematorium.

He shakes his head, trying to stay on track, thinks better of the head-shake action, but as usual, a bit too late, the VR headset not comfortable with the motion. He swipes away the programming interface to look at the model image, then switches over to the textures panel with a slight flick of his finger, his other hand resting on his lap. He's still not that comfortable with the haptic rings, but considering how much the two rings cost him, he's determined to master their use.

It's been a while since he's talked to either of his folks, but now that he's free camping on the south side of what's apparently called Monument Mountain, waiting for Nicky to let him know the Airbnb guests renting Nicky's folks' summer place have left, with Nicky then taking up residence and—God willing—him, too. Probably best he waits to call the folks until he's out of the woods. Ha. Out of the woods.

It might not even be an Airbnb, but it's some short-term rental platform, anyway. All he really knows from Nicky is the location, pinned now on his app. All he really knows is that the text can't come soon enough, since he's shit enough in the woods for a lifetime already. Yesterday, he stepped into someone's dump, some *asshole* who hadn't even bothered to throw dirt over it, or even a pile of leaves.

He removes his headset, the air cooling his now-uncovered eyes. Even in air conditioning, the headset tends to wear warm, and he tilts to his left, fishes out a handkerchief from the front right pocket of his cargo shorts and wipes around his eyes.

At least the 6G Wi-Fi signal is solid out here among the trees and bugs and other campers. The towers both in Housatonic and the main town's setup reach out this way, although apparently the nearby ravine is a dead zone.

A young person, a male, emerges from the scrub behind which the scattering of tents and tarps can be found. He's walking toward him. As he gets closer, Victor guesses the kid is mid-teens, not so big.

The kid nods and then holds up a side bag off his shoulder, some light canvas thing. "You want anything? I'm Rory."

"Okay. Um, what do you mean, 'want anything?'"

The kid just raises his eyebrows, responding with a *Really?* expression.

The kid steps closer, until he's maybe four feet away. "Kush. Ganja, or weed with speed, whatever you might like."

Victor waves him away with a quick "No, thanks," and with the tiniest of shrugs the youngster steps past and into the tree line behind him. Free enterprise. "An enterprising young man," he says to no one in particular. Kid must be a local.

He puts his headset back on and checks his phone's charge, seeing that it's enough for a couple more hours of work, anyway, but he'll recharge back at the Mexican place about a mile and a half down Route 183 and then Route 7, about a forty-minute walk. He'll recharge while nursing a beer and a taco or two, getting there right at dinner opening, before there's likely any crowd and his cheap-ass check total makes his seat a premium target for servers' complaints. Best keep the natives happy.

He checks the comms panel, and still no text from Nicky nor anything from the service. He'd love to know what the client thinks of the first batch he's sent him, but the deadline for the next batch is fast approaching.

"I'm in the Army now," he half sings. Hurry up and wait.

Chapter 24: Shoot and Scoot

July 3, 2035

"You talked direct?" Maker is asking John, *né* Jim, repeating the question he's already asked.

"Sure."

They're standing side by side, so he doesn't see John's face, but it's probably that same passive face but with some undercurrent of pride or subtle boastfulness he saw the first time he asked.

It's hard to believe any of this, but John has a level of detail that supports this possibility, as upsetting as Maker finds it. The operation must be more important to NOS than he'd thought.

Or they're just getting sloppy, or maybe Jim Boy is blowing one of them. This line of thinking's not good. Doesn't say anything positive about him, but he can't help it. It all raises a lot of questions, but a nagging one is *Why him?*

His own performance, his dedication can't be in question. He's been on the front lines for NOS since early on. Not from the earliest days that almost saw NOS end then, before it ever had much chance of carrying out the mission, before the reorg that recruited him, sent him to train, set him tests, including a weird one, online, that was later explained to him was an AI-based personality profiler. There were those long hours of conversation, talks about beliefs and values, about the war that needed to be waged against fossil fuels, about the guilty, the corporate malfeasance, the lies, the manipulation, the absurdly self-serving and life-threatening maneuverings designed to keep gas sales growing, and he had been found true.

But he's never been in the presence of even one Guide, never mind personally briefed by one, if he's to believe John.

He excelled with the training, the so-called boot camp, out someplace in the Southwest, he's sure, although he and the others had been hooded for the long journey there, out of Albuquerque, during what he'd estimated as four hours of driving to a nondescript western ranch house with more outbuildings than residents, he there with two others and two who were running the place. He was young then.

He's never again seen these others and he'd kept his identity secret and had never heard the real names of others, they were all just numbers, his reference number seven. He'd encouraged several recruits over the last four years, after he had spent enough time with these candidates to arrive at a decision, but he'd only ever seen Sylvie again, that one assignment that had kept the two of them together for some months and of course he'd known her real name and he'd told her his, but otherwise he's solidly followed procedures, the codes messages, the digital triggers for analog cyphers.

He carried out his objectives. He proved his ability to hit the enemy and hit hard. He took part in some of the big operations, before, that is, they determined he was good in the field, on his own, a source of the right results. He became something of a fire-and-forget agent who kept the faith, kept his silence, who knew how to succeed, how to get things done.

For an organization that values redundant mechanisms to maintain protective gaps among participants, that vets its field members—every member!—a thousand different ways, he's completely taken aback that he's paired with a guy who can't even maintain name discipline, and yet, here he is, this John-Jim, someone who's talked face-to-face with the very top, so he claims, the upper echelon itself providing the briefing that he's then shared with him. The source of this information is what most surprises Maker, this fellow operative confirming that he's been face-to-face on the briefing before he entered Mexico, and this is both improbable and impressive, even as it feels like a violation of protocol.

Learning that John has met someone in the NOS executive group in the real world, the so-called, near-mythical Guides, forces Maker to reevaluate this fellow operative. This forces Maker to reconsider his own value—is there now some lack thereof?—but he puts an end to such considerations, declaring these thoughts to be some residual selfish bourgeois bullshit, the sort of disease that runs rampant even while the world burns.

The two men are setting up for today's work, both hunching over the makeshift table—two wide boards placed across large plastic trash barrels, all brought in days before with the pretend construction crew. They're reviewing the images on the tablet, cycling through the seven sets of images that keep updating across ninety-second intervals, the feed coming from the tiny video camera they placed up on the roof the first night they'd been in place, four nights ago. The camera is on a motorized turntable, also barely wider than the low mount attached to the top of the roof access shed. The camera and motor are powered by a small solar sheet—one of those roll-ups that's become common enough to go unnoticed, just like surveillance cameras, Wi-Fi extender units, and air quality monitors or other such sensors, and any number of types of antennae, all so ubiquitous these are practically invisible to any attention.

They both are closely observing various rooftop areas across the street, where there's always some chance snipers could be stationed, or anti-snipers—that's what these members of a security detail call themselves, and for good reason. But the level of security is light, just as expected, just as John has been saying.

Maker can't help himself. "You mean, you've talked face-to-face?"

The camera image is once again on the roof of Secretaría de Gobernación, the southeastern area, one of the two spots where he would position an anti-sniper post, but it remains clear, like the other optimal post on the southwest roof. Should this protection be put in place, this would make the operation far more difficult, but they're clear on the contingency, with John sniping the roof-positioned anti-snipers. That's a more difficult challenge because even with suppressed rifles, any experienced personnel protection officer is likely to recognize the shot sound, and so John will have to reacquire the second target quickly and accurately.

He's not that experienced as a shooter and John has expressed this concern, even telling him his minimum accuracy rating is in the low seventies, certainly a passing grade as far as that goes, but short of his own mid-eighties, but this man knowing this about him is itself unsettling. He'd be open to sharing such information, after all, given the nature of the assignment and its level of difficulty, but to have this volunteered, that is discomforting.

Sack the fuck up. This should be seen as a positive, as this level of briefing is impressive and would speak well of the other information, its reliability, accuracy.

John also mentions his own UKD training results, and both are solid. The ability to acquire targets at unknown distances will be crucial should the protection setup they could face prove out. Each will have his own set of targets and will operate without spotter support, but this shouldn't be a problem, considering the relatively short distances, and he's already preset his scope for the most probable distance, less than two hundred feet from the roof or third floor, across the street, downward, but advantageously so from the roof, with better clearance of the vehicle. John will have the longer shots if the anti-sniper posts are present, but nothing anyone with basic shooting proficiency can't handle. Still, if there are anti-sniper posts to neutralize—

shoot dead—then he'll need to kill each of the two primary targets, which will be harder, the timeframe further compressed, since fast reaction by any security detail on the ground can be expected. The follow-up shot has to succeed within the pre-reaction period.

If there's too much security, the mission will abort, but if there are two or fewer anti-sniper posts, he and John will proceed by splitting the targets.

His text sounds and he glances at his phone, which is on the board table along with the tablet. He's overthinking the operation. The text says the targets are on the move, spotted leaving the National Palace, and another look at the southwest and southeast corners of roof across the street reveals no anti-sniper posts.

"Good intel," John says when Maker reports this.

How has this level of intel been acquired? From the cartels? But John having met with—been briefed by!—one or more of the Guides suggests the leadership could be in direct contact with one or more cartel sources. Must be all digital, non-contact connections. Has to be.

He's got no illusions about the cartels. They're evil, brutal, but their brutality is exponentially far less than what the fossil fuel corporations are doing. The fossils and their government dogs. Fuck them to hell.

"Ten minutes out," he says to John, and they both go over their weapons and check again that the black uniforms of the national police tactical squads are right, with tucked bloused trousers, and the uniform's material is stiff, black, some heavy poly material, and his has an odd, rotten smell, but faint, ignorable. He's inspected the uniform and thinks it's likely it's been taken off a dead man. There are two patches, but it could have benefited from another wash or two. He and John leave their automatic rifles unslung but check the magazines, belt attachments, and getting every detail won't matter, anyway, since cops anywhere tend to customize, and the bigger danger is to look too perfect.

They tug at each other's ballistic vests, settling them.

John suggests he swap belt position for the zip ties. Won't make any sort of difference, but it's easier just to do it than say anything about it.

He reminds John to clip the radio mic higher up. Only John has a radio, but that's not unusual. If they run into other police, John is better with Spanish.

They place the assault rifles near the roof access. They'll bring them with them when they go up to get in position when the five-minute mark comes. They do a quick final policing of the area, check the roof images one last time. Everything remains clear. Maker removes the tablet, removes the boards, and places the tablet into the barrel that has the incendiary explosive device at the bottom. While he's bent down, he activates the timer for twenty-seven minutes, just as redundancy. He'll detonate using the small controller in his front pocket. He stands up and checks the controller is set to safety, leans back into the barrel and sets the timer.

"No five-minute check yet, right?" John asks when Maker's done, and he checks the text and sees nothing new.

"Traffic, that's the thing," John says. "There's several spotters across the route, so when we get the five-minute text, it should be accurate."

He just grunts in reply, and they both startle when the text alert sounds. Maker looks at it closely, tosses the phone into the barrel. "Go, go, go, Jimmy-John," and they don the helmets and head up the ladder-like stairs to the roof.

The glare of the light assaults them, and John curses.

"Be okay," Maker says quietly. And they're both scanning, eyes narrowed to slits, and everything looks clear in the bright light. They settle into their positions.

The tar roof is boiling, but he uses a ratty blanket to protect himself, and a glance shows that John is doing the same with a long piece of cardboard pulled under him.

"I'm the executive, you're the minister," he reminds the other shooter. Was that a *no fuck*?

The two faces are clear in his mind. One of the targets is

a vice president of the American firm Castle Tower, here to sign off on a large investment partnership with some department of PEMEX, it's not clear which one, but the other target is an undersecretary from SEGOB, Mexico's version of Department of the Interior. The development deal is for Fast LNG 2, the second floating LNG facility to date, designed with add-on gas treatment and liquification modules, along with a power generation plant and accommodation for the workers. The jack rigs also have expandable dedicated floating storage units that can service LNG carriers.

The whole point of Fast LNG 2 is to support market expansion to Central and South America, but the facility can be moved to wherever it's needed, including back to the States.

There's again been congressional resistance to permitting LNG terminals, and the play here with this deal is likely to circumvent the hold on terminals. The intended positioning for Fast LNG 2 is off Altamira.

He and Jim, six feet apart, are both peering over the short-stepped wall at the front roof edge. The motorcade turns at the stone clock tower that sits in the middle of the intersection of Emilio Dondé and Bucareli. There's one lead motorcycle, lights flashing, and then two white SUVs making the turn, and then, after a small gap, another motorcycle with lights flashing, and that's it.

Maker stays silent. The line pulls up at the Casa Cobián gate, the two motorcycles, front and back, pulled into the middle of the street, blocking nonexistent traffic, and Maker steals a glance back up to the intersection, where the traffic is being diverted. The cars are sitting there.

The heat of the afternoon sun burns through the black polyester of the black uniforms, and he's sweating.

The doors of the second SUV open and people step out, probably aides, but before he fully scans them, the door of the front SUV is opening and the targets step out, their aides walking toward them, but the aides freeze as around each of the targets' heads forms a red mist halo, and everything is slow motion, the bodies dropping and then frenetic movement and shouts, and Maker and John are low-crawling backward until they reach the middle part of the roof. They remain low, crab-walking to the back, putting on their helmets and slinging the assault rifles, tossing both ropes out.

John pulls on thick gloves. Fuck! Maker's forgotten his, and the rappel is going to hurt, but there's nothing for it, and the two of them swing over the roof's low back-edge barrier and start down.

The cacophony of sirens arises, and some shouts from the street can be heard even as they are halfway down, the rope tight between Maker's feet, his hands burning.

Chapter 25: Offshore Wind Resistance

July 3, 2035

Jeannie Louise Smith feels like a dope and, because it's her seventy-eighth birthday tomorrow, like an old dope at that. She's taken on an assignment to review the East Coast wind farm projects—potential projects, at any rate—but even as she's working on the freelance article for *The Guardian*, the whole scene is suddenly in flux yet again. She's been scrambling to keep up, but this assignment, which should have been a slam dunk, is now a dismayingly fast-moving target.

She's sitting on her couch in the front room of her apartment near Cottage Street, sipping a cup of tea. The front curtains are drawn against the sun and the heat that's been peppering the Northeast for weeks, but the front air conditioner window unit is purring and she's plenty comfortable, temperature-wise, although her sciatica has been acting up again, adding to her usual aches and pains. Rain showers are expected later, but it's blue sky now. It's hot, but July hot, not heatwave hot. The NYC heatwave is proving brutal, the news full of stories, so she'll not complain.

She takes another sip and puts the cup and saucer down on the old rug she's been meaning to replace for years now, but domestic fussing is low on her list of priorities.

One small pot of tea is what she allows herself these days when it comes to stimulants. Her Adderall habit came to a head in a short hospital stay, two years back, with her diagnosis of rhabdomyolysis, which, as best as she understands it, is her muscle tissue breaking down and clogging up her kidneys. Since she's only got two kidneys, it's been a wakeup call for sure. A visit from public health services was another reason for her stopping, or more specifically their hint that she could face legal trouble, considering all her hijinks over the years in getting prescriptions.

She's been lucky. Getting herself back on track hasn't been the hellscape some experience with amphetamine addiction, but then she's always been a careful person. She's even been able to keep up with much of her *RE:CC* blog work and has kept her income steady with the bitbytes platform and has kept a lid on the whole mortifying potential scandal—*Hi, I'm Jeannie Louise Smith and I'm an amphetamine addict!*

She's had a long history with Adderall, but as a tool, not for any recreational high, and that's the attitude that led to her being hospitalized, because the physical consequences of the drug don't care if you're abusing it in a controlled manner for its utility rather than as an out-of-control, frivolous abuser. She only used Adderall to keep herself going when she'd take on too many assignments, been caught up in some long research and analysis spree, or been faced with yet another of a million deadlines she would have been hard-pressed to meet, but this has been years in the making. It came to her, there, the embarrassment, the humiliation, lying in the hospital with tubes stuck every which way in her, a crushing humiliation replacing her judgmental feelings regarding her brother, recently dead—finally dead—from his on-again-off-again opioid use, and there she was, no better.

Forgive me, my brother, she recites to herself, a habit she's taken away from the short stint of therapy she signed up for as she unwound herself from the impulses and drive to return to her old habits.

Her own habit could have made things difficult with The Laundry, the academic action group that's become important to her on many levels, including, of course, in terms of her sense of self. She managed her struggle on the QT, a mention of a bug here, some bronchitis there, when necessary to explain missed deadlines. She kept her recovery from these colleagues, and not because financially this work with The Laundry was important. Financially the work remains only indirectly beneficial, mainly in the form of plenty of great work related to this connection, but it was her shame she'd kept hiding. Much of what she's done with The Laundry across the years has been the sort of work she loves, work that digs into complex climate policy issues deeply, analyzes hard, and synthesizes well.

Last year, she finally came to the finish line on The Laundry project that has become dear to her, helping with an AI-driven mapping of dark money going to the multitudinous fossil fuel front groups, think tanks, and PACs. She's not exactly central to the effort, though, and her own work is done. But she's been instrumental in spurring early progress in identifying many of these groups and PACs, and with the exposure to AI that the project afforded her these last few years, nowadays she thinks of herself as a confident-enough AI wrangler.

She looks down at the small empty teapot and the cup and saucer on the floor and sighs. No coffee for her, no yellow plastic bottles full of tiny pills gained through lies and trickery, the focus of the ever-more-complex tales she fabricated for each new doctor, lies she told herself.

Unfortunately, her ego led her acceptance of this latest assignment, which is another sort of addiction and something of a backslide, but when the call from *The Guardian* finally came in, her white whale of a newspaper, the one where she'd never landed even one writing assignment, the one newspaper she admires for its coverage of climate change, it proved impossible to say no. She hasn't been taking on this sort of popular analysis writing for some years now, not for newspapers and popular periodicals, not that she hasn't refused such work in the past. Five years ago she hit her stride, showing up in *The New York Times*, *Rolling Stone*, *Edge*, and other top-level magazines and podcasts, and the recognition was good, but the money was only ever okay, and after she'd checked off her list of her biggest glory targets, she realized she didn't really care for the work. The publicity and fast-rising profile such assignments provided was nice enough, but such articles tended to demand that she ignore her policy and politics expertise.

But this personal Moby Dick has breached, and here she is. A dead whale or a stove boat. She scoffs. She's said yes, and she's going to have to do this the hard way, without her magic pills.

The story is on the latest developments in offshore wind farms here in the East, and unwinding the on-again-off-again-on-again trajectories of the various projects is painful enough to get clear. But her work with the dark money project has brought to life more complications, and while this should represent something of a coup, being the public face of the project's inaugural results presentation is daunting. In regard to the article she's working on now that the wind projects are back in full swing, the big news is a new case of behind-the-scenes manipulations by Big Oil. In just some cases, though.

The connections she, well, the AI project, has discovered are unbelievable.

The generally agreed-upon history of the big wind projects announced during the Biden Administration was that they'd fallen victim to Trump's hissy fits in his second term, with the two biggest energy companies, Encrecia and Optimius, due to start construction of huge offshore wind farms in 2024, but instead these projects were shut down. At that time, it looked like several major offshore wind projects were finally moving ahead, with agreements between Federal and several state governments having signed off and ready to pony up substantial financial support. But inflation and supply chain challenges of that period caused these companies to come back to the table to renegotiate energy purchase agreements upward, even while requesting that public investment be increased. Those controversial demands became moot, however, with Trump's reelection and what looked like concessions to the fossil fuel corporations, although that view was complicated by the fact that both companies had big ties to or were corporate divisions within fossil fuel corporations.

Now she has evidence that both companies intentionally sandbagged their own massive offshore wind projects. One piece of this is an internal memo found among the huge tranche hacked by as-yet-unidentified climate hackers. The memo described a "win-win" scenario should the wind projects be delayed or canceled, but the winners were not the public or the clean energy transition. The winners were clearly the companies themselves seeking to advance their position and profitability.

The win for the fossil fuel interests was that their delaying tactics provided them with years more of natural gas sales for power generation and build-out. That's the argument being made as the EPA and Justice Department consider whether civil or criminal charges should be pursued, although there's a court hearing about the admissibility of the hacked documents. Hacked or not, these documents show as clearly as possible that the two energy companies maneuvered to gain bigger profits from their other fossil energy businesses by delaying the wind projects.

One of these companies finally resuscitated their wind farm project and began construction in 2029. The other company, in its new corporate form, finally re-started its major wind project in 2032. Of course, this was at the time energy demand forecasts skyrocketed, and mainly because of server farms and AI requirements, but a new generation of natural gas power plants has been put in place already and more are in the pipeline. The new gas plants threaten more emissions while further retarding renewable energy transition progress.

All this is known, but what she's adding to the story are the findings from the dark money project that reveals connections of dark money to an organized campaign to delay the wind farms, mainly in the form of funding public relations companies who then used the funds to build astroturf campaigns opposing the wind farms. There are other wind projects, too, including Ocean Wind, off the Jersey shoreline, which have been dragging through the court system for far too long because of a stubborn cadre of NIMBY suits. That resistance should collapse as soon as the story of the dark money behind these groups gets revealed, with the money confidently traced back to fossil fuel interests. The other acronym, NOMOS—not on my ocean shoreline—hasn't caught on.

Her article will be the first general public victory for The Laundry's AI Dark Money project, which is fantastic.

As her research continues, she's been looking through her old posts, and one in particular is triggering. It all comes back as she skims that content, swiping through the rolling text on her tablet.

"The Dishearten Foundation and Their Acts of Lies" is the witty title. The post was originally written in early 2025 and was essentially a diatribe against The Heartland Foundation, a fossil fuel-funded climate denialist group with a history of obstructing solar energy development in Louisiana and other states. The Heartland Foundation was an active supporter of HB692, which was then before a legislative committee. The bill then progressed, then was passed, with then-Governor Landry signing the pro-gas proclamation recognizing natural gas as an affordable, reliable, and clean energy resource. Worse yet, the language in the bill defined any efforts to transition away from fossil fuels as "devastating" Louisiana consumers and economic growth.

Heartland Impact, the Foundation's advocacy arm, had been a prime mover behind the HB692 proclamation.

Entergy's direct involvement in the bill was never established, although the corporation was later identified as part of The Empowerment Alliance, a gas advocacy group, this discovery from notes of an executive committee meeting of the American Gas Association. The documented connection came from the very same alliance committee meeting where participants laid out industry plans to block state and local transitions away from gas and other fossil fuels, celebrating the Louisiana proclamation. "That's three down and forty-seven more states to go," appeared in the group's meeting notes. The Empowerment Alliance went on to push similar bills across the country, although by 2032, such further efforts had weakened into nothing, but the push to build ever more natural gas generators remains strong.

How many other pro-fossil fuel think tanks and advocacy groups has she highlighted—attacked, even—in her many other posts over the years?

"High Lies and Misdemeanors" is her working title for the *Guardian* piece, and the round-up of fossil fuel obstructionism will provide a compelling history lesson of malfeasance of the most serious sort. She has another great working title for the article: "Blowing Smoke on Wind."

Chapter 26: Deidre Under the Stars

July 3, 2035

She's living in a tent! Deidre's trying to figure out exactly what her feelings are concerning her current status. At best, she concludes, they're mixed.

She has an apartment lined up, or rather a fellow server at Farm Table is looking for a new roommate, the other roommate now, recently, an ex-roommate. She's got a funny feeling that the ex-roommate hightailed it because of some relationship trouble, whether with this very roommate or someone else, but she'll tread easy and hope for the best. First she's got to get through July, and this tent situation will help with her bank balance. Davin's being generous not charging her anything, his offer to set up a tent for her, a favor.

She has the use of the second-floor bathroom and has access to the house, just as if she was back to house sharing, except that a tent is her current bedroom assignment, but it's just for a few weeks. Her focus is to get the store up and running, which is exactly why she needs to keep her bank account balance up. If Alicia comes through with the loan, that will help. Fingers crossed, because she's trying to get the storefront's landlord to actually sign the lease she conditionally has. The new apartment she'll move into in August gives her an address for her landlord, so that's something else that should help. *Hi, I'm currently homeless, can we sign the lease?* But all's well that ends well, and the lease is guaranteed if Alicia comes through.

That's complicated, though, considering that they were lovers for a long spell, or at least the longest romantic relationship Deidre has experienced to date. For Alicia it was the first of its kind, in love with a woman, and that made things difficult in the end, Alicia uncomfortable with that, it seemed, although Alicia's work, instead of their relationship, had become all-consuming. It was a shame; the time with Alicia had been wonderful. Until it wasn't. The relationship had regrettably proved unsustainable. There's no blame or accusation, just lingering wistfulness. She closes her eyes and listens. She loves the sound of the rain on the tent.

The rain always makes her nostalgic and melancholy, but melancholy in a good way. She glances over at her notebook at the edge of the futon and is comforted by this. This mood is often productive for her writing, although her body is crying out for rest, so she sets an alarm on her phone and settles back, eyes closed.

She's moved her stuff into the store front from her erstwhile apartment, and the fact that she's completed this, the final small bags and boxes, just this morning, should be considered a miracle by her former landlord. She shudders. Don't even think about that creep.

Davin, on the other hand, has been absolutely great and has set up this tent for her and pulled a futon out of storage and there are plenty of blankets and pillows. The bed she's currently lying down on feels good, and the gentle rain is showing no signs of relenting. She sighs.

She has a shift at Farm Table tonight, but she's got two hours before she has to leave for it, and a nap is definitely in order. With the last few days of running around, moving her things, returning the rental van, arranging the logistics, yes, a nap is in order.

It's raining, and she feels the shift in her feelings, but maybe because she's thinking of Alicia, the feelings are a richer amalgam. She thinks of herself as a writer—although only published in small literary presses, and hardly the very best of them—and Alicia had been supportive, had been a first reader, had often been her exclusive audience. She writes poems, or something akin to that anyway, and usually they're about her stronger feelings and her confusion about her stronger feelings.

Deidre's no longer young, but, hey, thirty-one's not so old. Things take time—she'll figure things out. The store is an exciting venture.

If only she had someone with whom to share this excitement. She's dated and been in a few relationships since Alicia, but the lesbian community in the Berkshires—South County, anyway—is not only insular but too small, and she remains disappointed in love.

She'll have to go by her mom's apartment, where most of her clothes for the cold seasons are stored, if three moving boxes filled with her assortment of secondhand clothing shoved behind a couch can be considered storage. At least she's been moving her stock out of her mom's house to the store, although this could prove a challenge, even a catastrophic development, if the landlord pulls out of the lease agreement. She's got to figure out how to get to her mom's house now that Janice, her ex-roommate, is gone, along with her car.

Janice was a great roommate, but their friendship never fully developed, not to the point Deidre would have liked. There's something about sexual orientation that can put up a barrier between women, much like the problem of a girl just being friends with a guy, that old saw, that old barrier. She shrugs. *Que sera, sera.*

Deidre hasn't seen her mom for far too long, and she's been missing Mom. They've always enjoyed each other's company. Well, mostly always. There was that time, in her first year at BCC, living with her mom at her mom's previous apartment up in Pittsfield, convenient for its proximity to the main campus, but also because her mom had wanted to help with school costs. The free rent was a help. The free advice about the girlfriend Deidre had during the second semester, that wasn't welcome.

It isn't that her mother has a problem with her being attracted to other women, even if her mom has only just started using the term *lesbian* in the past couple of years. When, years before, Deidre had told her mom about her feeling that way, her mom had laughed, *No shit, Sherlock,* and had informed Deidre that she'd been pretty sure of Deidre's sexual orientation for a long time. *A mother knows,* her mom had said, and while Deidre had found this annoying, she was also relieved, having been worried about the potential reaction. But a mother knows other things, too. She considers her necessary visit up to Pittsfield to where her mom lives now, the current apartment in a better neighborhood and a nicer place than the one her mother had shared with Deidre.

Her mom also shared her opinion about Deidre's new girlfriend, Sand, during this time, telling her that the young woman didn't seem good for her, that the woman made her worry, was likely dangerous. But Deidre was in love.

Until, less than three weeks after her mom first talked to her about her girlfriend, Deidre was no longer in love but, instead, in fear, that experience with a far too mercurial personality who would push her to do things she had no interest in doing, that had reached breaking point. Deidre had been amazed by Sand's proposals that she shoplift or help break into Sand's former girlfriend's apartment, supposedly to reclaim money she insisted to Deidre had been stolen from her, the woman, the ex, a terrible person, abusive. In what turned out to be the last week of Deidre's relationship with Sand, her refusal to go along with the ideas and schemes drew more and more violent reaction, but the final trigger was when she found the prescription bottle of oxycodone, her girlfriend's argument that it'd been prescribed for her contradicted by the name on the bottle, and she knew that her mom had been right.

Manic-depression, or bipolar disorder, Deidre would

learn was the diagnosis, some months later, after Sand had gotten herself committed for observation after breaking into her previous girlfriend's place a second time, and after an onslaught of postcards and emails she compulsively wrote to Deidre, each receipt a stab in her heart.

Some think of Deidre as good-looking, not that she really believes it, even if she gets a lot of comments about her looks at Farm Table, often annoyingly. She's still young looking, with black hair that curls moderately to frame a symmetrical face with frank dark eyes and full dark lips, and skin that carries a hint of hard-to-determine ethnicity. These are descriptions that have been applied to her. Such compliments are surely just people being polite, not that she hasn't had some trouble with a couple of the other servers, one of whom volunteered that some guests think she is aloof, standoffish. She was shocked to hear that. She's sincere in her modesty, remaining simply unbelieving of her looks on some level, and encumbered by the long-held prejudice that only the rich can be beautiful. She thinks of herself as poor, but thinks that most of her peers are poor, too. She's just given up her apartment and is here, in a tent, trying to rest in order to go to work, and this only adds to the feeling of yet again having to scramble. There's always something.

She'll miss walking to work—the apartment she's just lost was halfway up East Street, and getting to work from there is an easy ten-minute walk to both of her jobs, each of which are on the west side of the Housatonic River, and both just off Main Street, the store toward the southern end, in the new mixed-use building a block or two past town hall, and the restaurant at the northern end.

She turns on her side, eyes closed, but there will be no nap. Still, resting helps, and the alarm gives her enough time to change into her Farm Table clothes and catch the bus at the bottom of the street, and she'll only be a bit late. She'll have to ask for a lift home from one of the other staff since the bus stops running at 8:00 p.m.

She figures things out. She's been working some job or another for a long time, whether babysitting or retail, and the summer after her sophomore year in high school she was a seasonal crew member of a landscaping company that had provided more than enough weeding work to last her a lifetime. She's always done what she could to help her divorced mom, but her mom has always worked so much harder, even if the result of such efforts of mom and daughter has always been no money left over. That's how she recalls growing up. Her sense of being on the margin much more real to her than the face or voice of her father, who headed out beyond the reach of family responsibilities well before she reached the age of two. Sometime in junior high, she realized that her fragments of memories of her father were far more likely manufactured memories, her father's face and her sense of his voice drawn from photographs and a bunch of well-worn stories rather than any actual recollections on her part.

Absent fathers and money worries were the same for many of her childhood friends, and so it was never all that unusual among a lot of the classmates she had known since kindergarten, or even among those she knew from the regional high school, where students from several nearby towns joined Great Barrington's students. Deidre has known forever that people could have money, and money enough not to worry about money in the sort of day-to-day way she and her mom did. Back then, still being shielded by her mom's hard scrambles, her classmates' parents who seemed to have money did not seem like a separate class of beings, and that included her best friend Caty and her folks. Caty went off to Brown right after graduation.

The greater divide, the divide that seems like some unalterable law of physics, was between the families that sent their kids to the public school system and those entirely and incomprehensively mysterious attendees of the private prep schools. There were many private schools long settled in various old Berkshire estates and scattered across

Northwest Corner, Connecticut, in fantasy campuses ever-expanding with sports facilities, private therapists, and new libraries and dining halls, along with the security required by any place that hosts the princes and princesses of the world.

For her, such schools were exotic and alien locales, populated with people different in kind from those people she knew, but as she grew older she came to more clearly understand that there were other divides as well, mostly still associated in her mind with a different kind of private school, including those where troubled children and adolescents were collected from near and far, those who were physically disabled or mentally impaired, or the broken result of drug-addicted adults or other home trauma or failed foster services. This awareness had begun to form as she was just starting high school, when her mom had gotten work as an aide at Hillcrest Center, one of several residential schools and care facilities within Hillcrest Educational Foundation. Both of them were surprised to learn that Hillcrest was the second largest employer in Pittsfield, and Hillcrest was merely the biggest of many such special needs institutions dotting the Berkshires.

And so, she began to understand more clearly how people could be a little different or a lot different, and unlike many of her compatriots, she appreciated that there was more than the local folk and second-home owners divide. She came to appreciate her own comfort and luck in comparison to those less fortunate, those who had become part of her mother's daily toil.

But differences came from many other conditions and situations and natures, she slowly learned as she grew into adulthood.

She still dislikes the word *lesbian,* and not because she doesn't accept her sexual orientation but simply because she doesn't like the sound of this word. Even the story of the Island of Lesbos annoys her with its grasping mythopoetic grandeur.

She likes words and she likes women, but the best words and the best women. Words have helped her to better know who she is. Words helped her through her confusion as a teenager, but even this period in her life seemed no stranger than that of any of her peers.

Deidre mostly thought herself fortunate back then, and she still does. She has long learned to embrace life on the economic margin, for example, turning secondhand clothing into thrift store triumphs. She took pride in those moments when a particularly striking ensemble gleaned from Goodwill might raise envy or admiration among some classmates or friends. And now, with luck, she'll make a business of this long-held talent.

The rain picks up, still gentle enough on the tent's fabric, but more noticeable, and now, in some reflexive way, she thinks of Caty.

In her high school days, it was by consensus that she and her best friend Caty preferred Caty's house after school, where, in her pretty bedroom, or sitting outside under the old gazebo near the house, they would debrief each other with increasing sophistication on who had said what to whom in the halls or cafeteria, and why, and what such interactions might signify, and talk of their dreams and plans. The preference of afternoons at Caty's was reinforced in part by Deidre's mom's difficult work schedule, but she knew well enough, even as an adolescent, that Caty's home was nicer and far less chaotic than the various apartments Deidre and her mom seemed always to be moving into and out of.

But all that worry about money isn't a big factor in her memories. What Deidre best remembers, what she likes to remember, is how she and Caty had loved the rain, stealing any chance to walk in drizzle and downpour alike, or standing on the Bridge Street span, both grasping at the jitterbugging umbrella and the steadying railing, while leaning over to watch the Housatonic dance and swell with its own hard rain meditations.

Caty loved the rain. Does she still? She last saw Caty when they were both freshmen in college. Caty was in Providence, at Brown, and Deidre at BCC, the local community college with its campus in Pittsfield, in pursuit of her associate degree in social work. That degree, she'd only slowly come to learn, would do little for her or any other who shared the poorly informed judgment to go that route. Or, certainly, the poorly informed judgment to take student loans to do so.

She's still working at the restaurant she worked at after finishing up at Berkshire Community College, although the number of shifts has expanded. Her other job, now gone, was assisting in the management of the tarot and crystals store, settling invoices, taking inventory, cleaning the store, rearranging the displays, and arranging special events. That job was easy and even pleasant in its parade of interesting and often-odd people, but it was barely enough to cover her rent and most other expenses, and then that disappeared, so Deidre and her associate degree in social work have the restaurant shift tonight, after her full day moving, and working to get the space prepared at the new store.

The rain's coming down hard now, but Deidre still loves the rain, and she'll think about Caty, who is now well past law school. She hasn't seen Caty for almost ten years now, and these days Caty only sends a card at Christmas, with a sketch of family news that includes her marriage.

The rain is drumming and she's thinking of Caty's bedroom up on Castle Hill, and more than that, she's now there again, sees Caty with her arms thrown over her face, her cotton blouse unbuttoned and pushed to her sides, and Deidre is sliding her own cheek down Caty's body, over her small breasts, over her stomach muscles, feeling Caty's quakes and tremblings, and she will once again hold her breath, *is* holding it, trying to stop this moment from fading into mist.

Chapter 27: A Conversation in the Dark

July 3, 2035

For the first week of July, it's hotter than expected, but then again, *hot* is relative. Compared to being in an actual heatwave, like the one New York City still suffers under, Davin's cool about the weather in the Berkshires. Here in his living room, he does possess some sense that expecting anomalies in the weather is something older folk like him have trouble adjusting to. On the other hand, with this season's weather, he's certainly gotten a head start in the garden, so there's that. The *free* garden, apparently, judging by the raids that have been happening and which are something he's far from cool about.

Marsha's already upstairs, early to bed, as usual. When she got home earlier, he talked to her about the garden raiders, and he came away with the impression she's more annoyed about it than he is.

"Give 'em hell," she told him when he let her know the plan for tonight.

But Jimmy and Cyn are visiting again, and that makes him happy. They've gone to Farm Table to have dinner and to bring Deidre back, the three of them friends since that time he first met Cynthia. Back when she was on the run from the people that had killed her boss, nine years ago.

He's sitting in the living room on the old couch, keeping an eye out for Cyn's car coming up to the parking area. He glances up periodically through the windows, the rain gone and the nighttime sky clear. As if conjured, he sees the sweep of the headlights, then, at rest, the car lights chirp off and three shapes make their way toward the house, silhouetted by the lone pole light that illuminates the parking area.

He wrote a book about the killing, although he doesn't think of the book much these days, seven years after its publication. Not many would-be readers think about that book, either. He's no longer wistful about what might have been, and he made some money on the early syndication deals on the article that had been the basis of the later book. That long article he'd serialized in *South County Interactive*, that hadn't made all that much money either, but it helped jump-start the syndication model that he built into the platform, and that model has been successful for the publication. Successful enough, anyway.

Jeannie Louise's *"Whether Weather or Climate"* work, managed by the platform, is a more recent, more successful, example, but he's not resentful, because he's got the deal with Alicia for a piece of any such action. While modest in any one instance, that income tends to accumulate, and everything he's been doing through *Berkshire Interactive* adds up and is helpful.

He watches the three shadows form into Jimmy, Cyn, and Deidre as they walk down the slope and approach the back doors lit by a pair of carriage lights.

"Hey, hey, Daddo," Jimmy says coming through the French doors, and he steps aside to let the two gals through, and then they're saying hello and Deidre is mentioning that she's got to get to bed, but she's turned toward the other two, so Davin only catches some sense of what she says, something about her heading out early to get to her new store. The new used clothing and whatever store that Alicia has mentioned she's helping out with a loan.

He's refrained from asking her if the two of them are back together, and the fact that Deidre is sleeping in the tent on his studio's green roof clearly suggests not.

Deidre disappears past the end of the couch, through the narrow double doors into the library, heading for the bathroom. She keeps her robe there, and she'll be back out, in the robe, after her night's ablutions, and outside to disappear into the tent. He appreciates the effort she makes not to intrude, but he's inclined to notice any intrusion, even minor or brief, like her bathrobe and a small makeup bag now in residence in his bathroom. He chalks his seeping annoyance up to his being an old codger, but at least he's making an effort not to show it.

Even putting up the air frame bed in his office feels like an intrusion, with his old recliner inconveniently pulled up snug behind his desk chair, but that's a small price for seeing his son and Cyn.

He gets up from the couch with a groan, picking up his empty rocks glass, the contents drained an hour ago as he sat reading while waiting for the kids to return. *Kids.* He laughs. Cyn is closing in on forty years of age and Jimmy's barely two years behind her.

"So, are you still game?" he asks Jimmy, and he sees Cyn glance at her partner, but Jimmy says he is, and Davin's relieved. An extra bonus with Jimmy and Cyn's visit is that Jimmy has agreed to accompany him, lights out, when—*if!*—the video cameras show a nightly visit by the garden raiders.

"What are you guys going to say to these… whoever you find up there?" Cyn asks, but she's looking at Davin.

"Uh, I don't know, maybe 'Do you know how to cook?'" but Cyn's clearly waiting for a more direct answer.

"I don't know," he says. "Maybe ask their names, ask them why they think it's okay to raid someone's garden, tell them to stop or I'll have to get the cops involved, that they're trespassing?"

Jimmy asks how serious the problem is in Great Barrington, letting Davin know that it's been making the news in Boston. "Yeah, that death the other day," he tells his dad, "some drug gang guy from Pittsfield? But this whole thing about the crowds, the reactions the different towns are having to it."

Has some Boston reporter or other been checking in on the stories in *Berkshire Interactive*? Is there a syndication opportunity here? Maybe not—the heat wave won't last long enough. He's caught up in his thoughts enough to miss something Jimmy is saying. "Sorry?"

Jimmy tells him that *climate refugees* is a term that's been mentioned in some of the coverage.

"Huh."

"Well, the right term would be *internally displaced people*," Jimmy adds.

"Huh."

"The heatwave, especially in the cities, it's run for a while, it's pretty bad. Maybe as bad or worse, even, than that one I went through."

Davin remembers that well. Jimmy had been in Chicago in 2026, when a heatwave hit the upper Mid-West, and had gotten himself back to Housatonic to escape it, and he'd come home with this young woman in tow, Cynthia, and it hadn't been long before they were in a relationship. Now nearly a decade, more, has gone by.

"Certainly, the death count is higher, but NYC is bigger than Chicago, for sure," Jimmy says. He looks over to Cyn. "You remember the latest?" but instead of answering, she pulls out her phone.

Deidre's out of the bathroom, stopping to get a hug from Cyn before wishing them all a good night and heading out to her tent.

They're silent, watching through the living room windows as she unzips the tent. She climbs in with another wave and zips the tent flap back up.

"Death count is two hundred sixty-seven," Cyn announces as she re-pockets her phone.

The two others just nod.

"I'm crashing," Cyn informs them, telling them that doesn't mean they can't stay up.

Jimmy tells her that he needs to do some things for work, asks if he can use the office desk and monitor, and Davin nods.

"Also, keep the camera pop-up windows active, let me know, we'll go up and check in on any guests, right?"

Jimmy smiles. "You stay up that late?" he teases, a long-running joke between the two of them, Jimmy a night owl and Davin, well, not so much.

Davin shrugs. "I'll stay here, reading, but if I'm in my bedroom and the light's out, don't worry about it. Just some free veggies for another day, right?"

Jimmy nods and he follows Cyn across the landing, where the office door is ajar on the other side.

Davin goes to the French doors, looks up toward the parking area to make sure the Airbnb guest's car is there and switches off the light.

He resumes his seat on the couch and gets back to his reading. Not even another chapter in, he can barely keep himself awake. Jimmy's still up, while Cyn is no doubt already asleep on the air frame, and he leans back to rest his eyes for a moment, but then Jimmy's somehow in front of him, asking if he still wants to do it, and it takes him a moment to realize that Jimmy's telling him there are garden visitors, that he's spotted two of them on the video.

"I'm up." And Davin's standing up, wiping at the drool around his mouth, blinking. He pulls out his phone. It's nearly one o'clock in the morning. "Early tonight," he tells Jimmy, who only shrugs.

He rolls his shoulders and heads toward the French doors, picking up an LED flashlight he keeps there. "Walk softly and carry a big light," he says to his son, and he quietly opens one of the doors and steps out onto the terrace, with Jimmy close behind. "Let's go up in the dark, use the flashlight when we get there, sound good?"

Jimmy answers with a soft laugh. "Sure."

There's enough light from the carriage lamp fixtures on each side of the French doors to make the going easy, and they both know the way, but by the time they're skirting the four cars up top, they're in shadow. Strange. Be's car's not there, although her Riggs shift is long over.

They're approaching the garden fence and Davin quickens his pace, snapping on the flashlight, closing the distance to the small greenhouse opens its outside door, and he's in a race with the man and woman in the garden, their stage-whispering growing as they approach the back side gate they've used for entry through the small greenhouse. They've left open the back garden gate, with its plastic covering that's part of the greenhouse envelope. They stop.

"Good evening," he says, and stops to wave away some mosquitoes.

"Uh, yeah," the young man says.

Davin figures he's early twenties, and with a quick flick of his hand, the flashlight reveals that the woman standing behind the young man is likely the same age.

He moves the flashlight back to the young man, the beam staying on his torso so that the light isn't glaring in the young man's eyes.

"Davin Caine. This is my house, property, garden."

The young woman is saying something, but not to him, and he can't make it out.

Jimmy's outside the fence on the house side of the greenhouse, but he's silent, pitch-perfect, a looming fellow saying nothing. Should Davin be feeling a touch bad for his garden raiders?

He flicks the light around again, seeing what the two youngsters have in their hands.

"Ah, early green beans," he says to the young man, who still has several dozen green beans in a drooping and transparent plastic bag. Shifting the flashlight toward the young woman, he nods. She's holding a handful of lettuce plants, dirt-clogged roots and all.

"Lettuce is starting to bitter," he says. "The recent heat, they're starting to bolt."

They seem not to understand anything he's saying. Not

worth explaining the concept of haricots verts, then.

"Come on out, I don't mean to trap you." He turns around and steps out of the small greenhouse but then turns back and asks them to shut the fence wall gate. He steps back away from the greenhouse door. He half-expects them to bolt, but they stop just outside the greenhouse door that they also dutifully latch.

"Names?"

The young man tells him his name is Jimmy, which makes the introduction of his son easy enough, Jimmy standing right by him now, and Davin nods at him. "That's my son's name, too."

"I'm Sam, Samantha," the young woman says. Her voice sounds tight.

"You guys free camping nearby, I assume?"

"Uh, yeah," Jimmy the Younger says. He describes how they're past the powerlines and maybe a quarter mile into the woods, and then he's apologizing and talking about how big the garden is, how great it is, even as he tries handing over the bag he's holding.

"Keep it. Just so you know, it's still early for the green beans." And now he concentrates the flashlight beam on the bag. "You need a lesson on not just when to pick them, but how, too. You've pulled some blossoms off with the beans, means you're reducing the yields."

The two young people are clearly uncomfortable. What exactly should he be saying?

"You've been sent to the principal's office," he starts in, surprising them.

There's Jimmy's soft, quick laugh. The two young people seem to relax a bit.

"Where do you guys live?" he asks, confusing them. "No, not camping, but where are you from."

"Uh, Staten Island," the young man tells him, but stops for a moment to slap at a mosquito. "Uh, we came up with my brother, he's got a girlfriend in Richmond, but there's no room there for us—"

"They had a fight," the young woman says.

"Yeah, uh, whatever," Jimmy the Younger replies, with a quick look at the young woman, who is waving away mosquitoes herself now. He turns back to Davin. "Got dropped off here, well, in Great Barrington, were going to take the train back, but—"

"We don't have the money and he doesn't want to ask his folks for it," the young woman says. She's still holding the lettuce in one hand, the other trying to wave away the mosquitoes.

"Hey," Jimmy the Younger says.

"Well, it's true," she says to her accomplice. "You're so stubborn about it, and here we are, like..." She gestures around and holds up the lettuce to his face.

The young man mutters something to her, but Davin can't catch it. He turns back toward Davin. "Uh, can we go?" The hangdog expression is raw, even in the dim cast of the flashlight's downward pointed glow. "I apologize, sorry about the garden, I can see how, well, sorry."

Jimmy asks them how much money they need for the train tickets. The young man stays quiet, but the young woman opens up.

"We're like thirty dollars short, thirty-five," she tells them, in a rush, "and it'd be nice to get some sandwiches or something, so fifty or sixty dollars would do it."

Even in the dim light, Davin sees that the young man is blushing. Jimmy tells them to hold on, he'll go in and grab some cash, and he sets off into the dark.

Davin is at a loss for something to say, but the young woman speaks up. "Can I grab our water bottles?" she asks, gesturing, and he flips the light toward the big water barrel under the water manifold he uses to water the garden. A gallon milk jug and a red-capped liter Coke bottle are sitting there on top.

"Yeah, yeah, of course." He tells her to use his flashlight, but she pulls a small one from her back pocket and switches it on.

She's back with the water bottles, the gallon handed to the young man, and then Jimmy's back, too, a bit winded.

He hands the young woman the cash and hands over a brown bag. "Doggie bag from tonight, pretty good, better hot but you'll like it."

She nods.

"Uh, thanks," Jimmy the Younger says, and he's nodding too.

"Heading back tomorrow?" Davin asks, and the nods are clear.

The mosquitoes are zeroing in, and with a "So…" they start moving toward the back of the property, and there's one final turn and a half-wave, and in moments their tiny flashlight is lost among the trees.

Jimmy laughs. "A real Farmer McGregor."

Davin scoffs. He turns toward the house and the flashlight catches the lettuce on the grass. He's about to say something but the mosquitoes are concentrating and so too does he, intent on the faster return to the bug-free safety of the house and bed.

"Farmer McGregor," Jimmy says again as he follows Davin through the door.

Chapter 28: Bug On, Bug Off

July 3, 2035

Maker hits the broken pavement of the alleyway. His palms are angry welts, and his left hand has broken skin from which a bit of blood is weeping. He brushes that palm on his pants and when he looks, the blood is hardly noticeable. The stinging pain, on the other hand, feels like fire.

The timer on his watch has another fifteen minutes or so left on it, set for when they get far enough. The explosion will accomplish two things, hopefully. The first is to provide distraction and confusion and the second purpose is to obliterate any traces of their presence. Of course, the explosion following the shooting will be plenty suggestive of where said shot arose.

"Ashes, ashes, all fall down," he intones.

The tablet and phone will be atomized and any forensic evidence, such as fingerprints and DNA, will be burned up, along with the sleeping bags, the backpacks, clothes, and litter of their four days. The toilet and the rest of the dirty plumbing have enjoyed a bleach rinse after the last relief before showtime. John's jerk-off tissues. Maker scoffs at the thought. Giving birth to a whole family of evidence, down the drain.

He thumbs the detonator. He hears a thumping noise back in the direction they've come from, the vague nature of the detonation surprising him.

They're walking purposefully, not running, and a back

door opens up into the alleyway. A dark-haired man, about his own age, steps through, startled by the sight of the two of them. But John's already on it, asking the man in what sounds to Maker like damn good Spanish, if he's seen anyone suspicious, and then telling him that he should leave, tell anyone in the building to do the same, to make sure that people evacuate, that there's been an explosion. Not that the wild-haired man needs to be told that, standing there, dumb, looking behind them at the flames bursting from the back of 98 to 100 Bucareli, and John's now shouting "*Ve! Ve! Ve!*" and Maker sees back entrances on both sides of the alley opening, people stepping out, and he takes up the call.

"*Evacuar!*" John is now yelling, alternating with "*Ve! Ve! Ve!*" both arms gesturing people forward down the alleyway.

They reach the entrance into Calle Tres Guerras 13, although Maker hesitates—the color is different from the briefing material, but it's definitely the same door. As he's turning to point it out to John, the door opens slowly, creaking, and Maker reaches in and pulls out a middle-aged woman. There's a line of others, mostly or all women as best he can tell looking into a dark space, and he points and yells "*Ve! Ve! Ve!*" but stops, worried about saying it right, but he's getting the point across. He doesn't have to say anything, really. The fear and panic is rising in the small group coming out the door, adding to the upset of the crowd that's now running down the alley, out to where it empties on Emilio Dondé. John's grabbing a young woman from the doorway, presumably asking if there are others in the building, and she's just shaking her head, and more cries of *Evacuar!* and *Ve!* get people moving. Maker and John step through the doorway.

A couple more people come straggling down the dark corridor, and now John's simply gesturing toward the ajar door, and one stops to ask the two men dressed as Mexican SWAT officers what's going on, but John just pushes this person, a middle-aged man, on.

The building is dark, but they have their standard-issue flashlights, and there's the sunlight from off the delivery driveway coming through painted glass windows and a loose-fitting door outlined with this light, and they push it open.

Maker looks down the length of this concrete run and there's the roll-up door at the other end, open, thank God, just like the intel said it would be, and the two of them start off toward it at a moderate jog.

"Cameras," he reminds John as they approach. The chances are good that there are other cameras and that their image gets caught somewhere along the line, but the farther they get from the scene, the less likely any investigator will do the work to seek them out. These days, there are just too many cameras to check. Or avoid.

Heads down, sunglasses on, they head up the concrete skirt to the iron gate, but they find this ajar and slip out, bumping into another pair of cops, but regular duty officers, and John starts informing them that people are evacuating but the officers need to call this in, there are likely many residents still in this block. The fire in the alley is getting worse, he adds in smooth Spanish.

Maker adopts the silent approach, nodding at what his companion is saying, and then the two of them are stepping past these officers, and Maker gives the closest one a hearty shoulder slap as he steps past. Then they're crossing the street, heading for a parking lot with vendor carts and people on benches, except now everyone is standing up, looking past the two of them, and Maker turns to take a look. Black smoke is boiling up past the block of buildings behind them and sirens, a mix of bleats and horns and old-fashioned alarm bells, provide the background sound.

They're now crossing through some sort of half-assed park, with its hard paving and open parking spots, its scattering of benches under thin, spare trees, the messy groups of vendors booths. All this contrasts with the line of three gleaming tourist coaches, but what's the destination? A half block or so down, there's Teatro Ciudadela, one of the biggest theaters—the buses must be waiting for the show to finish. A matinee?

There's a crowd of well-dressed people, a fast-moving line, heading down the street toward the buses, but he and John keep walking, entering Parque de la Ciudadela, a real park, well planted, a few degrees cooler with the shade canopy, and within three minutes, they're through to Balderas and there's the black van and they clamber in.

There's only the driver, but in the back there are clothes for them to change into, the value of the uniforms spent. Halfway through changing, John leans against the interior side of the van, then turns his head and throws up. The driver, a very young man Maker's never seen before and will likely never see again, mutters something he can't make out and John is apologizing, even as he finishes getting the uniform off, and then the two of them are getting dressed, packing the uniforms up into the bag that had contained the civilian clothes in which they're now garbed.

The acrid, vinegary smell of John's vomit accompanies them all the way to the safe house.

Chapter 29: Victor Victorious, Not

July 5, 2035

Victor is not loving the rain, now fiercely falling, his tarp inadequately wide to keep the wind from pushing the rain against him, the rain coming down in torrents that defeat the plastic sheeting he's added, and the drop cloth plastic keeps tearing away from the cheap clips he bought at the hardware store in town at the same time. He'd hoped to fix this very problem of inadequate shelter he experienced in an earlier, gentler, rainstorm.

The rain intensifies, a sudden burst. "Fuck, fuck, fuck!" He pushes his sleeping bag and the backpack with his clothes further into the fold of the tarp. His electronics, now wrapped in these clothes in the backpack for extra protection, should stay dry that way. He sits, chilled with the spray that accumulates on him and around him and further, the chill bolstered by the hits of dripping splashes off the tarp's edges, and he feels like shouting, raging, but then he laughs. It could be worse. He looks down at his T-shirt and at his cargo shorts. There's wetness, but nothing soaking. The temperature of the air is warm, and the moisture, the humidity, seems like a solid personal presence, so there's no real chill, just an impression of it under the rain's assault. But the rain is letting up, becoming gentler, then gentle, and he fixes the thin plastic sheeting, re-clipping where needed. He pulls a dirty T-shirt from the backpack and wipes up some spray from the tarp that's folded under him. Things could be far worse.

"Fuck." Better, too, things could be a lot better.

He assumed that Nicky, post-holiday, would give him the go-ahead, but the text informs him that the house is still rented out and the ADU, where Nicky sleeps, is still too crowded for any additions. His own suggestion that he relocate to Nicky's property has gone unanswered, which is too bad, because at this point, he really needs a shower and it would be miraculous progress to use a real flushing toilet.

At least he's not off in some crowded smelly restroom of a Brooklyn cooling center, the heat in New York still far too high to have him in his oven-like apartment.

And at least he's gotten his latest contract in on time, despite the circumstances, so victory there, but standing here, damp, now struggling to put his netting back over the top of the tarp now that the rain is done and the mosquitoes are coming back on the prowl, he's feeling anything but victorious.

Chapter 30: Earth Abides

July 8, 2035

John and Maker are in the third safe house, waiting to be moved one step closer to getting back into the States. Something seems off, though, since the rule of safe houses is to leapfrog one to another as fast as possible, post action. That's the best strategy, better than going long distances, because the sustained movement itself becomes a liability.

They've asked the men who are—what? Caregivers, helpers, babysitters, guards?—a whole range of questions, about schedules, about the border crossing possibilities, about who or what will accompany them through. Maker really doesn't want to be a mule, not for drugs. And herding migrants through also seems like an unnecessary risk. And creepy.

He laughs. He has no problem with shooting someone, or those other actions he's accomplished over the years, but babysitting desperate people trying for the American dream. Such help can only fail. There's no promise of the American dream anymore, not with an ecosphere racing toward its own destruction. Helping migrants, well, there's a sense of cognitive dissonance to it, shepherding those with hope, when he's a soldier of the despairing world.

His discomfort is more than just part of that feeling of responsibility, though. The cartels traffic in people, and it isn't just the coyote, the smuggling, the *pollero*, it is *fucking slavery*.

This term should be funny, an awful pun, but he's never felt forcing women, girls, boys into sex work to be anything other than a horror. He's dedicated his life to ending horror, the greatest horror visited upon man by man, the horror of a planet so altered that everyone would suffer and die, and animals, plants are going extinct, places are becoming inhospitable, deserts, floods. People responsible for this, those who would have everyone drink their deadly oil, breathe their poisonous fumes, those people are rightly punished and the worst of them deserve to die.

He takes a long breath. He can too often get caught up in the specifics of any task, the details of any operation, but now, post action, he can come back to himself, his core, his dedication.

After what he learned last night, though, this exercise has gotten harder. Sometimes innocent people get hurt, but there's no pleasure or joy in collateral damage, only regret that circumstance has put them in the wrong place at the wrong time, that the war in which he fights has far greater numbers dealt death by those he fights.

He's made peace with his own righteous anger long ago. He's been driven to battle against evil, an evil so stupidly mendacious, so grounded in short-term gain for so few at the expense of so many. He's given up college, given up a life of normalcy for this fight, but he learned in his three semesters studying Jeremy Bentham, and John Stuart Mill, and Moore, the twentieth century ethics philosopher, although to his annoyance, he seems to have forgotten that philosopher's first name.

Not that there's any life anywhere in these times that could ever truly claim to be normal—that's clearer than ever. Not when the earth itself is twisting, morphing into something dead, something that doesn't nurture but negates. The illusions of normalcy of those dooming the world demand to be shaken. He has long hoped his acts, and the actions of his brothers and sisters in this war, are charging the true price to be paid by those who he's dedicated to attacking.

John and he should have been on the move already. John and he should have separated after the first safe house, that's standard procedure, but instead, they're cooling their jets, just hanging out, waiting.

Biff will come by. Biff will have some answers. Whether he will like those answers is a different question.

He doesn't like NOS working with the cartels. He understands the expediency of it—NOS needs certain things: guns, cash, different kinds of help with some illegal actions, logistical support for complex operations, and their own capacity is limited. Such things and such assistance are hard to come by, necessarily involves criminals. The cartels are terrorists by nature, hurting and killing innocents, ruining lives, hurting the world in their own vicious ways. A helping hand expects help in return, unfortunately. Spending the last three days stuck here in a small grimy house is even more unfortunate, although at least they're past the hood stage, and he and John are free to walk around. There's the smell of farmland, and the quiet, too, and he's been allowed to sit at the back windows up on the second floor of the building, where the vista is one of agricultural fields, a group of buildings like warehouses, and big trucks, sometimes diesel, blat and sigh along the road behind him. They've been allowed outside, too, within a large walled compound. They're in a rundown house at the spare end of the compound, with neighbors spaced far away, but the walls mean only the roofs of these other houses are visible. Yesterday, in the afternoon hours, there was the far-off sound of a soccer game.

Along the road out back there are big transmission lines and towers. Ironically, they aren't far from Tepexpán. He glimpsed a road sign from the back of yet another van, the one that brought them here. This one had painted windows, but enough scratches of the paint gave him glances of the passing world, and enough to catch sight of a city sign. In his autodidact life, he's read of Tepexpán, where an old human fossil was found, Tepexpán man, at least ten thousand years old, and the fossil may be a woman, but either way, the fossilized remains showed a clear cause of death: trampled by a mastodon. Interesting. He hadn't known mastodons had ranged so far south, but with the Ice Age, maybe Mexico wasn't that far south of the ancient and unimaginable glacial sheet that had crushed much of the northern continent.

There was controversy about the discovery, and the whole thing remains conjecture by the academic community as far as he knows, but how odd it must be to be an academic. He's read about a mammoth kill site that was near Tepexpán, where the giant mammals were driven into bogs where they were severely slowed, to be killed by groups of men or, perhaps, women. Are mastodons and mammoth just different names for the same creature or actual distinct species?

He's had a lot of time to read over the last few years. He would read now, as they wait, if he'd brought along a book. There's not a book in the house, English, Spanish, or otherwise, or at least that's what the two men sharing the house with them tell him, and he's not inclined to press the point.

He has imagined what it must have been like to chase mammoths into bogs, poking them with the hunters' fluted points, likely obsidian, if he remembers that right, Tepexpán a source of this stone.

Do these two men, who as yet have given neither he nor John their names, and who appear to have grown increasingly nervous as the three days here pass into the fourth, know about Tepexpán and obsidian, or of the old fossil of a mastodon-trampled woman? Neither of these young men, one his age probably, the other still a teenager, he'd guess, seem open to any conversation, although as of yesterday, they've begun to share their *cerveza*, the drinking of which seems their primary activity and interest. That and pacing around, and glancing at him or John. Their pacing is growing.

The waiting is a pain, but at least these men aren't frightening exactly. Most people he's met from the cartels, as terrifying or bizarre as some may be, aren't burning down the world. The men he's met, some, anyway, have a value system, with its brand of loyalty and standards, opaque or not, all in support of family, group, tribe, even if many are weird, unusual, even alien. These two are indistinct, almost normal. Some, like Biff, the contact he's worked with over the past eight months, seem normal, or normal enough. Biff is someone who would pass the have-a-beer-with test. These two, no.

He and John are told only that Biff will be coming by, and at least one man always has them in his sight, inside or out in the compound, the pistol each carries tucked into their belt, one looks like a Sig Sauer P320, but the other looks like a knockoff, maybe of a CZ 75. At night, he and John are shooed into a room where the windows are nailed fixed with a six-inch gap for air, the door latched, and it wouldn't be hard to butt the door open, but it wouldn't be quiet.

John's gotten chatty again with him during these last nights. John is not exactly reliving the operation, but his first night seemed like a debrief. Last night was different, though. Last night was surprising. John talked about the delay and the nervous babysitters, and he talked more broadly about NOS's relationship with the cartels, and the operation just past, the specific reasons behind those targets, and as he talked, the depth of his knowledge became ever more obvious. Maker hadn't known that the Mexican minister John had as a target was Subsecretario Gabriel Bernal, Secretaría de Gobernación, with his brief in petroleum and most other matters pertaining to fossil fuel. He only knew what the two targets looked like, or barely more than that—their names, and that they were signing some sort of oil deal, that these two targets were fossil fuel criminals.

"We've gotten so much help because CJNG wants

Bernal gone," was the first revelation. Maker had almost asked what the initials meant, but with a flush it dropped—*Cártel de Jalisco Nueva Generación*, and only then had he understood that NOS's cartel connections extended to this, the fiercest of cartels, the cartel that has consumed other cartels, including one that first controlled the illicit petroleum economy, a victory in the second *Triángulo Rojo of huachicol*, the epicenter of fuel theft, as John explained to him. John told him running battles have been fought in the state of Guanajuato, where the main cities of Salamanca, Irapuato, and Celaya form Mexico's El Bajío Industrial Corridor, and where financial losses from fuel theft are more than a billion US dollars, annually.

Fuel theft has become a primary concern for the country's economic and political stability as the number of illicit taps and diverse ways to pilfer fuel increases, and The Ministry of the Interior, or *Secretaría de Gobernación*, has been fighting against them.

"Subsecretario Gabriel Bernal is leading this fight," John said. "Was leading."

"We're doing wet work for the worst of the worst of the cartels," Maker responded.

John shrugged. "They're in a good position, have been an effective financial source, more cash than they know what to do with, I think."

Anyone who pays attention to the news would know who they are, and Maker's been spending time in Texas and the Southwest, where that news is hard to ignore. CJNG controls the ports of Veracruz, Manzanillo, and Lázaro Cardenas in the Gulf and Pacific, which means they're now the main access to global illicit goods supply chains.

He'd assumed Sinaloa was his source. He'd assumed that Sinaloa was the main cartel with whom the secret army of NOS worked, that Biff was the face of that cartel for him, and what felt like a thousand questions flooded him then, in the dark of that night room, dim sky the only illumination.

He managed to ask one. "They're the source of those

precursor chemicals?" He began to explain the work he'd been doing, but John knew all about snapdragons, another shock, and it wasn't just that he knew but that he reported how thrilled they were with their new toys, that and two other items he's built, including the very incendiary device he used just days before.

"How the fuck do you know about that?" But his world was already turning upside down as he began to suspect the answer.

"You're a fucking Guide," was the only answer he got, to John's growing grin, but that grin faded when he asked how it was that he, a Guide, was in the field. "That blows just about all the protocols."

He managed not to add that John, né Jim was *way too fucking young*.

They talked for an hour more, maybe longer. He had trouble sleeping after, his thoughts racing with what he'd learned, which was that Jim was here because CJNG wanted him here, as simple as that, and because they could demand this, get such young hands dirty. Not *as a sign of good faith,* as Jim had explained. Like hell.

By the time Jim started talking about how NOS ranks were thin, how Guides were doing more and more in the field, Maker had passed through confusion into despair. Jim talked about how the cartels were asking for more and more and were giving them lots of money to recruit others, but not for NOS, not exactly, but as operatives for the cartels to move more freely in the States.

NOS wasn't what Maker had thought, and must not have been for a while.

He kept his own counsel amid his restless and weary night.

Today, tired and anxious from his night and from his new-found knowledge, it's impossible to tell whether the two watchers are Sinaloa or CJNG, but it's clear, in the light of this day, that something unnerves them too.

Chapter 31: The Selectboard

July 10, 2035

Last night's Selectboard meeting ran far longer than usual, and this morning Davin's at his desk trying to write it up for *Berkshire Interactive*. Both he and Alicia have already talked about the meeting, her calling far too early this morning, and she's eager to get the story out. Unfortunately, going back to sleep won't be an option.

Last night was unusual in every way. The room was overcrowded, and for only the second time since Davin Caine, city reporter, has attended, the meeting required a second room to be set up, for overflow. Considering the topic, this easily anticipatable need could have been addressed in advance, but instead, this had added yet more time to the evening's proceedings. The extra time taken to arrange this was significant. That extra time, that half hour of mindless delay, he'll never get back.

He's a bit sorry this morning that he's ever felt attending civic meetings is boring, a thing to be endured as one of his responsibilities. This morning he can only yearn for boredom because after last night's experience, boredom seems the better part. He normally likes the sense of the town's activity that he gets from such attendances, even though there's tedium to survive. Still, his gig as nominal town governance reporter gives him some sense of connection with his community, and this remains a good thing for him and pushes back on his tendency to become isolated. Another of his opportunities for connection is his growing mentorship of the ever-changing parade of new reporters Alicia brings on, but those are specific connections, and more intimate ones that deal with the various personalities and types of people who wish to write for *Berkshire Interactive*. There seems little consistency in the writing abilities and intelligence he comes across in this capacity, but this activity is exhausting in a whole different way than the marathon of anxieties and just plain weirdness of yesterday's meeting.

For one thing, last night the crowd insisted on rearranging the meeting's set agenda, and after some initial resistance on the part of the chair, rearranged the agenda was. The topic on the audience's mind was what should be done with the too many strangers doing too many unwelcome things in town, about unhoused people, and about crime, discomfort, and anger, and all these were part and parcel of the last agenda item under "new business," until, of course, that topic became the first item by popular demand.

The agenda item itself sounded innocuous enough, but then, agenda items often do. Chief Sullivan was on hand, although after the angry tone of the public comment period escalated and then escalated even more, the police chief seemed to regret being there. Fletch was there, as usual, and she came in for a lot of pushback too.

He doesn't know how to begin his article about last night, but he starts typing.

> "The police are impotent," one of a cascade of speakers said, or shouted, and that occasioned perhaps the hundredth gaveling of the night of July 9, during the regular meeting of the Great Barrington Selectboard.

It's okay, but it's not the right first line. A more

traditional approach is required. He types:

> At a regular Monday meeting of the Great Barrington Selectboard, the topic of the night went by various names: trespassers, shoplifters, street beggars, plague, and so much more, after the members of the public present forced the board to bring agenda item IV to the fore.
>
> The agenda item in question read as follows: "IV. Discussion of recent police reports and criminal complaints, and citizens' notice of incidents of public solicitation, loitering, disruption of the public peace, sleeping and camping in public spaces, and trespass."
>
> This reporter left the meeting after the Selectboard had managed, finally, to gavel to a close the free-for-all discussion of the first item discussed, said aforementioned Item IV...

A little too wise guy-ey, probably, but he'll keep going and deal with the flippant tone in the next draft, as needed.

> ... about the crowded streets and by-lanes...

He shakes his head—he's a fucking country squire, apparently—and deletes the Anglicism.

> ...crowded streets and alleys, and our town's pocket parks, and, yes, even the gazebo behind the very place this meeting takes place was a named location among

> many, where various examples of poor behavior, vagrancy, petty crime, and flagrant trespassing were cited. The public comment period followed the straightforward and dry instructions of the board to town manager, Marion Fletcher-Gray, to request that the police department prepare a report on these problems. But when moved and seconded, the result was a rush of citizens' scrambling to get their own three minutes of comment. More time than usual was spent organizing the line for public comment.

He scoffs. He *is* a country squire! He suspects his strange frame of mind and his abandoned consideration of using the word *queue* is directly related to his lack of a good night's sleep.

> As far as this reporter knows, the Selectboard may well still be in session, working to resolve all the other, more mundane matters that were pushed for later attention, his having left with the still-grumbling crowd at the close of vote on this agenda item, at an hour not regularly seen at these meetings, a touch past midnight.

> The public comments contained repeating themes across the more than sixty residents who wished to speak, but discomfort, inconvenience, and gobsmacked disbelief at any number of things witnessed were

common. Those provoking these comments are, of course, the young men and women newly arrived in the town, most often up from the city in escape from the heatwave, and most often without fixed lodgings. Certain members of this "horde" (as one speaker put it) are also represented in police actions, and next week's police log seems likely to be a very long read.

The opinions expressed were hardly uniform. Some speakers called for patience and care regarding these visitors, reminding those in attendance that the number of deaths in New York City due to the ongoing high temperatures is at a count well past three hundred. A check of the official city index reveals that overnight the number of heat-related deaths has climbed another three dozen, although the majority of the new deaths are from an HVAC failure at an unregistered retirement home in Yonkers. Others reminded attendees at the Selectboard meeting of heat hazards across the affected areas, which now extend southward below Washington DC and westward, closing in on Detroit.

Many other speakers, though, called for the town's attention to what is occurring locally, and while no official tally was made of the numbers on one side or the other of the

> matter, sentiments seemed overwhelmingly negative in tone. One speaker called for the police to enforce "border checks" along town lines, while another responding to this proposal suggested that it represented a lack of understanding of the Constitution.
>
> Tempers in the chamber ebbed and flowed and the chair's gavel saw hard duty in keeping any civil decorum. The issue of housing, or, more to the point, the lack of housing, was raised by several of the speakers, including two who accused the town of a prevailing NIMBY attitude, and one spoke in reference to a housing project proposal that had failed to pass zoning approval in April, noting this was one of a string of defeats for the large lot at the corner of Mahaiwe Street. Of more practical value were suggestions that the town allow tent cities and provide porta-potties, and while these recommendations had support, there was little agreement on where a tent city might be located.

The tent city proposal was interesting on its merits, and there's value in thinking through the planning for the concept, but what became clear during the comment period was that nobody seems willing to have this present in their own neighborhoods. Owners of restaurants and other businesses in town pushed for consideration of the fairgrounds, a long-unused and slowly crumbling set of buildings in one section of the Housatonic flood plain. These buildings have recently been demolished, this site of about a hundred acres being prepared for new apartments and a commercial center. But there was strong pushback, too.

The idea of a tent city makes sense, and he is curious to see if this solution moves forward, but the town will be reluctant to spend money on such a short-term response to a heatwave condition that's likely to clear soon, or soon enough. Several other speakers made the suggestion that the park behind the town hall be similarly used, but the several residents from The Hill, a well-off neighborhood just on the other side of the tracks, used their three minutes to express their opposition to the use of that location.

He could pull up the CTSB video, but he doesn't bother to check if the video is yet available. The community cable station is notoriously slow in posting anything in a timely manner, and despite the fact that what's posted is the live broadcast, rudimentary post-production, mainly adding titles and index, seems to take forever. Another reason he doesn't bother to check for the video is that if, improbably, it's already available, this will add a lot more work for him.

He finishes up the piece, reviews it, makes some edits, and sends it off.

It's barely past 9:00 a.m. He could go back to bed but—dammit!—he's got to turn the apartment for the new guests coming in. This has to be done by 3:00 p.m. Is Be at Riggs today? He'll hear her when she's up, though. It would be nice to have her help, since, when working together making the beds, vacuuming, and all the other cleanup, it takes less than two hours, not counting the wash. Laundry is his life.

His phone rings again and it's Alicia.

"What's up?" he asks. "Did ya get the article? Sent it in five, ten minutes ago."

She's gotten the article, but she's got news, too. "Just heard over the scanner, there's been a killing, just happened, probably around 2:00 a.m., they think."

"They" must be the police. Alicia has something of a direct line to the police chief. Is this something the chief encourages or simply can't escape? She's already filling him in about the dead man, young, one of those up from the city. He died of injuries from a beating by several young men, as yet unknown to her by name, but local.

"One apparently Sheffield," she adds, telling him that the others are likely from Great Barrington, but it is all still unconfirmed.

He tells her he can't get to this story for a day or two. This should get her looking for another writer for it, but she lets him know that he's not going to write up the story. Thank God.

"I'm thinking Marcus," she says, referring to one of the new editorial interns. "He up to it?"

Davin's shrug can't be seen, since the call's voice only, but he tells her that this could work, keeping his reservations to himself. Young Marcus is not the best writer, but then that's what editors are for. Then Alicia surprises him.

"I want you to rewrite, well, write a new version. We'll run with the story you've sent in, but I want you to bring names and quotes in from the video of the meeting, capture the anger you suggest in the first piece, but make this real—"

"Got it, got it." It's obvious, really, and that had been his instinct, but he hadn't wanted to put in the time, and now, somehow, he's agreeing to a deadline that will be hard to meet but possible, even with his apartment turn. He also has some questions to answer from the gallery in Hudson, and that can't be put off either. But the more you do, the more you do. "Yup, yup, yup."

Chapter 32: The Fast-Flying Fury of Fisticuffs

July 11, 2035

"Boy," Fletch says to no one, since she's alone in her office at this moment, the utterance reflecting her sense of confusion. Or maybe it's a form of prayer.

Given that a Timothy Walloch of 1401 Atlantic Avenue, Brooklyn is in the morgue, it might be for him, but it's as likely for the town. Morgue. Is that some mislabel from all the police procedurals she's watched over the years? Anyway, his body's in whatever that space is called at Finnerty & Stevens Funeral Home, waiting for the Massachusetts Office of the Chief Medical Examiner. OCME is involved because its purpose is to investigate the cause and manner of death in cases of violence, unnatural causes, or natural causes requiring further investigation, and the young man, found beaten to death in the early hours of the previous day, clearly falls within the category of a violent death.

The OCME is sending out personnel from the regional office in Westfield. The Great Barrington Police Department will "interface" with the ME and the staties, according to Sullivan, who's done well with keeping her apprised of developments, although she could do without the cascade of jargon. So far, she's resisted creating a glossary.

Interface? Why can't real language be used, like *working with* or *helping*? She's not sure why she's fixating on the language being *utilized* around this death, fits right in with the could-be glossary, but then everything feels strange, off in some fundamental way, the town in some hush. Or it could be just her.

Sullivan has five young men in custody, and the district attorney and a gaggle of ADAs are heading down from Pittsfield, and apparently there's a request for public defenders from two of the young men, the other three already with lawyers. Bond hearings are scheduled at Southern Berkshire District Court, right here in Great Barrington, a ten-minute walk away from town hall, on Gilmore Avenue, a quiet street, with modest homes making up the rest of the neighborhood. She's got a friend who lives on the same street, a fact which has no material application to this situation.

She's got to call Alicia Soares, *Berkshire Interactive*'s publisher and editor. She wants advice about how to handle this problem, how to get ahead of it, the messaging that could help citizens toward some positive perspective so that things don't get worse. Kara's already told her the phone calls to her office are still running hot and she's asked that Kara set up a citizens' comment line, and screen them close to real time in case there are people she should be getting back to. So far, the tenor of the messages, some twenty-seven of them, run the gamut of pro-prosecution and law and order and sympathetic tolerance. Some of the calls coming in are painfully self-righteous, some simply painful. *Free the Great Barrington Five.*

She likes Alicia well enough, and they enjoy a good working relationship, sometimes just chatting about the town and goings-on, off the record. Still, she's got to remember to listen more than talk. Alicia's online effort is pretty much what goes for a local newspaper these days, and that sort of undertaking has its own agenda. Relying on goodwill is a recipe for trouble, PR-wise. Still, she can probably use the exclusive angle to motivate Alicia, but there are plenty of other sources in a town like Great Barrington, so she shouldn't overplay the exclusivity offer.

Manipulate, with the leverage on exclusive access. Some balance of trust and suspicion on her part should see her through if she thinks it through.

The last murder had occurred not long after she took the job, and Alicia had run headlines about gangland slayings and other overly dramatic slants.

There's that killing up in Housatonic, too. *Great Barrington, Murder Capital*. She sighs.

Kara is keeping a list of media interview requests, and *Berkshire Interactive* is on it, of course, but network affiliates and the Albany and Boston media market are showing up on the list as well. There is one unknown publication or news streaming platform or whatever it may be, but all she knows so far is that the request comes from Brooklyn.

When the DA's office gets here and does their thing, only then, according to Sullivan, will a decision be made on a 58A, and she was short with him for not explaining what that is, although she then felt a bit foolish when he told her it is a dangerousness hearing in lieu of a regular bail, and necessary for the defendant or defendants to be held without bail. If so, the defendant or defendants thus found to be too dangerous would be placed in the Berkshire House of Correction, he then explained, until such time as trial commences or bail appeals succeed.

All the boys—men, actually—are local, and she only knows one by name, having met him at some party at one of her neighbors' homes, an aging couple, Sam and Missy Waterton, whom she loves to have close by, two houses down. Sweet and thoughtful people.

She's seen this young man around the neighborhood in the ten years she's been in her house. She thinks of him mainly as a teenager, but probably wouldn't have remembered his name—Joey—if that hadn't been part of Sullivan's report, but she does remember his helping his folks with mowing the lawn and shoveling snow, and he seemed a perfectly fine fellow. He moved out some years ago—three or four?—for Westfield University, maybe. Did he ever graduate? She does remember Sam and Missy telling her that he applied for a position in the fire department.

They hoped she'd put in a word, she assumed at the time, but they were too polite to ask outright, and she promptly forgot. She's pretty sure the application didn't ever advance far enough to come to her attention.

Joey Waterton is one of four of the five being charged, if Sullivan's assumptions prove out, either with accessory after the fact, or conspiracy to commit murder, or other charges related to direct involvement with the killing itself, whether manslaughter or murder. It all depends on whether it can be shown that they participated in the act or aided in the cover-up, he told her.

It's not as if she hasn't known people in trouble with the law, with DUIs and the occasional domestic assault, but homegrown killers are a black swan occurrence. The first and last time she actually met her neighbors' son was three years ago, at Sam's seventieth birthday, and seeing them together, close-up, she was surprised that they'd had their son late, an only child, only now twenty-three years old, if she's heard Sullivan right. Missy, who's younger than Sam, must have been in her early forties when she got pregnant.

She can't imagine he or the three others will be held without bail, but more likely released under some condition like GPS monitoring or a curfew.

It isn't even two full days since the vitriolic Selectboard meeting, and the violent tone and threats that made up much of the public comment now seems ominous, predictive of this assault.

She leans back and hits the intercom, Kara, her administrative assistant, coming into her office without any lag. The cast of anxiety on the young woman's face is disturbing, but Kara is tough despite her young years.

"Okay," Fletch tells her, "Let's get Alicia Soares in as soon as we can. I'll call her."

Kara nods.

"We're going to need to come up with a statement, but something generic. We don't know much in the way of facts yet, but that's going to play out today."

Kara nods.

"Run the comments through speech-to-text, create a written record."

Kara looks confused.

"The comments phone log, all the messages, any others for a while."

Kara nods.

"Also, I'm expecting an update from Sullivan, and the DA is coming down today. There's the bond thing at the court probably later today or first thing tomorrow." She stops. "Um, notes maybe?"

Her charades-like motion with her hand, mimicking writing, gets the point across, and Kara steps out and comes back with a pad and pen. Fletch repeats what she's been saying and adds a few more items, including that Kara run the comment line messages through AI for checks on a speech-to-text, and keep updating as new messages come in.

"Make sure that you review these, though. We don't want to misquote, right?"

Kara nods.

"And check the spelling of names and addresses, double check these through the town rolls."

Kara, usually unflappable, seems unusually upset.

"What's going on?" she asks. "I mean, yeah this is terrible, but—"

"Yeah…" A nod of encouragement from her gets Kara going. "My younger sister dated two of these guys, went to prom with one of them."

"Oh boy. Yeah, everyone is feeling awful about all this." Another nod sends Kara off to her tasks, closing the office door as she goes.

Berkshires in a nutshell. Housing prices are high and job opportunities for many townies are low, the high interest rates persist and that's no help, and the whole county still coasts close to economic depression. Worse without the out-of-towners, the tourists, the second-homeowners, but it's hard to try to tell anyone that.

She reaches for her phone.

"Prom dates and provocations," she says as she's punching in Alicia Soares's number.

Chapter 33: Dreaming of Be

July 12, 2035

Davin is still bleary-eyed from the Selectboard video, but he's gotten through it all and has sent Alicia the revised article sprouting quotes and attributions.

It's been a busy time, and he still has to get back to the Hudson gallery, since he hasn't gotten to that task yet. There's nothing demanding, and mainly he has to fill out a form about his preferred name and the titles, dimensions, and suggested prices of the five pieces he and the gallery have arrived at, although the gallery has made it clear it'll keep the option open to raise them. It's mostly busy work, including listing the materials used in each piece, although, with his sort of assemblage, such lists can be quite long and confusing. Maybe gallery visitors will play Where's Waldo.

Fortunately, he's got all this information somewhere, so his real task is finding the various files. Unfortunately, he's managed not to be quite as disciplined with his folder and file conventions as he is with those he uses for his other work.

Unfortunately, thoughts of Be and what happened in the studio keep intruding. He's not going to count the number of days, not going to obsess. Except he does. What should he think about it?

He's always thought her attractive, and that's been right from the beginning, when he interviewed her about the house share, but he's also always put that perception into its own lockbox, because a relationship with a house sharer is a bad idea, of course.

He sees again her wink as she backed into him. The stirrings of an erection, no automatic occurrence at seventy years of age, come to his attention. Jesus. He's completely flummoxed. What if he's reading too much into all of this? What if it's all just a joke on her part, a good-natured tease, nothing more?

She's been more and more helpful in the studio. He likes her suggestions about his work and likes that she'll wait for him to ask before she says anything.

He takes a long-drawn breath. He loves talking with her and he's under the impression she enjoys talking with him. He feels like a goddamn teenager.

She's been caught up in her three-day intensive schedule at Austen Riggs, so tonight's not a good time to talk with her, to try to figure out *Lockbox or not.*

She still has curves, rising into a smaller waist, up into strong shoulders and those masses of dark curls.

Jesus. He takes another deep breath.

Lockbox or not?

Chapter 34: Wait, Wait, Don't Tell Me

July 12, 2035

It's been another three days, but Biff is finally here, and Maker has plenty of questions for him. Except Biff doesn't seem to have any answers other than to say they're waiting for someone.

Biff's an odd fellow. First there's Biff, the name the guy goes by, that seems entirely incongruous, but considering that he's calling himself Maker Dewers for this particular go-around, Biff may simply be something picked out of a hat by this man. Biff certainly doesn't look cartel always dressed like a middle-class Mexican, except that today he's shown up wearing a decent suit, lightweight for the heat, but this only adds another element of incongruity. Another thing that is off is the shocking fact that he is still at the safe house, days and days beyond the usual protocol. He and Jim-John, should have been brought back into the States days ago.

Is Biff maybe someone quite different than he's been assuming? Jim-John has certainly turned out to be something that shocked him, which is that he's one of the fabled Guides, those top-echelon leaders of NOS, supposedly unknown by their real identity, even one to another, but then Jim-John, who doesn't appreciate the moniker, has told him his real name: John Seward, originally from Astoria, Oregon, where his father Stewart Seward, a Methodist minister, died when John was three. Maker managed not to ask if the father had killed himself because of his name.

John's mother, who still has not been mentioned by name, remarried, and it was Jim-John's stepfather who had gotten him involved in climate change work. The divorce put an end to his relationship with his stepfather, but the climate action continued. How his involvement with NOS came to pass is unclear, but Maker's reluctant to ask for details and clarifications because, as best he can figure it, it could be that there was a sexual relationship with one of the NOS Guides. Advancement through some sort of *back door maneuvering*. There's no point sharing the joke, of course. Queer or not means nothing to him. He doesn't care, but it's been embarrassing, the way Jim-John has kept talking about it, and now he knows that there's a Guide named Alex, or was, anyway. The way Jim-John refers to the man makes it unclear if he's alive or dead. He hasn't felt the need to risk hearing more details about the relationship, current or past, as it may be. There are other more interesting things Jim-John's mentioned over the days they've been waiting.

What he does closely heed are Jim-John's complaints about the state of NOS, the declining cells and members, the drop-off of missions, the money problems. That surprised him, initially, the talk of NOS's slow diminishment—he's never once entertained the possibility. The longer and longer delays in assignment targets he's been seeing, and his working solo for the past two years, the slow arrival of money, this all makes better sense now. But he's been so caught up assuming that these were consequences of ever-evolving operational security.

Ass, you, me. Disappointing. Maybe he doesn't understand the world he's placed himself in quite as well as he thinks. No One is Safe, sure as shit.

Jim-John's told him a lot over the days spent waiting in the safe house, but there are things he doesn't need to be told, such as the appallingly young age of Jim-John, who has already mentioned he's just turned twenty-two years of age a couple of times. Another surprise is how much the guy likes to talk about things, including things that should be withheld for operational security, like his statement that the number of Guides has been dwindling. His own understanding over the course of his decade of involvement is that there are seven Guides, although that's only ever been the common rumor. Jim-John has told him that there are now only three. This means that one-third of the top echelon of the NOS structure is here with him, a Guide sent out on a field operation.

Biff comes up the stairs, back from a walk around the compound, and Maker again asks about the long wait, but he just gets back an odd smile. Then, as the sounds of approaching vehicles drift in, the smile disappears and Biff is snapping orders at the two Mexicans who have been keeping company with him and Jim-John over this long stay.

He doesn't care for their change of expression, the usually slack faces energized with anxiety or worry, dread even?

He moves to the front window where Biff looks out, and sees a three-vehicle convoy of SUVs billowing dust behind them, turning into the compound, where there are armed men waiting.

"Wait is over my friends," Biff says, but Jim-John hasn't bothered to come to the window, instead staying slumped against the wall, eyes still closed. "El Escorpión," he adds, with a serious nod to Maker.

Chapter 35: Whoops, I Did It Again

July 14, 2035

Well, it's happened, Davin is thinking, and the thought isn't without some trepidation, but the sheer—What? Exuberance? Excitement?—of the turn of events in the studio the day before.

He's up in his small bedroom on the second floor. He feels like a kid, at least in some ways, in the way, for instance, that feeling in love drives the ability to think over the edge and beyond restraint, and since yesterday he's been forcing himself to slow down, to breathe, to steady himself.

It's not love, though. He's too old to think that way. The whole thing is comical in its way—feelings take time, time to develop, time to confirm and test, yet he's out of time. It's all inexplicable.

He and Be were in the studio yesterday. She was doing some prep work on a new mass of clay, but he was there to put together an artist statement for the Hudson show that had finally come through, and he moseyed around the various works he was to include, testing his statement against the particular collection, and pretty much like always when it came to talking about his strange sculptural works, he couldn't claim whether the draft statement was good or dreck.

After hemming and hawing, he asked Be for her opinion and she left her wedging top, covering the big clay lump with a wet rag, and stood reading the statement page out on his big worktable, the two of them standing side by side.

The house was empty and the latest Airbnb guests were due at the close of day. He hadn't spoken to Be since the incident in the studio some days before, when she'd flirtatiously backed into him as he helped her move one of her large architectural slabs, and he was hoping to figure out some way to test the competing theories of *interest* or *joke*.

"This is really good," she told him, and then asked him to read the statement out loud, a technique for reviewing the flow, a technique he well knew, if seldom practiced.

He cleared his throat and began. "My art is made out of the material created in the headlong rush of materialism: recoveries from forgotten trunks, drawers, and boxes, gleanings from estates, flea markets, and tag sales, and items revealed and retrieved from streets, sidewalks, and trash piles—"

"Start with the title."

"Yeah, okay, makes sense," he replied, wondering at his rising heartbeat. "Assemblage, Found Objects, Utility, and Intentional Presentation."

She nodded approvingly, flashing a thumbs-up.

"The material includes media—photographs, slides, cards, prints—"

"From the start. Begin again from the start."

"My art is made out of the material created in the headlong rush of materialism: recoveries from forgotten trunks, drawers, and boxes, gleanings from estates, flea markets, and tag sales, and items revealed and retrieved from streets, sidewalks, and trash piles. The material includes plentiful media—photographs, slides, cards, prints—to say the least. But there's more. The written and printed records of personal and public lives are also copious, from the informational sort, such as diaries, letters, books, documents, and magazines, to the many and various recording products, such as films, records, and tapes.

"Not surprisingly, these objects are powerfully infused

with nostalgia. Even physical objects with which viewers are not personally acquainted—such as an anonymous fourth-grade class photograph or an unfamiliar piece of costume jewelry—are likely to have meaning projected onto them by the viewers. This projection is a fundamental element of any and all art forms, of course. What may have changed over the last century is that everyday things have become aesthetically objectified through the work of artists such as Joseph Cornell, whose work is seminal when it comes to found objects and assemblage. Not only is Cornell's work achingly beautiful, but, together with surrealists such as Marcel Duchamp and Man Ray, Cornell was central to ushering in a new concept of media where 'everyday' things become as much a medium in building art as clay, pigment, pen, paper."

He paused to look at her.

Be looked back, with a gentle smile, and a nod for him to continue.

He read on. "I think of my own assemblages as 'image poems,' where, just as happens in poetry, images are presented in a way that allows them to be experienced swiftly by the viewers. 'There is always a phantasmagoria,' said Yeats; and the word suggests the rapidity of a shared dream experience, even as it suggests the inability to directly describe such perceptions.

"By bringing a utilitarian function to my work—however formal or improbable—I hope to further elicit the participation of the viewer. Many of my pieces use lighting elements for just such a purpose. Another strategy is to make the objects' arrangement more artificial through the finish and workmanship of an applied furniture-making process. Indeed, many of these pieces are, in their own way, furniture or made in part from furniture fragments. In fact, the impulse toward recycling and reuse is an important one in my work, even if the nod to worldly stewardship carries this to an absurd form. Craft, too, plays a central role in the work, as I strive to mix the flotsam of our lives—'kipple' in the words of Philip K. Dick—with artisan techniques that are a reaction to the commoditization of our age."

He stopped again and his glance was reward enough for the pause, although it was a bit of a challenge breathing, so he took a deep breath. She nodded again for him to continue.

"The elements of absurdity in my work are, I hope, apt, not only given the associations among assemblage artists, surrealists, and dadaists, but because it provides another irony—commercialism, the keystone in our world of material excretion, is mocked. Like the Popeil Veg-O-Matic sales pitch 'But wait! There's more!' and with that I can state that many of these art works are not only sculpture 'But also a lamp! Now how much would you expect to pay?'

"Is that too stupid?" he asked with another glance toward her, but Be just gestured for him to continue.

"Absurdity notwithstanding, the aesthetic experience of the objects and the combinations and presentations themselves are not ironic, but rather, a simple reflection of an openness to and a hungering after beauty, even in such otherwise ridiculous, nostalgic, or everyday objects.

"In the end, I hope, my work reflects puzzles of a larger sort, an effort to wrestle with the most basic struggles in which we are all engaged: consumption versus conservation, paying attention versus being overwhelmed, mass commodity versus individuality, nostalgia versus presence, despair versus grace."

The studio had one of those moments of deep silence, but one quickly interrupted by Be's light laugh.

"It's great, really great!"

And then she was leaning in and on tiptoes and kissed him on the lips, and he took her by her shoulders, the statement printout still in one hand, and she leaned back in and the second kiss grew long and forceful, their tongues dancing with growing frenzy.

"Let's go to your bedroom," she said when they stepped apart, with the wink that drove him crazy.

Now he looks around at the small space, a room with monk-like furnishings. He's sitting on a slipper chair tucked into a corner, crowded against a small side table, the chair encroaching on the deck entrance door. When he's reading, he'll usually sit in one of the small armchairs in the library outside his interior door, or in the somewhat ratty old recliner tucked into the corner of his office, but because of yesterday's events, he's looking at his bedroom in a very different light.

The inviolate rule about avoiding romantic relationship with a house sharer has been broken, but it feels right. As right as his feelings can be in their mix of joy and anxiety.

He must be an idiot, but he doesn't feel like an idiot. He's head over heels; he's ecstatic, but he's worried, too. He really doesn't know that much about Be, although that seems impossible with them sharing the studio. But while they've had some great talks about art, both his and hers, she's only been in the house a half year, a bit less. Is she seeing someone? She seems to be out of the house often, but he's never thought to ask where she goes, and why would he?

Chapter 36: Playing the Cartels You're Dealt

July 14, 2035

Central casting goes through Maker's mind the minute El Escorpión walks in, flanked by tattooed men with assault rifles and strapped with pistols and knives, and he's pretty sure that's a machete he's glimpsed, but the sum of these men's tattoos pales in comparison to El Escorpión's.

Biff has hustled them downstairs, into what one might call the living room, if for no other reason than there are armchairs there, and they haven't sat but are standing, somehow knowing not to claim a seat yet. It's as if Biff is beaming instructions directly into his brain, but in reality, he's simply picking up the nonverbal cue of *Holy shit!*

El Escorpión steps across the room and with a nod takes the one upholstered armchair.

Maker jokes to himself that *he* wanted that chair, trying to dissipate some of the tension that's rippling through him, but he's producing hysteria more than calming humor.

Biff gestures for him and Jim-John to sit, and Biff and El Escorpión exchange fast Spanish. Maker doesn't catch a word. Apparently, Jim-John does, and he's rising, his hand out toward El Escorpión, but the tiniest gesture of his hand has Jim-John sit back down.

El Escorpión says something to the room and all the others except Biff and the two of them clear out. El Escorpión says something to Biff, who nods.

"We want you to understand," Biff says, and he's

speaking to Jim-John, "NOS is ours now."

What the fuck!

Jim-John, whose full and real name is John Seward, blinks but nods. El Escorpión and Biff are both keeping their eyes on the younger man. John Seward looks like he might actually cry. Bad idea. El Escorpión says something else, but he doesn't look at Biff this time.

Surprisingly, John answers. "Yes, yes, the agreed-upon routes, the destination targets, special operations."

El Escorpión says something else—something about a coyote? The guy covered in tattoos is speaking quickly and Maker finds him hard to follow.

John nods. "Yes, transport. Better cover and we'll bring in your goods and what you supply us. We understand."

Smuggling? Human trafficking? What the fuck else?

He's feeling ill. Maybe he's sweating, or noticeably more so. Calm the fuck down.

He can't stop himself from staring at El Escorpión, who says something short, but Maker doesn't catch it.

Seward tells him that all the points in the agreement are set, but then he says this in Spanish, prompted by the slightest frown on the tattooed face, or Maker thinks so, anyway.

"And NOS gets support for what we need," Seward says, using English to keep Maker in the loop but then repeating himself in Spanish.

El Escorpión flicks one hand, dismissively.

Biff is the one to respond. "When there's time, opportunity, we're priority, *sí*?"

Seward echoes the sentiment. "*Cuando haya tiempo,*" and then "*Aprovechar la oportunidad.*"

The man in the armchair seems to expect more.

"*Si, la prioridad,*" Seward adds, pointing at El Escorpión.

The tattooed man is addressing Biff, who replies, and Maker can't follow much, except he catches *Maker* and he sits up straighter.

El Escorpión is grinning. "*Fabricante,*" he says with a

nod toward Maker.

Maybe his current *nom de guerre* is less clever than he'd thought. He's wondering exactly what the tattooed man means, but he is a fabricator, that's one of the things he loves to do. He's rethinking his prior enthusiasm.

El Escorpión stands up and gestures toward the front door. Biff tells them to come along, and El Escorpión's hand is at the small of Maker's back, pushing him forward, almost a caress. His confusion is rising, but it gets worse when a man gets pulled out of one of the cars, men dragging the half-stumbling man, one of the men covering them with a pistol, and when they have the man standing between them in the middle of the compound, forty feet away, each arm held by them, El Escorpión barks out something and another man brings out a modest sized box. The cardboard top is opened and there's the snap dragon.

El Escorpión nods, and Maker picks it up, and then the detonator, waiting for further instructions.

These come from Biff, behind them, who's been speaking with Seward almost non-stop since they've come outside. "Try it out, my friend. Go, place this on the man's arm." He points to the three men some distance away, the fourth man, with the pistol, standing relaxed nearby.

He doesn't have to guess who or what they mean. He holds up a finger, *wait*, and he reaches into the box and grabs the small radio detonator, then shows El Escorpión the safety, pointing out the safe position and then the armed, mimicking an explosion. He makes sure the detonator is on safe, waiting for El Escorpión to nod his understanding.

"Keep it on safe until I'm clear," he says to Biff, who translates for El Escorpión, who laughs, clapping Maker on the shoulder, and then the grin disappears and he gestures for him to get on with it.

Maker finds himself walking faster than he'd like, the pumping adrenaline spurring him forward. He gets to the three men, and he tries not to look at the man being held, but the man's terror-crazed eyes, showing white, are unavoidable as he gestures to the man's arm, then he holds his own out, the one that holds the snap dragon.

With some struggling that includes one of the men striking the terrified man's head, the man's arm is outstretched and Maker takes a breath and snaps the copper shell links on the man's arm, up near the elbow. He manages not to gulp his relief, the device snapping just about perfectly.

He walks back to El Escorpión, and halfway he passes Biff. Biff's asking the man questions, but Maker's ears are staticky and he can't make anything out.

Seward steps next to him, on the other side of El Escorpión. "*Cuentas extraterritoriales,*" he tells him. "Something about offshore accounts, and now asking for routing numbers I think."

The conversation goes on. Biff has a pad of paper out, jotting notes, and then there are more questions, and then Biff pulls out a phone and is working that for several minutes.

The man between the two others now seems to have calmed down some. El Escorpión calls a man over and says something to him and the man starts off toward one of the buildings on the far side of the compound. Biff gestures toward them, holding the phone up and the other hand is thumbs-up, and then he's back talking to the man.

Seward leans forward and then straightens back up, talking low to Maker. "Something about the guy's family, I'm pretty sure."

Biff's walking back toward them. The two men who had held the man are behind him. The man stays where he is, but there are two men, each many yards away, both with rifles still trained on the man.

Biff says to El Escorpión, "*Vale. Todo está bien.*"

All good. Even Maker knows that.

El Escorpión pulls the radio detonator out from a pocket and thumbs the safety.

"*Alto!*" Maker shouts. That's not even the word, but

he's busy pointing at some of the men, gesturing to them to move back.

El Escorpión squints at him

"*Espere,*" Seward and Biff say almost simultaneously, and they're taking some steps backward and El Escorpión is now grinning, stepping back too, with Maker right at his heels.

"*Aqui*?" El Escorpión asks after they've gotten much closer to the safe house walls, and Maker nods, turning, screwing his face up in agony, and El Escorpión presses the radio button on the detonator and the blast staggers Maker. When he looks it takes him a moment to make out where the man is, a dark shape on the ground.

El Escorpión's grin looms. The tattooed man gestures for Maker to follow him, already stepping toward the blast area.

The body seems intact for a moment, the leg and side facing them still clothed, but when he walks around with El Escorpión, he sees that the other arm is gone, up to the man's shoulder, and much of the side of the torso is open. A large amount of the man's liver is visible past some jagged ribs, and part of the lung. He stares, frozen. He throws up.

El Escorpión laughs and claps him on the shoulder, saying something to Biff, and then the man he sent to the other house is back, with an insulated bag, and El Escorpión is pulling out some wrapped things and tears one open.

"Popsicle?" he says, offering Maker an orange one.

Chapter 37: The Meat of It

July 18, 2035

Cynthia is riding along in an EV from MMEAT's small fleet, this one new enough and she practiced enough to let the car pay close attention to the road. Except she's about to leave Route 7, passing out of Stockbridge to take the shortcut that connects to Route 183 down to Housatonic.

Route 183, which is a narrow two-lane highway that follows the Housatonic River, is both too curvy and too narrow and tests her faith in the driving assist functions of the car she's in, so she toggles to full manual as she turns on to Glendale Middle Road. Within moments she's going past a golf course that sees a bit too frequent flooding, from today's glance of a recent aftermath, at any rate.

It's pretty, this drive, and the leaves are completely grown out and already taking on the dusty tone that reminds her that summer is starting to show its age. If she takes the time to pay attention, anyway. She's concentrating on approaching traffic as she stops, looks both ways, and turns on to 183, more country lane than highway.

She's meeting up with Jimmy at his dad's house, the second time in two weeks, her coming from a week up in Middlebury, where MMEAT still is headquartered, and Jimmy, out from Boston, where the two of them have a top-floor apartment on Comm Ave, the four flights of stairs providing regular aerobic workouts when she's there.

Jimmy's gentle complaints about her apartment in

Middlebury have started up again. It may be time to listen, and anyway, she's feeling *small potatoes* these days about her need to be on site, but that's fine. MMEAT is going gangbusters these days and the more people—and farms and food chains and restaurants—get involved, the less she's needed on site, even if she is now director of the whole shebang. She's hired great administrative staff, and in the last two years, the effort to encourage farms to consider regenerative agriculture has been gathering momentum. The campaign to get the people to eat less meat and explore cultured meat substitutes has also been advancing.

She's reluctant to shift her focus where she must shift it, and that is toward direct political work. Lobbyist is not how she's always thought of herself, not at all.

She's due down in Washington next week, a round of meetings already scheduled. MMEAT is pushing for inclusion in the carbon credit clearinghouse, and on the regenerative agriculture side of the ledger, there remains strong resistance. They have to argue about sequestration measurements, and those measurements aren't yet adequately systematized, which is why she's heading down, to rally funds to develop metrics and means, but she's not looking forward to this new role. She and Jimmy will overnight in Davin's Airbnb, otherwise offsetting any cost by providing him with a tax-deduction. It's not like they're taking business from him, unlikely as it is he would have guests to sign on to an odd two-day gap in reservations. She's glad of this gap because the air frame mattress that he's put up in his office makes for difficult sleep, not that she'll tell him that.

It will be nice seeing Davin and nice to provide receipt for the tax-deductible donation of the apartment furnished to them on official MMEAT business. This is one perk of working for a 501(c)(3).

The next morning, while Jimmy's visiting with his dad, she'll be attending a round of meetings with some South County farming organizations in the hopes of getting as many of the near dozen on board as possible, so that when she's pitching the right NGOs and the Feds, this backing will send a stronger message. She's due to visit two local farming operations, too, and both are proponents of regenerative agriculture, and it will be helpful to lay eyes on these operations so the concept isn't so abstract. She's been in intensive study mode, and while she has long understood the tenets of regenerative agriculture, she now finally feels confident to hold a conversation on the subject.

One of these farms is in Great Barrington, and she's had some solid contact with the owner. She suspects the owner there may be better at publicity than actual carbon reduction, but then, the whole point of the fundraising is to support the development of techniques to assess the carbon sequestration, something that's proven to be quite a challenge, to date. The other farm she'll be visiting tomorrow is in Sheffield, and it will be her first in-person contact with that operation. There's been email and some videoconferencing with the Sheffield people already.

She's meeting the executive director of ReGen Berkshires tonight at the farm-to-table restaurant that's enjoyed a long run, but maybe that has to do with its name: Farm Table. She knows the place, has been out for drinks there with a couple of Davin's young house sharers. She remembers one such time, especially, since that was back when there was likely a local threat to her, as she'd been told while rather tipsy, only after they'd all returned to the house. And just two weeks ago, it was nice seeing Deidre.

She hasn't thought about that time in 2026 for quite a while, but she's not surprised to be thinking of it now, that whole mess of a time when she was a person of interest in the killing of her boss, a killing she actually witnessed, causing her to flee. How many years ago *was* that? As she's passing the small hydroelectric power plant off on the right, nestled into the river, she counts out the years. Nine years ago. A lot has changed since then.

The best change was her building a life with Jimmy, but

she's also done well at MMEAT.

When she helped start the nonprofit spin-off of Climate Progress, the penetration of meat substitute products had barely registered in the market, not even breaking past the 1 percent mark. These days, market penetration is closing in on a double-digit presence for meat substitutes or, as MMEAT most recently prefers to call this category, *smart meat*.

She frowns. This latest effort hasn't been gaining enough traction and is the third attempt at general category branding. Even the several biggest producers seem cool to it. Fake meat, lab meat, 3D-printed meat, cultured meat, none have caught on, and the public remains too easily confused about exactly what this type of product is, despite some recent sales growth.

Really Smart Meat, she thinks, frowning. The concept of meat not from butchered animals remains a hard sell, cell culture produced through fermentation processes being a puzzling concept. She's been to countless labs in the last three years and, increasingly, actual production facilities, too, and even she still has some fuzziness in her understanding of how the processes work.

It's complicated. She finds it fascinating, too, but what makes her an enthusiastic booster is that she truly loves the products now widely available. She's never been a fan of Impossible Burgers or Beyond Meat, not that these types of meat substitutes aren't an improvement over more traditional products, typically bean-based or mushroom-based or some sort of soy. These products just aren't that good of an improvement, although she's long appreciated what those companies have been trying to do with animal husbandry greenhouse gas reduction.

She needs patience, and that has never been one of her strengths. She feels good about her recent onboarding of a new assistant director who is aiming at restaurant adoption of synthetic meat, arguing that this remains one of the most effective ways to introduce the product category.

Real Meat is real meat is the other tagline they're testing against Smart Meat. They've been AI generating seemingly endless versions of messaging. *I love meat, Real Meat* is one of those versions, which continues with some version of *and I love my planet, too* or *Climate change is real, too*. The AI close-up images of the *Real* Meat dinners are impressively staged like photos from cookbooks or in-action videos, with the people featured in them eating with gusto. Still, they've decided to bring in food photographers because the AI images, while impressive, didn't seem quite real enough.

Food porn. This is a running joke around the office. Well, except for among the vegans or strict vegetarians. She's had that discussion with her newest assistant director, when the issue of cooking traditional meat and *Smart* Meat on the same grills gets raised by the purists. Her assistant director is determining whether this is a bug or a feature. *Real Meat* or *Smart Meat* or whatever catches on for the product category is actual meat cells, just muscle and fat cells that have never been part of an actual animal, printed up on special nutritionally positive matrixes, and for the life of her, tastewise, there's no real difference. Which is fine with her. It's a good sign that *Real Meat* comes across as no big deal.

What's more important to her is that she's a big deal to Jimmy, and he to her, and that still feels good, even though they've now been together for almost a decade.

Jimmy met Cyn's twin brothers early on, and they liked him immediately, which was a good thing because it was becoming clear that she and Jimmy liked each other and, in fact, were kind of crazy for each other, even if Jimmy had taken to calling her his *Old Lady* during or shortly after that first weeklong trip on the Green Mountain Trail.

She laughs. This *Old Lady* tag was Jimmy's way of getting back at her for her taunts about how out of shape he was for a big guy, barely handling more pack weight than her. She was two years older and proved far better on the trail.

That had been a very good week indeed, and she, to this day, remains somewhat shocked about how intimate it had been in every way and their comfort with that, with the stinky socks and limited hygiene, the trailside relieving, the bouts of trail mix gas in the middle of the night in the small tent and the double sleeping bag they shared. And the sex. Her fantasy of great bear sex was improved by the reality, for all the clumsiness in the tent. Maybe because of the clumsiness in the tent. She smiles, thinking about it. Sex had never really been fun for her, or funny, before.

And the math wasn't wrong, Jimmy figuring out that he was a month shy of being two years younger, and it's *just the facts, ma'am,* and this wasn't and isn't an issue for him or her, at least outside of his wisecracking.

She'd met up with Jimmy in Boston, a few weeks before that backpacking trip, back when they were both being interviewed, or rather reinterviewed, or quite possibly re-reinterviewed, ad infinitum. That time this took place at the FBI Boston field office, just another odd experience, shocking in its tedium and not at all like anyone raised on crime drama would have expected. Jimmy had come east for two job interviews, scheduled around the FBI's attention.

Real Meat, she decides, making a mental note to cancel further market testing, going with her gut. She's passing the Monument Mills, still mostly empty after decades. Nothing looks changed, really, and she's taking the turn and climbing up Davin's weirdly steep driveway, glad to see what must be Jimmy's rental up in the parking area.

"Home again, home again, jiggety jig."

Chapter 38: Holy Tornado

July 20, 2035

Fletch has felt impending doom from the very start of her day, with the check on weather and the red band alert for high wind warnings. Reading the details of the forecast did nothing to ease her concern, the forecast being for a line of thunderstorms building up against the high-pressure system that has been capping the heatwave continuing across lower New England and New York and now out past Detroit. New York City remains in triple digits and there's some potential for the conflicting fronts to break the weather pattern, but projections break even on whether today's weather racing toward Massachusetts and upper New England will disrupt the multi-state dome of high pressure and deliver an end to the heatwave.

Throughout the morning, she has cleaved to her pessimism of the last few weeks as more people have come from the city into the Berkshires to escape the heat and cause her problems. She's looking over today's report from the police department. Next to that printout lies this morning's tally of citizen complaints to town hall. This list has only grown, except for that one day following the young man's death, but the complaints have been ever more frequent since. One of her afternoon meetings is to get an update on the case, and her last scheduled item for today is an interview with an online news agency out of New York.

She scolds herself for drawing a blank on the name of

the dead man, but she'll look this up when she gets a moment. Not remembering is disrespectful. Having this sort of senior moment regarding the name of the person recently killed in Great Barrington could come across as callous, and therefore a political liability. It's awful having to think this way, but she's learned over the years it can be the little things that possess an outsized power to create problems.

Nothing little about this to him, though. This gets her thinking about the five young men from here and the potential life-ruining consequences. Timothy Walloch. That's his name.

She sighs. She has a lot to do today, including her now-expected calls and emails in answer to some of the complainants, but Sullivan, who also serves as the town's public safety liaison, wants an answer about what messaging, if any, should be sent out via the town's alert system, and whether this should merely emphasize and repeat the National Weather Service's current severe weather watch.

She knows that at some point the heat wave to the south of them will break and the bump in population here in South County will moderate, but now there's this weather watch to claim her attention. If you don't like New England weather, just wait five minutes. Hopefully fast-changing political weather is equally likely. The sooner the heatwave smothering New York City is over, the sooner she can get back to the more normal worries about parking and regular public safety and taxes. There's a meeting scheduled for this afternoon with the town counsel about potential civic and criminal enforcement strategies should the waves of surplus visitors continue for a while more.

She takes a moment to email Sullivan back with her recommendation, which is to use the town's announcement platform to make sure as many people as possible know about the existing weather watch. She's barely begun composing the email when she gets an alert on her screen that the watch has been upgraded to an alert, and a moment later Kara tells her Sullivan's on the phone, and he's telling her about the status change, and then there's the echo of an alert notification that ghosts her own. She looks at the update, alarmed, and now they both are talking about the shift to tornado alert.

She asks Sullivan to issue this update immediately and she hangs up, but she's barely had time to push her chair back and take a breath when the emergency tone on her phone sounds, and sure enough, there's the update. She stares at the text for a moment.

> TORNADO ALERT in effect until 1:00 PM EST, July 20.
>
> The National Weather Service has issued a Tornado Warning, at 9:48 a.m. for the following areas: Northwest Connecticut, including all of Litchfield County; Berkshire County, Massachusetts, south of Pittsfield; western portions of Hampden County, Massachusetts, including the towns of Chester, Blandford, Tolland, Granville, Russell, and Montgomery; and the southwestern portion of Hampshire County, Massachusetts, including the towns of Huntington, Westhampton, Easthampton, Southampton, and Northampton.
>
> HAZARD: Damaging Tornado and hail possible, with lightning and heavy rains.
>
> SOURCE: Radar indicates conditions for wind shear and rotational development.
>
> IMPACT: Flying debris will be dangerous to

> those caught without shelter. Mobile homes may be damaged or destroyed. Damage to roofs, windows, and vehicles will occur. Tree damage is likely.
>
> PRECAUTIONARY/PREPAREDNESS ACTIONS: TAKE COVER NOW! Move to a basement or an interior room on the lowest floor of a sturdy building. Avoid windows/Stay away from windows. If in a mobile home, a vehicle, or outdoors, move to the closest substantial shelter and protect yourself from flying debris.

The skies, already dark, grow darker, and a sudden crack of lightning makes her jump. She goes to her window. Thunderclouds are pushing northeastward over the town, and gusting winds whip tree limbs back and forth, the growing frenzy throwing leaves and small branches into flight. More lightning and close-by thunder and the skies darken further behind the sudden curtains of rain.

Her computer sounds another emergency tone.

Chapter 39: If a Tree Falls in the Forest and Nobody Hears

Midday, Saturday, July 21, 2035

Davin looks at the backyard and notes that the wind hasn't damaged the sunscreens. They'll have held because these screens were new last year, with several years left to them before the UV damage weakens the poly fabric too badly. Some of the plants, including the better part of a row of tomatoes, have been pushed down by the wind, but he's already determined that there's little actual damage beyond the need to re-stake some of them.

There are branches and leaves still scattered about, but cleanup is straightforward. A tree near the end of the property has come down, and he'll need to cut away some of its limbs, but nothing pressing. All of his careful water redirects, swales, and drainage systems did their jobs, although the main drain outlet just past his bedroom deck has created something of an erosion channel on one side of the landscaped beam-and-flagstone steps down to the front yard.

Deidre's tent did fine through yesterday's storm, and he made sure to check this first after the storm passed in the early afternoon. A couple of her anchors failed, but she has so much in there weighing it all down that there's been little change in position. The studio's bump-up framing likely offered some protection from the wind, too. She slept there last night *like a baby,* she mentioned before driving away early.

From all that he's read, Great Barrington has been lucky with the storm, although the Market 32 supermarket has taken damage, as have several other structures near or in the same plaza. The unstable system of low pressure descended from the front coming in from the northwest, clashing with the high-pressure front that was keeping the city and other parts southward under the heatwave. Looking at the weather recreation graphics this morning, it looks like the two weather systems collided, with the unstable system bouncing off the other.

Except, of course, the wind shear and sudden updraft created rotation conditions, and a tornado formed a short way past Great Barrington's downtown's east end. The tornado followed northward, east of the river, damaging the shopping plaza, shredding some roofing and tearing off some solar panels before skipping along Blue Hill Road toward the elevation to the east, not quite cresting Three Mile Hill before skidding back down toward the river. This tornado, which has been classified as an F1 after some debate, was only one of several along different parts of the weather front's path. The one in Great Barrington knocked down a swath of trees near Three Mile Hill, then shifted slightly westward, bringing it to Monument Mountain's summit before petering out over the wetlands of Agawam Brook on the other side. The tornado never got to the Stockbridge town line.

His own house and property have been largely spared because the tornado stayed east of the secondary western ridge of the Monument Mountain structure known as Flag Rock Ridge, flowing along the ridge of Peeskawso Peak and up and over the mountain. Still, he appreciates how close his house was to being damaged, Flag Rock standing proud up the high slope of the westernmost side of Monument Mountain, little more than a half mile away and five hundred feet higher in elevation. Not spared, however, was a group of free campers on the southern face of Monument

Mountain, where a wide belt of trees was knocked down as the tornado climbed upward toward the peak.

Yesterday afternoon, he was among the first to learn about the camp and its ordeal, with two people coming out from the woods in back of his house, seeking help, and he had called it in after making sure he could give useful directions to the rescue services. There remained hours of daylight, and the sky had cleared completely, so he got into his hiking boots and sprayed on some permethrin for the ticks. He headed back out with the two young people, a man named Victor and a woman named Vicky, which, of course, reinforced his sense that they were a couple, but he learned otherwise quickly enough.

He offered a number of the campers emerging from the fallen trunks and heaps of foliage the use of his backyard for the evening fast approaching, and he helped search among the branches for scattered bits of kit.

Seventeen people followed him back to the house.

Chapter 40: Robbie Rolls Over

Saturday evening, July 21, 2035

Robbie Gray feels like a kid. He feels like he's skipping school, although, of course, there's no school, but it's a mixed feeling. There hasn't been school for decades, of course, but the hovering presence of authority and obligation is gone, and the sense of freedom is intoxicating. He feels like a kid hanging out in a secret hideout, which is a few back rooms of one of the many mill buildings in the Monument Mills complex in Housatonic, mostly empty, a mix of giant stand-alone structures and adjoining smaller buildings like the one he's in. These rooms are in the back building, away from the street view, and kept dark at night with windows that are covered by a bewildering assortment of blankets and comforters, dusty, ratty. About a third of the windows that look out back have thin sheets of plywood nailed up on the inside. Some of these windows would once have looked out on other buildings when the mill complex was at its height, but now there's just open space, rubble strewn and with patches of weeds and small saplings.

He hunkered down here during yesterday's storm, but apart from some rain driven by wind gusts through old rattling windows, the old building he's in survived just fine. About the worst of it was the soaking of one of the makeshift blackout curtains. The power failed, but that wasn't much of an impediment, since Benjamin had several battery lamps, and they didn't need much light anyway, spending the storm hours getting high and having sex. Much like today.

There's plenty of other, less exciting feelings in his new situation, too, including that he has to think about getting a job, although not in any pressing way. His work on the book about the Great Barrington Mohicans, of which he still hasn't decided whether it's a work of fiction or non-fiction, isn't going to pay rent. Not that rent here is pressing. He moved in several days after leaving his house, but the space is a squat. This is hardly a solid arrangement, even as enamored as Benji may be at the moment.

This also does nothing to help him avoid his sense of being in trouble. It's not just the trouble that comes from blowing up your life, not just from not being sure where he might be sleeping tomorrow. This is trouble that can come from the end of a gun.

He keeps reassuring himself that it's all in his head.

The adult part of him, the part he's been in the process of blowing up for months now, has been feeling in trouble, and well before Marion caught him with the woman, the yoga pal of his wife. The sex was unmemorable, as was her name.

She was the third person he'd started fucking, before being caught. It was as if he simply woke up one morning and was screwing around, but the first circumstance, the older woman, Clare, who he met at a Mahaiwe Theater function he attended with Marion in the spring, had asked him for his number right there, in front of Marion, saying she would text him about his writing, that she was trying to write, too, and she invited him to her house a few days later—a very nice house, as it turned out. Way better than Benjamin's squat.

Clare was far wealthier than he'd first assumed, although it later made sense, considering it was a Mahaiwe event. The house tour she offered him that day was of great interest to him, of course, but what proved of greater interest was her placing her hand on his chest, there in her bedroom, telling him how beautiful he was, running her hands over him. He was surprised he didn't feel embarrassed or self-conscious, since these were his typical reactions when some woman might allude to his looks. He'd developed a long habit of ignoring such comments, dismissing them as politeness or matronly, but something else happened that day.

He snorts. Of course, being in the woman's bedroom was hardly the typical situation. Not hardly. They had fucked all afternoon. He went down on her after the first time he came in her, and she grasped his head, one ear had her nails behind it, her other hand in his hair. He hadn't even known he had that hunger. He shakes his head. This is not true, not really.

What he hadn't known was that he'd been holding his breath for so long, for years now, married to Marion. Was this always the case, right from the start? A marital quid pro quo neither of them acknowledged or, more likely, ever understood?

He sighs. He's been casting about for weeks now, out of control, and this is, in its way, much more familiar to him, even if he hasn't considered it for years now. His early life in Worcester was one of abandon. Not one of hustling, just good times, and then one of his friends worried he'd gotten AIDS, which Robbie was confident, at least on the outside, wouldn't be the end of the world, not with the treatments that were emerging, seemingly by the day.

But he had crashed with fear and dread. He did get tested, and the results were negative, and then two weeks of celibacy later, he got tested again, with the same welcome result. But the fear never left him. A year later he met Marion and they married before that year turned.

But this hunger now is a hunger long ignored, long thought gone, long repressed, a life he had put away. Sitting here in a half-furnished squat in a Housatonic mill building, he's finally clear about this hunger, and he welcomes it.

He's waiting for Benjamin to return from what passes as a bathroom in this place, down the dim hall lit with a battery LED lantern, a small washroom with a doorless toilet stall, a stained urinal, a tiny, begrimed sink, a blotched silver mirror. It once had been a restroom for whoever made whatever in this building, something for floor workers, maybe, or more likely front office people, since where Benjamin's rooms are looks like old office space.

He'd ejaculated over Benjamin's naked chest, Benjamin trying not to swallow, which made it all the messier.

He feels another erection suggesting itself, but he ignores this. Benji had gotten angry at the mess of it all and probably won't want to fuck around now.

Although he could go down on him. Show him how to do it right. He looks around for Benji's bag of dope, knowing that the thirty-something-year-old man is hornier when high, but his thoughts shift, his heart beating faster. He's again thinking of what he saw those weeks ago while waiting for Benjamin to show up, to get back from whatever it is exactly he does at the Co-op, running much later than usual—some inventory thing.

It was glimmering dusk, like now, the stars starting to peek. The lights inside the squat were off as he stared out the window at nothing, simply drifting.

And then the sole door at the back of the adjoining building had burst open and he was looking at something that resolved itself as three arguing men, three men half tucked in the doorframe, with light being cast past them from inside.

The shouting had flared, a sudden crescendo, one man walking further out from the door, turning back around, his arms out in front of him, hands set as if miming against an invisible wall, the two others following. One was shouting, cursing, the language Spanish, but off somehow, maybe Portuguese, and the curses were unintelligible and snarled, but the gun that fired into the first man was completely clear.

That one shot still rings loudly in his thoughts.

He'd stood in the dark room, transfixed. The horror of

what he'd just seen seemed artificial, but then he worried he was too close to the window and possibly visible in the last of the fading light and he'd stepped back into safety. But he kept watching. The other man, the one without the gun, began shouting at the shooter, and then took to swatting him about the head a few times, still cursing.

"Fucked up, man," the other man said after he stopped his blows. The English words were clear, the accent no hindrance.

Two more men came rushing out through the door. The light from the doorway illuminated the scene, a tableau he can still sharply see, and as he watched, he sensed the other man was in charge, the shooter someone under him. The boss told the two others something and they went off, back with a pickup truck within moments.

The shooter was told something, and he went back into the building, returning with a tarp. Three of them maneuvered the body onto the tarp as the other man, the boss, watched, and then they manhandled the clumsily wrapped body into the bed of the truck.

The other man was clear in the light, not tall, but with wide shoulders, maybe a weightlifter—that had crossed his mind at the time. Hair dark and tightly cropped, a strong chin, dark eyes, dark brows, but the nose oddly aquiline, off center. He'd gotten a good view of the three others, too.

He can't recall any detail about the dead man other than the posture as he was shot, the position of his hands.

And then he'd spotted the young man Rory, a boy, really, in the scrub trees lining the river, well beyond the end of the mill building from which the men had emerged. Rory was looking on, observing it all in the shadows, a dim, silent apparition. Rory, the person he and Benjamin buy drugs from.

He looks around, taking himself away from these thoughts and the underlying unease that what he saw still produces in him. He's struggling with going to the police because that will involve speaking with Marion. Getting involved in a crime case will blow things up and he does feel bad about hurting her.

Even worse than the threat of discovery is that any prospect of involving himself will hurt him. These last two months he's been feeling free. He's been feeling like he's finally living his life, and getting involved, going to the police, well, that's trouble.

Benjamin's coming down the hall. The dim light behind him puts him in partial silhouette, but he can see that Benjamin's shorts are hanging low, one hand pulling on the waistband, and as he comes into the light Robbie sees that Benjamin's penis and testicles are hanging over the front band, penis enlarged, swaying as he walks.

Robbie snorts. Guess he's not so mad about the mess.

Chapter 41: A Game of Four-Dimensional Psychic Chess

July 22, 2035

The first email Davin reads this morning in his office is a reply from Jeannie Louise Smith, responding to one of his regular check-ins. These days he thinks of Jeannie Louise, or JL as he's become accustomed to calling her, as a friend, or something close to it, although the relationship continues to have something of a fraught side to it, too, like when getting her to meet deadlines.

From the very start, she's seen her contributing to *Berkshire Interactive* as more option than obligation. He can't really blame her, though, since the fees she gets from *BI* are okay but hardly great, especially compared to the sort of assignments she's enjoyed for years, running pieces in *real* publications. Even her newsletter, or whatever such things are called these days on bitbytes, is producing better income, she's told him, although she didn't mention just how much income that may be. Without the free subscription she gave him for *RE:CC,* he wouldn't read any of it, and given its high level of technical vocabulary and arcane political and policy critiques, he's still not reading all that much of it, free or not.

He's still expected to corral her work for *Berkshire Interactive,* though. This ongoing duty is something of a grandfathered one, and given that she's almost always busy with professional work that pays, or pays much better, anyway, he's often hard-pressed to press her too hard. Still, despite his shift in responsibilities toward editorial rather than platform, babysitting her has been more a matter of repeatedly readjusting schedules and deadlines.

At least that was the case until last year, when her regular contribution became "Whether Climate Change or Weather," the output of climate modeling she regularly follows, but applied hyper-locally, regularly updating climate change attribution of the local weather.

Hyper-locally. He's always liked that term, even if he didn't coin it, not when it comes to the type of newspaper—*hyperlocal information platform*—that he's been instrumental in setting up for Alicia Soares, the owner-publisher-editor.

He's proud of the sorts of features they've developed together, but of late he's especially gratified by bringing forward "Whether Climate Change or Weather." He's far from clear if JL plays any role in the AI platform that models complex attributions, but she's connected enough to have access, or at least enough to regularly update the "Whether Climate Change or Weather" index.

During Jimmy and Cyn's visit, Jimmy explained how important this attribution capability is, and that it's likely that this ongoing project will be increasingly important for at least some of the climate court cases going forward. Jimmy tried to explain, anyway, but the two had to get going early enough this morning, and he remains hazy on the concept.

The fact that he can't come up with the right description—*AI system* or *platform* or whatever is the right word—is more than clear enough evidence that Jimmy hasn't gotten much of anything through to his level. As best Davin understands it, the challenge has been that in such complex systems as weather and climate, determining causal connections between extreme weather events and climate change has been too hard, but with the new AI modeling system, causality now enjoys higher confidence. His son explained that, as yet, the one-event, one-climate attribution consistency remains elusive, but that the system's sufficient statistical confidence is gaining ground in court cases. His clearest understanding is that Jimmy seems to think this is a big step forward.

He's got a couple of things to do in his office, but he's up out of his chair, pacing. He's hoping he'll get to his studio, but this gets him thinking about his years of work for Alicia, which started up not long after coming out of COVID, the original contract work gained when the divorce was already underway.

Back then, he hoped to spend more time in his recently built art studio, the bump-up roof portion with all the small windows that he now finds himself looking at from his office window on the second floor of his house. The structure was built into the same slope the house had been built into a hundred-some years ago, the house which he rebuilt, more or less, making the old Greek revival duplex an energy-efficient, draft-free home for Gwen and he and their son, Jimmy, who, at the time of the move out of Cambridge, had been going into ninth grade and then off to college as the marriage was unraveling. The studio, the last big building project, is mostly underground, its green roof half is on the same level as the second floor of the house, which, because of the slope, is ground level on the east length. The green roof is covered by what he likes to think of as the terrace, where a bit of lawn, on which Deidre's tent now resides, and bluestone pavers run along the length of the second floor living room with its French doors.

The purchase of the property was a bad choice, he's long concluded in retrospect. The renovation work had been exhausting and long running, and that was before he finally got around to excavating a big chunk of hillside and pouring the studio's insulated concrete forms. All the while, he'd kept up with his work as consultant and analyst on content management and other varieties of digital content technologies. His intention to escape such work was part of the motivation for his move out to Housatonic, but that didn't exactly work. He made an effort to build his consulting work more locally, working independent of the small consultancy he'd joined some years back, but the only real victory was with Alicia, the intense younger woman who remained determined to make her editorial mark in the Berkshires, especially after losing out as editor in chief of *The Berkshire Record*, the last independent weekly, sold to a new owner after all her hard work building readership and staff. Almost as soon as Davin met with her about platform specifications for developing an online version of *Record*, she was out of the job, the first to be laid off by the new owner.

Then COVID, and then the divorce consumed him, but as he learned later, Alicia's own life course had also changed radically, with her husband's death. Her husband had been quite successful as a day trader, or so Davin's gleaned over the years. Alicia was left with something of a small fortune. She recontacted him, and before long the new platform capabilities were being defined and then he'd managed the RFP process. The combination of template-driven content ingestion and a robust ad tracking system had been the right choice for the online... What's the term? Hyperlocal information platform.

He'd only signed up for the scoping and setup of the platform, but somehow Alicia kept him interested and open to more and more work with *South County Interactive*. The divorce was an economic factor then, too, and he's scrambled for years to knock back the mortgage, using his big house—bought out from Gwen—to take in house sharers to keep him mostly on the plus side of resources, although a baker's dozen of years back, his involvement with the interactive newspaper had begun at the worst of his years of financial worry. His biggest income still comes from his work for *Berkshire Interactive*. His savings have grown, albeit slowly, and now he's getting his social security and is on Medicare.

He looks at the grass growing against the studio's bump-up and the front railing that keeps people from stepping off the green roof onto his studio parking slab below. Where he's set up the tent for Deidre, it's close to the house and gives her good access to his second-floor bathroom. After some consideration, he'd decided not to put the inconvenience on the house sharers, and besides, the tent won't be there long.

Beyond the tent, he notices, this grassy area is long overdue for a weed-whacking edge trim.

While his art income remains modest, he's had the last couple of years brushing the ten-thousand-dollar mark. Well, eight thousand, nine hundred-something, last tax filing. The year before that had been a good one, just over the ten-thousand-dollar mark. This year's sales income will largely depend on the two shows he's lined up for. He still doesn't have any ongoing gallery representation.

He continues his role in the ongoing management and development of the *Berkshire Interactive* platform, although now his contribution is mainly getting the right contractors to implement upgrades and tweaks. However, his other work has expanded. Within months of getting the then *South County Interactive* platform up and running, he was writing stories, and then, somehow, without his exactly meaning to, he'd taken to helping Alicia with more and more editorial work, and this continues. The work's enjoyable, except for pressing deadlines, and he especially likes serving as town reporter, covering the usually boring Selectboard meetings and the like, but it makes him feel more connected in the community, and that's a plus.

One regular irritant has been working with JL, and not because she's lousy or lackadaisical with what she does, but just the opposite. Alicia was lucky to get her attention, never mind her work, considering her national reputation—*international,* really—a reputation that has only grown stronger over the years. With his own odd and demanding amalgam of work—wearing different hats with *Berkshire Interactive,* including platform expansions, and his writing and editorial work—he's more sympathetic to JL's workload, maybe even empathetic. Also, admiring and a bit intimidated, too.

They run a lot of stories these days about climate change, or more about climate action, really. Massachusetts and the Northeast have been productive in clean electricity build-out, although sometimes there's still opposition to a solar farm, here or there. Last year there was a stink about siting batteries too close to the middle school, where the adjacent new solar fields would more conveniently tie into storage, but that problem has been resolved. They've also run a series of stories on the new push for hydroelectric, but often the dam restoration happening along the Housatonic is built more for flood catchment and control than for power generation. Still, with the new class of in-flow stream turbines emplacements, the extra generation was an easy sell.

Corralling her these days no longer feels like a full-time job. Her "Whether Climate Change or Weather" she tends to keep on schedule. She's dealing with almost automatic content, though, simply correlating the week's past weather and submitting this to the climate platform modeling to which she's got easy access. She's tried to explain it all to him, something about attribution modeling that's some part of the larger modeling platform. He still doesn't get it, but the result is that she provides a weekly index of what recent weather in the Berkshires can be attributed with high confidence to changes in the climate of the planet.

It has become a popular index and the links and visits to it are solid numbers and the ad revenue and attention traffic are strong, so Alicia is happy. The AI system JL has access to, whatever exactly that is, means that she's been able to build up other opportunities, and through *Berkshire Interactive*'s syndication engine, she's providing similar indexes for many other locales. Win-win. The balance of fees goes to the author, but Alicia, or, rather, *Berkshire Interactive*, gets a piece of every syndication transaction.

Of course Alicia loves him, considering that the

publication platform he spec'd for her had anticipated such business potential, his arguing early on that a flexible and modular content management and distribution system was the way to future-proof new business opportunities. The argument was difficult, since he had to convince her that more money spent early would save money and make money later.

"Whether Climate or Weather" makes it clear that the heat wave hovering to the south has clearly flagged climate change as causal, not that anyone needs an AI platform to inform them of this. The growing number of dead is enough to convince anyone that things are out of whack.

He sits down at his desk and checks email again and then closes his laptop. His new monitor, a forty-four-inch curved Magic Touch, blinks off automatically. He doesn't need to turn off the motion rig he often uses to hand-gesture various functions and operations when he's doing VR, because he hasn't bothered to turn the control box on this morning, nor put on his wrist sensors. He's gotten pretty good at using the rig, but he only goes as far as using it with the monitor interface. He can't get used to the glasses, with their heads-up displays that make him feel like he's always moving back from the flitting images and fast-scrolling text. He has mixed feelings about the new tech, including all the various interface options for VR, but then again, the way he uses his laptop is what he's used to, and for the most part it works just fine. Still, he gets a kick out of hand gesturing through files, and his voice transcription is unbelievably helpful, although he still reviews and changes up a lot of the AI's best guesses on what he meant to say.

He looks at the small black motion rig box he hasn't bothered to use today. It drives him crazy sometimes, being with people who are on their glasses, and it doesn't really matter if they're using VR goggles or smart glasses, although the VR headsets always make him scoot out of the way of anyone on the move with them. Old fart.

"Dagnabbit," he's saying as he stands.

He also isn't one to be on constant speaking terms with his smart phone. He still mostly brings up the number from Contacts or Recents in what he thinks of as the normal way, except he well knows he's the nonnormative user these days.

Now when he calls JL these days it might as easily be about a cocktail party coming up, or to see if she's up for a walk, or to get more about that AI Dark Money project that's so fascinating to him. She's still a tough nut to get a personal read on, but she remains interesting as hell. That Cynthia is something of a fangirl helps his own reputation with her, nor does it hurt that Jeannie Louise likes what Cynthia is doing up at MMEAT. Well, he's learned a lot.

He heads down the stairs to brew a pot of tea. In the kitchen, he waits the requisite steep time. What does he have to learn now? What does he need to figure out? He'd love to talk with someone about Be and all his feelings, but he can't quite believe this can be real.

He wants to call one of his oldest friends, one who was very helpful talking sense to him as the divorce moved forward, but the years have passed and this friend is recently diagnosed and figuring out his own more existential challenges, a matter of medicine and choices, not a matter of the heart.

Chapter 42: Community Care

Sunday, July 22, 2035

There's a Selectboard meeting tomorrow night, and while Jeannie Louise has never bothered attending any, she's thinking a lot about what is sure to be the hot topic, which is how the town can control the wave of unwanted visitors up from the city.

She's annoyed about all the negative reactions she's seeing from many of her fellow GBers in the community letters in *Berkshire Interactive*. She's annoyed enough that she's decided, to her own surprise, to attempt an editorial on the matter, not that she's bothering to ask Alicia if this is anything she might want. She can always post it as a community letter, worse case, although there her editorial might get lost, one among many. Of course, she expects this will run as a featured editorial, but whatever.

"Community Care" is her working title—and a good one at that—since its ambiguity reflects the basic question "Is a community that only cares for itself better served than a community that cares for itself and for others?" In fact, she has this as the first line. The second line is "In this age of climate change consequences, caring for all is the necessary first step to caring for ourselves."

She looks over her current draft. There's a brief primer on climate migration, citing what she realizes are too many examples, so she makes some deletions but keeps the current Pakistan-India problem. She's also keeping in the last several years' counts of North and East African deaths as migration passages are attempted, and she's included a sub-count for infants lost in this time period, but she decides to forgo any discussion of the political developments, including seemingly ever-growing electoral successes of far-right European parties.

Blood and Sand, God help us. She laughs. She means *Blood and Soil*, the far-right cry, taken from the Nazis. Blood and Sand is a cocktail and about the only thing it has in common with Nazism is that both came into existence in the 1930s. She had a Blood and Sand at one of Davin's cocktail parties, and she liked it, but she had to endure his short lecture, of course, including that it's a fussy drink to make, requiring careful measures. He was right. The one time she tried to make one, the results were disappointing. She still has the bottle of Cherry Heering, mostly full, and next time he throws a cocktail party, she must remember to bring the bottle as a gift.

She'll write up a brief summary of the situation at America's own southern borders and use that to lead into the instance of the mini climate migration that the southern Berkshires and parts of the Hudson Valley are experiencing.

She may be late to the game, considering the long-range forecasts show the New York City heatwave is finally likely to dissipate, but the topic of why anyone should care about anyone else in regard to climate change is important. She's heard of several examples of community members acting with care for the wayward New Yorkers.

One of these examples is Davin, who mentioned earlier in the day, during a phone call about assignment deadlines, that he let some of the free campers set up in his backyard, people caught up by damage from the tornado two days back, the squat camp in the woods affected by the storm, with trees down around some of the tents. At least that's what Davin told her, an eye-witness account. Good on him.

Will he be having a cocktail party for his new wards? Not likely. She would have gotten an invite.

Chapter 43: The Vagaries of Vagrancy

July 23, 2035

Davin's at another Selectboard meeting and this one is entirely about the Brooklyn Hipster Invasion, so named by some wag. He can't recall who, but it's easy enough to find out, since this showed up in a community letters section. That part of *Berkshire Interactive* has been one of the quiet successes, although this section is not at all quiet. "The Letters" is especially frenzied these days, with opinions about what to do about the current situation. The submissions range widely, both in the spectrum of opinion and level of volatility. One recent theme has been to demand the police arrest such unwanted visitors for vagrancy, or as vagabonds or tramps or, in one especially bile-filled letter, "scum." Running negative about four to one, although he hasn't done the actual count analysis.

Jeannie Louise published a surprisingly moving editorial just this morning, although he wishes she hadn't mentioned what's going on at his Housatonic House on the Hill. He's received a couple of emails from friends, and all to the positive, but still, he'd rather have run silent on this particular contribution.

My little fiefdom, feudal lord will travel. It's an old joke, a play on a black and white television show, *Have Gun, Will Travel,* but really, no one gets it anymore. Whether or not any of his new guests want to help out on the property is entirely up to them, but most of them took to cleaning up the storm's debris, and one meticulously restacked a tumbled-down portion of the firewood stack, but then, they've been free enough in using this wood, building fires for cooking and heating up water. For the latter, he's supplied an enormous enamel pot, one meant for big lobster boils and such, even though he has no idea how he came into possession of this particular thing.

He's treated them right, he's pretty sure. Didn't bring out graham crackers and marshmallows for s'mores, though, did he? No Hershey's.

It's another crowded meeting tonight and this time he's ready for it to run long, and this time he'll write down the names of public commentors. He finds himself torn between some sense of dread and boredom, although the evening may very well carry entertainment value. If people shouting one another down is entertaining.

He's printed out the agenda sheet just before leaving for downtown. The agenda items start with a report from the town counsel. He's no longer confused about where he comes down on the subject. He's got thirteen *Brooklyn Hipsters* using his backyard as an impromptu campground, with his blessing, and that's in addition to Deidre's tent, but Deidre is close to the house, and the sets of mismatched tents and tarps are out back near the east property line, behind and to the side of the garden. The very garden that one of the campers, a guy by the name of Victor, has called *Garden of Eden*, and the term for the temporary settlement has been adopted by others there. Eden. Funny, but also moving. He's getting to know some of his campers more than others, but they all seem like nice people, good kids.

The chair calls the meeting to order and then recognizes McKenzie Grant, the town counsel. After the typical preliminaries of thanking the chair, the other members, and the town manager, he begins.

"General Laws, Part IV, Title I, Chapter 272 of the Commonwealth of Massachusetts addresses issues of vagrancy, a few of the sections, anyway, but the very concept of vagrancy is inapplicable in most cases. From my conversation with Chief Sullivan—" There's enough shouts from the audience that the chair is already on the gavel, asking people to settle down. The muttering quiets. "The most directly pertinent are Sections 69 and 70, which name 'vagrants' specifically and define conditions and methods for detention or arrest, but case law clearly defines a vagrant not only as someone in public without housing, but specifically without any permanent housing at all, and that's simply not the case in most, if not all, interviews by our police. The people visiting Great Barrington have a confirmable residence, most often in the New York Metro area."

"They're sleeping on the sidewalks!" someone shouts from the audience, but Davin can't see who has interrupted, and the gavel is sharply knocked. The chair warns that any attendee deemed unruly will be removed.

"The other case law definition of vagrant is to be unemployed as well as unhoused, and again, interviews show that the vast majority of these visitors do work, including remotely," McKenzie says. "At least some are actually working while here."

There's some murmuring, but no outbursts.

"The General Laws are interesting, and there are specific means and directives for law enforcement to act, but not simply by assessing someone as a vagrant—well, I suppose there are likely unhoused unemployed people meeting conditions of vagrancy, but when one looks at case law, in practice this is an impractically high bar."

The chair asks if McKenzie's done.

"No, not yet. I'd like to address a couple of related points if I may."

He gets the nod to go ahead.

"There are many instances where police may make arrests without warrant—that means a judge needn't have issued a specific arrest warrant, but instead the police officer is within his or her statutory rights to detain or arrest, but these all apply to public infractions." He looks down at his notes for a moment. "If I may," he says, looking toward the Selectboard, "here's a good example. 'Section 59: Ordinances or regulations relating to streets, reservations, or parkways; alcoholic beverages; profanity; arrest without warrant. Whoever remains in a street or elsewhere in a town in willful violation of an ordinance or bylaw of such town or of any rule or regulation for the government or use of any public reservation, parkway or boulevard made under authority of law by any department, officer or board in charge thereof, whoever is in a street or elsewhere in a town in willful violation of an ordinance or bylaw of such town or of any rule or regulation for the government or use of any public reservation, parkway or boulevard made under authority of law by any department, officer or board in charge thereof, the substance of which is the drinking or possession of alcoholic beverage, and whoever in a street or other public place accosts or addresses another person with profane or obscene language, in willful violation of an ordinance or bylaw of such town, may be arrested without a warrant by an officer authorized to serve criminal process in the place where the offense is committed and kept in custody until he can be taken before a court having jurisdiction of the offense.'"

The room, with all its crowding, seems stunned into silence by the droning recitation, better than a gavel, but someone's saying, "Blah, blah, blah," and then someone shouts, "So make a law!" and the pounding of the chair's gavel recommences.

He himself has been growing somewhat stupefied with this recitation of law, but the sharp gavel takes any such somnambulistic leaning away. Why would McKenzie bother reading out statutes?

"The sections of law here address various situations, including"—and he glances at his notes again—"'Section 75. Whoever, without authority, removes flowers, flags or memorial tokens from any grave, tomb, monument or burial lot in any cemetery or other place of burial shall be punished by a fine of not more than one thousand dollars or by imprisonment for not more than six months,' and then there's, in effect, littering, and there is language of 'Tramps' and 'Vagabonds,' all with proscribed actions, so the police can find probable cause and make arrests, but it doesn't make sense, really, and means going in front of judges, here in District Court, and that takes time too, and even if so warranted, what? We put these people in jail up at Berkshire Correctional, which means we're now dealing with the Sheriff 's Office, questions of capacity, and, uh"—and here he pauses to look over at the board—"Uh, possibilities of civil suits against the town."

People in the audience are whispering and Selectboard members are talking among themselves, too.

McKenzie continues. "Two things to think about. Say one of these out-of-towners we're worried about drops a wrapper and refuses to pick it up, you want the police to arrest him? How about if a Great Barrington citizen does this, are we going to start arresting everyone who drops a gum wrapper?"

Someone in the audience says "Alice's Restaurant" and that's quickly followed by a quiet "Rapists, fatherfuckers, motherfuckers," and that's funny, the reference to native son Arlo Guthrie's album still a touchstone for the region. Some others are laughing and the gavel bangs once. The room again quiets.

The chair ignores the audience and addresses the town counsel. "Recommendations?"

"Arrest only with clear probable cause and only for significant illegal acts, just like you'd do anyway, for anyone breaking a law. The vagrancy angle is more trouble, not a solution, not with all the case law from the last four decades."

The chair, a red-faced man named Arnie Wetheren, is nodding, and then he announces housekeeping guidelines, including a prohibition against shouting, and a strict time limit, and adds that any of the board can call for an end to public discussion, and then he asks McKenzie to remain available for questions. His expression shifts to a grimace as he opens up the floor to public comment, some mix of despair and surrender.

Davin laughs, but just a quiet nose sniff, nothing like the full-out laugh he feels bubbling up inside. As the line for public comment grows, though, his own expression may come to mirror Wetheren's.

The first in line is his neighbor from up the street, and the man, Donny, is looking over at him, then back to the board as he begins.

"What about other agencies, like the Health Department, or Zoning?"

Davin's heart rate increases.

"I have a neighbor, he's got a bunch of these people camping in his backyard, who knows the sanitation situation, possibly dangerous. I'm just two houses up." Donny's back to looking at Davin from across the room.

Davin feels like he's radiating a blush, but keeps his expression neutral, or so he's hoping. Fuck. Asshole. Should he get up to speak? He considers the propriety of joining the public comment line. He's there as a reporter, though, so best not to, and besides, the line is already twenty people long.

He's missed some of what Donny has been saying, but fortunately, Wetheren gavels and calls time, and yet another person approaches the reluctantly released public comment podium. The comments that follow, from person after person, are very much along the same lines as Donny's, which is that *these people* think they can do anything, they're taking advantage, and they're ruining everything about the town.

Chapter 44: Pipeline to Hell

July 24, 2035

Maker and John and a third NOS member, who's given his name as Frederick, but who John more often calls Phil, are sitting in a hot trailer in Vista Del Rio trailer park right off Route 83, and Maker's asked John a couple of times already if there's been a change in protocol about using real names, but John always just shrugs. This is hardly a comfort. He's very uneasy knowing that John knows his real name is Allen Randolph. The Guides have access to this information, John has informed him. John has also mentioned a few times that if he plays along, if he does what's being asked of him, he'll be a Guide too.

Becoming a Guide is the last thing on his mind. Ever since spending those long days in the compound somewhere northeast of Mexico City, in the final safe house after the last assignment, he's finding himself thinking everything about NOS has changed, including that the cartels now expect NOS to serve them. Meeting Scorpion King, as he now thinks of the tattooed man that showed up at the compound that last day, he had carefully watched how the man acted, and the ruthlessness he saw, the cruelty, the delight, that's all plenty good reason for a bit of rethink. Not that he shares this with John. John, although shaken up by that last day before they were smuggled back into America, seems on board with the wholesale adoption of NOS into the cartels, whatever exactly the cartels are, since the different ones, once vicious enemies, seem all one now. The enemy of my enemy…

He's sitting on the double bed, in all its rattiness, while John and Frederick-Phil are up at the other end talking about, when he strains to listen, old teachers. The enemy of my enemy is stark fucking bonkers-ass crazy. The remnants of that body after snapdragon had been used… He shudders.

The cartel boss—the tattooed man—wherever on the roster he sits, that guy was baroquely evil. Maker tries to compare this to the evil of the fossil fuel companies, the executives in charge, the investors, the institutions, and that is deep evil, clearly, but with its abstract power. That evil is not close-up, not personal, not in intent, anyway. More monstrous, certainly, in scope, in its pervasive, destructive doom, but what he saw there in the compound was personal, direct. What he saw there was terrifying.

In some ways, what he's seen in Biff is scarier. Biff is smart, educated, at least in languages, but logistically, too. Biff is far more than a translator or messenger, but high up in the cartels too. Biff is the architect of the NOS conversion, or at least one of them. Has to be. This sort of operation has to be from high up. He doesn't trust Biff at all. They're not friendly acquaintances, not anymore, never were, he realizes. The friendly tone, the middle-class appearance, the show of education, that had all helped fool him, but it's a new day now. He doesn't trust their new assignment, either. It doesn't make sense, not when you look at it carefully. He's been asked to build a pipeline submarine, a tiny one, and Biff talks about new smuggling opportunities. He talks about the big aqueducts that cross the border in a dozen places, how getting this right could mean a long period of safe transfer for high-value items. He's supplied him with schematics for such aqueducts, complete with valve systems, control mechanisms, and inspection ports.

NOS has done something similar before, the LNG terminal in Southern California, arguably their biggest blow against the Machine, but pipe conveyance doesn't make sense for anything that needs volume. Biff has supplied him with the casing, and even this seems off, too thin, too likely to break up, lose seal and inundate the contents. The actual contents will come from Biff, who's due here this afternoon, but he's been given a blank that's claimed to be the same shape as the final insert. Biff claims sensors are the main inclusion so that the package can be tracked, but when he raised questions, Biff's true self finally came to the fore.

"You're not the only smart person," Biff snapped.

It wasn't what he said, though, as much as the tone of seething impatience and anger at being questioned. He didn't have to say more. What he meant came through loud and clear: *You work for me.*

Maker rubs his face with his hands, the grit of the place noticeable on his cheeks as he does so, and his hair feels stiff.

He worries about being caught, killed, or put on trial, imprisoned. He always tries to take care and stay in the fight. He'll get caught some day, but with NOS as he sees it today, this seems likely to happen sooner, not later. Now he's working for a boss, not a colleague, not a fellow fighter, not a warrior against the demise of the world. What happens to their fight?

He gets up off the bed, the two young men in front turning toward the movement. They watch as he settles himself at the makeshift worktable, a long sheet of plywood cut to a three-foot width, anchored to the wobbly dining table designed for double duty as a supplemental bed when broken down. It's a crappy work area and it must be ninety degrees or more in the trailer, the cooling system wheezing and uttering a series of small thumps every now and then.

It turns out that John and Frederick-Phil are both from the same high school, something of bosom buddies. This is what he's learned listening to them talk, and before the first three days pass trapped in this mobile home, with a barely working air conditioner, Maker now knows all about the two. This isn't wanted knowledge, but there you go. And what exactly does this mean for him?

He's finished the *fish* device. It's barely ten inches across, with a semi-oval cross section, the propulsion system an aluminum tube added to the thin metal casing with brazing, the three points of contact on the casing each a worry as he did them, concerned about piercing the thin shell with the torch as he heated up the joining metal.

He looks it over: good job. He learns a lot from these kinds of projects and now he can add brazing to his skills. After Biff shows up with the package, he'll settle it in and seal it inside with a series of small screw bolts all around the middle edges, the soft gasket hopefully keeping the water out. The propulsion tube is more for direction and orientation, since the waterflow in the pipe itself will be the main motivator, but the shape of the tube, with its small electric propeller and drag fins, will keep fish moving forward front first.

He looks at the ancient kitchen clock that belongs to the trailer, placed haphazardly above the metal entrance door, There's two hours, more or less, before they expect Biff.

Every morning, in the three days they've been here, he's corrected the time on the clock, which creeps fast almost a half hour over the course of twenty-four hours.

The instructions are that John and Frederick-Phil will use the Blazer after fish is set. They'll drive to the access road for the pipeline, a water supply pipe whose aquifer source point feeds Beyerville and water truck services but then runs all the way to the new Army base southeast of Kino Springs and across the border. Access to the new pipeline is rough, the construction road hardly there, oftentimes simply following dry washes. He's pored over Google Maps, and knows that the pipe loops west, then southwest, following contours and low hills all the way to the camp.

He draws a blank on the official name of the new base but it's already mostly referred to as Camp Oasis. Trucks and other Army vehicles come down Route 83 through Beyerville, and where they're coming from is unknown, but any such vehicle, when traveling southward, is Camp Oasis bound. The local businesses, such as they are, are thrilled with the traffic.

There's the distinctive sound of a Hummer from the close-by highway, then another one.

"Hey, you guys all set?" he calls toward the front of the mobile home trailer. Another review of their tasks makes sense, since, as best he can tell, they've been mostly trading high school stories.

Over the last two years he's been out on his own with little contact with other NOS members, and since the Mexico City operation, he's shocked by how much things seem changed in the organization, the organization for which he's supposed to be thrilled to be named a Guide.

Even the hits the cartels helped them with, with great intel, good weapons, and a solid action plan, turned out to be as much for the cartels as a blow against Big Oil—much more. Just what is NOS really these days? John casually mentioned that the cartels have big money tied to fossil fuel theft, the equivalent of hundreds of millions of dollars, anyway. And the assassination of both the American oil executive and the Mexican minister seems like a win for NOS, a blow against PEMEX, a blow against the petrostates, another guilty party taken down, but John also talked about how the cartels have been getting pushback from the interior ministry.

But whatever power struggle is underway still means, even if this fuel is stolen, it's simply being sold into the marketplace by new owners and not disappearing unused.

He argued that the two of them have contributed to more carbon spill, basically, down Mexico way, but John just shrugged and talked about the LNG terminal. "Stopped, or at least delayed," is what he replied. What the fuck is he doing? This has become the number one question for him.

"You want to review your steps," he mentions again. "Go time is"—and he looks at his more accurate watch—"in less than two hours."

"Yep." At least the two are picking up the pages of instructions and diagrams and are looking over them.

"Tool kit?"

John looks up and nods.

"Yes?" he asks again.

"In the car, in the car."

He's not worried about John getting annoyed. He's more worried about Biff becoming unhappy. The image of the destroyed body, the body he helped destroy, stutters into his thoughts.

His role is staying back here, packing up, doing a site clean, the big sprayer bought at Tractor Supply all ready with the bleach mix, good to go.

"Any questions, any at all, now's the time," he says.

Now that Frederick-Phil is with John, the two of them look even younger. They nod, and mumble a reply. They'll ask if they need something made clear, but it's straightforward. They know how to find the pump valve station, they have a drawing of the inspection hatch, the procedures for shut down, opening and closing, and the sequence for turning it all back on. Worst case, they can call and he'll walk them through, but the intention is to run silent. No need for adding more ammunition to any potential investigation, cell towers being what they are—geolocators.

The camp downpipe might experience a slowing of water for a few moments and, worst case, some air splutter, but that's not an issue. The whole place is full of soldiers, not water supply engineers.

If all goes as planned, the package will be retrieved on the Mexican side, at least this was what Biff had intimated, but Biff hadn't answered any questions for him. It's always good to be skeptical about operational security, that kind of caution never hurts, but this is a whole different sort of doubt—a lack of trust.

He continues to keep this to himself, even as he worries that Frederick-Phil, who is clearly not a Guide but in fact a new recruit, might also know his real name. At least he only knows this young man's real first name, but he's waiting to see if John messes up and ends up mentioning Phil's last name, too, and he can guess it won't take long before he learns this and who knows how much more. The three of them will be up front in his truck's cab, the even older Blazer a leave behind. They'll be on the road for hours and hours before they reach their first stop.

John is so bad with basic protocols. NOS must be really hard up. And here he is, stuck with these two, in Beyerville, Arizona, and they're supposed to keep outside activity to a minimum, and the only activities available are sweating and walking. The town of Beyerville is a long walk to nowhere, but then, out here everything is a long walk. John has driven the beat-up 2005 Chevy Blazer to either the Safeway or Walmart in Nogales, Arizona for food groceries. Maker has twice gone with John on a different type of supply run, making the circuit of Home Depot, Harbor Freight, and Tractor Supply Company, and then a final stop at a local plumbing supply shop. They've managed to collect everything they needed that he otherwise didn't have in the truck camper. Money isn't a problem, not with the cartel connections. Is that a good thing or a bad thing?

He glances up at the clock, a square shape with a faded plaid frame, the lens of the clock scratched and cloudy. The time is approaching T-minus an hour, give or take.

Chapter 45: Latrine Duties and Porta-Potty Politics

July 26, 2035

Victor is telling Davin that he'd planned on staying with a friend, at the guy's parents' second home in Great Barrington, but it could be Sheffield.

"The problem is that my pal, idiot that he is, also invited others," he says as he and Davin stand near the garden fence, out toward the back of the property.

There are four tents, and one Rube Goldberg setup of tarp and mosquito netting that's the current residence of the young man he's speaking with. There are ropes Victor has borrowed from him to string up his shelter, although these are in not quite understandable arrangements, twisted around various limbs of the one tree at the edge of his property that was downed by the winds a few days back, the winds from the near-passing tornado, the tornado that had mowed down swathes of trees near where Victor and others were escaping the heatwave, up from New York.

Brooklyn, in the case of Victor, as Davin learned a few minutes earlier. The forecasts are predicting that the heatwave will dissipate in a day or two or three, depending on which weather app he looks at. With the crowd of tents up here in the back, he's been scouring the weather forecasts, waiting for the day everyone returns to their regular lives, including him. Every one of his *refugees*—that's what he's calling them, both in his thoughts and in any conversation with them or others—seems a decent sort, some friendly, some less so, but considering what these young people have been through, up to and including the brush with *a goddam tornado,* a touch of petulance is understandable.

He's up in back, having overseen the delivery of a porta-potty, and the delivery crew of two have gone, but not before plenty of grumbling about the delivery spot. The driveway was too steep, except, of course, after they drove up. The spot was too far back, except, of course, it wasn't, but the price imposed is a broken branch of one of the peach trees the truck clipped backing up toward the back of the property to place the toilet unit where Davin wanted it. The crew was made up of a corpulent older man and a ratty-looking youngster, younger than any of Davin's refugees, and both had been unpleasant in their own unique ways.

On the other hand, they literally have a shitty job. He's only half-listening to Victor, letting out a bit of a snort, some half-laugh that catches the young man's attention.

"What?" Victor asks.

"Yeah, sorry, just thinking of those two," he says with a vague wave toward the big blue box. "A shitty job, but there's something I need you guys to do, more or less a similar crappy task."

Victor waits for more.

"That latrine trench you guys dug out the first day, it needs filling back in now that we have the porta-potty thing here, is that something you can get some help with?"

"Yeah, no problem," Victor tells him. "Great improvement in accommodations, sirrah."

The lingo's a bit pretentious, but then Davin was once young, too.

Neither of them can see the latrine from where they're standing. The latrine was dug at the southeast corner of the property, as far away as possible from the collection of tents. Victor's tarp setup is the closest to the latrine, but still a good thirty feet away. What the two of them *can* see is a privacy screen for the latrine, another tarp that hangs over a rope from the corner garden fence post that runs up to a tree branch that's been pulled down to fix the other end. The tarp's bottom edge is tucked under the dirt pile from the trench excavation, so the privacy function works. A board, the latrine seat, spans two five-gallon buckets left over from years ago, when he used the joint compound in some interior wall work. Now these buckets are set upside down on two big pieces of plywood that span the trench. The setup seems to work, or at least he hasn't heard of any accidents, although he wouldn't be surprised if the narrow slit is sometimes missed, but that's what the garden trowel is for. A branch has been pushed into the ground to hold a roll of toilet paper, and there's a third bucket, upright, with water for washing hands, and a towel is draped over the top of the garden fence.

He's allowed the use of the second-floor bathroom for showers, and he's run three loads of laundry for his charges, but he feels fine keeping access to the house restricted. He has his house sharers to think about. And himself. Sharing his bathroom with a crowd is not his greatest wish—far from it. He's gotten to know the group of campers out back, well, some more than others, and they seem trustworthy enough, but access to the house is by permission, and they've all been good about not asking for too much.

Victor tells Davin again that he was supposed to be staying with his friend, but even there it might have been camping in the yard, there being too many for the house, which wasn't the main house but an ADU on the friend's folks' property, the main house rented out.

"The last text I got from my pal," Victor says, "is that there's now septic system problems, so no complaints here."

Davin says nothing.

"I'm saying thanks, actually." Victor grins. "And I'm happy to do that with blisters!" He picks up the shovel that Davin has brought back out from the garden shed, shoulders it, and executes what is probably supposed to be a sharp, parade ground left face and retreats toward the latrine.

Hopefully the heatwave is going and he can get away with the one-week porta-potty rental. Perhaps he'll get to enjoy the same grumbling crew at pickup.

There are some of his folding chairs scattered about near the tents. A young woman sitting there waves at him. He starts toward her, and she gets up and walks toward him.

"Sarah, right?"

She nods, continuing her approach. "Nice garden." She's now standing near, but her eyes are on the garden, looking beyond the small greenhouse that doubles as the back gate. "I really appreciate – we appreciate – your letting us use it. The green beans are really coming in, the zucchinis are great, I steamed a whole bunch yesterday for six of us. Yum."

"You had butter?" He hadn't offered any – it hadn't even occurred to him. "Salt? Pepper?"

She nods. "Brian had salt and pepper shakers, and Victor came back with some butter, bought from Taft Farm, I think. A feast."

Sarah knows her way around a garden and has been helping some of the others learn to weed and harvest.

"I appreciate you guys working the garden, it's looking great."

She seems about to say something, but she nods instead, and Davin turns to see a man walking up the driveway. He has no idea who this might be or why he's here, but the man is carrying a bound folder.

Davin walks over to meet him, the two meeting halfway up into the parking area. Davin looks down, notices that there's need for some weeding here, where it's always a constant battle keeping weeds from overtaking the three-quarter-inch crushed stone that makes the surface of the parking area. Great. Another weed whack job.

"Good morning," he says to the stranger. "And you

are?"

This question seems to flummox the man. He's about Davin's height, heavier, and is wearing a polyester short-sleeve dress shirt of some blue-purple color Davin hadn't until then known existed.

Rubbing the top of his head seems to revive the man's sense of self.

"Uh, yes, Stephan Devole, I'm the health inspector for the town, for Great Barrington, and, uh…"

"No restaurant here," Davin says lightly.

The health inspector sniffs out a laugh, or so it seems. "Yeah, no, of course not."

Another pause ensues.

"And how may I help the health inspector today?"

"Yeah, no, there's been some complaints about sanitary conditions over people camping here."

"Okay."

"In your backyard," the other man says, or asks.

"Donny, Donny, Donny," Davin says, looking at the man, but there's no change in expression. "Is it my neighbor down the street?"

The man merely shrugs.

He resists shrugging in response, although the impulse is oddly fierce.

"So, again, what can I do for you? This an official visit? You have the right to just come by, no warrant, no judge's order, no whatever?"

The man's shoulders slump. "No, nothing like that, this isn't official, just trying to help, make sure there's not a problem, something that could make people sick, or some liability for you, public safety."

The man tells him that he'd like to see the backyard and check on conditions. Oh jeez. He gestures to the man to follow, and they walk up to the back. Sarah's in the garden, half-hidden by the plants, but she waves. There's another of the young women with her, but a bit farther up a row of purple top turnips. He can't think of that woman's name. He may not even have heard it.

There are clothes flopped over the top fence frame. The two men stop at the fence, both looking through at the garden hose manifold, with Devole taking a moment to run his eyes along the length of hose that runs off back toward the house. There's a short hose off the four-spigot manifold that's been pushed through the fence, the nozzle's trigger used to hang the end of that hose up on the outside of the fence. The big enamel pot is below, half-filled with clear water. The two items of clothing near this part of the fence, it turns out, are towels.

On the inside of the fence, almost under the manifold, there's an upended plastic rain barrel. Davin uses the butt of the barrel mainly as a work surface for filling watering cans from the short hose that's currently pushed through to serve as a water source for the campers. There's a wrench and a scattering of hose gaskets across the bright blue plastic bottom.

"Nice garden," Devole says, and Davin just nods. "These things,"—he points at the sunscreens strung well about the fence tops, still in the breezeless day—"I'm seeing these more and more. They really work?"

"Yeah, great. You remember that hailstorm, two summers ago, right? Damaged a lot of crops, but these things really help."

Devole grunts and turns away, looking at the tents.

"Helps with too-hot weather, too. Pricey, but worth it, that's my opinion," he tells the man as they walk toward the tents.

The tents are out toward the back property line, and two people, a man and a woman, talking, are sitting on the folding chairs near the impromptu fire pit, an occasional tendril of smoke rising. Ken and... not Barbie but... Bobbie! How could he forget a name like that?

The health inspector looks at the porta-potty and then he's veering toward it. He stops and reads the maintenance label and then returns to Davin's side.

"Ken, Bobbie," Davin says to the two sitting near the nearly dead fire pit, then nods his head to Devole. "Health Inspector of Great Barrington. Any plague to report?" He instantly regrets making his wisecrack, but the two laugh and tell him it's all good, and then he says, pointing, "I see Victor's working away. Any others around?"

Bobbie tells him that she's pretty sure everyone else is away, maybe for lunch, and that Carl—he draws a blank on which one of the still-confusing group of faces is Carl—is going to Taft's or Market 32 for some food.

"Not Market 32," Davin says at the same time Devole is saying that the supermarket is closed. Davin's read that the damage from the storm is severe enough that the store's going to be closed quite a while, the parent company having decided to do a full renovation.

"Yeah, right," Bobbie says. "Carl said it was closed."

Devole touches Davin's arm and nods toward Victor and they close the distance. Victor ignores them for a moment, intent on tamping down the dirt he's filled back in in the former latrine. Some of the tarp has been pulled away and swung over the top rope to get it out of his way.

"Hey," he says. "All done."

Devole looks around, eyeing the ropes holding up the tarp, sees the stick with the toilet paper lying on the ground, the bucket with water, the still-fussing Victor. "Latrine?"

"Dead body," Davin quips, and the health inspector finally cracks a smile.

"Porta-potty's good. How many people, how many, uh, guests you got at present?"

Davin tells him he believes thirteen is the number.

"One porta-potty, no problem. Fresh water?"

Davin points to the manifold and the hose running back toward the house. "I expect these people will be heading back home soon." He says. "The heatwave is lifting in a couple, sounds like."

"Yeah." Devole nods. "A bad one. Last I heard, death count is over twelve hundred, metro, and that doesn't even count all the carry forward problems, kidney disease spikes, for example, or the late finds."

"Late finds?"

"Yeah." Devole nods. "Sometimes weeks, the smell is the usual alert, old people living alone, dehydration leading to falls, or don't have their medicine, whatever, heart attack, but the person doesn't have anyone checking in."

"Yikes."

"Early on, years ago, I was EMS in Troy, before the career change, before coming to the Berkshires," he tells Davin, but he's looking off into the distance. He shakes himself and turns back to Davin. "I had two of those calls over six years, but the guys in the city? Now? There will be dozens. Hundreds, maybe."

They start walking back toward the house.

"Hey, thanks," Devole says, back to rubbing the top of his head. "I appreciate the tour, the cooperation. I can go back and report that there's nothing here, no problems."

They reach the top of the driveway, and he sees that Devole has parked his car down lower in the driveway, at the big front steps. Fortunately, the current Airbnb guests are out, likely most of the day. Fortunately, the current couple in residence find the story of the campers, the refugees from the heatwave, interesting. Fortunately, the recent tenters out back, his good deeds, have kept in the background—a curiosity to the guests, not a problem. Reviews, reviews, reviews. He's proud of his Superhost status, and that comes from good reviews.

"Quite the driveway," Devole says, starting down, with Davin following.

"Yup."

Sometimes the steepness of the driveway does get mentioned in reviews, but he's always sure to mention it when he sends out confirmations and directions.

They get down to Devole's car, and Devole stops and turns back to him, his hand out. "Really appreciate it," he says, and there's something of an awkward handshake, but that may be because Davin's on the first of the big stone steps now, looking down.

"Squeaky wheel, right?" the health inspector tells him.

"Squeaky asshole, maybe, right?"

The man smiles. "No comment."

"The floor's squeaking," he says quietly, watching the man let himself drop into the car, but his comment has clearly puzzled the guy.

Davin waves it away. "Just something an old friend used to say," he says. "Private joke."

The man nods and pulls the car door closed and starts backing down the driveway.

Davin waits for one final wave, and the car disappears down the road.

"The floor's squeaking," he repeats, and smiles. This was something an old carpenter, who worked with him on some interior finish projects years ago, used to say whenever he'd passed gas.

Chapter 46: The Case of Climate Cases is in Your Court

July 30, 2035

"I think this is important," Jimmy says.

His colleague Manny Mederia is standing off to the side, behind him, looking over his shoulder.

They're both staring at one of Jimmy's three monitors, and Jimmy reaches up and taps a line of code. "This."

He's sent the code, what he still thinks of as the *code bomb,* to the National Cyber Investigative Joint Task Force. The FBI is the lead investigation body, but in a recent telephone call with the NCIJTF contact person that Jimmy's been talking to, the guy inferred NSA involvement, but in a sort of *nudge, nudge, wink, wink* sort of way. It's been a trip for him, this peek into the world of high-level cybercrime and law enforcement. The Cybermen, the C-men, that's one of his jokes.

"I'm confused," Manny tells him. "What exactly am I looking at?"

Jimmy highlights the string of code he's showing his colleague. Manny isn't an employee of NoNolo but is one of NoNolo's clients. He's an IT contact from The Massachusetts Office of the Attorney General. He works in the AG's Enterprise and Major Crimes Division and was brought in because of the legal documents that gathered evidence for a number of court cases against various fossil fuel corporations, including eleven class actions shared with a number of other states and at least one RICO prosecution. Jimmy finds his stories fascinating, and his long-running interest in cyber security has been reinvigorated. It doesn't hurt that they tend to meet at microbreweries.

The AG's office is a few blocks away, and the two men have become pals lately. After a couple of pints, Manny is inclined to grow loquacious and he has plenty of fascinating stories of cybercrimes, local and international, and Jimmy loves hearing them. It helps that he has a solid background from his work in IT, and he's been even more immersed in cybersecurity issues these days, fortunately, before the hack attempt. He's told the story a hundred times—or at least, that's how it feels—about the close call with NoNolo's own backup hack. He enjoys the dramatic aspect of the story, and it all ends well, NoNolo coming through like the hero of an ancient tale, slaying the dragon, saving the day, the legal documents entrusted to the clearinghouse safe in the end, his company able to restore the clients' own backups. Even thinking about the close call now makes his hands start sweating.

"One of the agencies," and he pauses, trying to recall which of the alphabet soup of agencies he's gotten this recent file from, but he decides to say Task Force, foregoing the full run of letters, because the National Cyber Investigative Joint Task Force is the umbrella agency that coordinates more than thirty co-located agencies from the intelligence community and law enforcement. He's emailed and talked with people from some of the thirty agencies at one point or another over the six weeks, but he's lost track of the different agencies. He meant to keep his contact logs up to date, but that went by the wayside within the first couple of weeks. The rain of conversations and emails from various agencies about what's happened has been at times overwhelming in and of itself, but working with the clients, assuring them their documents were safe, and packing and sending off backup refreshes, that's been exhausting.

"One of those in Task Force—if you want, I can look at

the email," but Manny tells him to continue with his explanation.

"So, there are tells in coding—habits, reused code, country of origin indications, suggestive, anyway, but the task force has a catalog, a backlog of various cyberattack code, whole libraries now, and they do pattern recognition, some sort of analysis, anyway. They're pretty sure the code that hit you and the others, well, and us, except," he gestures a thumbs-up while pointing to himself.

"Jesus," Manny says, shaking his head, and he seems to find his antics funny, but then he grows serious. "Well, I guess you are the hero, big guy."

Jimmy scoffs and continues his show-and-tell. "So, this string is one, and I've gone through and highlighted some of the other indicators, those include syntax, too, apparently, but I'm clueless on that with this… I'm not supposed to be mentioning this to anyone, so, you know."

Manny nods.

"There's some sort of ongoing analysis still, not that I could tell you what that is, it's a mystery to me, and it's likely this will all be public soon enough, but what they've determined is that it's the Ukrainian group BD, which I only just found out stands for *Bryhada Donósnyk*, and that means something like *tattletale brigade* or *informer group*."

"Yeah, BD, they did the Revolution Windmill system hack, right? But they work for the Russians?"

"The Russians had quite a few Ukrainians doing hacking during the war, that whole Donbas thing, Russian speaking, some aligned with Russia. Or with their money."

"Right, right," Manny says. "It's hard to imagine, with the treaty, the whole recovery of the territory, the whole Ukraine patriotism culture." Manny's talking about the Ukraine–Russia war resolution, halfway through the return of the Democrats to the White House, seven years ago now. How fast things go by.

"Well, money is still a weapon, right?" he says to Manny. "But the wind farm hack, the one that brought down parts of New York, that was BD, two years ago. A bunch more actions, too, it seems, mostly nothing anyone like us would ever have heard of, but BD has ties with Russia, does a lot of work for them, and a history with some of the Gulf nations too, Saudi Arabia for sure."

"Petrostates," Manny says.

Jimmy just nods. "Here's the thing that's really QT. The task force is building a case for money transfers between America's Energy Independence, that new, well, newish, PAC, the one that funded a lot of campaigns in last year's midterms, remember?"

Manny shrugs.

"There was a big blowup because they'd emailed a disinformation flyer to Americans for Energy Independence, the solar group, and Climate Covenant did a special event on it, national coverage."

"Yeah, vaguely," Manny says.

"Sorry, my dad's really into Climate Covenant, so maybe I heard more about it."

"So, the connection?"

Jimmy stands and Manny reflexively steps back. He pulls out his phone. "I'm done for the day," he tells Manny. "Beer?"

They're on their way out of NoNolo when Manny reminds him he's still waiting for an answer.

"Evidence of money transfer between AEI and BD," Jimmy finally answers.

"Huh. Fuck. How certain?"

Jimmy just shrugs and points across the street to the newest microbrew pub in downtown Boston, and makes a beeline for it.

Manny runs to catch up. "I hope they make a hell of a case," he says, holding open the door as Jimmy steps through.

Chapter 47: A Harper's Ferry of One's Own

August 1, 2035

Maker thinks having the three of them crammed into the front seat of his old pickup makes it crowded enough, but after six hours of driving, the front seems more crowded than ever.

The F-150 is old enough to still sport a bench seat, or old enough to have once been bought with low trim options. He likes that he has a bench seat. Sometimes he'll pull over and catch a nap, stretching out a heck of a lot better than in a reclining bucket seat, especially in this old Ford, no extended cab and without much space behind the seat to recline a bucket seat if he had one. There's a bed in the camper, but a quick cat nap there would mean having to rearrange all the shit that clutters up that space.

They'd taken East Patagonia Highway out of Beyerville as soon as John and Frederick-Phil got back, the trailer stinking of bleach. The only delay was the wipe down of the Blazer, but he was good at this sort of thing, efficient. The luggage, such as it is, was already stashed in his camper. They were gone within fifteen minutes.

In another fifteen minutes Patagonia Highway turned into Arizona State Route 82, and they followed that until Whetstone, and within an hour and a half they were on I-10 near Benson.

The conversation was light enough between John and Frederick-Phil, bleeding off the adrenaline of the operation.

Frederick-Phil was passing some foul gas, or so John had accused him, but the windows were down, the air rushing through the cab, and Maker was left in relative peace in the welcome turbulent roar.

By hour three, they were in Road Forks, New Mexico, stopping for gas. The sun was low and the desert chill was coming on and the windows up. That was the end of any peaceful drive.

Maker turned on the radio, less interested in what he'd find on the dial, more interested in keeping the two young men quiet. A news station caught their attention as they approached Albuquerque, the news at the top of the hour, and the news was about Camp Stewart-Sousa, and it was then that Maker remembered the actual name of Camp Oasis. The name of the camp was the top news item, and the news was that it had been attacked by armed cartel terrorists, overrun, with casualties likely reaching over one hundred, though the reports were still coming.

"Holy shit," John said. "We fucking did it!"

Frederick-Phil joined in with other inane comments.

That triggered Maker and he shouted out, asking if they'd known this was the plan.

"No, but, you know," John said, with Frederick-Phil nodding.

Maker kept listening. Many had been killed execution style. Fuck. He gripped the steering wheel tighter, listening to the dawning awareness of the other two that their operation must have been part of this larger plan. They were awed, but giddy, excited.

The story came out in pieces, updates breaking into the programming. The camp had been overcome by a debilitating illness earlier, one of the reporters on the scene breathlessly reported, and watch stations were undermanned or with ill soldiers incapacitated, other soldiers making a stand, but the speed and force of the attack had overwhelmed any effective defense, until a redoubt had been formed in a small part of the base.

The two younger men were chittering on, excited, nodding, a high five.

"Hey!" he shouted, and they turned toward him. "I want to listen. Jesus."

He turned up the radio. The Governor of Arizona was talking about deploying National Guard, and she was followed by an Army spokesman whose name Maker didn't catch, the two others still vibrating, still chattering.

He thought about stopping the truck and kicking them out, but the odds were bad, two against one. He thought about smashing his fist into John's face, but that wasn't recommended going down US 25 at seventy miles per hour. He thought about screaming.

Facts and details kept coming as the press conference continued. An unknown quantity of weapons and ammunition had been taken, many vehicles stolen, this had been a highly coordinated operation, investigation teams already on the scene, some poisoning agent suspected, medical personnel on the scene, soldiers evaced, satellites and drones dispatched to track the retreating attack force. Twelve enemy combatants killed, a hundred four US service personnel dead or wounded, preliminary information.

The reporters' questions came at a fast pace. Were US forces in pursuit? Was Mexico cooperating? Why had communications failed? Another military person was answering these questions. It appeared that a sophisticated jamming suite had been deployed, so requests for assistance had gone silent.

They were on I-25, heading north to Pueblo, Colorado, a safe house of sorts, or maybe more. John was cagey even while hinting Maker would get his contributions acknowledged, officially become a Guide.

He snapped off the radio, telling the other two that they could listen in later, for updates.

On the CanAm Highway, they are just entering town limits for Truth or Consequences.

They have another six and a half hours to go.

Chapter 48: Bedtime Stories

August 27, 2035

Deidre is in her new apartment and she's happy enough to be out of the tent, although many nights this prior month, she's slept at the store, too exhausted and too stranded to head back. Already, though, the other roommate is exactly the sort of trouble she's feared, an odd neediness and mixed signals that just spell *Run!* But she can survive it. *Friendly, distant, empathetic, emphatic,* she recites, her words to live by.

It was nice of Davin to make the tent available. She was one of his first house sharers. *House sharer,* he'd been insistent on using the phrase. Probably still does.

He's a nice guy, a bit nervous, maybe, but fair and good-hearted. Her first time moving in happened just after his son Jimmy and Cynthia arrived, retreating from the 2026 Chicago heatwave, and there was that trouble Cynthia was in, not that Deidre had heard much about it, nor had she asked. At least not until weeks later, while Cynthia was being interviewed by a whole lot of different people—cops, the DA, others.

She liked Cynthia. She was impressed by Jimmy. The three of them went out a couple of times. Actually, they'd picked her up at work, some drinks after. This gets her thinking, as she bustles about her new place, checking doors and windows, about what she needs to do about a car. A van? She doesn't like using her mom's car, and that's hard to schedule anyway, with her mom's work, especially that second job where she needs to be on call.

She needs to get to her circuit of thrift and secondhand stores, and Brimfield Flea Market, all that. Janice, her old roommate, was always generous with the use of her car, but her ex-roommate has moved home to Longmeadow, back with her folks.

Maybe just an e-bike to get around, and she can always rent a van when needed. She'll figure it out. The loan from Alicia will help. Already has.

Alicia looks good, not much changed, even though it's been more than five years. The check was handed over at Alicia's familiar offices, all business, the agreement a simple typed one page with generous terms, although Alicia's lawyer had been present, and a notary.

But she herself has changed, past thirty now, and finally, it seems, she's building something. The life of a server may finally end, a businesswoman now, although she'll still take some shifts at Farm Table for a while. She still feels young, and she's just a pound or two heavier, but she gets enough flirting and compliments at Farm Table. That's a hazardous way to keep her confidence, but she manages to keep the *players* at bay. She shakes her head. Friendly, distant, empathetic, emphatic.

She has an invitation from Davin to one of his cocktail parties, one of the three or four that he holds every year, and she picks this up off the couch that doubles, when folded out, as her bed. She checks the time. She's got to get going. She hasn't been to one of those cocktail parties since the first time she lived there, from where she'd later moved out to live full time with Alicia and then moved back in for a few months after leaving her.

This still bothers her. She's lived since with a small seed of disappointment, disappointment that Alicia hadn't been comfortable being in love with her, had buried herself in her work on the business. She's since dated, but nothing, no one, has stuck. She's lonely.

Enough. She wants to go to the party, if only as a way

to thank Davin again and to see Marsha, odd as Marsha may be, although the other one, the new one, Be, seems like fun company and hopefully she'll be there. The other house sharer, Charlie, she's only heard of, since he was away the whole two weeks or so she was tenting, but she might meet him, might not. Be's a hoot, a fine-looking woman, maybe fifty, or younger or older, she'd never asked. She also hasn't asked anything about the looks and glances she's caught Davin shooting Be's way or the flirting Be does with him. Of course, maybe she's reading too much into the looks and glances.

She had dinner with these two house sharers and Davin once each of the two weeks she was there. It's a tradition of sorts, a weekly dinner for everyone in the house, especially when the garden is high. She laughs quietly, thinking of Marsha and her pride in the garden, and all the food preserving going on. She found herself amazed at how a meal might take place amid all of the sauces cooking and vegetables blanching, but each of the dinners was wonderful, cooked by Davin, and well worth rearranging her Farm Table schedule to enjoy.

Of course, that last week had the campers out back, but they all headed back two or three weeks ago, or whenever exactly the New York City heatwave finally ended. Always a strange situation at Davin's.

She's got to get going if she doesn't want to be late, so she locks up and gets to the corner where the BRTA bus runs past her apartment just a block past the Brown Bridge, in an area west of the damage from the storm a month back. The bus stops and she climbs on.

Her thoughts fill with all the tasks she has to do for the store, including figuring out the actual opening day so that she can promote the store well. She's caught up still trying to puzzle out the window display she wants, going back and forth on two ideas, liking one, then liking the other more, and on and on, and it's enough to make her crazy.

She takes a long breath and looks around. The drive

down Route 183 toward Housatonic is both familiar and new, but she's excited about the party. And nervous.

She'd met Alicia at another of these cocktail parties, her very first. That was in 2026. Nine years ago!

She'd been introduced, shifting her cocktail glass to her left hand to offer Alicia her hand. There had been the tremor of contact, and she'd broken out with what she's sure was a deranged grin.

"Are you a friend of Jimmy's?" Alicia had asked and she'd said that she just boards with Davin, and it's a recent thing. It felt like she was unable to stop looking into this woman's face, taking her all in, to the point of barely breathing, and then she saw Alicia looking at her, really looking, all over, and she caught her breath and took a sip of the cocktail that had appeared in her hand, looking at Alicia over the glass, and Alicia looking back at her, and they both started laughing.

"So, which is your room?" Alicia asked her, and she suddenly felt very shy, but she told her that she'd show her. Stepping through the library and entering the old guest room she'd taken over, she pulled her bedroom door shut, and turning, was pressed back into the door by the force and frenzy of their kiss. She sighs.

She looks up and sees the old transit barn that was once part of the mills, a low brick structure on the left, the river behind, her drop-off spot coming up fast. She's jumping up, pulling the stop and marching up the short aisle to the front. She says goodbye to the driver, one of the regulars, and hops down, right at the foot of Davin's street.

She starts up the street on a rising gradient, although the driveway, already in sight, is steeper yet.

A horn sounds behind and she jumps, the car pulling up beside her.

It's Alicia, who rolls down the window on the passenger side and leans toward her, grinning. "Need a ride, young lady?"

"Hey." Deidre pulls open the door, and then an

awkward silence accompanies the car engine's strain as it crests the parking lot. Alicia noses it into a parking space. It's a nice car. She's ridden in it many times, but now it's been years. It's an old BMW 5 Series, still using gasoline, but Deidre appreciates the quality of it, the style. She appreciated a lot of quality and style when she lived with Alicia, but she was more interested in maintaining her independence, often discouraging Alicia from buying her clothes, other things. But the loan, that's not so independent.

"I know I've thanked you for the loan, you know it's appreciated, but this was really important."

"How is the store going?" Alicia asks, and Deidre explains the forming promotional efforts and her thoughts concerning opening dates.

She's looking around, recognizing some cars. They zoomed past Davin's car on their way up the driveway, his car tucked into a tight space in front of the studio. There's Jeannie Louise's old hybrid, Marsha's electric motorcycle locked to a post Davin probably put in for her, the motorbike covered. Be's car is there, and there are two vehicles she doesn't recognize, but one might belong to the never-yet-met Charlie. What she thinks might be Charlie's car could also be the Airbnb guests' instead, and she suggests to Alicia that they park on the grass, telling her that Davin can get anxious if there's not easy parking for Airbnb guests. Alicia starts the car, reversing to a spot quite a lot farther back than she needs to be, almost up against the garden's big front gates.

"Whoa," Deidre says, craning to look backward. "This is good enough." She turns around and sees Alicia looking at her, an expression that's atypical. Is Alicia annoyed by her directions? Or maybe it's about the loan?

"I've really missed you," Alicia says, and then more comes rushing out and they talk and cry and laugh and kiss, and they never get to the cocktail party.

Chapter 49: The Restraining Strain

Saturday, August 28, 2035

Fletch didn't go to the cocktail party at Davin's the night before. She had other things to do, important things. And she didn't feel like going to any kind of party. Pity party? She laughs quietly. Going with her lawyer to see a judge to get a restraining order against Robbie isn't the right preparation for acting casual at a party. She's been hunkered down at home instead, reviewing what's happened.

She picks up the mug of tea and takes a sip, but frowns. It's cold. Again. This is her second mug, made to replace the first one she allowed to get cold.

Earlier this week, Robbie was at the police station, and from what Sullivan told her, not entirely voluntarily. He was asked in to speak to them about the shooting in Housatonic in June. He's been hanging out in some sort of squat, with some guy from the Co-op—*a homosexual*—a Bernie or Ben or some such name, and if she's heard the last name it's lost to her now. It's understandable that she's upset. And not tracking everything exactly, that's understandable, too.

Cellus, Benjamin Cellus, that's his name.

The chief dropped by her office, and she recognized the courtesy. According to Sullivan, Robbie's been staying with this thirty-one-year-old Benjamin Cellus and had been there, *there* being the place of where the killing of the man found in the river had taken place, but Robbie didn't come forward of his own accord. According to Sullivan, who told her under the strictest confidence because it involves a minor, Rory Ouelette, sixteen, Robbie was a witness to the shooting. Sullivan had gone on to describe the kid as having been expelled from Monument Mountain High School for selling drugs, and likely homeless, likely still dealing, likely getting his drugs from Andres Coelho's gang. If she's remembering all Chief's told her right. This Rory, also saw the killing but saw Robbie for a moment as the events—a member of Coelho's operation shooting another member behind the mills—played out.

She asked him which mill building. She's familiar with those buildings, having entertained two different development plans for the overall property over her time as town manager, although neither moved forward beyond the preliminary presentation planning and architects' site plans. The building was one once owned by the town, taken for back taxes—a tax lien foreclosure.

The property is a ramshackle collection of connected buildings that the town sold to a developer, and with great relief. The developer still owns it, she's pretty sure, and the taxes are getting paid, but nothing has moved forward with that targeted project, the interest rates remaining too high. That's what she's been told.

Cook's Garage, that's it. The name had a life well beyond the long-past owner, but in small towns, old names of things tend to stick. A part of the property is used as a storage site, she told Sullivan after she realized which building was involved. There had been a gallery studio space there a few years, too, but the building has remained largely empty for years, none of it yet sprinklered.

According to Sullivan, Coelho is apparently using some part of it as a "stash house." The use of this slang by Yorkie Sullivan struck her as odd, even absurd, but she was letting herself focus on stupid things, a defense she uses when stressed.

This is all much worse than Robbie being a philanderer.

First, fucking around town. Now drugs, homosexuality. Jesus. The chief has been kind.

The circumstance was that Robbie was staying at this squat on the first floor of one of the attached buildings, and he saw the killing, as did Rory, who saw Robbie. But Rory was recently arrested and he had his public defendant inform them that he had information to trade for dropping the charges, and the DA got involved. A deal was struck, but only because Rory had insisted that there was a collaborating witness, which is when the name Robert Gray came up.

"How did this high school kid even know my husband's name?" she'd asked.

The chief's response was simply to raise his eyebrows and give a half-shrug with his hands and Fletch knew at that moment that most everybody knows about Robbie, the wild man, the husband of the town manager, kicked out, all kinds of problems. And now he's gay, lives in a squat, takes drugs.

Sullivan talked more, telling her that Rory knew him, had met him, that Benjamin Cellus, produce manager at the Berkshire Co-op, was a regular customer.

They went to the building the day of Rory's affidavit and arrested Benjamin on suspicion of criminal trespass and for drug possession. The second charge may or may not stick, the chief told her, since it was marijuana, but they're still waiting on the state lab to get back to them. Rory often sold speed-laced dope, apparently.

Robbie's currently without charges, but they're holding him as a material witness, and they've threatened him with full charges if he doesn't cooperate. Robbie has been able to identify three of the people involved in the killing, and one of them is Coelho.

Robbie is due in front of a judge, Monday, for his own affidavit, or whatever exactly they do to draw a warrant for Coelho and the others, so Monday is Public Knowledge Day. Any time she thinks of the news getting out, she gets sweat pinpricks under her arms.

She had those same feelings in front of the judge yesterday, getting the restraining order. She'll file for divorce sometime next week, only waiting for her lawyer to confirm the appointment.

Two murders in one year. Although it may be that the beating death of the young man from Brooklyn will be charged as manslaughter, if that makes any difference. Everyone's waiting for the trial and the date hasn't even been set yet.

Two murders in one year. The expanded police budget for the next fiscal year seems like a done deal now.

Great Barrington, Murder Capital of the World.

Chapter 50: Maker Makes His Escape

September 14, 2035

Maker is angry, angry, angry, but it's a new species of anger. He's long lived with his virulent hatred of the world burners. He's acted on his confidence that fossil fuel corporate executives, the main financers, and the key supporting companies are guilty and that the least anyone could do is exact damage on their tools and vengeance on their persons. It is right.

He's leaning against the tool shop, on the exterior back wall that is now casting its full shade over him, an essential need given that he's back at the Ranch, these nine years later, all the way back to his orientation and training as committed NOS personnel. He knows where the Ranch is located, no hoods and triple turns or other disorientation techniques employed for him this time heading in.

He, John, and Frederick-Phil drove here on John's directions after a stayover in Colorado Springs, right after the Pueblo misdirect, where they left the truck and walked out under the cover of the following night, after some much-needed rest. Showered and shaved, sporting new clean clothes, they were picked up under an overpass, and then switched again in a parking garage, those cars stolen randomly by a sixty-something woman with gray frizzy hair she wore like a cap. She had another passenger for them, which surprised him, but John seemed to expect it.

She dropped them off in an old hangar out by Falon,

east on Colorado 24, in what looked like an abandoned small airport called Meadow Lake, some buildings down to their concrete pads, others still sound, but almost all of them open.

The new truck, an extended cab electric, was waiting within. They transferred their meager luggage and some water and snacks for the road and waved goodbye to the woman as she backed out of the hangar.

They took a different route out, and he could see that the airport had once been bigger and that some buildings were occupied, but no airplanes were visible. They got back on Colorado 24, but only for a short distance, then they were on a series of old grid roads that stretched on, doglegging back westward toward Interstate 25 and up toward Denver, where they picked up Interstate 70, and after hundreds of miles and a fast recharge or two, they switched to Interstate 15.

"Las Vegas!" the new passenger, an even younger guy than the other two, yelled out as they merged on to that interstate, and that was something of a shock since the teenager had been largely quiet most of the way, nervous enough, Maker guessed, because he was going to the Ranch for the first time. The teenager was called Joe, and Maker assumed it was a false name, John back to being serious about security protocols, and he also only ever called Frederick-Phil just Frederick, the whole time they rode.

He did most of the driving, and only he and John shared the one set of directions. The two others knew they would be hooded at some point, but each gawked as they drove through Las Vegas, noses pressed to the windows, occasional shouts or comments from one or the other when they thought they spied a structure they recognized.

They'd been on the road for twelve hours, give or take, when the hoods came out, just after the last stop for food and a charge, south of Vegas, stopping at a tavern that proved neither fast nor good but was near a charging station and a grocery store. They took their time shopping, he and

John, for a long list of supplies that John had somehow received.

The two others were hooded, back in the truck, after the supplies were stashed in the truck bed under the folding tonneau cover.

John's cell phone, which then was the only one, was put in a Faraday pouch. He gave verbal directions, only lefts and rights and stops and starts, no street or highway names or numbers uttered, except that he told him to go north on Route 146, the exit they first took off the interstate, but the next half hour, he was given a series of doglegs and reversals that saw them back on the interstate, heading south.

Maker thought the ruse transparent, but then again, he couldn't have told anyone the location of the Ranch the first time he'd been there, because of his own hood experience many years before. John had him take an exit off toward the town of Jean, and they used the small town's grid to sow more confusion, but they ended up back on Interstate 15, which didn't seem all that confusing to figure out, even for anyone hooded.

But he drove, saying nothing, and was then told to get off where there was no town, but after he drove west, then north, he found himself in a huge parking lot, golf greens on the other side. John was taking over driving and he barely had time to appreciate the surreal scene as John retraced the route back to the interstate.

The last stretch wasn't too long, but he was glad to not drive. He was beat.

Once in California, they got off at Nipton Road and drove for less than half an hour before turning onto a dirt road. He saw some RVs and, more bizarrely, what looked like marina storage, with at least a half dozen boats sitting in a rough cleared lot, baking in the hot desert sun. The dirt road ended at the Ranch, another fifteen minutes on.

At night, he thinks he can hear road traffic beyond these hills, but he might just be imagining it. He's trying to figure out how he can leave without getting caught. There are enough guns around here, and he's sure that announcing he's done will not do.

There's a new person in charge of the Ranch. He never knew the previous Number One all that well, and he never heard of the guy passing, but then, it isn't like NOS has a company newsletter. The Number One he knew was as much a warrior as he is, but the same doesn't seem true with this one. It could be that the guy, who also wants to be addressed as Number One, just plays things closer to the vest.

The shade is starting to work away from the back side of the toolshed, but he's got time. There's a wide wash, or a geological remnant of one, anyway, out behind the property, and the vegetation here is nothing more than tiny clumps, sparsely spaced all the way to the foothills. He's got no idea what those hills are called, but he's heard they're on the Nevada side of the border. Good siting, being this close to a state border. If there's a raid it would come from the road, and, with sufficient heads-up, someone here could scramble and go for the border. There's a garage that has three all-terrain vehicles.

He walks back around the building, opens the big door and goes inside, the light dim compared to the big sky he's been staring at for the last twenty minutes.

He goes to the center of the room, where a huge hexacopter drone sits on sawhorses, the tarp that covers it when he's not working on it crumpled nearby. The chain is slung up out of the way, since he's not using the trolley track to lift and slide the drone outside. Not yet.

They've been having him do drone work. He's qualified, or qualified enough. Although he didn't work on the drone attack on the Eagle Refinery, he got involved with NOS shortly after, and his drone team succeeded with some good hits. Unfortunately, those attacks have spurred refineries and other vulnerable targets to develop anti-drone defenses, and since the Defense Department was full out on this for their own purposes, the private businesses taking on the contracts for the oil companies had a solid jump start. The drone attack on the Eagle Refinery was crude, simple, and within months most similar targets had installed audio-pickup warning systems, including the best-selling such system, Audio Eyes. These systems were simple and inexpensive, consisting of a ring of what were basically cell phones, all networked using the telephone networks, and then later independent Wi-Fi relays were added by some, for redundancy. Those drone sensors fed into Software as Service platforms, where AI analyzed audio for the tell-tale sounds of drones, and countermeasures would be deployed on detection. Knocking out commercial drones is easy enough if you're covering a relatively small area, and the inability to hide soundwave profiles from AI analysis means the where and when of drones are quickly determined. Many refineries take up five or six acres of land, but it's easy enough to inexpensively cover ten times that area.

There was no longer much opportunity to sneak in a drone attack after that.

Drones can still be effective for anti-personnel attacks, though, and he had some victories there for a while. Anti-personnel attacks. He shakes his head at how easy it is to slip into impersonal language. Killing people, assassinations.

That wouldn't have worked in Mexico. Too much cover and too many trained for protection against drones, at least that had been the assumption.

At the Ranch, he's been researching the latest commercial offerings in anti-drone protection. NOS—or Number One?—wants to get drones back in the game. Or the cartels? He's wondered about this a few times already.

Of those he's investigated, his favorite counter-drone system is the Dragin, a large drone equipped with a sweep net that it deploys as it approaches the attacking drone or drones. Some of the options carry surprisingly large net dimensions. The Dragin drone, like most of the other commercial systems, uses its own sonic sensor system for drone target acquisition and simply catches up the attacking drone's twirling propellers in the net. It's not much of a contest. There are other methods, too, including the communications disruption approach and even a drone-mounted system that resembles flak cannons, although this gets complicated in populated areas. There's even a mini-missile system awaiting FAA approval, among other agencies, and the trade press he's scoured seems to think this is unlikely for commercial markets, despite the claims of soft projectiles. Nerf anti-drone guns. Huh.

The challenge is that sensor or communication disruptors on the attack drones are simply too expensive and add too much weight as an anti-anti-drone tactic, throwing off the cost, distance, payload factors for an attack. Adding speed is unproductive, too, since it's hard to mask the position and tracking of an incoming drone, the audio systems very impressive in their analytical intelligence.

There are plenty of soft targets where a wide deployment of anti-drone systems doesn't make economic sense, and gas lines or fuel transport of various sorts are examples, but the high-value targets are refineries, terminals, and tankers, and NOS hasn't had a successful attack using drones on such targets for four years. One could always attack a tanker from a floating platform such as a boat or ship, but the major channels' lanes have their own sensor nets, and going out beyond the nets means ocean atmospherics that aren't kind to drones, and it would be far too easy for the drone base platform to be caught. The other problem is the limited damage inflicted with the drones used by NOS. That very first attack, which had lit a portion of the refinery's fuel tank farm ablaze, turned out to be beginner's luck.

He can admit to himself that he loves this sort of research, and the Ranch is well equipped with internet connections. It isn't fiber they're using but a satellite system, maybe Starlink or Kuiper, or maybe even something else. He hasn't followed this market for years. He's not interested in asking, either.

What he is interested in is figuring out a way to leave the Ranch. Nothing he's heard here or tasks he's been assigned make him feel better about what happened at the border.

Young kids, soldiers. There's a lot wrong with America, but helping to kill Americans not central to the continuing fossil fuel firestorm—that was wrong. Innocent people get caught up in NOS operations at times, sure, but this was a whole different scale, a whole different operation and he's sure that it's only for the cartels. They stole a lot of equipment and armament and ammunition. A fucking fire sale.

And NOS helped, and how was this even close to holding to their mission? Getting funds, yes, getting help, yes, but the price was too high.

There's been no mention in the news of NOS in relation to the border raid, but that means nothing. Investigations could be ongoing and those sorts of things get played close to the vest. Any of them could have been identified, or triggered some query, anyway.

He's less afraid of that than he is about being here, though. He's less afraid of that than being a newly anointed Guide, not that this seems to make much of a difference in his actual standing.

He had raised the border incident—huh, fucking massacre—indirectly, cautiously, but he saw that this was a subject Not to Be Mentioned. That had come across clearly. The old "enemy of my enemy" gem was said and "If we are going to continue" was uttered, the discussion ending with the always-effective "You got a problem with this?"

Not me, sahib. Fuck you.

He's finding he has a big problem with a lot of things he's seeing. This is not the Ranch of yesteryear, that's for sure. The main house, to which only Guides are invited, has been built out and the living is easy. There's a media room, and, sure, he can understand teleconferences and briefings and reviewing videos NOS might want to make or study, but as best he can tell, this is mainly a deluxe entertainment center. The kitchen looks like something out of *Architectural Digest*. The place is powered by a big solar array with batteries, and that makes sense, but what's with all the capacity? The main house is now a power pig, that's his guess. And much of it looks new. He'd love to ask John about it, Guide to Guide, but John seems neck deep in it. He won't risk it.

His own quarters in the old bunkhouse have been updated and are comfortable, and at some point, someone built a new bunkhouse, but that seems to be empty except for Frederick and Joe. He's supposed to be teaching explosives and remotes, and he's got no idea what John is actually doing besides spending time with the big guy, although he guesses John is doing the sort of protocol training with Frederick that he has to attend. John the teacher. That's a laugh. He shakes his head, remembering how sloppy the young man also known as John-Jim can be. And John-Jim knows Maker's real name, but sure as hell not from him.

Some of the protocol material is actually interesting. Communicating through text chats in multiplayer online games is a new development he's been updated on, and he'll admit this seems a lot better than the book-based cyphers he's always had to use. They change the games regularly. There's a list of games people have to memorize, and they must change over to the next one every twenty-seven days.

Focus on what's important. He could take off, maybe with the truck they arrived in, but where then?

He guesses that Number One knows the routes in and out, but *he* sure as shit doesn't. The closest foothills would probably be the safer way. But he doesn't know about the RVs, and maybe one or all of them are sentinels, or there could be sensors or hidden video cameras on the road back to reach the highway, ready to be triggered.

He looks at the giant drone. He's tested it already using the FPV gear. He's tested the gross weight lift. The idea is that this will be the carrier drone, fast on approach, and moments before intercept, it will release smaller drones carrying their own payloads before destroying the counter-drone.

The carrying capacity is twenty pounds above his body weight. The altitude he can reach is great enough to get a good sense of where to head.

He goes to the workbench and picks up the prototype of the attachment mechanism for the smaller carried drones.

He's got a plan.

Chapter 51: One Point Eight, Be Be Delilah

Thursday, November 8, 2035

Davin is waiting up by the parking lot, having just done some raking out back. He's waiting for Be to come back from work. He's mostly been cooped up in his office, first getting out the Ad Leads report for October, a tedious but well-worn task, and one with consistent good news for *Berkshire Interactive* and for him, too. His original deal with Alicia is still honored, the positive results giving him a small percentage of the ad revenue.

And then he's had email with the Hudson gallery, and while the sales have been decent, the end of the show is approaching and the owner wants to know if he could drop some of the prices and what piece he'd like to have remain at the gallery after the close of the show. That turned into an awkward telephone conversation when a surprising suggestion came up that Davin consider letting a friend of the gallery see about doing some corporate placement, or corporate interior designing maybe it was, but the money deal sounded bad.

He'd gotten lost, after that, looking over the latest from Climate Covenant, and with the 2036 election cycle starting to spin up, this made sense, even as he knows this will be ever more time-consuming as the months tick toward the election, now officially less than a year away. He particularly focused on the tax reform platform potential. Adding sensible tax reform makes clear sense to him, anyway, as a de facto climate issue.

Who should pay the most for climate progress? That was proposed as a key talking point. He's taken part in the group's members' poll, and he knows that defining the right stance on tax reform might be used to help determine the rating of candidates and Climate Covenant Action's campaign support.

He's staring off into nowhere, leaning on the rake. He's thinking about what he read this morning and he suddenly laughs.

It's a good sign when a candidate effectively encapsulates the basic point at issue. Representative *something* Leyland, from Ohio's First District, with Cincinnati as the base, has included in his submitted information to Climate Covenant a great phrase regarding estate tax reforms: *Death to the free tax ride huge wealth has been given for far too long*, or something like that.

He looks at his wristwatch. He shouldn't have more than a few minutes' wait, but it's a bit chilly and he heads for the house. He leans the rake against the wall near the French doors and goes in. He settles himself in the big club chair by the fireplace. There hasn't been any use of the fireplace but tonight seems a good candidate.

With this cold weather, fall seems at an end, although not calendar-wise, still being some weeks shy. This colder weather is welcomed by many, since the summer—its heat and humidity—has been recorded now as the hottest on record, although this is hardly surprising, as the previous twenty seasons saw fourteen of them setting heat records.

Most scientists, he knows, are saying a 1.7 degrees Celsius rise in average global temperature is now here, although there's a big controversy, or battle, really, in fixing the degrees of warming. The smallest group claims it can't yet be known if 1.5 degrees has been exceeded, there being a ten-year span during which the average has to be maintained and that this period is still short one year. The mainstream rejects this as overly conservative, since this year is on course for 1.7 degrees and the two previous years clocked in at 1.6 degrees and 1.67 degrees, but the views in the middle are all over the place and he can't really be sure what the exact measure is.

But then, he's not a scientist. He follows the news and has been paying attention to climate issues as much as possible for some time now, but since there are disagreements among the scientists, who knows? There's a vocal minority who are called Hansenists by some. Depending on whom one talks to, these are either cranks or prophets, forecasting 1.8 degrees above will be the new global temperature average next year. Their earlier warnings, back in 2025 or 2026, have been tracking well. None of it is good news, be it conservative, radical, or Goldilocks middle.

But there's progress. Climate Covenant looks well positioned to help keep at least a small majority in the House and Senate, with many candidates lining up with climate pledges, and those statements are fact-checked against their records. There's been a lot of great legislation passed since the Democrats retook the White House and Congress back in 2028. The last seven years have seen a big build-out of solar and battery infrastructure, and many of the big wind farms off the Eastern Seaboard are already online, with some of the others soon to be. The GREAT Act is in its fourth year, and grid expansion seems finally to be closing on the capacity targets.

Last year, his solar panels and batteries joined a VPP, and the electricity rate that he pays has finally dropped. *I love my virtual power plant participation*, he recites silently, mimicking a recent promotion campaign, alliterative jingle and all. *Lower prices and I need to do virtually nothing at all!*

The workforce development alone coming out of the GREAT Act has helped shift employment upward, right along with The Sea Wall Act, which has mutated in its aims as it starts to shift from mostly planning to construction. Fewer cities are building to hold back the sea, and more funding is going to relocation projects that are coupled with housing. Many of those projects are part of the solar build-out, too, solar roofs mandated when practical. As yet, though, only a few such projects are finished and occupied.

Will Jimmy and Cyn go through with moving, once that right part of the Boston Wall is complete? It will be years before they'd move in, probably many years, but they have their spot staked out with a deposit.

Through the glass French doors, he sees a car coming up the driveway. It's the current Airbnb guests parking up and he pushes himself out of the chair and goes outside to say hello. And listen to them complain about the weather, no doubt. This is the last rental of the season, and anyone with any sense knows that these days the weather in November could be nice or not.

"The apartment alright?" he asks as they wend their way toward the side of the house. Just past his deck there are the stairs that drop down into the front yard, with a pathway leading to the front porch and the apartment entrance.

They tell him it's all wonderful, "a cute place," and thank him for the hospitality, but whenever he hears "cute place" he interprets it as meaning "too small."

The many pictures of the apartment and the descriptive copy make it clear that the second bedroom is tiny, more along the lines of a Japanese coffin hotel, not that he uses that phrase, but the clever Murphy furniture turns a twin bed into a work desk, so there's that.

"Brrrr," the woman says to him, looking back as they step past his deck, with Davin keeping them in view.

He goes back into the living room, another glance at his wristwatch. He sits back in the club chair. Within moments he's up, getting himself a drink, a small bourbon with ice, and after disappearing down the steps to the kitchen for the ice, he's back settled in the chair, the big cube clunking as he sits.

It's cold enough for a nice fire in the fireplace, but he's

nervous about the talk he wants to have, needs to have, with Be. It's chilly, though.

The elevation of Berkshire County means that some of the highest areas have recently experienced heavy frost and light snow, and everyone has been surprised by the advent of unseasonably cold weather at the very end of summer. Then a nice Indian Summer settled in, with one large rainstorm passing along with the change in weather fronts, and he and Be picnicked up on Monument Mountain. One part of the trail as they started hiking down their counterclockwise route held a good view of the summer's tornado path.

Back at the house, they'd tick-checked each other and then showered together up in the third-floor bathroom, the only bathroom, with its clawfoot tub, that makes a two-person shower at all feasible.

He's not fond of double-showering, especially up on the third floor, where he finds the poly shower curtain that hangs from the overhead ring clingy, but that exercise in personal hygiene had its good points.

He smiles. They'd had the house to themselves and made the most of it, including the rare use of her bedroom, one door up across the hall.

The forecast today is for the latest cold stretch of weather to continue, some sort of jet stream anomaly dropping hints of colder, arctic air over the Northeast.

Thanksgiving is coming up and that's always a hard holiday for Davin, even all these years after the divorce. This Thanksgiving looks to be harder—no pun intended—thanks to Be.

He continues to surprise himself, acting the schoolboy lover, less often using the ED pills that he found sometimes helpful in his previous dating. But then again, he and Be aren't exactly dating and that's been exactly the problem, though not for her.

He's been planning on speaking with her, but she's been working and then she was gone overnight, back this morning, but with just enough time to change for work. And wink at him and serve that grin that launches a thousand different feelings in him.

He puts down the whiskey glass, barely any left, but the block cube still useful.

He grabs the canvas firewood carrier and goes back out, spinning left to where a wood crib is built against the house. He fills the carrier twice, loading a large heavy wicker with the first load and setting the second load against the short wall that ends at the edge of the French doors. He builds a fire, and that's a pleasure, his care and attention directed to the task, the tinder under the kindling shoved in under the fire grate with prods and additions until the small split logs he's carefully placed under two larger logs in the grate catch fire.

He grabs the glass, walks into the front part of the library, and pours more bourbon.

He's just sitting back down when he sees Be's car pull in. He stands and approaches the door. There's just enough light to see that it's her car, the body and shape of the car still visible against the headlights and brake light glare.

He grabs the remote from the fireplace mantel and thumbs on the parking area light and the LED landscape lights the run down from there.

She waves. His heart is racing, and he's hoping he's not showing flushed. His feelings are already mixed between his need to have this conversation with her and a stirring erection. Down boy. The joke fails to lighten his mood.

He sits back down, then stands up again as Be comes through the door.

"Hey there," she says brightly.

"Hey."

She takes off her jacket and seems ready to go off, whether to the kitchen or upstairs, so he says, pulling out the ottoman that he'd pushed aside when he built the fire, "Can we have the talk I've been asking you about?"

"Sure." She tosses the jacket onto the couch and sits on

the ottoman, turning to look at the fire. "This is so cozy."

Now Davin doesn't know what to say, his thoughts only halfway formed suddenly, but he knows what's bothering him most. Confusing him. She has other lovers—she's been upfront about being polyamorous, not that she'd said anything the first few times. He's sure that she wasn't trying to hide anything. He'd never thought to ask.

He looks her over. She seems tired, but she looks lovely, nonetheless.

He clears his throat. "You know I'm crazy about you."

She smiles, places a hand on his knee, bumping right up against the ottoman.

"I think you're wonderful," she says, but a hint of a frown appears. "What's going on?" she asks, the hand withdrawn.

"I'm crazy, that's what. I think about you all the time, love the sex, try not to think about those others."

She seems to stiffen, so he places his hand on her arm.

"The main thing"—No, don't say this!—"The main thing is I'm worried we're too different."

That's not it, or not exactly. He wants emotional connection, yes, to be friends, but something more. He only sees that this is what he can't have, not with the others, and he knows he's judging, or will be seen to be. He can't seem to get this main point out.

"How are we so different?" she says in a neutral tone.

He loves her! He wants her to love him! He wants to build a life together! He's keeping his own expression neutral, or hoping to, anyway.

Of course it's absurd, of course he's too old, certainly too old, anyway, for her.

He wants to be wanted. He wants to have someone. Be.

"Is this about my being polyamorous?" she asks quietly.

He sighs. "Well, I'm still trying to figure this out. I know you aren't hiding it from me and that you don't, uh, share, overshare, whatever, and that's considerate, but there are other things, too."

"Like?"

"Well, like the climate thing. I've tried to get you interested, get you thinking about everything that's going on—"

"But that's not who I am. I know about it." She laughs. "Well, some, anyway, but politics isn't my thing, demonstrations, just thinking about it, it's just all crazy."

Why is he talking about climate? But he can't help himself, apparently.

"I mean, we're talking 1.8 degrees warmer, and that's not the end of that, and there's a need for everyone—"

She holds up her hand to stop him. "This is about me remaining unattached, not a couple."

He picks up his whiskey from the side table, the ice gone, the bourbon watered, but his sip, which turns into a gulp, which turns into a bit of a coughing fit, is a hedge against speaking too quickly.

He clears his throat. "Well, I want to build a life, I want to do something in this life to help." He pauses. "The poly thing, it seems like you don't want to be serious with me—"

"I've seriously fucked you, right?"' she says sharply. She softens. "It has been, can be wonderful. Is," she says, her tone now neutral, but her eyes tell a different story.

"But how serious can you be, fucking, having sex with so many others? What life is that?" He's lost her, can see it in her shoulders and in her slackened face. Her face is always animated. It's one of the things he loves about her. And there are things he doesn't like.

"You want me to move out?"

He knew this could, would, come up. He doesn't think that this would be fair in any way.

"No." He looks into her eyes. "No, of course not, you're an excellent tenant, you've done nothing wrong, and this is something else, so not relevant to you staying here or not. I just feel confused, I guess I want more, I want to build a life—"

"I have a life."

He nods. *How serious a life?* is what he wants to ask but doesn't.

It isn't that she hasn't told him about her life. There was an earlier conversation, one in which he insisted on knowing who else she's in a relationship with. He'd managed not to react when he learned there were two women and three men. And him. She doesn't see one of the women often—it seemed like even just once a year, but she's important to her, apparently, just like he's important to her, she'd said. One of the men is similarly rare—once, twice a year, but she wouldn't provide more about him. The two others are friends she sometimes has sex with. Each man is nice, and everything is open.

He masked his feelings then, stunned by what she'd told him, feigning nonchalance.

They had great sex that night, he recalls, but that simply upsets him, thinking about that.

"Huh. I may not entirely get it, hell, I don't seem to entirely understand what it is I want from you."

Be stretches her back straight, looking directly at him.

"More than tenant with benefits," he says, trying for some humor, but it comes out dripping with disappointment, because it's more that he wants.

She stands. "Davin, you're a sweet guy, you're a very nice man. You're a good fuck, too." But she's now stepping away from him.

"I've loved spending this time with you."

He manages not to look at his empty whiskey glass. He knows what's coming.

"But I can't give you what you want." Her eyes are wet, but she turns around and strides across the living room, scooping up her jacket and disappearing into the landing and up the stairs to her bedroom.

She can't. He sighs and his eyes are tearing up. He sits back, deep into the club chair, having incrementally crept forward as they talked.

He closes his eyes, listening for sounds from upstairs.

He opens his eyes and brushes them clear. The fireplace has burned down to coal and ash.

Chapter 52: Operators are Haterators

December 23, 2035

He's on site, working, but there's some delay with the next cable feed, so he's just waiting near the base of a giant transmission pylon.

His thoughts drift back several months to the more or less twelve-mile flight, and Allen had never been so terrified. He still wakes up sometimes, even these months later, when the images and sensations leak into his sleep, of that unstable drone lift from the Ranch to Primm, Nevada, even these months later.

All things considered, he looks back at his escapade with pride, even if he'd scrambled in panic to find the center of balance on top of the carrier hexacopter drone. He sometimes wonders if his days as a skateboarder, back before high school, had helped.

The gyro stabilizer's feedback had been for shit. He kept his center of gravity low, and his need to keep dead center was crucial, too, because the whirling blades were never much more than two feet away, and with his shifting around to balance the drone and the resultant dips and sways, he got dangerously close to one or two of the props as he sought to place his center.

After steadying the drone, he popped the drone up to get his bearings, and the setting sun's glinting off the three Ivanpah concentrating solar arrays west of the interstate was easy to find, and he could keep the interstate, which led into Primm, in easy sight even flying low. He'd kept the town's lights in sight and the blank space of the large solar farm east of the town, and fourteen minutes later he was setting down near the southwest edge of the solar farm, where he would find dirt roads leading into town.

His ears rang. The joystick controller was far harder to use without the heads-up display, and that surprised him. He hadn't added much as a seat, and the two crossbars were harshly uncomfortable over the twelve or thirteen miles. He was desperately in pain for the whole of the flight, but he figured that a good sign, since a sore ass was better than a bad gash or a crash to the ground. He mostly flew low, the terrain perfect for that, just needing to clear the scrub and rocks and small rises, so he kept his altitude above thirty feet as best he could, minimizing clouding trails of dust. He'd set out toward the close of evening, and the flat landscape carried enough light from the setting sun to illuminate his path.

He'd set up the test with Number One, hoping that the noise of the flight when he left would be assumed just that, a test, and he wonders even today how long it took them to figure out he was going.

He'd seen no sign of alarm in his few quick glances back, and he never had to try to evade anyone from the Ranch who might have been looking for him, so he still thinks they hadn't thought much about it until he was well underway and they weren't able to spot him in the falling light atop the carrier drone, thirty feet up, heading for Primm.

He set down before getting too close to Primm, not too far from a house he hadn't spotted on Google Maps when planning the route. The house was out on the outskirts, a trailer home, the man and he looking at each other as he zoomed overhead.

Thank God for Nevada. It's a now regular invocation for the live-and-let-live mentality.

He'd walked into Primm covered with dust, but a few

slaps made him presentable, and it was good cover, too, he guessed. He'd studied Primm on Google Maps, and in detail down to Street View. He's always had a good sense of direction, and he found exactly where he wanted to be. Back at the Ranch, he'd cleared the browser history and cache and hadn't printed out anything.

He discovered Primm Valley Boulevard right off the dirt road, walked past a big two-story apartment complex to his left and the Primm Valley Casino Resorts on the other side, until the road intersected with the street with the underpass below Interstate 15, and within ten minutes he was looking at Flying J Dealer Travel Center Plaza, a good-sized truck stop close to another big casino and a massive five-story parking garage.

He was struck by the number of sizable parking garages in this out-of-the-way place, but he figured these were for the various casinos and that these, and the town, must be some sort of destination thing. He briefly considered trying for a ride from an outward-bound gambler, but he stuck with his trucker plan.

On the third conversation looking for a Las Vegas-bound trailer truck, he succeeded, and he was heading north on the interstate, telling the driver more details about how he needed to get to Las Vegas because his girlfriend had gone and he had to get to her before she did something stupid.

Cash from the stack he'd taken from the ranch certainly didn't hurt his request for the lift.

Later, he started using the two debit cards that he'd gotten from NOS over the years. He was supposed to cut up any and all such cards after the particular operation they'd been assigned for, but he'd secreted them, kept them nonetheless, and he was relieved to find that they still both worked. He emptied both accounts and had nearly two thousand in funds. The ATMs in Las Vegas had large limits.

It was time to become Allen Randolph again.

He's ended up in Tyringham, Massachusetts, at least for

now. He contacted his mother, asking for her to send him a package he'd years ago stored away that contained his driver's license, passport, and his old bank account details, not that he was sure it would still be available. The driver's license needed renewing, for sure.

That call was difficult, his mother alternating between crying and yelling, but he made the best of it he could, his mother at times vehemently accusing him of abandoning her or hurting her and of being an awful son, a terrible person—he was precious to her, how dare he treat her like this, and when could she see him?

He ended up spending a week with her at the old resort they used to go to as a family. NOS wouldn't know about that, and it was a help that she had moved to a new place, so even if they had the resources to try to find him that would hamper them a bit. If, of course, they were pursuing him at all. They'd probably retrieved the drone.

It was good to see his mother. He'd always been more of his dad's son, but after his dad died, he'd grown, if not closer to, then more tolerant of, his mother's emotional and needy personality, and the week they spent together had been pleasant enough. If lying to your mother constantly, which he'd been doing a little over three months ago, is ever a pleasant pastime. It had been easy to lie, but then he's been practicing that for a decade.

The story he settled on with his mom was that he'd gotten involved with a woman, a woman he finally, only recently, concluded was crazy, her insistence he cut off family ties just one early indication. The years passed, and he felt ashamed and was thinking it might be best to let things lie, but of late he'd realized the absurdity of that thinking, and here he was, back, sorry.

He had no trouble concocting the story, the woman's name, her backstory of abuse, the towns they'd lived in while he worked odd jobs, mostly handyman. After their big fight, the woman stole his tools, his car. That was a nice touch.

He got his REAL ID driver's license, that indeed has expired, as has his passport. The best thing he got, though, was news about a high school pal that his mom ran into when the friend was back visiting his folks. He'd been asked after, and his pal told his mother that if Allen was interested, he could see about work on the electric grid, that he would be happy to link him up, that there was a big demand for skilled workers.

He laughs. The recruiters are hungry, that's true. His old high school friend wasn't anyone close, and he works out in Colorado, but he'll have been eager for the national recruitment bonus he expects if Allen Randolph stays an Electric Sector Modernization Plans man long enough.

Within a week he had a phone, a shared house, and a job in Massachusetts as an ESMP man, part of the Commonwealth's block grants. Just the bottom rung, just a day laborer, basically, but if he did well, he'd be on the pension route, the sky the limit, that was the pitch.

One of the guys he shares this small farmhouse with is a work colleague, and as usual the two of them were up early this morning, him riding along on the way to the Ludlow site where more new lines are going up. He spent most of the ride going back over something he's put together for the job, seeing if he's come up with a way to improve it.

He finds the technical challenges fascinating. Fortunately, he's got a great supervising manager, Mike, who's thrilled by his talent. They've been working with the new line jig he's figured out, one that will save time and money, and his manager is already hinting at patents, although Allen doesn't think the tweaks are good enough for that, and besides, he configured the new jig while working. After working hours, sure, but using the company tool shop he has access to.

But it works. Mike thinks this can save a chunk of time raising new lines, and he's ecstatic.

It's not even 11:00 a.m., and he's already getting bored

with his latest effort, his tool hack succeeding without a hitch. Already he's thinking about other ideas. He wants to do more.

He's been shocked by how much build-out toward the renewable energy transition is underway. The US has been almost meeting its 2030 carbon emissions reduction targets, and only two years late. Already it looks like the progress is accelerating and it's well on track to come close to the 2050 goals. The revised goals, anyway.

He'd been a fool with NOS, he sees this now, but back when he started, fossil fuels were ascendant and companies were moving forward with establishing as much new infrastructure as possible to lock markets in, including scores and scores of natural gas generators. The sunk investment argument of the fossil fuel fuckers had seemed unassailable. Why build out renewables while fossil fuels covered the growing power demands already?

The time of Trump had driven him mad, that's what he thinks now.

Now Big Oil isn't so big anymore. Still dangerous, but it's becoming clear the tide of electrotech economics is too strong for the fossil fuel industry to swim against, and fuck them anyway.

But these days he's torn about the many things he's done as a member of NOS. Not that the bastards, the fucking world-eaters, don't deserve it, but there are better ways to contribute. There's Climate Covenant, an organization he was barely aware of, those years buried deep within his demimonde. He's been trying to catch up and finds himself astonished by the political efforts underway, by the success.

It's cold enough to see one's breath, but the winter work coveralls they each wear are warm enough.

"Hey, Randolph!" Mike calls out over the radio, shaking Allen free from his thoughts. He can barely make out Mike's wave from down at the latest strung pylon, a good two hundred feet away.

Allen glances at the top of the pylon he's under and sees

the crown lineman wave.

"The pickup set on the wire?" asks Mike. Allen can almost make his actual words out all the way from the cable truck, an odd echo-like distortion against the radio's speaker.

"Yup, that's affirmative."

There's the check-in with the crown, and the lead line starts rising, pulled by the improved rigging unit, rising toward the top frames of the pylon he's standing under. He keeps an eye on the power cable as it rises, following the lead. It's like a massive snake, a pipe in the sky. Magnificent.

"I'm going to get the next lead set," he radios to Mike, who tells him that's a go, but he's barely set off when Mike radios back.

"Some folks here, asking for you."

Allen sees a group of men, two in suits, three dressed tactical, with XM7s. From two hundred feet away, he sees Mike point right at him.

He walks toward them and the group of five men walk toward him.

He learns, in the next few hours and days, that the Ranch has been raided. He learns that Jim-John has cut a deal.

He finds himself thinking a lot about the last time he saw Biff.

He'd driven up to the trailer, but hadn't gotten out of the car, a new G-Class Mercedes, one of those off-road luxury SUVs, and Allen went out to greet him but stopped short. He could see through the tinted glass of the flat back window that Biff was talking to someone. He stood there, off the right back bumper and waited, looking over the SUV and puzzling over the technical crate up on the roof rack, dark green, with markings he couldn't make out, and then he stepped forward as the rear passenger side cracked open and Biff climbed out.

Maker greeted him. Biff looked annoyed and seemed about to say something, but the driver's side passenger door opened. A man stepped out. He had black hair, cut short, seemed neither old nor young, dressed in a black guayabera with a wide stripe of tan and black on the front starting from each shoulder. As he stepped around toward the back, Maker saw that he had on black dress pants and leather shoes. He looked to Allen as if he was playing dress up as a priest. He looked Chinese.

Biff turned to the man, calling out *Jiahao*, and the man's being Chinese was confirmed when Biff said something in a short burst of what Allen had thought was Mandarin, or Chinese, anyway. The man answered back but took another step toward the back of the car.

He'd nodded and the man nodded back, but Biff was already at the back door, and resting one hand on the spare tire's metal cover, he swung it open. As he reached inside for the package Allen expected, but glancing past him Allen could see a large cardboard box. The box bore the word *Shoghi* and Chinese characters, and then Biff swung the door back shut.

The man said something to Biff, who answered in the man's own language, then turned, carrying a bag, and nodded to Allen to lead the way into the trailer.

Allen set to work, taking the contents of the bag and settled it into the fish. The shape he knew from the blank he'd been given, but the material was the same: simple cardboard, cut and taped to form the right shape.

The workmanship, he noted, was sloppy, and as he settled it into the fish, one piece of cardboard had come undone, and he could see two vials and some electronics. He could smell something quite familiar to him, not exactly, but very close. He knew it was the smell of some type of plastic explosive. It wasn't overwhelming, and he gently lifted another span of cardboard and could see the lump was tiny, with thin wires leading out behind it.

He was still looking when Biff hit him on the shoulder and said, "Curious Cat." The tone brought the meaning clear.

He finished securing the covers, checking the seals and the strapped-on battery for the propulsion unit, turning it on to see the propeller spin. He handed the empty bag back and Biff asked him if the others knew their instructions, and he only nodded.

The very last time he glimpsed Biff was through the small side window of the trailer as Biff and the man he'd called Jiahao climbed back in, after which their driver took them away.

Allen knows Shoghi is a Chinese maker of electronics, known for signal jammers among other things. He'd spent time studying jammers during his early drone days and while he didn't know the exact model, from the big case up top, he knew the rig was a long-distance scrambler.

What do the authorities know about NOS and the cartels and the links to China?

He's starting to see a plan.

Let's Make a Deal! he silently shouts, but without any of the television gameshow exuberance he was endlessly blasted with at his grandmother's house. Monty-something.

And now his thoughts are racing, the Shoghi logo blooming into a desperate hope, but this moment of relief fades into a flashing image of the destroyed man lying in the Mexican compound, the snapdragon's blast-shattered ribs, arm gone up to the shoulder, the shoulder gone, the stripped open liver.

He manages to stop himself from vomiting.

He breathes slowly, intentionally. He concentrates, hoping to quiet his mind. He's imagining the face of the young woman he recruited and who he may have loved. The face looms, but what was her name?

No one is safe repeats on a stuttering loop.

He's trapped in an endless mist of misery.

No one is safe.

Next up in The Steep Climes Quartet, *Farm to Me*

Chapter 1: Creeptime for Germany

Early April, 2047

Tom Meyer is looking over his field, the latest one he's putting into production under the new guidelines, as if this isn't all a pain in the ass, at least the process, the rigmarole and hoops he's had to jump through, the studying for certification for the credits, but by now all this is becoming more routine.

His son is supposed to be here giving him a hand, but there's no surprise to him that Robbie is a no-show. Again. He'll have to do the grid samples on his own, since the pre-certification samples are due by the end of the week.

He looks over the windbreak shrubs just starting to green, the brown and rust hues of the wintered branches tangled together with newly tinged swollen leaf buds and emerging leaves that are still more hint than promise. These windbreaks were one of the things that had caught his eye when he was on the lookout for the right farmland. The positions and compositions of these windbreaks show the wisdom of the farmer who'd put them in a hundred years ago or more, probably.

The row of windbreak shrub across the narrow field isn't doing much to break any discomfort this morning, the chill of the spring day cutting, but the weather is supposed to break starting tomorrow, so he's out here laying out his plans for putting his last field into registration. This field is his farm's most modest in size, and the one closest to the house and outbuildings. The other largest fields are already registered and already earning credits the last year. His total acreage is nothing to boast about, but he feels like he's finally getting the hang of the regenerative agriculture processes and with this last field getting ready for registration, all his tillable fields will be fully registered.

"Huh," he says, amused by the old language that seem immutable. *Till*, that word no longer applies. He's been aiming at an A-level registration and he's been no till for the minimum time, four years. He thinks it's funny that it's harder to get his mind around the proper terminology than it is for him to make the actual changes in his farming techniques.

"Un-till death do me part," he says to the empty field he's standing in, the cold shadow of the winter still finding the open entrances in his jacket, nor is his mesh-backed give-me cap doing anything to keep his ears warm. What does warm him is his thoughts of last year's yields, especially in the west field where the beets, carrots, and potatoes did well, loving the organically built-up soil that kept roots moist even through the dry spell that wrecked the production for his neighbor Timmons. Timmons, who had tended to laugh at the shift Tom's taken with his own truck farm. Timmons hadn't laughed much the most recent time he'd seen him, after he'd told Timmons about the yields. He'd known full well that Timmons had suffered in last year's harvest production relative to his own record-breaking harvest, but Meyer thinks he's been polite not rubbing his success in Timmons face.

Well, except he'd taken the time to do just that, back last October, when spotting him at the new bar and taco place, the once-and-future Cantina 229, a place that he'd seen go through several iterations back when he and Milly used to rent a month in the summers in Monterey. The restaurant back then had been a high-end restaurant, then a casual one, and for the last several years it had gone back to what was basically a Mexican joint, albeit with the bones of a once-great bar still extant, a disconcerting incongruity he enjoys. He'd met up with John Large from Ledges Farm for a quick post-mortem. Large had been a big help getting him and running the regenerative agriculture switch, and he was there to buy him a thank-you drink for all his guidance over the previous seasons. But seeing Timmons, he couldn't resist the dig, and he offered to buy his neighbor a drink, citing the carbon credit payout for 2046. Large had noticed, though, and made it clear he'd thought it a jerk move, his mentioning the credits payout.

The payout should be even better this year, god willing and if the fucking creek or some freak of weather don't rise.

He can admit it had been a jerk-move, but then again, fair play as far as he's concerned, with Timmons being about as nasty a neighbor as can be, and growing up in New Marlborough in a family that goes back a few generations is no cause for the sullenness and derisive comments directed at him when he purchased the farm eight years ago.

He keeps forgetting how insular the locals are and he keeps forgetting he's not thought of as a local, even though he's serious about his farm.

He himself might have been something of an asshole too. He'd been pretty raw at the time, the new signs of success, previously long absent, had brought up a few demons. He'd long been competitive, he well knows, but he thought he was done with that different version of himself, one he thinks of as Before-Tom, when he'd been atop of the world, all that success in his earlier years that had kept him and his family living in the city. But Before-Tom had crashed when his much-vaunted skills at arbitrage had succumbed to AI, and his belief that he'd be safe as a high-level analyst whose reputation still was riding high with his predictive modeling work. So much for being able to figure things out and see patterns in the marketplace, never thinking for a moment that his predictive modeling could be fed into and greatly improved upon by the newest AI platforms.

He took the golden parachute and his own good trading wins and became a gentleman farmer, licking his wounds in the hills of New Marlborough.

The saving grace for him was the effort it demanded to make a go of the farm, and he found himself intrigued by the challenge, even if the first couple of years had seemed like one failure after another, to Timmons's delight.

Now he's the one laughing. Better yet, he's enjoying his life more than he'd ever had in the city, despite the hard work, or maybe because of the nature of his hard work. He finds himself surprised when he thinks of his former life. What had he been thinking, giving Timmons a hard dig last fall? Before-Tom had been knocking on his psyche's door, looking to reclaim dominance, ugh.

He's tried to take Large's castigation to heart. Mostly, anyway.

He's mapped out the field already, the simple drone and camera rig more than enough for photogrammetry to produce dimensions and topography, identifying the minor slopes and other features of the field that can make a surprising difference for crop planning. He'd layered biochar here in early 2046 and then followed this with a layer of ground leaf meal for winter coverage.

The soil is testing well. Lot's of microorganisms and wriggly little bastards and the PH scans well except for one depressed section of the field where extra moisture has ticked the soil acids over toward the high side. The baseline samples he's collecting today should pass muster.

It's hard work, but he enjoys it. His wife Milly has made the shift too, and is happier, even though the work is tougher. He takes the lead on the farm. She's using her management experience directing Elder Services two towns over. The pay is shit, but she's thriving.

He grins, thinking of last night, their weekly date night,

down in Great Barrington. For a farmer's wife, she's still pretty damn hot.

But his grin fades as he texts Robbie again, still ghosted. He tries the phone, which should have the added benefit of shocking the kid, but it goes to voice mail. He's guessing Robbie's down at the Southfield Store, likely chatting up the barista, a new conquest if he's read Robbie's own grin the last time they'd talked.

Or he's still asleep, another long night of session gaming, which really seems odd considering that his son is almost twenty-one years old, but then his son hadn't made the shift to country living all that well. He'd been in his teen years when the move happened and it's like he's never recovered. His being back home after graduating college doesn't help, Tom assumes. He also assumes that Robbie's lackluster career as an undergraduate and the modest GPA isn't helping. One would think that a degree in mechanical engineering could be helpful around the farm, but testing that theory requires some show of interest first.

Tom starts walking back to the house. He's got to finish up the field plan, although he's already decided on leafy crops, with an emphasis on spinach, despite the traditional difficulty in the growing zone. But then, of course, that makes the crop that much more valuable, fetching good prices. Spinach uber-alles.

He sees a truck pulling into the driveway. It's that damn Wagner fellow, back again to bother him about switching to his food distribution service, promising the world if only he changes over. The worst thing about Wagner is how he thinks he gives a crap about their so-called common ethnicity, both German-Americans, both three generations in, both grandfathers children of German soldiers after the war, sponsored by the same Dalton, Ohio church helping out with the displaced persons problem. At least Wagner hasn't made the argument that their grandfathers come in the same DP charity tranche.

Tom wants to keep his options open with the various

food distributors serving the Northeast market, but so far he hasn't heard anything from Wagner that causes him to think there's any advantage switching from the distributor he's currently contracted with. Consolidation may work for Wagner but there's no advantage for him.

It's all the same sausage no matter how you slice it, shared stupid German heritage or not.

And there's something about Wagner that rubs him raw, not that he can put a finger on anything specific, more like a hunch.

But then he's been pretty successful with his hunches, hasn't he?

Chapter 2: Not a Dry Eye in the House

Early April, 2047

Davin Caine is standing outside Great Barrington's Berkshire Eye Center waiting for RAT. Here in town the wait is typically short, although in Housatonic, there are often fewer units ready on demand.

He's not thinking about the rural autonomous transport on its way to bring him back to his house in Housatonic. He'd simply pressed the RAT button on his smart phone, although he'll more often think of the RAT button as an app, but then he is also old-fashioned and still uses the touch screen, not the AR interface. When you are eighty-one years old, being old-fashioned is just being.

He'd find this funny, the sort of bon mot or clever turn he's known for, or was, back when he was doing more writing for *Tri-Interactive*. But now, except for the occasional opinion or observation piece, he's not really writing much these days. He's still on the masthead as contributing editor, but that's just Alicia being nice. Or maybe just getting her money's worth.

He'd started with Alicia, originally helping her set up the platform for *South County Interactive,* the sort of self-erecting content platform and advertising management system, and that's been well over two decades now, although his role has been diminishing more and more as he himself diminishes. It's been years since he worked as the system admin and these days keeping on with the technology is someone else's business. Got to get back to Raphine on the latest specs she's sent, but he's pretty sure she sends this on to him as a courtesy. Time to tell her to be less polite.

He's mostly a mentor to the new staff and the interns that he calls *slaves,* although he does this as a test for humor. He takes his responsibilities more seriously than he should, but mentees working for experience for small stipends demands value in return and he's conscientious enough about this. Mentees. He's never liked the word. He's never liked the whole no-pay/low-pay bullshit of interns instead of hiring employees, but the gig economy has long gone giga economy, although he can't remember where that expression is from.

It's a beautiful day, late April, a bit nippy even, but that's New England. He peers at his screen, moving the phone close to his face. His eyes are dilated and the sun is painful when he inches the dark glasses up to check that he has, indeed, pressed RAT.

He has. He's got only a few destination buttons, including the Tri-Interactive office downtown, various doctors and therapists, and his son Jimmy's place in Boston and his daughter Skip's house in San Diego. The RAT system is simple, from the user's perspective, something like a point-and-shoot camera, back when such things existed. Push the button and the destination buttons come up or you tell RAT where you're heading. No scheduling. No route planning. All that is figured out on the back end and always optimized. RAT is specifically for rural spaces and there are versions for urban called OUT, which he's pretty sure stands for Optimized Urban Transport, but either works with the central platform. He's sure there are differences based on the special needs of rural-versus-urban, but he's got no real sense of what that might be. If he wants to visit Jimmy, he pushes that destination and the system comes and picks him up and presents the full travel itinerary and he just follows the directions provided. A single occupancy vehicle might show up, or a multi-passenger one, depending on timing and coordination, but out here in Berkshire County, especially in low density areas, the single occupant variety is the more likely. There's just not enough people moving about at the same times and destinations, until, anyway, you get to the closest relevant public transportation network. Where he is now, on Stockbridge Road, his RAT might drop him off at the regional bus stop, but maybe not the closest but the one with the best pick-up time and it's all real time data. The RAT often enough brings him directly home without the intermediary of the regional bus if the timing doesn't work.

Home. The house goes by the name he's used for years, which is the Housatonic House on the Hill, the name works well for his Airbnb apartment that takes up one half of the first floor. It's a strange enough place, built sometime in the late-nineteenth century, and built into a steep slope, steep enough for the second floor being at grade on the east side. Housatonic, a part of Great Barrington, is where the Housatonic River valley squeezes close in. Mills, now repurposed, were built there for the resulting water power of rapids as the river narrows.

He can see the tops of some of the mill buildings from his second-floor office. He can see only a couple of the buildings, but from the top floor there are some glimpses of other of the buildings, and at certain times in the seasons, afternoon sunlight can reflect off the solar panels of the various flat roofs of the mills and poke a person in the eye. He's not on the top floor much, since that is where the bedrooms are for the people who live at the Housatonic House on the Hill.

He's distracted, all sorts and varieties of thoughts popping in his mind only to be replaced with other half-images or memories, but mainly he's distracted by the news from his eye doctor. He barely notices the RAT moving stealthily toward him, and he looks up only when the RAT beeps its arrival.

The Rural Autonomous Transport screen tells him that it will deliver him home directly, and while that's not uncommon, it's a big relief today. He's got a lot to process about what he's been told following his routine annual eye exam and the solitary ride is better than jumping on to regional buses, better than being around others.

Dr. Maroni is worried that the latest retinal scan more clearly indicates early signs of macular degeneration, especially in his left eye.

He's symptom-free, fortunately, and it is possible that the gene therapy trials might work out, not that he's a candidate, not yet, anyway. All watchful waiting at this point. The current treatment involves a sharp stick in the eye, as he had joked, when Maroni talked about choices. Not funny, but that's the way he is with odd news. Make a joke first, think later. The needle approach is likely not more difficult that the two cataract surgeries, at least he thinks this is something Maroni said. His condition could be slow to develop and never amount to any real problem, Maroni said. It seems likely that the condition is the better of the two options. Dry-macular degeneration, the doctor kept repeating to him during the consult, is slower and often less completely a center field vision degeneration that the wet-macular degeneration version.

He likes being able to see. His art is detail-filled, his odd assemblages require precision placement of tiny objects and often intricate mounting solutions, at least the series he's just started, a series that he is very excited about.

He's seeing just fine, at least as well as most other

eighty-two year olds, glasses used for close-up work.

He sees that he's turning off Route 7 where Route 183 splits off toward Housatonic. He's supposed to be getting the apartment read for the new season.

Remain calm. Do not panic. Do not pass Go.

Fuck me.

He's sure his vision is okay at present, but hearing the diagnosis, the trees and houses and river he's passing all look out of focus. The river seems swollen, no doubt because of the hard rains a few days back, the Risingdale dam catchment used to control potential flooding downstream in Sheffield.

Cry me a river.

He laughs, but it is sardonic, of course.

Not a dry eye in the house, he tells himself.

About The Steep Climes Quartet

The Steep Climes Quartet is a four-book literary climate fiction series that examines the near- and mid-future consequences of climate change as experienced in recurring characters' lives and through the lens of Berkshire County, Massachusetts.

Visit Amazon or https://davidguenette.com/ for information on where to buy *Over Brooklyn Hills* and the other books in The Steep Climes Quartet, including the many non-Amazon places where you may purchase this book.

The climate change science, technologies, and politics in the books are grounded in long-term and in-depth study, rejecting needlessly gratuitous exaggeration for realistic extrapolation designed to help readers identify with their own likely experiences of near-and mid-term futures. This climate crisis is terrifying enough, but might this be a future that remains open to our own agency and the potential in working together toward solutions?

Book One: Kill Well

In *Kill Well*, it is 2026 and the nation is still reeling from second-term President Trump's oil-centric chaos, but the pro-Democrat mid-terms has helped rebalance the federal government. There are still plenty of climate activists working hard, too. Cynthia is a young woman on a trip with her boss, a V.P. at Carbon's End, a ClimateProgress.Org spin-off aimed at accelerating fossil fuel divestiture, but on the way to a meeting with an investment group near Mojave, she witnesses his murder, and someone is trying to pin it on her.

Panicked and terrified, Cynthia is on the run, moving in and out of disassociated states echoing a childhood trauma re-triggered by what she's seen. She's obsessing to find a place she might be safe, and Great Barrington, in the Berkshires, has good memories for her. Meeting sixty-one-year-old Davin Caine's son, Jimmy, who is homeward bound on the North Shore Limited,

Cynthia ends up at Davin's Housatonic house, and a great news story for the interactive newspaper Davin has helped start lands in his lap. On the other hand, a contract killer comes to the Berkshires, looking to finish the job of making it look like Cynthia is simply a suicide post-murder of her putative lover and boss.

Book Two: Dear Josephine

Dear Josephine finds now sixty-four-year-old Davin Caine frustrated by the constant game of financial catch-up he's forced to play to keep his Berkshire County, Massachusetts, house. It's 2029 and the Republican Party is continuing its losing streak, and new climate bills and regulations are passing in Congress and getting signed. Like many, Davin's also still struggling past the legacy of Trump and high energy prices and jumps in costs for insurance policies are just the latest challenges. He must take on more paying work at the online newspaper service he helped design and spend less time in his art studio, and with food prices that keep increasing, his vegetable garden is more important than ever.

And then Hurricane Josephine, the earliest and strongest on record, hits Florida's Gold Coast, and the devastation of South Beach and the Miami Metro area and the count of the dead and the displaced staggers the nation and spurs the pending The Sea Wall Act legislation and its potentially enormous budget.

In national news there's the developing story of a series of murders and a possible terrorist organization calling itself *Kill the Rich,* but it just may be that fossil fuel-funded operatives are also using this as cover in the latest behind-the-scenes effort to influence and control key legislation. Meanwhile, Jeannie Louise Smith, a national climate change politics analyst who lives in Great Barrington, and her researcher- and professor-filled collective, *The Laundry,* is applying AI to uncover sources of dark money, triggering a level of pushback that is far from academic, even while a new and violent climate group, *No One is Safe,* is making the news.

Book Three: Over Brooklyn Hills

In *Over Brooklyn Hills,* it is 2035, and six years have passed since The Sea Wall Act was enacted, thanks in part to the exposure of The Kehoe Institute's criminal efforts to push the goals of an informal group of the extreme wealthy who hold vast fossil fuel interests. For Davin Caine, now seventy years old, the economy finally has some bright spots, including ongoing renewable energy infrastructure programs that are relieving unemployment and chipping away at the country's carbon footprint. But these efforts are expensive, and for many, including Davin, the cost of living remains expensive too. He's become more politically active and is now a member of Climate Covenant, an organization that pushes the renewable energy transition, but the fossil fuel industry has its own ideas and still possesses the means to carry there to fruition.

On the international front, China has grown belligerent as it tries to recover domestically from the worldwide recession that has stunned it, and America's expanding efforts to build out renewable energy infrastructure in the Global South is part of the rising tensions between the two powers. Mass climate migration adds fuel to the fire with border wars raging in a mix of allied nations. America's own escalating conflict on the southern border finds the climate terrorist group No One is Safe playing a troubling role.

Even the Berkshires is having its own migration challenge with increasingly shocking numbers of young and economically marginal New York City residents trekking to the relatively cool hills of the Berkshires to escape the brutal summer heat of the city and power cost demands for vital air conditioning. Vagrancy laws are referenced, but many of these young adults work, and the plethora of smart glasses and VR headsets that let them work anywhere. Great Barrington's attempts to deal with the wave of "free campers" an out-of-control housing crisis, and a spike in petty crime results in an "us versus them" response, and civility and basic rights hang in the balance.

Book Four: Farm to Me

In 2047, twelve years after the events of the previous book, *Farm to Me* sees eighty-two-year-old Davin Caine losing sight of his dreams, literally, as his worsening macular degeneration is making it difficult for him to continue his art. Climbing all those stairs in his house in Housatonic is getting hard, too, and he's having trouble believing he shouldn't sell the house and studio and move somewhere more sensible.

But where? Costs are still high, even with clean energy infrastructure driving down energy costs. More and more extreme weather events demand costly responses and are starting to hurt markets and take noticeable bites out of the U.S. GDP. Food costs—

beyond what Davin needs out of his garden—are levelling off, at least locally, with more and more local farms in regenerative agricultural production as the movement toward local economies grows deeper roots.

But where there is business opportunity there is conflict, and *Tri-Interactive,* the expanded online news and information service Davin still occasionally works with, has been hearing rumors about a play for consolidating the local food distribution business, and it's looking more and more like extortion is becoming part of that play.

Davin's been mentoring some of the newly expanded *Tri-Interactive* staff of writers, and when the young reporter chasing a story about shifting affiliations among small food distribution companies dies in an unlikely accident, Davin finds himself caught up in a hometown conspiracy. It's complicated for him because he's long known Marion Fletcher-Gray from covering town politics over the years she's been the Great Barrington town manager, but it looks like the town may be choosing the wrong side.

Acknowledgements

Thanks to all those who have contributed to this book's existence, from casual conversers to beta readers and attendees at my climate presentations throughout the region. I am grateful for the help.

A special acknowledgement is due Louise Holtby of Holtby Editorial, who served as copy editor, but also much more. Her close reading, attention to detail, and impressive skill with the mechanics of language helps make *Over Brooklyn Hills* that much more readable, which means that she'd faithfully executed the prime role of the editor, which is to serve the reader. This book is far better off for her efforts, including her patient but persistent argument to streamline the third-person POV style I'd used in the first two books of the series. After my previous experiences with other editors, I've concluded that working with her is so much more collegial, relaxed, and, most important of all, effective in improving the text. The Steep Climes Quartet has one more book to go and you can bet I'm lining Louise Holtby up for that book, too.

Speaking of gratitude, a big shout of appreciation for my dear wife Mary Ann Palermo, who has exercised plenty of patience along with encouragement, plus the occasional gentle dope slap when I've let the anxiety of the publishing business in these odd days get to me.

Thanks go out to my old friends, of whom these days are correctly referenced as The Ancient Ones, and who have been tolerant—and even supportive—of all my talk about climate change and the long-running project that is The Steep Climes Quartet. These people include David Rivard, Dianne Cella, Nancy Silva, Mark Ouellette, Phil Sego, and my sister Elaine. A special tip o' the cap to my younger brother Michael who, even when my doubts about the work abound, has been especially heartening in his listening, reading, encouragement, and comments, and despite his knowing me for so long he has been one hell of a help getting the manuscript into shape.

As always, the connections to my daughter and son and their families are crucial touchstones in my life and work, and ever more so with my granddaughter, Magnificent Mae, her younger sister, Celeste Emma, and, at the time of this writing, a grandson on the way.

I fervently wish all of us grownups manage not to make too big of a mess of this precious world for these and all other children, and that we do our part healing this world as best we can.

About the Author

David Guenette is the author of the climate fiction series, The Steep Climes Quartet, a four-book literary climate fiction series with *Kill Well* published in September 2023, *Dear Josephine,* published in Spring 2025, and *Over Brooklyn Hills,* published in Spring 2026. There's a lot of writing yet to do for the last book, *Farm to Me,* so that publication date is TBD.

You'll also find more information about the series at *https://davidguenette.com,* where he writes extensively about the climate crisis and the technologies and policies pursuing the Electrotech Revolution, as well as news about talks he gives about climate change. At the website, sign up via the contact form to notification of new posts and updates on the series. Guenette also publishes through Substack, *The Steep Climes* (*https://substack.com/@davidrguenette454046*).

He worked in book publishing as a developmental and acquisitions editor before shifting his focus to digital publishing, long serving as a journalist and editor for electronic publishing trade periodicals, and as a consultant and electronic publishing business and technology analyst. While undertaking a deep energy retrofit of his house in Berkshire County, he combined his background in digital technologies and his growing understanding of building science and house renovation and retrofitting processes to found Retrosheath, a start-up that aimed to reduce cost for energy efficiency improvements in the built environment.

He lives in the Berkshires and is part of Citizens' Climate Lobby (Berkshires Chapter) and 350Mass.Org (Berkshire Node).

www.ingramcontent.com/pod-product-compliance
Lightning Source LLC
LaVergne TN
LVHW100510110826
845146LV00002B/581

* 9 7 9 8 9 8 8 5 0 5 5 4 9 *